THE
STARS
AND THEIR
LIGHT

OTHER TITLES
BY OLIVIA HAWKER

THE
STARS
AND THEIR
LIGHT

A Novel

OLIVIA HAWKER

LAKE UNION
PUBLISHING

Published by Lake Union Publishing, Seattle

www.apub.com

Amazon, the Amazon logo, and Lake Union Publishing are trademarks of Amazon.com, Inc., or its affiliates.

ISBN-13: 9781662511066 (hardcover)
ISBN-13: 9781662511059 (paperback)
ISBN-13: 9781662511073 (digital)

Cover design by Ploy Siripant
Cover image: © Joaanna Czogala / Archangel; © Diana Robinson Photography, © Jim Henderson / Getty; © ISOVECTOR, © Marina Sun / Shutterstock

Printed in the United States of America

First edition

First, he was aware of light—so white and sharp it seemed to come from everywhere, to be everywhere, above and below, cutting through him as a sunbeam cuts through a windowpane, and emanating from within, from the place where the physical substance that had once made him had once existed.

Then, in the next heartbeat, he felt a golden weight in his arms. He was holding something precious, cradling the unseen burden against his chest, though the concrete and the physical meant nothing in the brilliance of that flash. His body didn't exist—not the arms that held, not the heart that beat, not the ears that heard the voice that didn't speak but moved inside him, in the same deep place from which the light had come.

What you see, you do not see, *the voice said.* And all that you see, you see truly, for the truth is all, and all is within you.

Now open your eyes and look.

He looked. And the world he had known, a well-behaved world of simple order, of laws of nature and laws of man, broke into words disconnected from meaning, shattered into the shards of a dropped mirror, and each silver-white piece went spinning by his awareness, their facets reflecting the past and the desert and the future and the night sky, and the faces of people he knew, and three red circles in snow, and the faces of people he didn't yet recognize but knew all the same. And his own expression, slack and stricken by something too holy to be called wonder.

Olivia Hawker

TRANSCRIPT pages 1–3

INVESTIGATION OF ALLEGED STIGMATIC ISABEL
CAMPBELL BY BISHOP FRANK MICHAEL COTE
OCTOBER 30, 1947
ROSWELL, NEW MEXICO

BISHOP COTE: Thank you all for being here today. Before we begin, for the accuracy of our records, I would like to read the names of all who are present. Father Vernor Kerry, priest of this parish. Sister Mary Agnes, an extern of the order of Poor Clares, who have recently founded a new monastery here in Roswell. Rosa Morales Campbell, mother of the subject of our investigation—and I understand your husband, Roger Campbell, will be joining us later this afternoon, ma'am, when his duties at the Army airfield have concluded.

ROSA CAMPBELL: Yes, Bishop, that's correct.

BISHOP COTE: Thank you. And finally, of course, Isabel Campbell, seventeen years old, a student at the local high school.

ISABEL CAMPBELL: Everyone calls me Betty.

BISHOP COTE: Very well, Betty. Why don't we begin by affirming that we are in fact here to investigate your claims that you have experienced the stigmata, a spontaneous appearance of the wounds of our crucified Lord—

BETTY: They aren't my claims. They're other people's claims. I never said it's . . . what you say it is. I only want to know what's happening to me.

ROSA: Betty, dear, don't interrupt the bishop.

BISHOP COTE: That's quite all right; occurrences such as these can be highly upsetting and disorienting. We all hope for the same thing, Betty—to understand what's happening here. That's why I've come all the way from Santa Fe to speak with you. You are willing to talk about your experiences, aren't you?

BETTY: *(pause)* I guess so.

BISHOP COTE: Very good. The best place to start is at the beginning. Tell me about the first time you had this experience.

BETTY: It was the night my dad came home.

BISHOP COTE: Came home? From where?

BETTY: From Mac Brazel's ranch, I guess. Wherever the Army sent him. Wherever the saucer went down.

FATHER KERRY: Pardon me, Your Excellency. This town has suffered some unusual . . . shall we say, *disruptions* over the past few months. Rumors of something that crashed out in the desert, an aircraft or a weather balloon . . .

BISHOP COTE: Yes, Father, I know. The story was in all

3

the newspapers in Santa Fe. If I were a betting man, I'd wager that the story made the news across the whole country.

FATHER KERRY: It is only a story. Rumor. The Army was quick to investigate, and they confirmed that the crashed object was ordinary weather-monitoring equipment from Alamogordo.

BETTY: It wasn't a balloon. Every kid in town knows what weather balloons look like. If you find them and turn them in, the Army pays you twenty-five bucks. Some of the boys at my school have rodded out their cars just from the money they've earned by picking up balloons.

BISHOP COTE: If it wasn't a weather balloon, then what do you suppose it was?

BETTY: *(pause)* I don't know. I never saw the crash, myself. But my dad saw it. He went along on the recovery mission, to find the crash and clean it up. All I know is the way he looked when he came home that night.

BISHOP COTE: And how did your father look?

BETTY: Scared. I've never seen him like that before, kind of staring and jumpy, like something had frightened him out of his wits. He wouldn't tell me much. But that was the first time I . . . the first time it . . . that was when it happened. To me. For the first time.

CHAPTER ONE

July 3, 1947

By the time Roger Campbell got back home, nothing remained of the day except a deep-blue glow in the western sky. The stars were coming out above Roswell. A few kids played on the sidewalks, lighting off firecrackers in anticipation of the next day's celebration. Each time one of the firecrackers burst in a clamor of noise and colored light, a jolt arced along all of Roger's nerves at once. He remembered the lightning from the night before, the boom of a thunderstorm so close it shook even the cement bunker walls of the radar room at the airfield. He remembered that light—that rapid, dancing light—flashing from here to there across the radar scope. That was all he wanted to remember. If he could stop himself at that point, erase every subsequent detail of that day from his memory, he would do it. But there was no forgetting something like this.

As he turned off Main Street into the sleepy comfort of his neighborhood, he could feel the metal in the pocket of his uniform jacket. That scrap of debris was thin as paper and weighed even less. Impossible, that the fragment should drag at him now, weighing him down like lead, digging into his side with the solidity of iron or stone. But he did feel it. All the long drive back from Corona—seventy-five miles in the back seat of an Army car, with Captain Cavitt in the front seat and Colonel Blanchard beside him—the scrap in his pocket had nagged at his conscience. If anyone found out he'd taken it, he would be in real trouble with his superior officers.

An honest man, a loyal lieutenant colonel of the United States Army would have added that scrap to the back of the jeep carryall with everything else, all the debris the Army crew had scoured out of the desert. And more than debris. That *thing*, whatever it was. It wasn't that Roger was dishonest—far from it. Nor was he disloyal. But twenty-four hours hadn't passed since he'd been called to the ranch outside Corona, and already he was struggling to fit the pieces of his memory together, struggling to comprehend. The scrap in his pocket was proof of what he'd seen—proof that he hadn't lost his mind. *Like a huge dishpan smashed into the earth. Some Soviet invention, or a Japanese spy craft. That thing. Whatever it was.*

Roger pulled his car to the curb outside his house, shut off the engine, and sat for a while, watching the neighborhood. All those quiet, ordinary homes, their windows glowing. It seemed like a cruel trick from a distant god that everyone—his neighbors and his family, and the town, and everyone beyond it—should carry on with their everyday lives, sleepwalking through this old reality, which Roger knew, now, was held together by nothing more substantial than threads and suppositions. What kind of disturbance would it take to blow apart this mass delusion of nice, ordinary, secure American life? Not much. After everything that had happened since the thunderstorm blew across the desert, he was damn sure it wouldn't take much.

Next thing he knew, he was stepping through the front door of his home, dropping his key ring into the old, chipped ceramic dish that sat on the nearby bureau. The framed pictures of his wife and children stood there, too, all of them smiling. He didn't remember leaving his car or walking up the path through the summer-warm darkness. He was skipping across the face of his own life, his awareness dipping down now and then into the slower currents of ordinary reality while the rest of him was still stumbling up there in the stratosphere, through the maze of the day that had just passed.

His daughter called from the kitchen, "Hi, Dad. Mom took the boys to the park so they could set off their fireworks. They didn't want to wait till tomorrow."

And then he was in the kitchen, suddenly, improbably—for it was improbable that something as mundane as kitchens and homes and quiet towns should exist in the same world in which that *thing* in the desert existed. The rich, comforting smell of his wife's cooking filled the room. And Betty, his girl, sat at the table with one foot folded beneath her, bending over a textbook, a rolled tortilla with cinnamon and sugar half-eaten on the plate beside her.

"What are you doing?" Roger asked. "It's late. And it's summer. You don't have any homework."

"I need to study, anyway, if I hope to get into college. Junior year starts soon, and I've got to start making applications . . ."

Betty looked up at her father, then faltered, fell silent. Something was wrong. She could see that right away in his sober expression, his distant, stricken eyes.

"Dad? What's the matter?"

Roger didn't say anything. There was nothing he could say, not without violating the oath of silence Colonel Blanchard had required before he'd been permitted to leave the base and go home. But he could *show* Betty. And he needed to show someone. He needed to, for a moment, lay down the great burden of having witnessed the impossible. He needed to see someone else's reaction, know that he hadn't lost his head, know that what he'd seen had been real.

He drew the scrap of metal from his pocket. Flexible and thin, it weighed nothing in his hands and picked up the glow of the kitchen's light with a curious intensity, reflecting his own image with an unsettling vibrancy of color and form.

Betty rose from her chair. "What in the heck is that?"

"Something I found in the desert."

The girl approached her father slowly, stilled by a caution that had no evident provocation. He held nothing more than a piece of trash,

7

as far as Betty could see—a bit of aluminum foil or a piece of paper coated with some shiny substance. But as she drew nearer, everything seemed to grow dense around and within her—air and time, thought and breath, laden with a weight of importance the girl had never known before. There was a pounding in her ears, her own heartbeat, but something hummed behind that rhythm, like a chord of music rising to a crescendo, and she felt that every fleeting, mundane moment of her life had been guiding her, somehow, to this.

She reached out to touch the object. No more than a fingertip brushed its smooth surface before she flinched back, for a stab of pain shot through her hand—through both hands at once—and she looked down at the two bright wells of blood rising, as if she held a garnet in each palm.

Betty screamed.

The drifting detachment that had plagued Roger for most of the day vanished with his daughter's cry. He forgot the piece of metal, dropped it on the kitchen floor, took Betty's hands in his own. He pressed clean kitchen towels into her palms, exerting enough pressure to stanch the flow of blood.

Betty collapsed into her chair, her hands held together as if in prayer, the towels bulky between them. "What do I do?" she demanded, wide-eyed, pale with fear. "What do I do? What do I do?"

"Calm down," Roger said. "You only cut yourself. It was sharp . . ."

She held his eye, silent and accusing. Both of them knew she hadn't cut herself.

"Don't tell anyone about this," Roger said. "You can't. It'll make trouble—for you, for me."

"How am I supposed to keep people from seeing?" She eased up her grip on the towels, examined one palm—and melted into tears again.

"Hang on," Roger said. "I've got just the thing."

He led Betty up to his bedroom. At the back of his closet, the green trunk waited, full of his old Army things, artifacts from his years in the war. His fingerless shooting gloves were all the way down at the bottom of the trunk, but he dug them out and held them up for Betty's inspection.

The gloves made her cry all the more. "No one wears stuff like that, Dad! Not even the boys."

"It's either the gloves or bandages—and then you're going to have to answer questions, Betty. You're a smart girl. You can convince your friends that you're trying to set a new style."

It took more wailing and protestation, but Betty saw the sense in his plan and stormed off to her bedroom with the gloves tucked under her arm. She slammed the door, and he left her to confront the shock on her own. What else could he do?

He returned to the kitchen then, stood looking down at the fragment of metal where it lay. From this angle, his reflection was a blur of darkness amid the glow of bouncing light.

He should get rid of the thing. It had hurt his little girl, done something to her that Roger couldn't explain. He shouldn't have taken it out of the desert in the first place.

But even as he told himself all that, Roger knew he wouldn't part with the metal. It was important. For all he could say, that scrap of debris might be the most important thing in all the world.

He looked, because the Voice told him to, through wheels inside wheels, through pillars of smoke and flame. A dim and distant part of his mind understood that nothing was flowing past him. The scene before him was as still as abandonment or death, but these rapid images that bombarded him—they were knowings and memories, the remembrance of moments that had passed and, somehow, a deep and familiar remembrance of what hadn't yet come to be, but would, as surely as the sun rose, as surely as he breathed. He saw light through a ring of trees. And the brown-white-black motion of a bird's wings, and the deep sorrowful eyes of a woman, her smile hidden by a veil, and her voice, like a bird singing: Once, we called them angels. *He saw waves breaking on the curve of a bay. Heard the roar of fighters and bombers far above the Pacific, and in one ear he heard his own voice:* It's not malfunctioning, sir. *In the other, his own voice:* I've never been much of a Bible reader.

Nothing real rushed past with the force of a breached dam or a meteorite burning down to earth. Memory, knowing—not real, and yet more real than his body, than all the time that had carried him to this point. And at the paper-thin, featherlight boundary between what was real and what couldn't be, he was struck through the heart by a hot, sweet fire, like the flame that martyrs the saints, a revelation of the close, quiet presence of the divine.

Through the lack of sense, he found words. He named what he was seeing, and then he could see it all so clearly.

Chairs—seats. Like a pilot's seat in a fighter plane. But smooth and white, made without seam or rivet. And the flat mirror-blackness of screens, not unlike the screen of an oscilloscope, but different somehow—greater.

All of this—the whole object, the whole thing*—struck him the same way. Resembling in every respect everything he had ever known, and, at the same time, despite the paradox and the contradiction, different and greater and more.*

TRANSCRIPT pages 16–17

BISHOP COTE: Mr. Campbell, thank you for joining us. I know you're a busy man.

ROGER CAMPBELL: It's no trouble.

BISHOP COTE: Can you tell us about yourself? What is your employment, for example?

ROGER: I'm a lieutenant colonel in the United States Army.

BISHOP COTE: You served during the war, I presume.

ROGER: Yes, sir. I led one of the signal aircraft warning battalions in the Pacific.

BISHOP COTE: A service we all appreciate, I'm sure. And I assume it's safe to say that you have plenty of expertise in assessing airborne phenomena.

ROGER: *(no answer)*

BISHOP COTE: Colonel Campbell, you helped with the recovery effort after the weather balloon went down in the desert—isn't that so?

ROGER: I don't see what that has to do with my Betty.

BISHOP COTE: Well, that's what we hope to get to the bottom of, Colonel.

ROGER: See here, I agreed to talk with you church men to make my wife happy, but if you ask me, this supernatural stuff is nonsense. All I want is for this misunderstanding to be cleared up once and for all, so folks will leave my family alone.

BISHOP COTE: Has your family been harassed, Colonel?

FATHER KERRY: The Campbells have become the focus of some unwanted attention since word got out about Betty's . . . experience.

ROGER: People coming in the middle of the night, turning my front lawn into some sort of damn shrine.

ROSA: Roger, language, please.

ROGER: Beg your pardon, men—and you, too, Sister—but I've had enough of it. It's turning our lives upside down, and life has been hard enough these past few months without the town fanning rumors about my daughter.

BISHOP COTE: What do you mean by that, Colonel—your life has been hard enough?

ROGER: I'm not at liberty to say.

BISHOP COTE: I understand that a fellow of your profession, in your position, must be cautious about what he says, and to whom. Is there anything you can tell us that might help make sense of what your family is going through now?

ROGER: There are too many rumors already in this town. Too much nonsense.

FATHER KERRY: Are you referring to the stories about the flying saucer?

ROGER: It was nothing but a weather balloon.

FATHER KERRY: That's what you believe about it?

ROGER: That's all you'll hear from me about it.

CHAPTER TWO

Summer of 1944

"Sorry, Colonel." The young, lanky private stepped in front of the flap of the signal tent, barring Roger's way. "Command gave orders not to let anyone inside except the four members of this unit."

Roger eyed the kid. He was young, and no one Roger recognized. He must have arrived at the outpost earlier in the week, while Roger was still at the command muster down in Finschhafen, being briefed on things he would rather not have known. The tent guard might be green, but he was meticulous about obeying orders—something to be commended, in the balance. You couldn't be too careful about the sensitive information that flowed through a signal aircraft warning battalion. Roger was glad to have him.

Still, the kid needed to be put in his place.

"What's your name, son?"

"Jepson, sir. Private first class."

"Then let me tell you something, Private Jepson." Roger drew closer to the young fellow, as close as he could stand in the dense equatorial humidity. "I *am* your command, you numbskull."

The private wilted with embarrassment.

Roger heard a familiar laugh from inside the tent. That was his best radarman, Harvey Day. "Let him in, Jepson," Harvey called. "He's all right."

"Sorry, sir," the guard squeaked, sidling out of the way.

Roger gave him an encouraging slap on the shoulder. "Good man, doing your duty. Keep it up, son."

The tent was small and crowded with equipment. The air inside, charged as it was by the heat and hum of electronics, was even more sweltering than the surrounding jungle. The plotter and radio operator—the other two signalmen who made up the unit—stood to salute Roger as he entered.

"Don't you dare get up, Day," Roger barked at his radarman. "I want your eyes on that scope."

Harvey laughed again. "I wasn't planning to get up, sir. My eyes never leave my scope, not as long as I'm on duty. You'll have to go without proper respect from me."

Roger chuckled, mopping his face with a handkerchief. "Nothing new there."

The others returned to their duties. Roger pulled an empty stool closer to Harvey and sank onto it, eyeing the oscilloscope for himself—its concentric rings of precise measurement, the smooth, clockwise sweep of its indicator band. "How long till the squadron is within range of the target?"

"About twenty minutes, sir," the plotter answered, "assuming the tailwind holds."

Roger gave Harvey a subtle nudge with his elbow. "About to see some fireworks on that scope, Day."

"I just hope it's over quick."

"You and me both."

Roger wanted all of this to be over quickly—the capture of the island and this damned interminable war. He hadn't seen his family for over two years. Not a minute passed that he didn't think of them—his wife, Rosa, so witty and lovely and warm in his arms. His two boys, big enough now that they'd want their dad around for games of catch and fishing trips and man-to-man talks about life's biggest questions. And his girl, Betty, who would be fourteen soon. Hardly a girl any longer, she was growing up into a young lady, full of modern ambitions and fiery drive, but without her father to look after her.

Damn this war, anyway, he thought, *and damn every war.* What good was this to anybody? Men blowing each other to smithereens, flattening cities, setting islands on fire. And all of it getting worse by the day, with ever more horrible weapons. Sometimes he lay awake at night, listening to the jungle chattering and crying around him, and he wondered what this crescendo of destruction was leading to.

If not for the human connections he'd made out there in the Pacific, his duties would have been unbearable. Signalman Day was one of those fellows who lifted Roger's mood with his easygoing presence. Seldom had Roger met a man as coolly accepting as Harvey Day was. The bright, thoughtful radar specialist took every turn with an unflappable air of *c'est la vie.* A fleet of Martians could land in the middle of their SAW battalion, and Harvey wouldn't bat an eye.

With another battle looming mere minutes in the future, Roger was more grateful than ever for Harvey's calm presence. He never could feel so fatalistic about any aspect of war—not with his family constantly on his mind, the ever-present threat that he might never see home again. But he had a friend here in the signal tent, and that was worth something. Well—he and Harvey might have been friends if they weren't in the middle of a war, if they had the leisure to think of anything other than winning, finally and for good.

Roger clapped Harvey on the back. "Send one of the boys for me as soon as you sight land."

"Yes, sir," Harvey said. "I'll send—"

He fell silent, which pulled Roger's attention sharply back to the scope. Three anomalous blips had appeared so rapidly they must have blinked into existence above the Pacific.

Harvey leaned into the scope. "I'll be damned. They're back. I never thought I'd see the things again, after the last time. I half convinced myself I never saw them at all."

"What's back?" Roger demanded. "What are those blips?"

For a moment, Harvey didn't answer. The radarman and the lieutenant colonel watched the dots hold their position on the scope. Then, as the circular indicator passed over one, it flashed across the field to its opposite side.

Roger lurched back, half-afraid the anomaly might reach through the screen and grab him. He'd been leading SAW battalions for years and was no stranger to radar. He'd never seen anything move like that on an oscilloscope—not once. "The system's malfunctioning," he said. "Shit. We'll hit that island in minutes. We can't have our radar go down now."

Harvey shook his head slowly. "It's not malfunctioning, sir."

"It has to be. Nothing can move like that, jumping, what, thirty miles, forty maybe, in less than a second?"

The radio crackled.

"Radar command," the operator said. "Come in."

The pilot's voice broke and hissed across the static. "What do you boys see on your screens there? I got some kind of bogey on my tail." A heartbeat later, the pilot's wordless shout filled the tent.

"Come in," the operator said. "Give us a report on what you're seeing."

"My God, there's three of them!" the pilot cried. "You see the way these fuckers are moving?"

Harvey muttered, "We're seeing it, all right."

No one heard him but Roger. "You're much too cool about this, Day."

"It's not the first time I've spotted these little guys. Watch now. See what they do."

The three bogeys flicked from one position to another, crossing the squadron's flight path, then swinging in behind the planes with a speed and precision that could only be called impossible. No aircraft moved that way—nothing in the American fleet, and nothing the Soviets or the Japanese possessed. Not as far as Allied intelligence knew.

"What in the hell are those things?" Roger demanded again.

"Some of the boys call them bogeys. Some call them foo fighters."

"Whose are they?"

"That's a good question, sir." Harvey offered no answer, beyond that.

A knot of dread tightened in Roger's stomach. He'd heard signalmen talk about foo fighters, but he'd written off the stories as stress-induced misinterpretations of perfectly ordinary radar functions. Unknown aircraft that moved in flicks across the sky and tailed the Army's fastest fighter planes seemed like the kind of legend that would grow amid the outsize strain of war. Yet there were three of them, right there on the scope, looking Roger dead in the eye.

"How often have you seen these things?" His voice had gone hoarse. He wished he had his canteen.

"They aren't terribly common," Harvey said, "but they come around often enough that I guess every radarman has seen them at least once."

The pilot's voice came scratching over the radio again. "Jesus, can you believe it? What're they doing out there? We're going thirty knots and they're keeping up with us, no wings, no exhaust that I can see—"

The bogeys disappeared from the scope, gone in a flash.

"Holy shit!" the pilot bellowed. "Did you see that acceleration?"

"Signal command to squadron," the operator said. "Confirm presence of bogeys."

"They're gone," the pilot answered. "Shot off to the north-northeast, all three of them. Fastest damn things I've seen in all my life."

"Tell him to carry on to the target," Harvey said. "The foos won't be back."

The radioman relayed the message calmly, but every nerve in Roger's body was still alive and burning with shock. "How do you know they won't be back?"

Harvey shrugged. "They've never interfered with a single mission. Whatever they are, they don't seem to be armed. And if they aren't exactly an Ally . . . well, they aren't against us, either."

"They might be"—Roger struggled to find some explanation—"an intelligence device. Spying on our aircraft, delivering information to the Japanese."

"I don't think so, sir. For all the times we've picked up foo fighters on radar, there's never been any link between them and a failed mission. I think they're just . . . curious."

"Curious?"

"About our planes. About us."

"You make it sound like they come from some other world."

Roger shuddered at the idea, pushed the thought away. As strange as the radar anomaly was—and stranger still, given the pilot's panicked reaction—the only possible explanation lay somewhere in the dense shadows that hung behind the walls of Axis intelligence. Roger had been briefed on the scientific advancements the Allied forces were making— the weapons they were building and testing, with the terrible heat of stars at their apocalyptic cores.

And we're supposed to be the good guys, he thought.

If America and Great Britain were hard at work on atomics, then God only knew what their enemies had cooked up in their secret bases and laboratories. Unmanned spy vehicles capable of leaping miles in a fraction of a second—why not? After all, the Allies could split atoms in explosions powerful enough to wipe entire cities off the planet.

Where will this end? Roger asked himself again.

He'd been asking the question too often lately, and he didn't like any of the answers he'd found.

CHAPTER THREE

July 2, 1947

That summer, the monsoon rains threatened to put the kibosh on fireworks. Late in the afternoon of July the second, one of those big, purple thunderstorms came stalking up from the south, but it didn't move on across the land, the way a monsoon usually does. By evening, the storm had settled firmly over Roswell, where it cycled through bursts of downpours and breaks where the children crept hopefully into their sodden yards, looking up at the clouds for any sign that the rain would soon depart. Basements flooded. The high school football field became a rectangular lake, dull beneath a heavy blanket of clouds. The streets were inundated until the gutters overflowed and a swift, deep current of brown water rushed everywhere through the town.

At the airfield base, three miles outside town, Roger wasn't bothered by the potential disruption of the holiday. He knew, though, that his kids would be disappointed if the rain stuck around through the Fourth. If the storm stayed on, the usual celebrations would be called off, and Roger could concentrate on his work. Since his return from the war, the Fourth of July had struck him as a kind of obscenity—a bluster of forceful patriotism that was a little too pleased with itself, and entirely too heedless of the cost that had been paid for all this extravagant freedom. Instead of participating in the ritualistic display of American superiority, he could linger in the radar bunker at the base, supervising as his men monitored the scopes for potential enemy intrusion over the nation's extensive test range. He and his unit would do what they did best: observe the serene privacy of the air above the desert bases where all those experimental aircraft were being made, assured of the enduring power and security of the USA.

As the night shift began, Roger entered the radar bunker just in time to feel a low throb of thunder shake through the muffling walls. He was pleased to see that Harvey Day was already settled at his scope.

Harvey wasn't from the Roswell area originally, like Roger was, but after the war, he'd been assigned to the airfield outside town. There was still plenty of work in the military for a good radarman—and now, with the Air Force about to split from the Army into its own autonomous branch, there was likely to be even more demand for anyone who knew what to do with an oscilloscope. That single unassuming airfield in Middle of Nowhere, New Mexico, was the center of all the action— ground zero for the flights and experiments that would bring the most cutting-edge aircraft out of the minds of engineers and into the hard, frank substance of reality. And not a moment too soon. If anyone had hoped the Soviets would curb their ambitions and retreat to their own territory to lick their considerable postwar wounds, that hope had been in vain. Another war already seemed inevitable, a fact that made Roger feel fifty years older than he was and weary, even in his sleep.

"Evening, Colonel," Harvey said—never taking his eyes from his scope, as usual. "How's the family?"

Roger smiled. "Just fine. Those two boys of mine are scamps. They're keeping their mother on her toes. They're in a panic over this storm, afraid it'll hang around all weekend and spoil the holiday."

"No danger of that," Harvey said. "Field watch radioed a few minutes ago, said the storm looks to be moving on."

"Finally. It's been a hell of a one. I'm surprised the town hasn't washed away."

"It's heading to the northwest now."

As if to emphasize the veracity of Harvey's report, another boom of thunder sounded.

Since nothing alarming was showing on the scopes, Roger went on talking about his family. There was nothing he was prouder of, after all. "That girl of mine, Betty—she's been studying all summer. Have you ever heard of a girl her age who'd rather have her nose in a book than go out with the boys?"

"Most dads would count themselves lucky, there," Harvey chuckled.

"I do, believe me. She's smart as a whip, that kid. And ambitious. She's got her sights set on college—wants to get into aeronautics, maybe rocketry. Betty's been wild about planes since she and her little friend put a model together back in—when was it?" He recalled the date, and the better part of his happiness evaporated. Just after Christmas of '41— that was when Betty had discovered her love of aircraft. Right before Roger had been called up to service. Right before he'd been forced to leave his family for the bleak, soulless grind of the war. "Anyway," he went on, "she's dead set on getting into a university, if she can find one that'll take girls."

"Good for her," Harvey said. "Coed colleges aren't as rare as they used to be. I'm sure she'll find a good school, if she's that keen on studies. I've thought sometimes I might try for a university myself—though I guess I might be too old for it now. Can't think what I'd do with a degree, anyway. Radar's all I know. I should probably stick with it."

In fact, Harvey had considered many different paths that might lead him out of Roswell. College or a gig as a mechanic in a friendlier climate—someplace where the summers didn't want to kill you and the rain was a gentle blessing, not these sudden, angry monsoon downbursts that sent every living thing cowering under shelter and made you sure a vengeful God was real and much too close for comfort. He'd thought of fixing up the old motorbike he'd found abandoned near the barracks, riding it all the way out of the desert, into the promising green hills of California. But what would he do there? What would he do in any other place? A curious inertia had tethered him to Roswell, a dull lassitude after the frantic pace of war. All these daydreams about other places never amounted to anything, never spurred him to any real action. He might as well remain there as go anywhere else. He had a purpose in the radar bunker.

Harvey lapsed into silence, focusing on his scope, and Roger settled at the radio desk with a two-day-old newspaper. Some half hour later, the thunder boomed again, but soft and distant this time.

Harvey said, "Sounds like the worst of the storm is beyond us now."

"Out in the open country," Roger agreed.

"What's the weather report like for the Fourth? Does that paper say? If another storm is coming and it's just going to rain again, the kids in town will probably set off all their fireworks tomorrow night instead. It's gonna sound like Okinawa, from town all the way to—"

Harvey's abrupt silence snapped Roger to attention. With a cold thrill, he remembered that day in the Pacific, when he'd visited the signal tent. Something about the intensity of Harvey's stillness felt the same, twisted the same knife in Roger's stomach.

"Colonel," Harvey said quietly, "I think you want to come and take a look at this."

Roger hurried across the room, leaned over Harvey's shoulder to watch the scope. There was a single white dot on the screen, exactly at the center of the northwest quadrant, maintaining its position as the indicator bar swept over it and around the scope again. Every speck of his attention, every nerve in his body, was trained on that small, white light. Maybe it was a malfunction caused by the storm. Such things were known to happen. But then again, maybe not. He wouldn't know unless it moved.

The blip did move. Between one sweep of the bar and the next, it jumped from the center of the northwest quadrant to the edge of the southeast. Then, just as suddenly, two more dots joined the first, arrayed across the black field.

Roger was sure now. Impossible as it seemed, out here in the desert, so far from the front—he was sure. "I'll be damned."

A fresh crack of thunder barreled across the desert waste, greater by far than the last had been. The cement bricks of the radar building shivered.

"Never thought I'd see foo fighters here," Harvey muttered. "Should we report this, sir?"

Roger was the guy who usually took reports of unexpected goings-on. He was the guy who was supposed to make the decisions. Only he couldn't think now what to do. He'd never imagined he might see those little white devils again.

"Let's see what they do first," he said.

His heart was pounding by then. His eyes were glued to the scope—to the bogeys. The dots flicked into one another's proximity, arranged themselves in a precise triangle.

"Jesus," Harvey muttered, "they're moving in formation."

"You ever see them do that in the Pacific?"

Harvey only shook his head, gripping the edges of the scope.

They watched the triangle of foo fighters leap from one edge of the scope to another, disappearing and reappearing across the field more rapidly than anything could move. Harvey reached for his dials, tuning frantically to pick up the next antenna in the array and keep the bogeys within sight. No sooner had he caught them again than they blinked once more across the field. Harvey spun his dials with shaking hands.

Roger's dazed mind finally caught up with what his eyes were seeing. The bogeys were maneuvering to avoid lightning as it licked from the clouds to the earth. The damn things must have been flying directly below the storm.

"They're using the storm as cover," he said. "It's an intentional incursion. Intelligence. They're trying to see what we're making out here—trying to get pictures or something, from our test flights of new aircraft." He spun away from the scope, scrambled for his radio, but the storm was interfering with the signal, and he couldn't raise anyone—not for long.

27

Still trying desperately for a connection, he watched from across the room as the V of white blips moved in a smooth glide to the northwest, hanging under the track of the storm.

"Keep on them," he said to Harvey—unnecessarily, for Harvey wouldn't have done anything less. But there was a strange, new desperation unfurling in Roger's heart. Something told him that if they lost sight of those objects now, they might never see the foos again. It wasn't only the concerns of duty or national security that drove him. An incongruous peace had come over him, a mesmerized fascination with the bizarre vehicles. The damn things couldn't be real, yet they were. And they had followed the American troops home from the Pacific. This wasn't a dream. It wasn't some feverish hallucination. Here were the impossible phantoms of his wartime service, thousands of miles from where they'd been before, flying in formation across the night-black desert.

Whether they were Soviet or Japanese in origin, Roger meant to find out, and turn the full force of the military against them. He hadn't gone off to fight, hadn't left his family for years, hadn't watched too many good men die to allow those treacherous Commies to intrude on American airspace with such arrogant impunity. He would make the bastards pay for shattering his illusion of peace.

Suddenly, the formation broke on Harvey's screen. Two of the fighters carried on in their coordinated glide while one sailed off at another trajectory. The A-scope responded in the same instant with a series of jagged peaks and valleys, radar waves bouncing off a confusion of solid matter—a bursting field of debris. A heartbeat later, a massive clap of thunder ripped across the desert. It shook Roger and Harvey both, right down to their bones.

Now, at last, Harvey tore his eyes from the scope. He stared at Roger, and for a long moment, Roger could do nothing but stare back.

They both knew what that thrashing signal on the A-scope meant. They'd seen it many times before, when enemy planes had been shot down—when Allies had lost their firefights, too. A downed aircraft registered the same on radar, whether it was one of your guys or the enemy who'd taken the hit.

"Damn it," Roger shouted, "if this radio doesn't pick up some signal, I swear I'll throw it across the room—"

"Come in," said a tinny voice across the static.

"This is Lieutenant Colonel Campbell in Signals," Roger said. "We've got a craft down, hit by lightning out on the desert."

"Sir," the radioman acknowledged. Then, a moment later, "What craft, sir? All our flights are grounded due to the—"

"The storm, I know," Roger cut in. "It isn't one of ours. It's a foo fighter."

A beat of silence. Harvey continued to stare at him, glazed and wide-eyed, more unsettled than Roger had seen him in their years of action together.

"Can you repeat that, sir?" the radioman said.

"You heard me right the first time. This is our chance to capture a foo fighter. Learn what we can about the enemy's tech."

About someone's tech, he added silently. *Whoever—whatever—made those bogeys.*

CHAPTER FOUR

July 2, 1947

That crack of thunder woke Betty first.

She sat up in her bed, looked in bleary confusion through the violet shadows of night. The coolness and the thick, mineral smell of the monsoon came in through her open window. The lace curtains stirred, and for a moment, she thought she saw something recede past the sill and out into the heavy, black night. It was a woman, a figure in flowing robes, with a ring of light around her ageless face. But when Betty blinked and rubbed her eyes, she understood that it had been only the tail end of a dream. There was nothing beyond the window but the clouds and the wind, and the great primal voice of the thunder muttering across the land. Her curtains stirred again. Alone with impressions she could barely half articulate—speed and distance and fire, and a sense of importance surrounding her, consuming her, a meaning as vast and ancient as the long, enduring sweep of the desert from one horizon to the other—she hugged her knees to her chest, and listened to the storm as it stalked its way over the sleeping desert.

Three blocks away, the thunder broke the persistent silence of the Lucero home, that dull, strained quiet that had filled its grieving walls for three years now. Jim hadn't really been sleeping. He'd been wavering somewhere between memory and dream, in a place where he could still hear his dead father's voice. *God put a brain in your head because he meant for you to use it, Jim.* The thunder frightened him, pulled him from that shadowy place where his father was now, back to reality, where his father wasn't. It was just a storm, and Jim wasn't a little boy any longer. He had no cause for fear. But the sound of the thunder was fear itself, the wave that shudders through you and shakes you apart, just when you think you've got yourself together. He thought of the great metal machines that cleave the sky. He thought of metal falling, and burning, the wild hopeless clutch of gravity. He left his bed, stole silently to his mother's door. When he looked in to check on her, he found her asleep, peaceful despite the emptiness at the other side of the bed, where Jim's father should have been.

The thunder swept across Roswell. Everyone who woke to its call also woke to a new awareness—of the bigness of things, and the small-ness of things, of the way the small and the great are contained within one another, and all contained in God's hand.

Cece Alvarado, already awake and sweating from the change of life, whispered comfort to her three little dogs and fed them tidbits of cheese to drive back their anxiety. And though it was a silly impulse, still she knew, as the rumble passed through her, that even a minor mercy to hum-ble creatures such as these was as good as the benediction of any saint.

Jake Carper, who ran the hardware store, jumped from his bed and looked out the window. He saw nothing but the close density of the monsoon sky. When his wife asked what was wrong, he answered, "Something's coming, Mary. Something big." He didn't know why.

The sheriff reached into his nightstand, made sure his gun was still there.

At St. Mary's Hospital, the nurses paused in their nightly rounds, listening to the storm, feeling its primitive force, and to each of them, the hospital itself seemed to become a transparent thing, its walls like panes of glass, so they could see far across the desert to a scene of terrible emergency and a white, blinding awe.

In a home at the western edge of town, Juanita Lopez heard the thunder and thought of her best friend, Betty Campbell—though she couldn't have told you why the storm brought Betty to her mind, nor why such a feeling of suffocating dread and deep, wounded sadness accompanied the thought. Nor could Juanita have explained the wonder that raced through her veins, an almost holy awareness, shivering with the sound of the storm. The girl went outside in her nightgown and found her mother in the front yard, mud up to her bare ankles, staring at the sky and smoking a cigarette even though it was the middle of the night.

"Mom," Juanita said, "what are you doing?"

"Praying," her mother answered, though she didn't look as if she were praying, and she said nothing more, only dragged at the cigarette and breathed smoke like a cloud of incense up to the sky.

The thunder moved through the rectory. Father Kerry woke with a cry of fear. His heart pounded so wildly that for a moment he considered calling for an ambulance. But there was no doctor who could remedy this—a crashing, bleak awareness that he had got it all wrong, that nothing as divine as God could be contained by tame lines of scripture, the rituals and ancient hierarchies of any church.

The echo of the storm moved from the rectory across the northern edge of town, past an old, white farmhouse surrounded by a ring of elms, through its empty rooms and through the souls who would soon occupy it, and far beyond Roswell, across the open range, chasing the path of the monsoon over miles of sage, over pale hills blushing with the brief miracle of desert bloom, to the ranch where Mac Brazel worked, tending sheep and cattle for its owners.

The strange persistence of the thunder drew Mac outside. His two young children followed. Together, they gazed in silence across the empty darkness to a towering monolith of cloud. Lightning licked down, again and again, illuminating the fat, purple curves of the storm's belly.

"What's that?" his daughter asked.

There was something odd about that storm. Mac could see it now. The bolts of lightning were coming too fast, one after another, strobing with a ferocity that seemed more determined, more intelligent than any storm had a right to be. Then he realized what had unsettled him about the lightning. It was striking again and again in the same place, as if drawn to some object or target. Lightning never did such things. Mac had never seen a storm like this, not in all his life in the desert.

"Get inside," he said to his kids.

"Why?" his son asked.

"Get inside," Mac repeated, "now."

He turned to watch them enter the small adobe shack that was their home—had to be sure they were safe, out of the path of this monster that was barreling toward them. When he was satisfied that his children were out of harm's way, he looked again in the direction of the lightning and found a different fire in the sky.

It was huge and burning, hurtling uncontrolled from the southeast, over the curve of the earth and straight toward the rangeland. *A plane,* he thought, frozen and staring, dumbstruck as one of his sheep in the slaughtering chute.

The object passed overhead, lighting the ground and Mac's house and Mac himself with the brightness of day.

He thought, *That's no goddamn plane.*

The next morning, as soon as dawn broke, he saddled his best horse and went out to find what he could.

He saw the scorch mark first, thirty feet wide at least, a black track of disorder clawed into the earth, still smoking from the fire. A chemical stench of burning overwhelmed the scent of the well-watered desert. His sheep flocked and bleated in a panic on the other side of the track. His horse refused to go near the burn, but he could ride parallel to it, all down its length, goggling at the pale, silvery shards of metal that had strewn themselves along the harrowed-up scar.

Then he saw the rest of it—the thing that was smashed and driven into the stony curve of a shallow arroyo. All he could do, for God knew how long, was stare.

CHAPTER FIVE

July 3, 1947

Harvey slumped on the bench outside Colonel Blanchard's office. The base had erupted into activity with the speed and fury of a kicked hornet's nest—privates running here and there, commanding officers barking out orders. Harvey let it all crash around him. Hours had passed since the bogey had gone down, and he was still easing himself into the truth. But there was no denying what he'd seen. The signals on his scope had been exactly like those he'd picked up years ago, in the Pacific.

Beside him on the bench, Roger ran his hands over his own face, for the fiftieth time or the hundredth, as if he might drive back reality by manual force. "Shit," Roger kept muttering. "Shit, shit, shit." Roswell's airfield was home to the only airborne atomics in the United States military. Whoever was behind the bogey—the Soviets, Roger assumed—they had to be looking for the Army planes that housed and carried the nation's A-bombs. Looking for the atomics so they could destroy them—detonate them, right there at the base, three miles outside town, three miles from where his family was sleeping.

"See here, you got no right to lay hands on me!"

That panicked squawk pulled Harvey out of his thoughts. He looked up to find a commotion nearby. Captain Armstrong, a redheaded giant of a man, and the famously unflappable Sergeant Roosevelt were frog-marching a civilian down the long hallway. Harvey blinked when he recognized the man—Mac Brazel, a rancher who managed a plot of land out near Corona. Brazel had joined Harvey for a beer now and then, when circumstances had brought them both into Roswell. He liked the guy—found Brazel to be one of those down-to-earth, honest types, if a little earthy and rough around the edges. He couldn't imagine what Brazel might have done to warrant a military arrest.

Armstrong and Roosevelt turned their prisoner abruptly, led him into a nearby room—one that contained a jail cell, Harvey knew.

When Brazel realized he was about to be detained, he yelped all the louder. "I'm supposed to have a lawyer! You got no right to detain me. Damn it, I was only trying to do the right thing!"

The office door swung open. Harvey and Roger both looked up, relieved to do something other than sit and wait. Colonel Blanchard gave a jerk of his head, a silent command to enter.

When they stepped inside, they found Captain Sheridan Cavitt bent over the colonel's desk, marking a topo map with a grease pencil. Major Jesse Marcel was there, too—a steady fellow with a background in intelligence and more recent experience with the nuclear tests out at Bikini Atoll. Marcel stood over Cavitt, hands braced on his hips and his brow furrowed, swaying restlessly from foot to foot as Cavitt drew on the map.

Blanchard closed the door. "Lieutenant Colonel Campbell, Signalman Day. You've both done great work with your quick report. Thanks to the coordinates you gave us, we've pinpointed the site of that crash."

"Is it a Soviet aircraft, sir?" Roger asked.

"That's what we hope to find out. The two of you are coming with us. We're taking a recovery crew out to investigate."

"My wife . . . ," Roger began.

"I've already told my secretary to call your wife and let her know you won't be home until late this evening. We expect it might take that long. You boys are going to need plenty of coffee; it'll be a long day, and you've just come off the night shift."

"With respect, sir," Harvey said, "what do you need us for?"

"Briefing," Blanchard said. "You'll ride with Major Marcel and me. And the captain. We want the whole story on the drive out to the crash site—everything you saw on radar, as much detail as you can give."

Harvey and Roger shared a long, cautious look.

"Nothing leaves this circle," Blanchard went on. "Not a word of this to anyone who's not on this recovery mission."

Roger said, "Pardon me, sir, but you don't need to tell us that."

Blanchard gave him a grim smile. "I'm telling you anyhow, Lieutenant Colonel. Don't you dare forget it."

By the time they neared the crash site, seventy-five miles outside Roswell, Harvey and Roger had both repeated the story so many times it felt like a liturgy. Blanchard and Cavitt took it all with an unsettling coolness, even the news that there had been three blips on Harvey's radar—two more unknown craft, at least, were still out there somewhere, doing God knew what. Major Marcel only scowled at the empty highway as he drove, sunk in his own dire thoughts.

Cavitt examined his map, then pointed to the road ahead. "That's the turn—that dirt road, there."

As Marcel's car left the highway, Harvey twisted to peer out the back window. A massive jeep carryall with a dark canvas canopy had followed them from the base. Its toothy tires dug into the saturated earth as it crawled along in Marcel's wake.

They traveled a good two or three miles from the highway, deep into the heart of Brazel's ranch, before Marcel hit the brakes with a curse. The dirt lane ascended a shallow hill just ahead—not a very imposing hill, for most of the land out there was nearly as flat as a board, but it was tall enough to block their view of the land that lay just ahead. At the crest of the hill, another car was stopped, and a man stood beside it, one hand shielding his eyes as he stared into the late-morning sun. He was a civilian, and he was entirely oblivious to the small convoy from the Army base, despite the rumble of the carryall's engine.

"Damn it," Blanchard muttered.

A moment later, he was out of Marcel's car, storming on foot up the road. Harvey and Roger shared a look, then scrambled out after the colonel.

"You there," Blanchard shouted.

The man at the crest of the hill spun in a panic. At the sight of the carryall—obviously a military vehicle—he began to pat frantically at the pockets of his trousers. He crept down the hill with reluctance, calling out to Blanchard, his mouth working rapidly as he stammered through an explanation.

"John McBoyle," the civilian said, "KSWS Radio in Roswell. I'm a reporter."

He found what he sought at last, pulled his wallet from a back pocket, proffered an ID card to Blanchard.

The colonel shoved the card back to McBoyle. "I don't care who you are. Get the hell out of here before I have you arrested."

McBoyle looked back up the hill to where his car waited, then turned once more to Blanchard with a stricken expression. "What is that thing?"

"None of your damn business, that's what. Didn't you hear me? Get out, or you're going to jail."

The threat pulled McBoyle out of his shock. "See here, I'm a member of the press. You've got no right to—"

Blanchard stepped up to the man, chest to chest. "It'll take me one phone call to DC, and I'll have your entire station's broadcast license revoked"—he snapped his fingers—"that fast. Now you've got thirty seconds to get your ass in your car and get out of here."

Still McBoyle hesitated, glancing uneasily at the slope—at whatever lay beyond it.

"One," Blanchard said.

The reporter scrambled back up the hill. He threw himself into his car, and a moment later, its engine roared to life. He turned awkwardly at the crest, skirting Marcel's car and the carryall on his way out of Brazel's range.

"Jesus." Roger watched the reporter's car dwindle in the distance.

Blanchard gestured at the carryall. Four men got out, stood at anxious attention.

"Two of you keep an eye on this road," the colonel said. "If anyone who's not in an Army uniform attempts to approach, drive them away. Draw your sidearms, if necessary." He turned on his heel, barked over his shoulder, "Everyone else, come with me."

The remainder of Blanchard's crew left the carryall halfway up the slope and gathered in a tight huddle, looking around the silent sweep of desert like a pack of hunted animals. The air still smelled crisp and lively from the previous night's rain. It was the kind of morning that usually inspired activity—birds winging and calling, snakes and lizards emerging from their burrows to bask in the sun. But an eerie silence had descended over the land. The only sound, the only sign of movement, were the brief gusts of wind that stirred the scrubby vegetation and whispered through the tangled branches.

Blanchard and Marcel led the crew up the slope to its crest. From there, the ground fell away into a deep bowl, a hollow entirely hidden from the road. Across that small valley stood a distinctive bluff, an arc of pale stone curving around the depression. When they saw what lay in the hollow, every man staggered to a halt. Not one of them could draw a breath, nor hear the wind. The sunrise blinked out of existence; every man's awareness of time and place was sucked into a yawning void of astonishment.

At the base of the curved bluff, something large and silvery white was smashed into the rocks and the broken sage.

Harvey was the first to speak. "My God."

A vast, still awe came over Roger—the catastrophic peace of a revelation. At his side, Harvey was breathing in short, ragged gasps. Roger reached out and clutched the radarman by his shoulder, not knowing whether he was trying to hold Harvey steady or keep himself from dropping to his knees in wonder and terror. Everything reeled around him—the desert, the endless morning, the substance of reality itself—revolving on the axis of that pale, unknowable thing, the stark impossibility wrecked among the stones of the ordinary earth.

"What is it?" A whisper was the best Roger could manage.

He'd thought they might find a plane of some kind—a very fast and unusually maneuverable craft, but still a recognizable airplane. This was unlike anything he'd seen in the sky, in all his years of training and combat. In fact, Roger couldn't fathom how the thing might have flown at all. Some thirty feet long and shaped like a giant snake's egg—or like the freight cars that carried chemicals in their cylindrical bellies—it possessed neither propellers nor jets, no visible means of propulsion. It had no wings, either, and no damage on its flank to show where a wing might have broken away. Aside from its crumpled nose and a sizable hole in its fuselage, the entire body was smooth, white, unriveted. All of a single piece.

"That's no Soviet plane," Roger said hoarsely.

"No, sir," Harvey said.

"We've got to go down and investigate," Major Marcel said. "Who's got the Geiger counter?"

One of the men from the carryall pressed the contraption into Marcel's hands. The major switched it on, and the machine gave a high-pitched whine. It began to tick out a slow, reassuring rhythm. No radiation detected—not yet.

The men crept in their huddle from the hilltop into the small valley, where the chill of morning shadows closed around them and dimmed the sky. No one spoke a word, and none could take their eyes off the wreckage. The craft, partway up the opposite slope of the depression, seemed to loom now above them—majestic, unconquerable even in its damaged and earthbound state.

"Somebody's got to go up there among the rocks and look for survivors," Captain Cavitt said.

"Survivors," one of the carryall men said. "My God."

Marcel jerked a thumb in Harvey's direction. "Signalman Day, you go."

Harvey swallowed hard. He was the most junior man present, which made him expendable, in the eyes of his military superiors. He wanted to refuse—his terror of the wreckage was quickly overwhelming any sense of wonder or awe—but refusal wasn't an option. Not for a mere signalman who'd been given a direct order by an Army captain.

"I'll go," Roger said. He put out his hand for the Geiger counter.

Harvey stepped in front of him. "No, sir. I've got my orders."

Roger watched his friend take the counter and pick his way toward the wreckage. Surely he was watching some bizarre film, not his own life, not the only real friend he had in this world inching toward the unknown. The chill and the dampness of early morning closed in tightly around him, and he drew one sharp, short breath after another, bracing for something to move, for the craft to rise with the same superior speed it had displayed on radar. What was he doing, allowing a good man like Harvey to do such dangerous work? Roger should have gone himself. Except that he had a family back home, a wife and children who needed him.

As Harvey moved among the boulders at the foot of the curved bluff, Roger called, "Be careful." It was all he could think to say.

Brandishing his sensor like a weapon, Harvey stumbled his way up through the ancient rocks and the gnarled roots of plants, through the scattered scraps of some pale, lightweight material, like Reynolds Wrap but stiff as steel. Other than himself, nothing moved. The absolute stillness made his skin crawl even as it filled him with a kind of worshipful dread. He drew within fifty feet of the crash, then forty. The Geiger counter clicked on in its steady rhythm. He inched a little farther up the foot of the bluff—closer and closer all the time, nearer to the heart of an unspeakable mystery.

Harvey looked around the boulder-strewn earth. He was braced to find the bodies of pilot and crew, but there was no sign of any person, living or dead. That was some small relief.

"Hello," he called.

Thank God, there was no answer.

Harvey was near enough now that he could touch the craft. He gazed up at it. Light bounced from the smooth curve of its fuselage, making his eyes water. He felt smaller than he had in all his life, an ant, a speck in the cosmic vastness of a universe that was far broader and wiser than he'd ever pretended it might be. The huge regality of that unknown object left him dizzy and sick with a staggering, breathless humility.

His eyes traveled along the body of the craft, and then he followed his own gaze, pacing down its length. It was easily thirty feet long, maybe more. One end—impossible to call it front or back—was buckled against the bluff, but the other side was mostly undamaged, save for the gaping hole in its eggshell skin. The hole was large enough that he could fit his head and shoulders inside. And his Geiger counter was still ticking along, registering no unusual radiation.

Harvey glanced back down the bluff. Roger and the rest were still there, watching him from the valley floor, small as toy soldiers.

He turned back to consider the craft again. He dropped to his knees beside the rent in the fuselage.

"Don't do it," Roger shouted from below.

For the rest of his life, Harvey wished he'd heeded those words. Because after he looked inside the wreckage, he was never the same man again. Or the world wasn't the same. Reality became the plaything of words and wind. All the sense and order of the world blew away like the storms of summer, leaving everything stark and scoured, half-drowned in their wake.

CHAPTER SIX

July 4, 1947

The reporter John McBoyle was useless for the rest of the day. He drifted around the radio station in an aimless daze until his boss sent him home to recover from whatever ailed him. McBoyle didn't sleep a wink that night, either. He paced his apartment until the small hours, scribbling notes about what he'd seen, crumpling them into balls, pitching them at the waste basket beside his desk, then writing it all out again. He didn't know what to call that huge, white machine he'd found smashed in the desert.

Mac Brazel had pounded on the door of the radio station some fifteen minutes before KSWS opened, pleading with somebody to come out and talk to him. McBoyle had done the honors, thinking he would find another dead-end story about petty theft or a squabble between neighbors—the usual line of business in a small, remote town. When he saw Brazel's expression—strained almost to the point of hysteria—he knew a bigger story had landed in his lap.

He didn't know how big it was till he'd driven all the way out to Brazel's land, and seen for himself what was smashed down in that depression below the bluffs.

For the rest of that day and all through the night, McBoyle searched his mind and his memory for a suitable description, any name to give the thing he'd seen that might make it concrete and rational. The only name that seemed to suit was one he'd read in a paper from Washington state a few weeks earlier, after a pilot had reported a bizarre encounter in the skies.

Flying saucer.

It was too strange, too mad, too impossible to be true. And yet, McBoyle had witnessed it.

Now he had to decide what to do about the story. The Army colonel hadn't made an idle threat—McBoyle was sure of that. His station might not survive, but he had a moral obligation as a member of the press. It was his duty to his fellow citizens to see that the truth got out.

When morning came, McBoyle poured his third cup of coffee and placed a long-distance phone call to KOAT, the sister station in Albuquerque. McBoyle was in luck. Lydia Sleppy took the call in KOAT's press room. He'd worked with Lydia before on stories of statewide interest. She was a sharp gal, full of a journalist's righteous passion for the truth.

"Lydia, thank God it's you. This is John McBoyle at KSWS."

"John! I haven't heard from you in weeks. What's the news in Roswell?"

McBoyle gave a shaky laugh. "Big—that's what the news is. I've got a hot story for the network."

He could hear the wheels of Lydia's chair squeal as she pulled in closer to her Teletype, the large, high-tech transmission device that converted typewritten messages to electronic signals and sent them down the telephone wires. Then a loud, grating hum as the machine switched on.

"Okay, John, I'm ready."

She wasn't ready, McBoyle knew—not for this. Nobody was. He said, "Listen, Lydia, there's no other way to say it. A flying saucer went down last night a little north of town. The Army has picked it up by now."

The Teletype grumbled amid Lydia's silence.

"Sorry," she finally said. "I don't think I heard you correctly."

"You heard me, all right. I wouldn't believe it myself if I hadn't seen it with my own eyes. But that's the headline, Lydia. 'United States Army in Possession of Flying Saucer.'"

She recovered herself quickly and snapped to work, as any good reporter did. He could hear her fingers on the keys, rapid and sure, rattling like machine-gun fire as she entered the message.

Then the sharp ping of an electronic bell, and a gasp.

Lydia's side of the line went quiet.

"Hello," McBoyle said into the receiver. He paced, as far as his telephone cord would allow. "Lydia? Are you there?"

She was still on the line. But she wasn't typing any longer. At the sound of the bell—a signal to indicate an incoming message—she had pulled her hands from the keys. Now she stared, astonished and more than a little frightened, at the incoming message as it assembled letter by letter on the scrolling paper.

THIS IS THE FBI. YOU WILL IMMEDIATELY CEASE TRANSMITTING.

"My God, John," she said faintly into her receiver. "What's going on down there in Roswell?"

After the craft was loaded into the carryall and the Army crew had scoured every last scrap of debris from Brazel's land, Harvey returned to the base with the rest of the men, where they were all sworn to secrecy on pain of court-martial and then released back to their normal lives, as if their lives could ever be normal again.

In his small room in the barracks, little bigger than the cell of a cloistered nun, Harvey slept heavily for a few hours. Thank goodness he didn't dream. He woke to the bright glare of day, showered away the sweat and tension of the past twenty-four hours, and returned to his tiny room with his towel around his neck, where he sat for a while on his narrow cot, taking in the simple, frank fact of his surroundings, the ordinary quiet, the evidence of life and Army operations going doggedly on despite the fact that American supremacy had fallen from the sky and burned a smoking trench across the desert. His window was coated, as always, with a veneer of dust, obscuring the expanse of the runways outside, blurring the distant mountain range to a thin line of purple. Harvey had stirred the air when he'd walked into the room. He watched dust motes turn slowly on invisible currents, glittering in the soft, persistent light—evidence of his own movement, his own presence. Proof that he, himself, was real.

All of this had been real. He had seen a foo fighter, not as a blip on his radar scope but as a thing of substance, physical, undeniable; he had touched it with his own hands.

He had looked inside.

When he tried to recall the moments after he'd leaned inside the fighter, when he tried to remember exactly what he'd seen, his mind reeled back and the memory collapsed into confusion. All he was left with was a vague impression of *wrongness*, a wave of sickness in his stomach, and a frantic awe that might, he thought, be something like a religious ecstasy. If he were a religious man.

He rose from his cot, stood in the heat of his windowpane, peered out through the dust and beyond the airstrips to the vast and ancient desert beyond.

Where had the fighter come from? Harvey asked himself.

He could think of a few explanations. None of them was the sort of thing a sane man would believe. But Harvey had looked inside the thing. He knew no ordinary answer would suffice.

Though the day was clear and bright, with no threat of another storm, the town of Roswell went about its Fourth of July celebration in a state of subdued meekness. The parade down Main Street wasn't as lively as it had been in years past. The marching band didn't sound quite so brassy, the cheerleaders from the high school didn't chant or pose with their usual pep. The mayor's wave from the back of a bunting-covered Cadillac was almost timid, and the flags among the crowd hung limp more often than they waved. No one could have said what caused so many spirits to sag. But every mind and heart in Roswell had been touched by a new awareness, a quiet acknowledgment of space that was larger than town or desert or country, of time that was larger than the here and now. It made the people of the town thoughtful and pensive. It made them look up to the great, blue arch of the sky and wonder what was on the other side.

By evening, when the first fireworks began to pop above the streets and the air was heavy with the smell of sulfur, rumors of a downed saucer were already wending through the population. This, of course, was in defiance of the oaths Roger and the other men had been made to swear. But what is an oath—even to the Army, with all its proven authority and power—compared to the thrill of a spaceship, or a time traveler's machine, or whatever might explain the mysterious object that had come down on the Brazel ranch?

Betty did her best to pretend that everything was normal. She couldn't get out of the big barbecue at the park, so she hid her hands in the bulky, fingerless gloves her father had given her, though the gloves made it difficult to eat her hot dog and drew stares and whispers from the other girls. When the story of a flying saucer made its way to Betty's ear, a sensation ran through her—not quite cold, but not exactly hot, either—a thrill of sudden understanding.

So that was what her father had found in the desert. That was where the scrap of metal had come from—outer space. Or from the future, depending on whom she believed, and she wasn't sure she believed anybody. Spaceships and time travelers had once been the stuff of magazine stories, nothing more than silly fun to entertain children. Now, she clenched her fists around the pain that still lingered in her palms, and she knew there was some truth in the stories. There had to be.

Something had to explain her affliction. There was a reason for everything. Wasn't there? That was what Betty had always read in her textbooks. That was what Father Kerry always said in his homilies.

If she could find the reason, then she could understand.

CHAPTER SEVEN

July 9–11, 1947

Evening had come again.

Roger lay in bed with his reading lamp on, ignoring the open book he held, scarcely registering the sounds of flowing water and Rosa humming in the bathroom while she washed her hair. A week since the thunderstorm, since the unknown craft went down in the desert. Night had followed day, and day had followed night, and women had gone on washing their hair and singing, and children had played, as ever, in the dusky streets when the worst of the summer heat had dissipated. And men had gone on guarding the secrets they kept. For the past week, as if this life were still the same, as if the word *ordinary* still meant something.

Roger lay, staring beyond the pages of his book and feeling the solidity of the walls around him—his home, his castle and his keep, where everyone he loved, everyone for whom he had sacrificed during the war, was safely within his reach. And he felt the long, black sweep of the desert beyond, a place as open and cold as airless space. For a moment, it all shivered around him, as if some vast power were about to suck it all away from him, out into the darkness—the bed and the walls, and Rosa's sweet, unconscious humming, and a father's instinctive impression of his children, so precious and small.

He heard Betty leave her room and descend the stairs. A minute later, the taps in the kitchen sink ran as she filled a glass with water. Roger tried to focus on his book, but all words were meaningless. He couldn't settle into his reading until he knew his girl was safely back in her room, where he expected to find her. Since that day in the desert— since he'd laid eyes on that silvery-white *thing*—he'd been possessed by a relentless fear, not for himself but for his family.

During the war, Rosa and the children were the banners under which he'd marched. He had gone willingly to fight and serve, determined to do his part—to do whatever was necessary to keep his family safe. Nothing he'd learned during his years of active duty had reassured him in the least. From his first briefing on the atomic bomb, Roger had understood that a terrible chain of events had been set in motion. The first domino had fallen in the nuclear test ranges of White Sands and Alamogordo. By the time Hiroshima and Nagasaki were destroyed, it was far too late to stop what was coming. America and the Soviet Union, and all their allies, were trapped now in a different kind of war. This one would be a conflict not of battlefronts and trenches, not of rifles and fighter planes, but of escalating technology, a race to build weapons that exceeded the power and horror of each that had come before. And the race would only grow tighter, faster, more urgent and desperate as each new weapon was produced.

Premonition blew through him, a bitter wind. It made him shudder. He could see the future unfolding in a long, straight path from where he stood—from where the whole world stood. The competition to make and possess the most indomitable weapon of all would require money, and plenty of it. That would mean more wars, for only active conflict could provide the impetus and the funding to maintain weapons development, thus ensuring that America's technology remained one jump ahead of the Soviets'. But these would not be wars like the one Roger had fought. The grim vision revealed to him small nations worn like puppets on the hands of greater powers. Countless lives destroyed merely for the sake of it, merely to keep the machine of war grinding along on its now inevitable course. The proxy wars would come. And then, the race of rocketry, to conquer and colonize the night sky. One domino falling after another. Once the Soviets had artificial satellites up there beyond the atmosphere, they would put atomic weapons up there, too. Bombs far worse than ones America had dropped on Japan would rain down from among the stars to burn away everything he loved, everything he was powerless to defend.

It was already beginning. That thing in the desert—it could only have been some Soviet device. An aircraft without wings or visible means of propulsion, a craft that could maneuver in ways that made a joke of physics. However the Soviets had managed it, there was no catching up with them now, even with the craft in the possession of the Army for study and reverse engineering. The dominoes had already fallen.

The low rumble of an engine sounded on the street below. It slowed and came to a halt outside the Campbell home. Roger set his book aside, got up from the bed, and peered out the window. An old pickup truck sat at the curb. A man got out and moved slowly up the path to Roger's front door.

He cast around for his old cotton dressing robe, but he'd left it in the bathroom. Rosa had locked the door, and it took a good deal of knocking and calling before she heard Roger over the sound of the rushing water. By the time Rosa let him in, her hair wrapped in the beehive of a bath towel, Betty had already answered the door.

Still knotting the tie of his robe, Roger nearly collided with his daughter as she came running up the stairs, wide-eyed and frantic.

"Honey," Roger said, "are you all right?"

"Someone's at the door," Betty said. "It's for you."

She brushed past him, and a moment later, her bedroom door slammed.

Roger hurried down the rest of the steps. Betty had left the front door hanging open, and there stood Harvey Day, hunched and shivering on the threshold. The man was all staring eyes and disheveled, sweat-stained civvies.

"Harvey," Roger said, "good God, what's happened to you? Come in. Let me get you some coffee."

He made Harvey sit on the sofa, turned on another lamp. Harvey winced at the light, and Roger noted the redness of his eyes. The guy hadn't slept in far too long. He shouldn't have driven all the way from the base in such a state.

"No coffee," Harvey said. "I came to talk, that's all."

"You need something to sharpen you up. Don't make me pull rank on you, Harvey; you know I will. Anyway, it won't take a minute."

In the kitchen, Roger set up the vacuum pot and filled it with a strong dose of grounds, knowing all the while that he was buying himself time as much as looking after his friend. There was only one thing Harvey would want to talk about. It was the same topic on which Roger had ruminated for the past week. He would have no answers to Harvey's questions. He had no answers to his own questions, and yet he hadn't stopped asking them—couldn't stop—from the moment he'd laid eyes on that inconceivable craft in the desert.

The coffee was ready all too soon. Roger drifted through the house, a ghost of himself traversing a landscape that barely existed. He handed a cup to Harvey, took a seat in his favorite easy chair. The coffee was strong and black. Harvey sipped it and jittered. A little splashed over the rim of the cup onto his dirty trousers. He didn't take any notice.

"It's been eating at me," Harvey said.

No need to go into specifics. Roger knew what he was talking about. Every man who'd been in the presence of the recovered craft would know exactly what Harvey was talking about.

"I've got to figure out what to do about it."

"Do about it?" Roger said. "I'll tell you what you do. You stick to the official story the Army gave."

One way or another—probably thanks to that reporter they'd found at the scene of the crash—the story had leaked into the press.

Not only the *Roswell Daily Record*, but several other papers across the region had blared headlines announcing that the Army Air Force had captured a flying saucer.

"The story that it was a weather balloon?" Harvey said. "Come on, Roger."

The Army had acted fast, countering the wild tale of a flying saucer with a calm, thoughtfully constructed narrative. The following day, the *Roswell Morning Dispatch*—rival to the *Daily Record*—featured the headline *Army Debunks Roswell Flying Disk as World Simmers with Excitement—Officers Say Disk Is Weather Balloon*. As a final touch from the heavy, authoritative hand of the Army, subsequent articles had included a photo of Major Marcel himself, in uniform, gingerly holding up the limp, reflective foil that was typically used in weather-monitoring craft.

That picture had been a setup, of course. Whatever they'd seen out there on Brazel's ranch, it was no goddamn weather balloon.

He wasn't prepared to say it was a flying saucer, either. There was no need to invent a Martian invasion when planet earth already had its share of dangerous enemies. The truth was much more terrifying than little green men from outer space. And public ignorance of the true capacity of Soviet weapons was the only hair-thin thread that still held society together.

"Yes," Roger insisted. "You stick to the Army's official story, and you *believe* it."

"*You* don't believe the official line," Harvey said. "God Almighty, Roger, you know what you saw—what *we* saw."

"That's not my point," Roger said, more calmly than he felt. "We won't know what we found until the engineers have had their chance to study it. Until then, we've got to keep the general population from panicking. Think about what might happen if people knew there were . . . *things* flying around our skies faster than any of our planes can travel, capable of doing . . . well, what we both saw them do on radar. Jesus, Harvey, it's like they can disappear and reappear a hundred miles away in half a second!

If John Q. Public knew the Soviets have that kind of technology—if they knew our military has no hope of defending them and their families against aircraft like that—there'd be riots in the streets. Mayhem. The overthrow of governments around the world. You could kiss any hope for a peaceful, ordinary life goodbye. If people find out the truth, then the whole idea of civilized society comes apart."

Harvey slouched into the sofa. He couldn't meet Roger's eye. "Maybe civilized society needs to come apart."

"Jesus, Harv, get a hold of yourself. That's not what you and I fought for."

"It's eating at me. The lie. The story that it was a weather balloon."

"You took an oath," Roger warned. "Remember that. You swore to uphold the Army's story, and you can't go back on it now. There would be consequences, Harvey. Real consequences, bad ones."

Harvey pulled himself together in that moment, sat up straight and met Roger's eye with his old, self-assured clarity. "I know I took an oath. I don't mean to break it. I don't give my word lightly, even under duress. But I can't keep serving in the Army, knowing what I do, knowing they're hiding the truth behind a screen of lies. Truth means something to me, too, Roger. And . . . and I know what I saw. I saw more than you did—more than Cavitt or Marcel or any of the rest. I can't just let them tell me I'm crazy. You know I'm not."

Roger sighed, pinched the bridge of his nose. "There might be a way out. I'm your XO; I can recommend you for a discharge, but that won't be easy, either. You'll lose your benefits. In a town like Roswell, where every family has at least one man in the Army, you'll be an outcast. You might have a hard time finding another job."

"Then I'll go somewhere else," Harvey said. "I don't care. I'll take another oath, if they want me to—swear never to breathe a word about what we saw. I'll deny I was ever at Brazel's ranch. I'll leave Roswell for good and never look back."

"That's the other thing," Roger said slowly. "You can deny you were there to civilians, but the Pentagon already has the reports. *They* know you were there—General Marshall, and Truman, and the FBI. You think they'd stop at anything to protect a secret like this? You'll be in real danger, Harvey. One word about this to anyone, and you could be a dead man."

"I know," Harvey said, calm now, almost his old, steady self. "I've thought about that, too. But I don't intend to tell a soul. No one would believe me, anyhow. Hell, Roger, you wouldn't even believe me if I told you what I saw. I'll take the discharge. It's my only way out now." He paused, then fixed Roger with a pleading look. "You have a piece of it, don't you?"

"A piece of it?"

"The saucer."

"God damn it, Harvey, you've got to come back down to earth. It was some Soviet invention, not a flying saucer."

"Whatever it is, you have a piece of it. While we were cleaning up the debris field, I saw you slip a piece into your pocket."

"That doesn't mean I kept it."

It was a feeble deflection, and Roger could tell by the keen narrowing of Harvey's eyes that his friend had seen right through the evasion. Of course Roger had kept the fragment of metal, or whatever the substance was. You didn't get rid of a thing like that—a wonder, a miracle, a horror.

"Let me see it," Harvey said. "Please."

"Harv, come on."

"You don't understand what it's like for me. I looked inside that thing, Roger. I need to know if it was real or not. If I'm crazy or not. I need to know."

Roger felt leaden, and fathoms underwater, as he pushed himself up from the easy chair. "Follow me."

He led Harvey to the kitchen, opened the closet that reached back under the stairs. He stooped to pry up the loose floorboard at the base of the water heater, withdrew the lead-lined box he had hidden in the cavity below. The Geiger counters had never registered radiation on any of the wreckage Roger and his men had recovered, but something about that scrap of debris had injured Betty's hands. Who could say what dangerous properties it might have? A barrier of lead seemed like the safest way to store that strange artifact under his roof, while keeping his family safe from any ill effects.

Roger opened the lid, held the box out so Harvey could look inside.

Harvey lifted the debris from its container with the reverence of a priest. He held the metal on his palm, and the surface reflected a blurred outline of his own head and shoulders, a distortion of himself.

Then he closed his fist, for no reason he could name. Maybe he wanted to destroy the artifact, break the saucer's hold over his scattered and fragmented mind. Maybe he wanted only to feel its substance, the sharp, sure presence of reality, as frank in his hand as truth was in all the world.

The metal yielded easily, crumpling into a tight ball.

When Harvey relaxed his grip, the thin metal didn't remain as it had been, but healed itself, unfolding flawless and flat. There was no line, no crease, not even the faintest dent to show that it had been damaged. It was as smooth and unmarked as the day Roger had taken it out of the desert.

"I'll be damned," Roger muttered.

Harvey said nothing but returned the metal gently to its reliquary.

Once Roger had placed the box back in its hiding place, the two men backed out of the closet.

"It's going to be okay," Roger said, though he knew it wasn't.

He walked Harvey to his truck, then stood in the street, watching as his friend drove away. The truck dwindled from a recognizable shape to the distant red specks of taillights, bright against the darkness of the town. Even after the lights had vanished, Roger remained in the street, resisting the urge to turn his eyes up to the numberless stars and the cold, deep darkness between them.

~

"I spoke with Major Marcel about your . . . situation," Roger said.

The two-man skiff drifted easily among the reeds of Mirror Lake. Sunset wasn't far off, and as Harvey shifted in the boat, pulling himself out of a pensive daze, the water broke and rippled around the skiff in reflections of deep, golden light.

"He's willing to grant you a discharge," Roger went on. "But listen, Harvey—it's got to be a blue slip. There's no other way to make this work, and the major is going out on a limb for you. He's risking a lot to get you out. I think it's the only chance you'll get."

Harvey digested the news calmly. A blue ticket wasn't exactly a dishonorable discharge, but it was the next worst thing. It was usually reserved for homosexuals—that, or men who'd completely lost their minds. The blue ticket meant a man was unfit for service, and Harvey supposed he was. If he was unwilling to go on serving a lie, then he was no longer suited for duty—not the duty the Army expected of him now. It didn't bother him so much, to be branded unfit. What worried him was the inevitable fallout. A blue-ticket discharge meant losing his access to a veteran's benefits. It meant the suspicion, maybe the animosity, of anyone who learned of it. Men who'd been given the blue slip often had a hard time finding work as civilians. They were deemed untrustworthy, generally suspect—and in a town like Roswell, where the Army was king and God, the effect would be ten times worse.

Roger spoke on, casting his fly casually and whisking it into the air again. "It was the best idea Marcel and I could come up with, between the two of us. It'll get you out fast, with no questions asked . . . unless you start talking."

"I won't," Harvey said.

"The major had to fudge things a little. Officially, they ended blue-ticket discharges on the first of this month, but Marcel wrote up orders and backdated your discharge to the thirtieth of June. He can plead slow mail, but if we'd waited a few more days, I don't think the scheme would work."

"Major Marcel could get into some real hot water for it," Harvey said.

"Don't you forget it. You owe him a real debt of gratitude."

"Why was he so willing to run that risk for me? I'm nothing but an enlisted."

For a moment, Roger didn't answer. His fly darted onto the golden water, and he flicked it back. Only ripples remained on the surface. "I think he felt bad," he finally said, "for commanding you to go and . . ."

Roger didn't finish the thought. There was no need. Harvey had lived and relived the minutes he'd spent approaching that ship until they wrapped and consumed his mind like eternity. And afterward, when he'd dropped to his knees, when he'd put his head and shoulders inside the wounded fuselage . . .

"Tell the major I'm grateful," Harvey said. "I'll take the blue ticket gladly, if it's my only way out."

Roger let his fly sink, fixed Harvey with a cautioning stare. "You'll still be in danger. You understand that, don't you? Without Army command looking out for you, you might very well end up with a target on your back. I mean it, Harvey. You know where they took that thing?"

"The weather balloon?" Harvey said wryly.

"They loaded it onto a B-29 and flew it to Ohio."

There was no need to ask where in Ohio. There could be only one destination for such a prize—Wright Field, the highly secretive base where captured enemy aircraft had been studied and reverse-engineered since the first World War.

Harvey gave a low whistle. "So they're going to try to crack all its secrets? Good luck to them."

"Men have disappeared just for mentioning some of the craft they've kept up in Ohio. And this is no German plane. The Pentagon won't hesitate to get rid of you if they think you're an intelligence risk. You've got to lie low, and most of all, you've got to keep your mouth shut. Not a word to anyone about what you saw. Take it to your grave, and you might be able to keep yourself out of danger."

"I don't intend to talk about it," Harvey said. "If I could forget the whole thing, I would. Anyway, I guess I've got more pressing concerns now than Pentagon spooks. I've got to find a job, Roger—for a few weeks, maybe a few months, and then I can move on. But I'll need a little money to get out of Roswell, set up a life someplace else. It won't be easy to find work with a blue ticket in my pocket."

Roger reeled in his fly and went on flicking the lure. Here, at least, he could offer some cause for hope. "Father Kerry lives on my street."

"Who?"

"The priest of our church. He's just bought that old, white farmhouse at the edge of town—bought it under the direction of the archbishop, I guess. You know the house I mean, out near the train tracks. The church wants to fix the place up right quick. I guess there are some nuns moving to town—coming down from Chicago, to start a new convent. Father Kerry told me this morning he's looking for a good, reliable man to do the work. Asked me if I know anyone who might fit the bill."

Harvey sat up so quickly that the boat rocked. "I used to do a little construction, back before my Army days. It's been years, but it'll come back to me. And I think it would be good, to work with my hands and back again, after all these years I've spent staring at radar scopes."

Roger nodded. He'd hoped Harvey would like the idea. "I'll recommend you for the job."

They were both quiet for a while. On the shore, the crickets had begun to sing their evening chorus, and the air was rich and comforting with the smell of damp vegetation.

Harvey eyed his friend as Roger cast his fly again, patient, withdrawn into the closed sphere of his own thoughts. He didn't want to break the peace—God knew, it was hard for any man to find a little quiet inside, after years spent at war.

But he also needed to know.

"Roger?"

"Yeah?"

"Do you think that thing we found in the desert really was made by the Soviets? Or by somebody else?"

The fly left the water, and Roger cast it out, pulled it away, cast it out in a simple, steady rhythm.

"Don't think about that right now," Roger said. "Just think about the fishing."

Harvey watched the ripples spread from the landing of the fly, and he listened to the crickets singing. The boat rocked gently as Roger cast his line again.

CHAPTER EIGHT

July 12, 1947

The smell of her mother's *carne guisada* had filled the house all day, but by the time the rich stew had simmered to perfection and Betty joined her family at the supper table, she found she had no appetite. That had been happening to her a lot lately. Since the night her father had come home from Mac Brazel's ranch, she had thought of almost nothing but the wounds that had appeared on her hands. This evening was no different. The question of what had happened to her and why had rolled around Betty's head like a marble dropped into a bowl, getting nowhere and circling endlessly upon itself. And now, as she stared at her dish of *guisada*, she almost wanted to laugh. How could something as prosaic as stew exist in this world alongside the momentous and the inexplicable?

At least the wounds on her hands had healed enough that she felt safe removing those ridiculous Army gloves. All that was left were two pink marks on her palms, perfectly round and so small that Betty couldn't believe, herself, that so much blood had run from them.

Her hands were healed now, but it had been a near thing. Only a few days before, long after the Campbell family had gone to bed, a stranger had appeared at their front door. Betty had been up getting a glass of water. When she'd heard the knock and answered the door, she'd found a disheveled man on the porch. He'd had the short haircut of a soldier, but his eyes had been wild, frantic, and yet somehow distant at the same time. Betty couldn't imagine that such a man might be with the Army. Yet the stranger had asked to speak with her dad. "I'm a friend of his from the war," he'd said.

Betty hadn't given him any answer, for the moment she looked in his eyes, her palms had begun to tingle and itch—then to hurt—dead in the center, exactly where the wounds had appeared. That had frightened her so much that she'd turned and run, just like a little girl. She hadn't even closed the door.

Yet when she'd reached the top of the stairs, Betty had taken herself in hand. She wanted answers, and maybe this was her chance to find them. It was a sure thing that no book or newspaper or radio program had yet yielded the comforting explanation she had sought. So she'd hidden in the shadows at the top of the stairs, hardly daring to breathe while her father and his odd visitor settled in the living room. Betty knew it was rotten to spy on her dad's private business, but she had greater concerns than mere morality. She'd simply *had* to know what the visit was all about, and why her hands had spiked with pain in the presence of that stranger.

The man's visit had yielded no answers, however, only more questions. It seemed as if that was all life ever gave—a well of mystery that grew darker and more fathomless the harder you tried to see into its depths.

"You've barely touched your supper, Betty."

The girl looked up, startled to be addressed, and more than a little annoyed at being pulled so abruptly from her thoughts.

Her mother was gazing at her with obvious concern. "Are you sick? What's the matter, dear?"

Betty flashed a quick look at her father. He held her eye with an unspoken warning. Roger knew his daughter must be eaten up by endless questions. God knew, he was suffering the same affliction. But it would be better for everyone if she said nothing, allowed the whole strange incident to fade into memory.

The girl scrambled for a likely excuse. "I've just been thinking about junior year—all the colleges I'm going to apply to. I guess I got caught up in my thoughts."

Roger cleared his throat, set down his spoon. "About that, Betty. I'm not so sure you should be chasing after college. Is it really a good idea?"

"Dad! What are you saying? I've wanted to go for years now, and you've always been okay with it. Don't you think I'm smart enough to get in?"

"I'm sure you could get in, honey, but I'm afraid it's not something I can agree to."

"For heaven's sake, why not? You never had any objections before."

The agonized look of betrayal on his little girl's face was almost more than Roger could bear. How could he explain to Betty that everything was different now—and do it without alerting Rosa to what had befallen their child? Certainly, before the incident in the desert, he'd had no reservations about Betty's interest in higher education. It was somewhat unusual for a girl, but Roger was sufficiently proud of his own progressive inclinations to hold no objection on the basis of gender. After all, it had been women who'd stepped up to work in the factories back home, manufacturing the aircraft and munitions that had won the war. His little girl could do anything a man could do; Roger was sure of that.

It was what *he* couldn't do that worried him. And now that he knew the astonishing power of the Soviets—now that he'd seen, firsthand, how sophisticated their craft and weaponry had become—he knew he was powerless to defend his family. And Betty seemed especially vulnerable to him, especially in need of his protection, ever since her unexplained affliction.

Roger fished desperately for a suitable excuse, one that wouldn't make him seem too helpless or foolish before his family. "There isn't any college here in town—not one that takes coeds—so I'm afraid it's out of the question, and that's that."

Betty scoffed. "You mean to tell me that you expect me to live my whole life in Roswell? Come on, Dad! You can't be serious."

He damn well was serious, and the more Betty pushed back, the more serious Roger grew—for he could feel the invisible threats closing around his daughter, around his whole family—the unknown dangers that waited out there, beyond the walls of their home. Betty was just a kid. She didn't understand, hadn't seen what Roger had seen in the war, in the desert. The girl had no idea how precarious this all was—the happy home, the stable life, the little, sleepy American town. But Roger knew full well that this blissful mirage was just that—an illusion. One day, the enemy would reveal their full power. The Soviets would fall on America with more of those wingless planes, the physics-defying fighters that could outrun the best jet engines America had at its disposal.

He said, far more calmly than he felt, "I don't want you off some-place where I can't protect you. Young women left to fend for them-selves against campuses full of . . . I know what boys are like at that age, Betty, and it's too dangerous."

"Boys are dangerous everywhere," Betty said flatly. "You think I don't know how to keep myself out of trouble?"

"It isn't only the boys—though I don't like the idea of that coed stuff, not at all. But say you go to, I don't know, Texas or California or New York, and the Soviets invade. What then?"

Betty rolled her eyes. "Holy cow, Dad. The Soviets aren't going to invade. And even if they tried, do you really think the Army and the Navy wouldn't see them coming?"

No, he wanted to say, *we wouldn't see them coming. That's exactly the trouble.*

Not even the brightest kid could understand what Roger had seen on the radar scopes, back in the Pacific. Planes that could leap across miles faster than you could blink. The girl had no idea what America was up against, how hopelessly outclassed the military already was.

"Besides," she went on, "what could you do if the Soviets did invade? Nothing, that's what. What could anyone in Hiroshima do when we dropped the bomb on them?"

It was the wrong thing to say. Roger tried to rein himself in, but it was already too late; he was at the point of boiling over—with fear, with restlessness, with a terrible, compulsive, directionless need to do something, do everything, shield himself and his family from an endless array of threats that he couldn't see yet nevertheless felt, like a ring of iron spikes hemming him in. Since the war, that feeling had never left him. It was always vibrating below his surface, a constant, exhausting vigilance that he knew wouldn't save him or anyone he loved. He couldn't help feeling it, all the same—couldn't shut it off. He'd tried, damn it; nobody knew how he'd tried. His face burned with the effort of holding back his anger. His fist clenched on the tabletop, and it was all he could do not to pound and shout, which would only set Betty to crying and Rosa to trembling and his sons, Billy and Andy, to hiding in their rooms.

Rosa stepped in smoothly. "What do you want to study, dear? Maybe it's something you can learn here in town, with a private tutor."

Betty turned her face down in a blue sulk. "I can't learn it here."

"But what is it? Maybe you can," Rosa persisted, as gentle and encouraging as ever.

"Aeronautics," Betty muttered.

The boys glanced at one another.

"What's that?" Andy said.

Betty answered her little brother flatly. "How planes fly."

Rosa gave a little sigh of disappointment. "I suppose you can't study that with a tutor."

Betty gathered herself again. "Listen, Dad, you can't protect me forever. I've got to grow up sometime and live my own life. And I don't want to be stuck in Roswell forever. I've got plans—ideas. I want to do something with my life, really *do* something, make a difference in the world."

The girl's brave self-defense swelled Roger's heart with pride—and choked him with the necessity of crushing her dreams. He'd always been proud of Betty's quick mind, her interest in science, and the girl deserved an opportunity to expand her horizons. And these were modern times. Why shouldn't his brilliant, sharp-witted daughter have her chance to change the world?

But he couldn't make himself say it. The thought of his child, his firstborn, being somewhere far beyond his reach when the bombs began to fall . . . no. The mere thought was more than Roger could bear. His fist tightened on the tabletop till his knuckles went white.

"You can do something from here," he said. "From where I can keep an eye on you and keep you safe."

Exasperated, Betty cast a desperate look at her mother, but Rosa shook her head in a silent warning: *Stop while things are still relatively calm.*

Every member of the family had been tiptoeing around Roger's temper since he'd come back from the war. He was never so easy to set off before he'd gone to the Pacific. Roger hated himself for the pressure he put his family under. If he knew how to stop worrying, if he knew how to shut off this fear, by God, he would do it. But lately, his own vigilant thoughts seemed to be the only things that were still holding the world together.

Under ordinary circumstances, Betty would have heeded her mother's warning. But nothing was the same as it once had been, and nothing was going back again. "I can't believe it," she cried. "Both of you are too prehistoric for words! We aren't living in the olden days. Women are going to go to universities and work at real jobs, whether you like it or not!"

"You can go up to your bedroom and stay there for the rest of the night," Roger said.

"For what?"

"For back talk and disrespect. And if I hear one more word out of you, young lady, you can stay in your room all weekend long."

"Aw, forget it." Betty pushed her chair away from the table. "Forget everything!"

~

Later that evening, the phone rang. A moment later, Betty's mother shouted for her, which was all the permission she needed to leave her room in defiance of her dad's order. Betty's best friend, Juanita Lopez, was on the line, breathless with the news that a pack of kids was going out cruising in the desert.

"Come along with us, Betty. Dwight Carey got his dad's old Special running again, and it's real cool."

"I think I'm grounded. I got my old man sore at me. He just about bit my head off; you should have seen the fuss."

Rosa had resumed her hand-sewing in the sitting room, content beside the mahogany Zenith with her favorite radionovela playing. She cleared her throat to catch Betty's attention, and when the girl looked at her, Rosa made a discreet shooing motion with one hand.

"Never mind," the girl said into the telephone. "I'll meet you at Vic's in half an hour."

After she hung up, Betty flew to her mother to plant a kiss on her cheek. "Are you sure? Dad'll turn into a bear again when he finds out I've gone."

"He isn't as angry as he seems," Rosa said. "He's only worried about you. And he'll come around about school; you'll see. You must try and be patient with him, dear. You know the war is still with him."

When Betty arrived at Vic's Drive-In, the last of the evening's light had faded from the sky. In the soft, violet luminance of a desert night, the scene stood out with a curious intensity, as if this time and place were all that mattered in the world—the gang assembled in the yellow glow of the restaurant's windows, the boys strutting around their cars, the girls perching on the hoods or the wheel wells, sipping Cokes and showing off their legs in high-waisted sailor shorts. Betty was struck by a sudden sharp awareness of her own youth, the freshness of a world reborn after the long, dark years of war. She saw, too, the gulf that existed now between her generation and her parents'. Whatever her mother thought, her dad was never going to relent on the matter of college—not if his opinions on the subject were tied up with his fears from the war. He might have come around over time if the crash hadn't happened—the saucer. Whatever he'd seen that day in the desert, the experience had left him stuck fast on the far side of a vanishing era. And Betty had no intentions of remaining with her dad in the moldy old past.

Dwight's Buick Special was a beauty. He walked Betty around the car, pointing out its clean, artful lines and the convertible top, which he'd lowered to underscore his own coolness. The car gleamed in a new coat of aquatone blue, candy-bright and slick as ice.

"Gee," Betty said, "it's really something."

Dwight leaned casually against the driver's-side door. "You should see her run. Hundred and seven horsepower, Dynaflash engine. She was my dad's pride and joy, but she got hit side-on by a truck a couple years ago, and she's been sitting all crumpled up in the garage ever since. Dad said if I could get the body straightened out and fix her up myself, he'd let me have her. I spent all last summer working on her, and now she's ready for her big debut."

"Then let's get going," Dougie Callers said. "I've been dying to see if your Special can outrun my Mercury."

The group began to sort itself, boys and girls piling into their friends' cars.

Dwight put his arm around Betty's shoulders. "Come on and ride with me. It's a perfect night for driving with the top down."

Soon she was tucked in the front seat of the Special, pressed close to Dwight, with Juanita on her other side. The back seat of the convertible quickly filled with more kids, and Dwight turned his car in an extravagant arc through the parking lot, the better to show off its metallic-blue flash. Then they were cruising up Main Street in pursuit of Dougie's red

Mercury. The roar of souped-up engines trailed behind, along with the howls of their friends in the other cars.

The gang left Roswell behind and sped into the black desert. A warm wind flowed over the windshield and tossed Betty's hair. For a while, she forgot the trouble with her father—forgot, too, the pink scars in the center of her hands and her other, private fears. She was just a girl that night, laughing with the wild freedom of youth and speed, unburdened by the weight of mystery. The cars careened along the highway, passing one another, their occupants waving and shouting. Engines and wind and the static of long, empty distance drowned out the music on their radios.

When they'd been driving for almost an hour, Betty shouted over the noise to Dwight, "Say, we're an awful long way from town. Where are we going, anyway?"

"Corona. Dougie wants to go out to Brazel's place, see where the saucer went down."

A sudden chill struck Betty in her gut. "Didn't the Army block the place off? There's no way we can get on the land."

"Nope," Dwight said. "Maggie Benson told Juan, who told Luke, who told Dougie, the whole place is wide open now. The Army hauled the saucer away, and since they've been telling the newspapers it was nothing but a weather balloon, there's no point in keeping the place blocked off. That'd only prove it *wasn't* a balloon. Some of the kids have gone out to the ranch and found little pieces of metal that the Army missed. They say it's from the saucer, but I don't know."

All too soon, the first car in the pack turned off the highway, onto an unassuming dirt road. Dwight followed. The road cut straight into the heart of the flat, empty land. Dust from the tires ahead blew through Dwight's headlights and billowed up the slant of his windshield. Betty squinted into the darkness, but she could see nothing unusual, nothing alarming on the vast plane of the ranch.

They drove far into the rangeland, until the highway was lost behind them. At the top of a shallow rise, they stopped their cars and tumbled out, the girls giggling and shrieking until the deep stillness of the place worked its way into their awareness. Then they all stood huddled together and silent, each aware for the first time of their own smallness and inexperience, the bright, bursting flash of life's brevity. The wind moved over the dry and ancient earth.

Dougie broke the sacred quiet first. "This should be the place. Everybody spread out and keep your eyes peeled."

Betty soon found herself alone on the dirt road as the other kids moved off eagerly across the rangeland, searching for the dim reflection of starlight on metal. She wrapped her arms around her body. She wasn't cold, but she was shivering. When she felt more alone on the road than she thought she might feel out there among the brush, she picked a direction and set off walking, dodging the spectral forms of cholla with their spiny arms.

The voices of her friends grew more distant, almost swallowed by the warm summer wind. Her father's voice came blowing out of her own thoughts, his going back on all her plans for college—it wasn't fair. How could she do it without her dad's blessing, without his money to see her through?

Far from the road, she stopped her wandering and looked up to where the stars arced in their countless thousands, describing the great curve of all that was and all that might yet be. It made her dizzy, to know that she was the smallest speck on a pebble of a planet, and yet she was somehow everything. The distance and multitude of the stars, the unfathomable reach of time in which their light traversed the emptiness of space to land, at last, right there, where she alone could see—it was a mystery more sacred than any she'd been told to believe by the priest or her mother. She wanted to understand. She wanted to know how far it was to the nearest star, and to the farthest, and to what lay beyond, the layers of light and dark that spread like ripples in a pond from herself out into the limitless perplexity of the universe. It was possible to know—Betty felt certain of that, with the stubborn, optimistic surety only the young can feel. It was possible, and she would know the answers, if she could find the right way to approach the mystery.

When her neck began to ache, she stopped staring at the sky and wandered a while longer. She could hear Juanita laughing, and Dwight's voice rising and falling in pitch as he talked to someone, and now and then a shout from one of the other kids. They all seemed so far away, so removed from Betty's private sphere of contemplation.

Something flashed among the roots of a stunted piñon, some ten feet ahead. It was a piece of debris, thin and pale, so much like the scrap her dad had brought home that it made her queasy and afraid. For a long time, she stood staring, hardly daring to move, as if the piece of inert metal were a scorpion or a snake. Had her hands begun to tingle, like they'd done when she'd answered the door to that wild-eyed stranger? Or was she only imagining the effect?

Betty forced herself to creep a little closer. The metal lay harmlessly on the ground, yet its very shimmer and sheen seemed to pull her in like the force of gravity. The sensation in her hands increased to a burn, then a throb that beat with the rhythm of her speeding heart. In her mind's eye, she saw herself bending to pick up the metal, and something hot and ecstatic crescendoed in her chest like a burst of song that wanted to be heard, and she saw, as if in a dream, a flash of sweet light consume her, just as her fingers touched the metal . . .

Betty staggered back, gasping. The scrap still lay on the earth, untouched. When she lifted her hands, her palms remained clean, the scars intact, thank God.

Dougie's voice came across the black waste. "Has anybody found a piece?"

Betty kicked dust over the scrap of metal till it vanished from her sight.

"No," she called back.

The wind carried the word away.

The white light and trembling fire of revelation didn't abate once he found the words. The shivering heat only grew inside him, for now that he understood what he was looking at—the seating and equipment of a flight crew—his awareness sped beyond, flooding into the space that had unfolded before him, and under him, and above. He looked up, felt up, but where the roof of the craft should have been, there was a limitless arc as high as the ceiling of Heaven. The interior walls of the craft reached to either side and back into the body of the bluff until the sleek, white details of their surfaces were lost in a glare of distance. Space and object and material, and the trustworthy framework of physics that had kept Earth moving in its orbit, all disintegrated at the precipice of a new reality. Impossible as it seemed—impossible as it was—a chamber the size of a football field was contained inside the thirty-foot-long craft.

The ceiling of that luminous room was arched and vaulted, the chancel of a saint's cathedral, and as he gazed up at its numinous glow, he felt the turning of a wheel around him, a wheel enclosed in a wheel whose countless thousands of celestial eyes opened wide to see him—him, humble and plain and small, at the center of this ring of everything that was and everything that might yet be.

Though it was morning and already hot, he thought of night, of stars, their distance and multitude, the long, dark wasteland of airless time that stretched between, only traversable by a single power: the engine of the will, whose fuel was the hunger to know.

TRANSCRIPT page 4

BISHOP COTE: Sister, it was you who brought Betty and her condition to the attention of the church.

SISTER MARY AGNES: Yes, Your Excellency. I've personally witnessed the girl's hands begin to bleed from wounds that weren't there before, when—

FATHER KERRY: One thing at a time, Sister. Perhaps we ought to begin your testimony by establishing your relationship to the girl.

SISTER MARY AGNES: Relationship? I don't have much of a relationship with Betty—no more than I have with any other person of this town.

FATHER KERRY: That is my point. The sisters have only been in Roswell a few weeks, Your Excellency. The monastery is newly founded.

BISHOP COTE: So you have no special knowledge of Betty—her habits or her character?

SISTER MARY AGNES: I know only that she is a child of God.

BISHOP COTE: For the record, Sister, please tell us who you are and how you came to be here in Roswell.

CHAPTER NINE

August 26, 1935

Before she was Sister Mary Agnes, her name was Patricia Walton, and she came from Chicago, Illinois.

That day was unseasonably gray and cold, miserable with a blustery rain that blew in sideways from the lake, a premonition of the autumn to come. She hunched under the umbrella she shared with her mother, but there wasn't enough room for both of them, and the rain kept gusting in to strike her cheek and slide under the collar of her coat. Her mother was talking—about nothing in particular, just talking with hardly a pause to draw breath. The sound of Mother's own words kept her thoughts at bay, Patricia knew, and Mother was anxious now, though she didn't want to let on. Patricia couldn't help but see it. She knew her mother well enough to understand what this nervous flood of words signified. And because there was no stopping her when she got into a fit of uncontrolled chatter, Patricia didn't try to listen. Instead, she repeated her name in her head, over and over, as they passed Sherman Park and turned west. Patricia Walton. Patricia Walton. Because, you see, it wouldn't be her name forever. Patricia Ann Walton. She said the name silently, so many times that the words lost all meaning. Certainly, the name no longer had anything to do with her. She became an emptiness, ready to receive the new self that God would soon pour in.

When they reached the high wall of red brick that surrounded the monastery, Patricia laid a hand on her mother's shoulder.

Mother stopped talking and looked at her, pale and sober. There were tears in her eyes. "You're sure this is what you want?"

"Yes, Mother. It's a calling. I can't explain it. This is what I must do, what God wants from me."

"I'm so proud of you."

They both juggled the handle of the umbrella as they embraced. Patricia felt like a rat, like some vile, small, unclean thing in her mother's arms. There had been no calling, no imperative in her heart that had led her to the religious life, the way it led other women. Patricia had made this decision as a practicality, a matter of self-defense. What Mother didn't know couldn't hurt her.

They were both crying openly now. Patricia didn't want to be the first to break their embrace. "It isn't as if we'll never see one another again," she said. "You can come visit as often as you like."

That was true, but it wouldn't be the same, and they both knew it. This was a monastery of Poor Clare, the religious order whose women lived in enclosure, barricaded from the rest of the world—all but a few select sisters who did the necessary work of interacting with those beyond the convent walls. When Patricia's family would come to see her, she mustn't touch or hold them, but must remain behind the ornate iron screen that kept the sisters separate from the world. A harsh measure, perhaps—but evidently, it was what Patricia needed.

One way or another, they tore themselves apart. Patricia left a last kiss on her mother's cheek. Then she turned resolutely away and passed through the monastery gate, into the gray-and-green solitude of the enclosed grounds, with the sound of her mother's grief trailing behind her.

The path was slick with the season's first rain, and it led through a heat-stricken garden to the steps of the great brick building. Everything about the place spoke of age—of a past far older than Chicago's. The sharply steepled roofline felt higher than two stories ought to have been, and the eaves were ornamented with gothic arches of brick that seemed to weep from the gables down toward the humble earth. A curve of pale marble stretched over the entrance. As Patricia stood looking up at it, one of the heavy oak doors swung open.

"Welcome, welcome." A nun stood in the dark frame of the doorway, beckoning and smiling. Her wide white collar and round face were stark against the deep shadows that hung in the hall behind. "You must be our new postulant. Come in; let's get you out of this rain."

The nun introduced herself as she took Patricia's coat. Sister Catherine of the Perpetual Sorrows, which seemed an ill-fitting name for such a kind woman. She was an extern, of course. No enclosed nun would have answered the door. That was too much contact with the outside world.

Sister Catherine led Patricia through a deep, calm stillness, the quiet of meditative prayer. The interior of the monastery held a more modest dignity than its outer façade. Simple panels of dark wood lined the walls, with no adornment save for the occasional framed image of Clare or Francis, the two founding saints of the order. The floor was tiled in humble, unglazed terra-cotta. Patricia thought the floor must have been cold under Sister Catherine's bare feet. No rug or runner was to be found anywhere. The only extravagance was the chapel. She passed its open door swiftly enough to catch a fleeting impression of the dramatic arches and pillars that framed the altar, heavy with gilding and vibrant with the painted images of angels and saints. The ornate majesty of the chapel and its luminous extravagance made it seem somehow larger than the building itself, as if it stretched into God's own infinity.

At another plain oak door, Sister Catherine paused and tapped. A moment later, Patricia was admitted to the presence of Mother Superior, the abbess who shepherded the women of this monastery with a gentle and loving hand.

Patricia smiled to see her. She had met the abbess several times at the discernment retreats she'd attended over the preceding months, as she'd weighed her options for a much-needed atonement. She liked the abbess, and was relieved that Mother Superior remembered her, too.

"Ah, Patricia. It's so good to see you again. Please, sit down. That will be all, Sister Catherine—thank you."

The door closed softly at Patricia's back.

"You've come to us today to begin your aspirancy," Mother Superior said. "Do you understand what it means, to become an aspirant?"

"Yes, Mother, I do."

It felt strange, to refer to anyone other than the woman who'd brought her into this world as Mother. But she would soon grow used to it. This was the least of the sacrifices she would make for the good of her soul.

"You must remain an aspirant for at least a year," the abbess said. "After that time, if you wish, you may enter your postulancy for another year or more, and then, if you still choose to pursue this life, you may take the novice's vows and become a sister of this order in truth—though you will still have at least two years of noviceship before you progress to junior vows."

"Certainly." Patricia hoped she didn't sound too eager.

"You're quite young to make such a commitment."

"I'm twenty-two, Mother. Younger women than I must have taken the vows. Anyhow, I'll have a few years to be sure this is the right path."

The truth was, she was already determined to make a permanent vow of enclosure. She would have committed herself to the order right then and there, if Mother Superior would have allowed it. This was her chance to set her soul back on a righteous road. A life of dedicated service in prayer would surely make amends for the grievous mistakes that had nearly damned her.

Patricia had always been the good girl her mother had taught her to be, obedient and conscious of sin, studious in avoiding the pitfalls of temptation. But after high school, she'd been swept away by the excitement of a new world unfolding. The craze for young women to enter the working world had gotten its roots in Patricia, despite her parents' best efforts at raising her along good, old-fashioned lines. She'd taken up work as a switchboard operator, and the sweetness of an independent, cosmopolitan life had soon intoxicated her, driving her straight out of common sense.

In the fast-paced, self-important dazzle of the working world, she had met too many fascinating men. She'd believed herself to be in love with one of them—John. Even now, after everything that had happened, her heart still ached at the mere thought of his name. She kept her eyes fixed on her hands, folded primly in her lap, as the abbess spoke of the enclosed life and the expectations of postulancy. But all her thoughts were with John. It cost her a wearying effort to push him out of her mind. He was the whole reason why she was here, why she'd been driven to such drastic measures. And still, she couldn't get that man out of her head.

In John's arms, she had found herself carried away by her feelings. She'd forgotten the very concept of sin, for with him, everything was pure and delicious as honey. Nothing was barred between them, not even the fullest expression of their affection.

And then Patricia had found herself in trouble. She counted herself lucky that the pregnancy had ended naturally, only a few weeks after she'd discovered it. But those weeks of cold terror and shame had been the worst of her life.

She'd been left appalled at her capacity for sin, sickened by how eagerly she'd fallen into temptation and lust—she, a good Catholic girl. Even now, damnation nipped at her heels, and she felt certain that nothing short of complete dedication to Jesus would make amends for her despicable weakness.

"I'm ready," she said when the abbess fell silent. "There's nothing I wish for more than to help the needy through constant prayer."

"Your faith is to be commended," the abbess said, smiling.

And again, Patricia felt like the lowest and smallest of creatures, the foulest ever to creep on its belly through the mud. Faith was the last thing that had brought her to the monastery. She had come to offer her youth and ambition as a sacrifice—a barter. Vows of enclosure and constant prayer in exchange for God's vouchsafement from the cold, black void of Hell. Oh, if she could do some real good for others, she wouldn't complain. A life of service would be a life well lived. But self-preservation was her real motive.

As for faith—she wasn't even sure that she knew the meaning of the word. God had always been a fixed and distant monolith in Patricia's imagination, the great shadow of judgment looming over her life. Nuns were supposed to come enraptured to their vows, burning with an unquenchable love, the devoted brides of Christ. Patricia felt no such burning—only a defensive need to dodge the swift hand of the Lord, by any means that might suit.

But it would never do to confess any of this to Mother Superior. So Patricia only offered a smile of her own, which she hoped looked suitably modest, and lowered her eyes in humble acceptance of the unwarranted praise.

Patricia Walton surrendered herself that day to Jesus. She traded the stylish clothing of a woman of the still-new twentieth century for the simple, modest clothing of an aspirant. The sisters welcomed her into a private sanctuary of camaraderie and prayer, and one year later, when she took the vow of a postulant, she discovered that the enclosed life wasn't as isolating as she had feared it might be. The nuns were good company, loving and patient, full of cheer. There was no shortage of friends to ease her homesickness and teach her the ways of a contemplative life.

The years of her early vows passed in ease and beauty—not the outward beauty of the material world, but the gradual widening of an inner landscape Patricia had never suspected her soul might contain. By the time she was required to advance to the noviceship or leave the order, there was no question of going back. She still harbored something too small and ill-defined to be called faith, but a genuine appreciation for the religious life was growing inside her. For all the bright temptations the world offered—for all she missed her family and longed for the simple pleasures of home—nothing could compare to the rich gardens of meaning that flowered now in her heart. Enclosed life offered an absolute peace, a freedom from everyday cares, which permitted, in turn, an endless meditation on ideas that had come to feel as essential as sunlight and fresh air. In contemplating the frailty of human nature, she came to understand and forgive her own weaknesses. And when Mother Superior proffered the noviceship, Patricia seized the opportunity with a good deal more purity of purpose than she'd had at the beginning of her journey. This time, she was reassured that whatever she presently lacked in faith would be amended with more time and prayer. God could work any miracle—or so Patricia had heard.

When she knelt at the altar and allowed the abbess to cut her hair short—a sign of her sacrifice to Jesus—she took the name Mary Agnes. *Sister* Mary Agnes. That was who she was now. Patricia Walton had faded into the past, somewhere back along the quiet, orderly chain of days that had made up her aspirant and postulant years. Sister Mary Agnes would proceed into the future, and the girl Patricia would remain behind, in the same place where she'd left the burdens of a marked and suffering soul.

Day and night, at the holy hours of Lauds and Sext, at Compline and Vespers, when she rose in the middle of the night for Matins, she prayed for all those who were caught up in sin, as she once had been. Month by month and year by year, as the war in Europe unwound like a thread from a rapidly spinning spool, Sister Mary Agnes prayed. Her noviceship passed, and she took her junior vow, replacing the white cap of a novice with the black veil of a true sister of Poor Clare. She prayed unceasingly for all the innocents who suffered, here and across the sea, where the fighting didn't cease but grew more terrible by the day—for even in enclosure, the nuns heard news of the war. She prayed for those who fought for a righteous cause, and that all those who'd done evil would repent and be forgiven. She prayed as word made its way into the convent of the terrible new invention that finally ended the conflict—a bomb that had harnessed the power of the stars. She prayed for the hundreds of thousands of lives those same bombs had taken. All the innocents had been caught up to the Savior's bosom, she hoped. Mother Mary, let it be so.

Sister Mary Agnes prayed behind her iron screen, behind her high brick wall, while the world went on without her. She had mired herself in a past that grew older and less relevant by the day. But she didn't see that yet. Years would pass before she would understand, in a blazing fire of revelation, how much she had given up, and how little she had gained.

CHAPTER TEN

July 30, 1947

Harvey gave his name and box number to the mail clerk.

"One moment," the man said, then disappeared into a back room.

Harvey fiddled with the chain on the counter pen while he waited. This was a new experience—picking up his mail from the town post, rather than at the airfield base, where he'd lived since the end of the war. Given the stigma of his blue-ticket discharge, he was lucky he'd been able to secure a post office box at all. He'd heard stories of men whose blue slips had barred them from damn near every facet of normal life, including such straightforward operations as receiving mail.

He was luckier still that his blue slip hadn't kept him from finding an apartment—though, if his discharge from the Army had been an honorable one, he might have landed a nicer place. Between the persistent grime, the rattling pipes, and the noise of Main Street below, the two-room hole above the hardware store didn't have much to recommend it. But it was a place to lay his head down while he worked at his new job, fixing up the old farmhouse at the northern edge of town for the local parish. Once his work there was finished, he would put Roswell behind him and hope for better fortunes in a place far from here.

The mail clerk returned with a few envelopes, passed them across the counter to Harvey, who tried not to look too excited by the return addresses. The *Fargo Forum*, North Dakota. The *Coast News* in Florida. The *Cincinnati Enquirer* had sent their reply in a fancy printed envelope complete with a bossed logo.

"Thanks," Harvey said, stuffing the letters in his trouser pocket.

Thank God, the walk was a short one from the post office to his new accommodation, for the afternoon was hot enough to blister. As he passed Ella's Bar, he nearly ran right into Mac Brazel, who was coming out with his wide-brimmed rancher's hat already pulled down low over his eyes.

"Say, Mac! I haven't seen you around town for a while."

Mac looked up with a twitchy speed. When he recognized Harvey, a little of his defensiveness melted away. Not all of it.

"Hey there, Harvey." Mac eyed him more closely, took in the faded denim work pants, the plain white T-shirt. "You're not in uniform."

"And not likely to be ever again. I've left the Army."

Now Mac held his eye with a searching, almost desperate intensity. Harvey offered a nod—*Yes, left the Army over* that. *You know.*

"I ain't gonna talk about it," Mac said.

"I wasn't going to ask you about it," Harvey answered.

Mac glanced around the street, fearful that someone might be listening, watching. "That's good—that's good. Better if you don't. You know they threw me in jail? That day . . . the . . . you know which day."

"I know. I was there on the base. I saw you being hauled in."

Mac edged up a little closer to him. Harvey could feel a tight, nervous energy leaping off the man like a static shock.

"Those two guys who nabbed me," he said, "the red-haired monster and that Black fellow—"

"I know them," Harvey said. "Captain Armstrong and Sergeant Roosevelt."

"Whoever they are. I only came to the base to report what I found. Figured the military ought to know about it. But those characters, Armstrong and Roosevelt—they said if I spoke a word about it to anyone, the government would have me put in the ground."

Harvey drew back a little, startled out of his composure. As a radar-man, he hadn't known either Captain Armstrong or Sergeant Roosevelt well, but his work had brought him into both men's presence a number of times. They were both imposing figures—especially Armstrong—but he couldn't picture either man making idle threats to a civilian's life.

Maybe, he considered then, *the threat wasn't idle.*

"Hell, Mac, you'd better do what they told you and keep quiet." He wished he had better advice to offer—to Mac Brazel, and to himself.

"I don't mean to do anything different. Nothing to talk about, anyway. It was just a weather balloon, right?"

Harvey offered a weak smile. His eyes slid away. "That's right."

"Got to get back to the ranch," Mac said. "It's deworming season."

"Take care of yourself."

Harvey watched as Mac hustled away.

He pressed on to his apartment. Roger's warnings rang in his memory, more loudly than they had before. *The Pentagon won't hesitate. Lie low, keep your mouth shut. Take it to your grave, and you might be able to keep yourself out of danger.*

If levelheaded, respectable captains and sergeants wouldn't scruple to threaten a civilian, they sure as hell wouldn't hold back on a blue-slipped outcast of Harvey's type. By the time he reached the hardware store, he was firmly resolved never to breathe a word about what he'd seen. Even if he couldn't stop thinking about it.

He ducked into the cool relief of the stairwell, climbed to his new bachelor digs on the second floor. The air inside was as stuffy and gray as ever. Opening his two windows did little to relieve the heat, but he did it all the same. The previous resident had left an old, sagging sofa behind, and Harvey collapsed onto it, tearing open the first of his envelopes.

The secretary at the *Fargo Forum* had enclosed a polite note with the folded front page from July 6. It was a beauty of a headline: *Report "Flying Saucer" Seen in N.D.: Mysterious Flight Still Puzzles U.S.* The letter from Florida yielded a smaller prize, neatly clipped out of a page. *Flying Saucer Sighted at Pender Harbor.*

The real gem was contained in the envelope from Ohio—another full-page spread, blaring in sharp black and white, *Flying Saucers Over Cincinnati: Army Aircraft Search for Mysterious Discs.* The *Cincinnati Enquirer*, a respected regional paper, had dedicated two different columns on the front page to the story. The left-hand column detailed the vigils of journalists in Oregon and California—and the F-80 fighters poised to scramble into defensive flight the moment the saucers were sighted again. The column on the right was of local interest. Its header read *TWO OF 'EM Seen Going North at 6 p.m. by Housewife in Terrace Park.*

Harvey checked the date at the top of the page. July 7, 1947. Like most of the clippings in his ever-growing collection, these stories, too, had occurred within days of the crash at Corona.

A rickety, secondhand coffee table stood before the sofa, and on its dusty top lay Harvey's scrapbook. After leaving the Army earlier that month, he had dedicated himself to the exploration of the one great mystery of his life. All his free time was now spent at the town library, amassing the names and addresses of newspapers around the country, and writing letters to inquire about any relevant headlines. He had expected the responses to come slowly, if they came at all. But he received letters almost every day, the envelopes fat with an abundance of evidence.

He picked up the book, settled back on the tired sofa. Keeping a record of the reports of saucers wasn't the same thing as talking about it. There was no danger, surely, in his book.

He turned the pages slowly, lingering over each, rereading the articles he'd recently obtained from newspapers and magazines, though already he'd pored over each one so thoroughly that he could have recited any story by heart.

First, the incident in the skies above Los Angeles, only months after the raid on Pearl Harbor, when a wary and ructious America had just entered the war. The appearance of unexplained lights off the California coast had set the city into an uproar. Anti-aircraft weapons had fired all night, thousands of rounds, and raid sirens had blared Los Angeles out of its sleep, into a full-scale panic. The photo from that article gave a shy whisper as Harvey passed his hand across its surface. The image, snapped by an intrepid reporter in the midst of the pandemonium, showed the bright-white beams of search lights cutting through the night sky—and dozens of lights, small and round like the blips on his radar scope, arrayed in a strange formation that no aircraft, American or Japanese, would use.

The next pages of his book documented the official response to the outburst in Los Angeles. It had only been a misunderstanding, the Army said, the governor of California said, President Roosevelt said. The objects in the sky that had inspired such panic had been nothing more than weather balloons. The response had been disproportionate, a case of wartime nerves running high.

Weather balloons. As if trained airmen and gunners—and good radarmen—couldn't tell the difference between a balloon's inert drift and the purposeful movement of an aerial threat.

The next few pages documented a rash of incidents in Washington state. Harvey had discovered the flap of sightings by chance, when he'd picked up a science-fiction magazine at the library, but he'd soon written to the editors of the cited papers, requesting copies of the relevant articles. Now here they were, carefully pasted into his secret book—the initial accounts of a private pilot who'd seen a train of luminous objects flying in formation above the Cascade mountains. "Supersonic flying saucers," the pilot had dubbed them, and the name had stuck. The objects performed maneuvers far beyond the capability of any known craft, halting and reversing course in midair, traveling at speeds of at least twelve hundred miles per hour, even leaping from one point to another in the blink of an eye, all without any evidence of exhaust—through no apparent means of propulsion.

From Washington, the phenomenon had spread rapidly across the country. July had barely reached its end, and already Harvey had collected dozens of clippings for that month, from almost everywhere, it seemed—Idaho, Texas, Arizona, Nebraska, Maine. Now he could add North Dakota, Ohio, and Florida to the list. There was almost no state that hadn't reported some inexplicable vision in the sky between late June and early July of that year. *More "Flying Saucers" Seen as Men of Science Ponder Serious Angles*, one headline read. But those men of science couldn't agree on an explanation, whether it was experimental aircraft or Soviet spies, the visible effects of atomic energy or good old-fashioned mass hysteria.

As far as Harvey knew, Roswell was the only town that could boast of having captured a saucer. Not that anyone in Roswell would admit to it now.

He turned to the final pages of his book, where he'd pasted the local articles. The initial headline trumpeting the Army's possession of a downed flying saucer was followed by that damned silly retraction, complete with the photos of Major Marcel in his uniform, calmly displaying the wrinkled debris of a weather balloon. The sight made Harvey sick every time he laid eyes on it. The Army and the government that commanded it knew damn well that there was something real here, something infinitely bigger than *weather balloons*. Crowned and anointed by their victory over the Axis, the Pentagon's preeminent authority might soothe a certain number of civilians into believing they never saw what they saw. Not Harvey Day. The book in his hands was all the proof he needed that he wasn't crazy, he hadn't been dreaming, he wasn't too stupid to understand what he'd seen and all the shattering implications it carried.

He pasted the new clippings into his book, then closed the cover with a meditative reverence. Then he kicked off his shoes, lay back on the sofa, shut his eyes against the intrusion of afternoon light, against the slow, heavy heat. But he could do nothing to evade his own memories. They were always waiting for him, whenever he was alone, whenever he retreated into darkness.

When he'd looked inside that thing, that object—the flying saucer—he had seen something he couldn't explain, something that couldn't *be*. And yet he had seen it. Harvey was certain of that, as certain as he was that up was up and down was down, that two and two made four. Sometimes at night, when he couldn't escape the fact of the stars, he would surrender to their power and stare into the blackness between them and wonder where the saucer had come from. Up there, maybe. Out there. Or, he sometimes speculated with a shudder of awe, from someplace much nearer. No matter how many times the question asked itself, Harvey never found any answer. By that time, he'd begun to accept the dull, heavy fact that he probably never would. Nor would anyone. A thing like *that*—the disorienting inversion of what is and what may be, the gutted bleed-out of an old, comforting reality—defied any human understanding.

But he was goddamn sure that it had been real. And it wasn't what the Army's brass insisted it was.

A *balloon*, for the love of all things sacred.

CHAPTER ELEVEN

August 19, 1947

After the sisters had observed the hour of Nones, the midafternoon prayer, and returned to their separate duties, a summer rain set in—the first shower to presage the changing season. Mary Agnes hesitated at the window of her cell. From her vantage on the uppermost floor of the old brick monastery, she could see the crowns of umbrellas bobbing just beyond the edge of the wall—passersby hurrying home from Sherman Park. The parade of bumbershoots in scarlet, blue, and sunflower made a poignant contrast to the heavy sky, the dull brick of the convent and its walls, the leaves of chestnut and oak rapidly losing their green at the tail end of a Chicago summer.

From that same window, Mary Agnes had watched the late-summer showers blow in off Lake Michigan every year. This gray bluster was no different from the others, yet it called to mind the rain that had fallen in another August, twelve years ago—a lifetime ago, when she had been a different woman. She remembered the cold drops blowing in past the edge of her umbrella, running down her cheek like the tears she had refused to shed. At the memory of her mother's voice—Mother's nervous chatter, filling the silence between them—a premonition of loss struck her, and the sharp pang of a regret she was seldom tempted to feel. True, her life in the monastery had been unusual, by the standards of a modern woman. But she had been safe here, all these years. She had held herself in perfect observation of the divine mysteries and had kept her soul unspotted by sin.

Why, then, was her faith still a small and distant thing?

Reluctantly, she turned from the window. The abbess had asked to visit in the still, shadowy office after Nones was finished. This was nothing unusual—Mother Superior often met with each of the sisters under her care, inquiring in her warm and comforting way whether there was anything she might do or provide. The abbess was always ready to offer balm to spirit or body—provided, of course, the material requests didn't violate the order's vow of poverty. Yet today, Mary Agnes anticipated the meeting with that same odd sensation of inexplicable loss.

It's only the dreams, she told herself.

She had suffered through the most terrible nightmares for weeks now—not every night, but often enough that they'd become a familiar occurrence. Dreadful visions of huge, burning machines that fell from the sky, plunging down on the city—on the monastery in particular—to obliterate the peace and safety that had surrounded her all these years. Prayer drove back the terrifying visions, but not for long, and never for good. Over the course of the summer, a low-grade yet constant anxiety had taken root inside her, an uncomfortable buzz of expectant fear that had no obvious antecedent and, apparently, no remedy. The nightmares had become so vivid and haunting that weeks ago, in early July, Mary Agnes had even been jolted out of her meditations during the midnight Matins prayer. On that terrible night, the vision of a fiery, mechanical thing seemed so real and present that she had looked up from her rosary with a horrified gasp, certain she would see the burning giant streak past the chapel window, braced for the sight of its apocalyptic red light on the gilded arches, the painted saints, the bowed heads of her sisters. But all had been peaceful and still. No one had noticed her fear. The plague of anxiety hadn't waned since that night. Now the nightmares were even making her dread a simple conversation with Mother Superior.

Mary Agnes set her mind to ignore the senseless terror. She passed from her cell into the long hall of the sisters' dormitory in a determined air of peace, hands clasped at the knot of her rope belt with a serenity she didn't feel. Shadows hung from the high ceilings, and rain murmured against the eaves. She descended the two flights of stairs to the ground floor, the banister of aged mahogany smooth below her palm, worn and polished by half a century of women's hands.

Beyond the gilded glory of the chapel, Mary Agnes reached the door to the abbess's office. As she raised her hand to knock, a sensation like an electric shock passed through her—a rapid, bursting certainty that she stood twelve years in the past, that she was Patricia Walton again, come to consign herself to the aspirancy that would lead her into this very life of enclosure. The folding of present into past left her dizzy and sick. Those cursed dreams had unsettled her too deeply. She would have to ask the abbess for advice. Surely among the ancient traditions of the church, there was a litany or a rosary to restore an unsettled soul to firmer ground. If anyone knew how to pray fear away, it was Mother Superior.

Mary Agnes tapped softly, so as not to disturb the quiet.

"Come in," the abbess said.

Mother Superior sat at her large desk, wreathed in the soft, brown gleam of polished wood. A scent of aged incense pervaded the room. Papers were spread across the desk, with a half-finished letter to one side, an uncapped fountain pen lying aslant its page as if the pen had just been dropped.

The abbess looked up with her nurturing smile. She gestured to the empty leather chair. "Dear Sister—please, make yourself comfortable."

Mary Agnes sank onto the seat, trembling a little and scolding herself for her foolishness. Whatever the reason for this conversation, there was no cause for alarm. Mother Superior was a lamb.

"How have you been these past weeks, Sister, since we last spoke?"

Mary Agnes almost confessed the truth. But as she opened her mouth, shame twisted inside. How foolish, to admit she'd been struggling with bad dreams. It was a child's complaint—and though she was among the youngest of the sisters, she was no child. "I've been well," she said, with only the slightest twinge of guilt over the lie.

"And how are you finding life here at the monastery?"

Mary Agnes blinked in surprise. A strange question to ask, after twelve years of dedication. "I find it very agreeable, of course, Mother."

"Have you ever longed for something different?" Mother Superior leaned over her desk with conspiratorial glee. "Have you thought, perhaps, that a change of scenery might be nice?"

The blood began to pound in Mary Agnes's ears. What exactly was the mother getting at? A change—certainly not! Change was the last thing that would appeal to her now. The predictable routines of enclosure had become the very framework of her life, the road map of her mind. And after so many years of enclosure, the monastery itself felt more like a home than the one she'd grown up in. Certainly, it was more of a home than the dismal apartment she'd lived in as a working girl.

"I don't understand," Mary Agnes floundered.

The abbess flicked through the papers on her desk, whisked one sheet from among the rest. "This is a letter from a certain archbishop. He wrote to me proposing the foundation of a new monastery. Naturally, I thought it was a lovely idea. And I had you in mind as an extern sister."

The routine hours froze in that moment—halted and then reversed. Time and tradition and all things that made up the cloistered world detached from reality, spun through Mary Agnes's head like snowflakes caught in an updraft. Unlike the enclosed nuns who lived apart from the world, extern sisters ventured beyond the convent walls, assisting priests, delivering host bread for the eucharist, and tending actively to the spiritual needs of the broader community. Mary Agnes had never considered seeking an appointment as an extern. She had entered the order with the express purpose of cutting herself off from the base temptations of the world. What good would there be to her soul if she ventured back into the wilderness beyond the walls, that unmapped forest of danger and sin?

"The archdiocese is in Santa Fe," Mother Superior said.

Mary Agnes searched her memory—childhood geography lessons. "New Mexico?"

"And the monastery itself," the abbess went on, "is to be established well outside the city. A small town called Roswell, far into the desert. Quite a change from Chicago, I'm sure."

Why did she recall that night in July, the rosary beads suddenly cold between her fingers, and the air so bitter as she drew a frightened gasp? She could almost see again the hellish red light that never came. She could smell a singe on the air, the smell of snuffed candles but a thousandfold—the smell of something burning.

With a will, she pushed the memory away. She wouldn't allow nightmares to frighten her. "God's light is needed everywhere."

"It's certainly needed in Roswell, according to the archbishop."

The abbess passed the letter to Mary Agnes, who scanned the note through her daze of ambushed surprise.

The town has gone through much that would test the faith of any man, the archbishop had written. *We fear that many will turn from the church. These troubles are unique to Roswell, as you will understand. A strong example of devotion will go far in holding souls to Christ and His eternal church before they can be lost. I know there will be much opportunity for the Sisters of your order to minister to the wayward and the confused.*

She handed the letter back to the abbess. "I will serve anywhere God sends me, of course, but . . . but surely I'm not the ideal choice for an extern, Mother."

The abbess's eyes wrinkled with amusement. "Oh? Why do you suppose that is?"

"I've been enclosed for a decade now, and even as an aspirant and postulant, I seldom left the monastery. In all that time, I've had no experience with the public—with speaking to anyone who's not a sister of this order. Sister Catherine of the Perpetual Sorrows would make a better extern for the Roswell monastery. She's been doing the job for years."

"Our dear Catherine is a woman of many talents; that is true. But we are none of us getting any younger, and Catherine is no exception. She will be sixty-five this November. An extern sister must be vigorous, physically capable. It's a role much better suited to a younger woman. Besides," Mother Superior said, smiling, "I've asked Catherine to serve as the abbess in New Mexico, and she has accepted. I believe she'll be a paragon in the role."

"Sister Catherine will make a fine abbess," Mary Agnes conceded. "But what about Sister Ann? She's still young, and—"

"No, dear, no. Sister Ann is a delight to us all, but bless her, she has a timid nature. An extern must be strong-willed, confident—capable of making decisions on her own. Always with the good of the order in mind, of course."

"And you think *I* am that!" Mary Agnes laughed bitterly; she couldn't help herself. "Confident. Able to make decisions on my own." Entirely too confident, if her shameful past was any indicator.

"I see those qualities in you, yes. I've always seen them, Mary Agnes. I know that after so many years in enclosure, the idea of venturing out into the world must seem frightening, but you must have more faith in yourself, my dear. You have more strength than you give yourself credit for. You're capable of more than you allow yourself to believe."

That's the trouble, Mary Agnes wanted to say. *I know all too well what I'm capable of, Mother, and you wouldn't like to hear the tale.*

And as for faith . . . if she had any—in herself or in God—she had yet to find it.

"Now tell me," the abbess said comfortably, "what is it you fear about the extern's life? Surely between the two of us, we can put the worst of your worries to bed."

"Oh, Mother, I . . . I fear temptation. Sin." She swallowed hard, willing herself not to cry. It was a fight she was rapidly losing. "I want to be strong enough to resist all the lures of the world, but I'm afraid I'm not. I *know* I'm not."

The abbess made a small, sympathetic sound and reached across the desk. Mary Agnes couldn't help but take her hands.

"My dear," the abbess said, "I won't force you to do this thing if you truly don't want to. But remember the words of Ecclesiastes: 'To everything there is a season.' The time comes for us all to grow, sooner or later, whether we desire that growth or not. God places us upon the paths He wishes for us to walk."

"There are times," Mary Agnes admitted, "when I wonder whether God is really paying attention. It's so easy to wander down the wrong path, no matter where He sets you. It's sinful, I know, to think such a thing . . ."

Mother Superior chuckled. "You're only a mortal woman, like the rest of us. Goodness knows, I've entertained the same thoughts, myself, now and then. But listen, my dear." She squeezed Mary Agnes's hands. "If you follow the path God gives you—if you hold to it with all your faith—then it will lead you to your true destination, in the end. It can't do otherwise."

A peace descended over Mary Agnes then—the only real peace she'd known for weeks, since the nightmares began. She lowered her face. "All right. I'll do as you think best, Mother."

And may every saint and angel protect me, she prayed. *Mother Mary, keep me to my path.*

CHAPTER TWELVE

September 8, 1947

Dearborn Street Station had appalled Mary Agnes, all noise and constant motion. The comings and goings of countless travelers echoed from the tile floors and soaring brick walls, and the tense, darting motion of strangers had left her feeling like a hunted animal. Huddled with the ten sisters bound for New Mexico, she had struggled to remind herself that she had once thrived in the bustle of the city. Or at least, she'd thought she'd been thriving, up to her neck in sin. Now she wondered how she'd survived her life before her vows. She'd grown so used to the meditative peace of the monastery that the din of a Chicago train station had frightened her as much as a glimpse into Hell might have done.

The train itself was an improvement over the station. The archbishop of Santa Fe had paid for two tourist sleeper compartments, which could house four travelers each in a cramped and spartan style. With five nuns to a room, they were packed in like sardines—but the sisters were used to one another's close company. The luxurious bedding made up for any minor inconvenience. The nuns were accustomed to sleeping on straw-filled mattresses with old, thin quilts. By comparison, the lumpy, compacted bunks of the train car with their thick woolen blankets seemed as decadent as feather beds.

Mary Agnes was smaller and slighter than most of her sisters, so she was chosen to share a berth with the doll-like Sister Ann. Once they were free from the oppressive noise of the station, a holiday spirit settled over the women. They chatted and joked as much as their vows of modesty would allow while they made themselves ready for bed. When the train's whistle sounded and it pulled out of the station with a hiss of steam, a startled silence fell over the car. The nuns gazed at one another, sober yet hopeful, as the car began to rock and the dark city flashed past the compartment window, faster with every moment. There was no turning back now. They had truly severed themselves from their mother house, and as yet, God was the only one who could say what the new monastery in Roswell would become.

In the upper berth, Mary Agnes and Ann giggled as they crawled over one another, trying to find some comfortable arrangement. Mary Agnes kept bumping her head against the curved ceiling of the compartment, and Ann nearly rolled off the bunk in her efforts to make room. Finally, they settled on lying head to foot—not the most dignified way to sleep, but it would have to do.

They lay for a while in silence, watching light and shadow play across the curved ceiling of the little rolling cell—the flashing red lights of railroad crossings, the all-night glare of Chicago, and then the intermittent brightness of towns that passed as rapidly as dreams. When the train left the last town behind and rolled out into the slumbering countryside, a deep, serene blackness filled the car—of night, of silence, of an emptiness ready to be filled.

"Mary Agnes," Ann whispered. "Are you still awake?"

For an answer, she gave Ann's shoulder a friendly nudge with her toes.

"I'm a little afraid," Ann confessed. "New Mexico. And a tiny town, in the middle of nowhere—not a city, like we've been used to. What will it be like, do you suppose?"

Mary Agnes said nothing for a long moment. She'd been asking herself the same question for weeks, since Mother Superior had called her to her office. The questions continued to multiply, the vista of what was possible growing wider and ever more complicated. But she had found no answers and didn't know what comfort she could offer to her sister.

Ann was waiting, however. Mary Agnes couldn't leave her to the silence.

"It will be a place like any other," she said quietly, "full of souls in need. Wherever we find one who suffers, we'll bring him comfort. What else would we do, no matter where God sends us?"

Ann soon drifted into sleep. The compartment below fell silent as the other sisters surrendered to the luxury of their mattresses. Mary Agnes watched the ebb and flow of shadow across the compartment's ceiling and waited for sleep to claim her, too, but it never did.

After a while, she clambered over Ann and groped with her feet for the ladder. Soon she was slipping out of the compartment, into the car's passageway.

In the tiny lavatory, Mary Agnes splashed her face with water. This did nothing to relieve the weight of the unknown. If anything, that weight had redoubled itself from the moment she'd stepped into the train station, into that shifting sea of humanity. There were far more questions outside the convent walls than there had been on the inside. She wondered, with a bleak thrum of despair, how she would ever survive this sudden calling to an extern's life.

She didn't return to her compartment. Instead, she drifted to the car's forward lounge, which was empty now. Every other passenger was in their bed.

Mary Agnes settled on a padded bench and pulled back the curtain on the nearest window. There was no telling where the train was, how far they'd traveled from Chicago. The countryside beyond the tracks was uninhabited, a long, black roll of earth unmarked by the glow of any distant town. The stars shone in bright profusion, so numerous here beyond the city that they seemed to hang like a vast and luminous tapestry, stretching from the arch of the sky to the humble land in a cascade of light. The stars held their places of fixed permanence in the heavens, so the land itself seemed to flow in a black current across the very hem of the sky.

She hoped Mother Superior had been right, that one only needed to walk the path one was given. She prayed that it would prove to be so simple, that she would be led to the truth if she held with all her faith to what she knew was right. She couldn't see a path out there among the darkness of the hills and fields. The only road that seemed to exist was the rail on which the train was running, and Mary Agnes was being conveyed along its course much too quickly for her liking.

TRANSCRIPT page 5

BISHOP COTE: Who else, besides Sister Mary Agnes here, has seen your hands begin to bleed?

BETTY: Just about all the kids who were at the sock hop, I guess. You can ask anyone.

BISHOP COTE: Would you like to give us some names?

BETTY: No.

ROSA: Betty, your manners.

BISHOP COTE: Why don't you want to give any names? Are you afraid that some of the other children might contradict your claims?

BETTY: No, I'm not afraid of that. I'm not afraid of anything. I just don't want anyone prying into my personal business.

BISHOP COTE: I don't understand what's personal about the question.

CHAPTER THIRTEEN

December 26, 1941

Betty Campbell stood in the exact middle of the street with her hands in the pockets of her new felt coat and her head thrown back so all she could see was the sky, the endless, inky blue-black of a cloudy night with snowflakes coming down in a mad, directionless whirl.

She wasn't afraid that a car might come, because this was the day after Christmas, and everyone was inside, having dinner with their families or playing with their brand-new toys, which was what Betty might have been doing now if she weren't eleven. Eleven is right in the middle of being too old to play with dolls anymore, but still young enough that you really want to. She was young enough, too, that she thought it wasn't fair. Not fair, that this was the saddest Christmas anyone had ever heard of, not fair that everyone had been dull and subdued the previous morning when they'd opened their presents. Not fair that at dinner tonight, Mom kept blinking the tears out of her eyes and even her little brothers didn't have the heart for their usual mischief. The whole of December had been simply awful since news came that the Japanese had dropped bombs on Hawaii. The war had felt comfortably distant and abstract for as long as Betty could remember, but now there was no hope that it might draw to some conclusion without Dad going off to fight.

All the houses down Twelfth Street had lights strung along their roofs. Betty resented the brightness, the gay colors. She put out her tongue to catch snowflakes. The sharp, smoky feel of the air and the close silence that attends a snowfall made her feel isolated and small. She might have been the only girl in the world just then—the only person in the world, left alone to face a grim and imminent future.

It wasn't fair. Dad had said many times since the bombing that no news had come from the command yet—not news about his unit, anyway—so there was no reason to get upset, not until there was a real cause for tears. But Betty was more perceptive than that. She could tell by the way all the grown-ups talked, furtive and low, that it was only a matter of time. When Mom and Dad whispered, they stood closer together than they usually did, like they couldn't stand the idea of being separated even by a few feet. Dad would be sent away, and he might not come home again, so there didn't seem much to be happy about, even if it was Christmastime.

Mom had convinced the boys to help with the dishes—which they probably only did because they felt sorry about the tears in her eyes—and no one noticed that Betty had slipped out of the house. She looked back from the road, and the soft, yellow light of the lamps allowed her to see right into the living room. There was Dad in his favorite chair, reading the newspaper as if this were an ordinary night, an ordinary time. The Christmas tree was a glory beside him, shining glass balls and garlands of the old, many-colored beads that Abuelita had strung on embroidery floss years before Betty was born. Tinsel fell like a summer rain from the tree's branches, cascades of silver. The sight disgusted Betty—everyone pretending it was going to be all right, when the biggest dummy in the world could see that nothing was ever going to be all right again.

She couldn't remain within sight of her home for another second. The snowfall was fresh, only an inch or so deep, but its smoothness over the familiar shapes and textures of her neighborhood combined with the transformative magic of night to make everything feel like a new landscape ripe for exploration. She set off up the street, walking right down its middle in her felt coat and rubber boots. It was better than staying where she was, watching from the outside while her family tried to cling to the falsehood of life carrying on the way it always had.

She trudged across the silent town for a long time, impressing the only footprints into the snow, glaring at scenes of happiness and security through lighted windows. She didn't notice that the snow had begun to fall faster, nor that the flakes were fattening and obscuring her tracks almost as quickly as she left them. By the time she realized her hands were too cold, even in her pockets, she looked around and saw that she was on an unfamiliar street, with no idea how far she'd wandered from home. Flakes had melted on her red pixie cap, and her hair was beginning to feel damp, her ears so cold they were aching. When she turned to look back the way she'd come, only her most recent footprints remained. The rest of the street stretched smoothly into a near, black distance.

A voice called from a nearby yard. "Are you okay?"

Betty spun, frightened, and found a boy close to her own age, leaning over a low wall of crumbling brick and adobe. He wore an old Army jacket with a woolen hat and a scarf wrapped all the way up to his chin, and he was looking at her with bright, curious eyes.

Betty began to cry. Suddenly, unstoppably, with huge, awful sobs that shook her whole body. She wasn't okay. Nobody was. And since the seventh of December, it seemed like she was the only person in the world who saw that clearly.

The boy hurried out of his yard and into the road, where Betty stood.

"Hey," he said, "it's all right. See? I won't hurt you."

She wasn't afraid the boy might hurt her. But she also didn't know how to explain these wracking tears, which appalled her as much as they did him. She choked out, "I got lost." It seemed like the most plausible excuse for her behavior.

"I can help you find your way home again," he said. "You don't have to cry."

She recognized him now, from school. "You're Jimmy Lucero."

"Yeah, that's right."

He was a grade ahead of Betty. He shifted the big Army jacket around so he could fish in the pocket of his trousers, and Betty watched from below her damp lashes, wondering at Jimmy. Older kids were supposed to be mean and a little scary, especially boys. At least, they never deigned to talk to the kids in lower grades, and boys of Jimmy Lucero's age weren't caught dead with girls.

Jimmy found his handkerchief and passed it to the girl. She dried her eyes.

"Isn't your name Betty?"

"How did you know?"

He shrugged. "I guess I've seen you around. Maybe at one of those Army picnics."

"Your dad is in the Army, too?"

"Sure," he said, "whose isn't? I guess it's going to be a long time before anyone has a picnic again. I mean . . . I guess you heard the news about Pearl Harbor."

When she returned his handkerchief, Jimmy said, "What street do you live on?"

"Twelfth."

"That's easy. I know how to get there; come on."

He set off at once, waving for her to follow. When she caught up with him, he loosened the scarf around his neck and handed it to her. "Here. You look cold."

"I'm all right."

"Aw, will you take it already? Can't a guy do something nice for a girl once in a while?"

Betty's cheeks burned. She took the scarf and draped it around her neck. It smelled pleasantly of damp wool and woodsmoke. "Thanks," she said.

"Look, I didn't mean to snap at you. It's just that I thought girls are supposed to get all mushy when you do something nice for them."

She laughed. "Mushy?"

"What were you crying about, anyway?"

"Being lost," Betty said.

"You were not. A little girl might get upset over being lost, but you're old enough not to cry over something like that."

She stuffed her hands deeper into her pockets, hunching against the cold. "I guess I was crying because my dad's going to go off to the war. Now that that thing happened in Hawaii, you know, with the bombs."

"I know how you feel. I've been thinking the same thing. My dad said there's no reason to expect it yet, but—"

"But they all expect it," Betty said. "You can tell by the way they talk and act. They expect it. It's going to happen."

The boy smiled at her through the sideways spin of the snowflakes. It was nice to find someone who understood.

Given Roswell's proximity to two important airfields—not just the one three miles outside of town but Clovis as well, where the Army's best fighter pilots were trained—most men in Roswell were enlisted. Those who weren't had retired from the Army long ago. Since the Great War, the town had practically become a military installation unto itself. Well, no one called it the Great War anymore. Newspapers and radio broadcasters and all the adults Betty and Jimmy knew said "the First World War" now, as if it were inevitable that this present conflict would swell to engulf the entire planet. Maybe that was so. Since news had broken of the ambush at Pearl Harbor, Jimmy hadn't been able to shake an image of the war as a monster, a vast, embodied thing, swallowing armies and towns and nations, getting larger and hungrier the more it consumed. And Betty had begun to think that even the penguins in Antarctica would soon have to pick a side.

They walked together down the street. The only sound was the crunch of their boots in the snow. The flakes were whirling down, swift and thick, and the world seemed to draw in around them, shutting out

Roswell and the enduring desert beyond, even pushing away the war for a while—that great, decisive weight which at other times they could feel rolling closer and closer with the inescapable authority of a god. In this private sphere of a shared reality, they could talk about anything they wanted.

"I'm worried about my dad, too," Jimmy said. "And sometimes I think maybe the war will go on for even longer, until I'm grown up, and then I'll have to go, too. They sent the boys off to fight, you know, in the last big war."

"Boys your age?" Betty said, astonished.

"Not my age, but not a whole lot older, either."

She didn't know much of anything about the last war, but she believed him. There was something about Jimmy's calm, measured way of thinking and talking that made him easy to believe. She had never really talked to a boy before—her brothers didn't count—and had certainly never walked home with one. It seemed a grown-up, ladylike thing to do, especially since he'd given her his scarf.

"Here's Twelfth," Jimmy said, turning at another corner.

"I didn't know I was so close. I didn't recognize anything with the snow. Thought I'd gone all the way across town."

"Say," Jimmy said, "I got plans for a radio-controlled plane as a Christmas present. Since we live so close, you should come over sometime and help me put it together."

Betty drew herself up with a sudden new excitement.

Before she could answer, however, Jimmy said, "Never mind. That was a dumb thing to say. Girls don't like model planes; you like dresses and dancing and flowers and stuff."

Betty laughed again. "Those things are all right, but I like planes, too. And it sounds neat to put one together."

"It does? You really like planes?"

"Sure," Betty said. "I think all the time about what it must be like to fly in one. To be up there in the sky."

"My dad's a flight engineer in the Air Corps," the boy said, proud yet shy. "I've gone up a few times with him."

"Gee, that must have been something. I've read some great things about rockets in those magazines they get at the library—*Amazing Stories* and *Weird Tales* and all the rest. But those are made-up stories; they aren't real. You know what I read in the newspaper the other day? That in ten years or less, people will travel in jet airplanes. That's got to be real; you can't print made-up stories in the newspaper. My dad said so. Can you imagine? The paper said that jets will be able to cross the ocean in hours. Why, we could fly from here to anywhere in the world!" She paused, kicking at the snow. "If there wasn't a war, I mean."

"I believe it," Jimmy said. "The Air Corps is making jet planes. Rocket planes, too. My dad told me all about it, and he would know."

"Rocket planes?"

"They can fly higher than jets, and faster, too, because they don't need oxygen the way turbines do. The higher you go, the less oxygen there is, so you have to mix chemicals together to make your fuel burn."

They grinned at one another, and for a moment, all the fears that had made the future seem so bleak and inevitable receded.

"What do you say? Do you want to help me put this plane together, or not?"

Betty nodded eagerly. Then she gave him back his scarf. "Guess I'd better get inside."

"You know where I live now. Come over on Saturday afternoon, and we'll get started."

From then on, they spent every minute together that their parents would allow. While the world resigned itself to war and their fathers made their grim preparations, while their mothers wept and voices on the radio grew more emphatic with patriotism, Betty and Jimmy retreated to the sanctuary of a shared purpose.

In the garage of Jimmy's home, with an old oil heater beating back the chill of a desert winter, they pored over instructions and sliced into sheets of balsa wood with the care of surgeons. Jimmy's dad had allowed him to set up the old gramophone in the garage, and they spun records by the hour, Glenn Miller and the Andrews Sisters, the Ink Spots, Duke Ellington and His Famous Orchestra, the horns and the swingy drumbeats loud enough to stifle every thought that wasn't for the Good Brothers' Guff they were assembling.

They talked about jet engines and rocket-propelled flight. They talked about the journeys they would take when the war was over and they were a little older—to England and back in a day, to Paris, to Moscow, to the moon. They talked about the weird tales and amazing stories they'd read in library magazines. Everything except the way their private worlds were coming apart at the seams, the contents of their families and lives sucked out into the airless void of the unknown.

Betty left assembly of the engine in Jimmy's hands. She didn't trust herself with all that metal, and the soldering iron scared her. She painted the Guff instead, red with precise black stripes across its wings, a jaunty star under the window, right where the pilot would sit. Jimmy pronounced it sharp, which made her glow with pride.

On an evening late in January, when the sky was pale with the approach of night but not yet dark, the model plane was finished. Both children had spent the day at the Air Corps flying school outside town, saying goodbye to their fathers as they boarded the planes that would carry them off to war. Their mothers had wept, and so had they—but now, as they maneuvered the four-foot model through the gate of the high school football field, they didn't think of their tears or their worries. Nor did they dwell on the rumors of Japanese rocket planes that could fly much faster than the fragile American craft that carried their dads in their bellies. All their attention was trained on the model with its small, finicky engine.

Jimmy tested the breeze and set the model carefully in the grass. Betty watched, shivering with anxiety. After all this time and work, maybe their plane wouldn't fly. But when Jimmy threw the ignition switch on his radio transmitter, the model's engine came to life with a loud buzz, and the propeller pulled the contraption through the gathering dusk, faster, faster, its nose lifting to the sky.

They ran in the plane's wake, shouting, laughing. The engine was loud enough to drown out their noise. When the model rose into the air, it left them far behind on the small, simple earth.

The plane worked perfectly. Barely visible against the dusk, it defined sweeping arcs of elegant space and pirouetted in defiance of gravity. It rose and fell and rose again in giddy parabolas, up there among the night's first stars.

CHAPTER FOURTEEN

September 22, 1944

At his father's funeral, Jim Lucero's biggest concern was holding it together so no one would see him cry. Not for his own sake—he didn't much care if the guys made fun of him or called him a sissy, not with his dad so recently gone—but for his mother's sake. She had taken the news hard. She'd barely spoken a word since the Western Union messenger car stopped outside their home last week. The somber, white-gloved driver had emerged with a stoic greeting, and in his hand was the telegram no wife or son in America wanted to read. Jim was determined to give his mother his strength now, even if he felt too weak to carry the weight of his own grief. Still, he would do what he must. Just like his dad had done.

All through the funeral service, the contents of that damned telegram kept running through his head—its stiff formality, its stark, unavoidable words.

> *The Secretary of War desires me to express his deepest*
> *regret . . .*

Before the altar, Father Kerry was speaking of the gentle salvation of Jesus, the promise of life everlasting that waits beyond the grave. Nonsense. No one knew what happened after you died, and the facts were probably as blunt as the words in that telegram had been. When you died, you just stopped. That was it; it was all over for you, like the flick of a light switch. The burning brightness of being alive, of being you and being real. And then, in an instant, nothing.

> *The Secretary of War desires me to express his deepest regret that your husband, Second Officer Salvador Lucero, was killed in action on seventeen September over the Philippines . . .*

He was holding his mother's free hand, which was so cold and motionless it seemed that she was already dead, too. She kept wiping her tears with a handkerchief, but more always fell, so many that Jim thought she was crying for both of them. He wished they didn't have to sit in the foremost pew of the church. Because there were heaps of flowers below the altar, but no casket. There had been no viewing—for which Jim was secretly grateful—and no wake. His father's body would never be recovered. Shot down in a firefight off the northern coast of Luzon.

It was time again for prayer. Jim helped his mother onto the low, padded kneeler, then arranged himself at her side. His prayer beads hung lifeless in his hand.

Throughout the Rosary for the Dead, he didn't pray, but thought instead of his father above the vast, gray Pacific, which Jim had never seen. In his mind, the ocean was a veil through which the final mysteries passed. He could see the water as his dad must have seen it, wrinkled and shining, like one enormous sheet of foil, wrapping the planet all the way out to the hazy geodesic curve of the horizon. It wasn't fair, that the earth from above was all his dad had seen these past two years. It wasn't fair, that Jim hadn't seen his father at all while two years of life had gone by and the war had dragged out to a set gravitational permanence. And now he would never see his dad again. His father had gone past the veil of the ocean, into the unknown darkness on the other side.

The prayers kept going. The rosary beads became numbers in Jim's hand. Numbers, like his father was now—a statistic, another man lost to war—like Jim would become, himself, one day soon. There seemed little hope now that this war would end. In three short years, Jim would be old enough for the draft, and then he would be sent off to fight and die and become a number, a bead on an endless string, so commonplace that no one remembered his name or Second Officer Salvador Lucero's name, or anyone else's. Only the numbers.

But if this were to be Jim's fate, at least he would accomplish one thing. He would remember his dad, if no one else did, honor his memory. Dad had been so proud of his work as a flight engineer, proud that it was his knowledge that kept the planes running, even when disasters struck midair. "It takes brains to do this job, Jimmy," Dad used to say. "God put a brain between your ears because he meant for you to use it."

There on the kneeler, with the priest droning the comfortless liturgy of death, Jim found a purpose for his life—however much life remained to him, before the war took him, too. He would use the brains God and his father had given him. He would become an engineer, just like his dad, and if there were any flicker of light beyond the grave—if some scrap of his father's soul remained in the waves and whitecaps of unbeing—Jim would make him proud.

He made up his mind to leave high school and get into the New Mexico Military Institute, Roswell's Army academy. After that, he'd go to a university, like his dad had done, and study aeronautics. Maybe even rocketry, like he and Betty Campbell used to talk about when they'd built the old Guff together. And once he knew all there was to know about the physics of flight, he would join the Army, help make the world a safer, better place for everyone. Until the war took him, too.

The prayer finally came to its end. Jim helped his mother up. After the priest had admonished them all to go in peace, Jim stood by his mother's side while friends and neighbors and people he didn't know came to kiss her cheek and take her hand in sympathy.

One slender figure in the crowd had come to speak with Jim, however. Betty Campbell wore a dark, plaid skirt and a black cardigan sweater, and between the sweater and the tidy waves of her black hair, her face stood out with the paleness of porcelain. She seemed an other-worldly messenger, and Jim half expected her to produce an envelope from the pocket of her skirt, another telegram with the worst kind of news.

Betty wasn't sure if Jim would remember her. Their friendship hadn't lasted long past the winter of '42, when they'd flown the Guff together. Once he'd gone on to high school, they had found themselves in separate spheres with no cause to interact, no common interest to share. But she had watched him through the funeral service, from the far end of the chapel. The stoic set of his shoulders, his upright posture in the pew. She had tried to think of something to say to him. What could anyone say at a time like this?

"Hello, Jimmy."

He didn't have the heart to tell her that he was just Jim now. It didn't really matter.

"Do you remember me?" Betty asked.

He smiled, though he didn't feel like doing it. "What kind of a question is that? Of course I remember you."

"I just wanted to say . . ." Betty floundered. Every expression of sympathy that came to her mind seemed so false, mere platitudes. "I'm real sorry," she finally said. "It's just awful, and I'm sorry, and . . . and, well, I guess I'll be praying for you."

Her own rosary was wrapped around her fist, clutched like the hilt of a dagger. It almost made Jim want to laugh. It didn't seem as if Betty had any more use for prayer than he did. Somehow, that did give him a little comfort. He hadn't expected to find any today.

"Thanks," he said to his old playmate. "I mean that. It was good of you to come."

A thick, miserable pressure was filling Betty's throat, burning in her eyes. Her father was still alive. She didn't wish any ill on her own dad, of course, but she also felt obscene, standing there before Jim and his grieving mother, a living embodiment of the luck that had abandoned the Lucero family. She needed to make some offering of humility. She sensed that, and reached impulsively for the first thought that came to her mind.

"Do you want to go fly the old plane together? You know, the way we used to?"

The moment the words were out of her mouth, Betty wished the floor of the church would open and swallow her whole. Jimmy's dad had died in an air fight. The last thing he wanted to think about now was planes.

"I'm sorry," Betty said. "I shouldn't have . . ."

"It's okay." Jim took her hand briefly, the one that wasn't trying to mangle her rosary. "I can't, though." He lowered his voice so his mother and her friends wouldn't hear. "I've got to stick by my mom. Tonight will be hard on her. Tonight, and for a while, I guess. But I'll see you around."

"Sure," Betty said. "See you around."

Long after the funeral had ended and the whole town had gone to bed, Betty slipped down the stairs of her home and out into the still-warm night. She walked alone to the high school, to the football field, and pushed at the gate until she could squeeze through the gap, despite the padlock and chain that secured it. The field seemed to stretch before her into an ever-unrolling procession of darkness. She walked until she was somewhere near the center of the field, and then she sank to the turf and hugged her knees to her chest and looked up into the far, cold infinity of the sky.

There were hundreds of stars overhead. Millions of them, one for every life lost to this war, and one for all the lives that were yet to be cut short by bullets or bombs or the horrors of German camps, or the grief that comes to suffocate you in your own bed, far from the front lines. The stars were real, but God didn't seem to be. How could He be the benevolent force of love the priest and the Bible claimed Him to be, if He could allow all this to happen, if He could allow a good man like Jimmy's dad to be taken in a flash of fire?

She wondered what it must be like, to fly up there among the stars. And what it must be like to come down, uncontrolled, the engine of your plane a hopeless whine, the stars stretching into white lines that rush past the dome of your canopy, the last of your reality a streak of fire at your tail.

Imagination failed her. She couldn't picture anything beyond that—the fall from the sky, the clutch of gravity like God's own hand. When she tried to comprehend what came after, she met with a blankness inside, and her thoughts dwelled there for a long time, going nowhere, seeing nothing but the sky. Death was the one great border, the unchangeable fact that hemmed in and defined life. Beyond that boundary, anything might exist. Heaven, if you believed the church and the priest. Betty wasn't sure that she did. Or a new life—countless new lives, the soul (whatever that was) multiplying into a deep infinity, like when you hold two mirrors in your hands and step into the magic space between them.

Or nothing, nothing at all, which somehow felt more sacred to Betty than anything she'd ever heard at church, because if there was truly nothing beyond that final boundary, then everything in life was elevated to the level of holiness. Everything, no matter how simple or mundane, had a value far beyond gold. Even the dense, choking sadness Jim and his mother were feeling. Even the last, burning fall from the sky.

She watched the stars in their teeming thousands. The distance between Earth and the nearest star was greater than Betty could comprehend. She knew that the light from some of those cool, bright points in the blackness took thousands of years to cross the void of space—millions of years. Scales of time that made her dizzy, evidence of a vastness beyond this small, fragile planet that turned her into a pinpoint of improbability. Yet she found it easier to stare into that mystery than to look at the bright divinity of an ordinary night, with its ordinary grief, with the feel of Jimmy's hand still lingering in her own and the pull of gravity in her heart. The stars and their light were very far away. But she could name them and count them. They were here with her, in the realm of the living, where everything was sacred, even the unknown.

CHAPTER FIFTEEN

September 12, 1947

That week, Friday was a long time in coming. The hours of the school day were a dull slog, and Betty had sat tapping her pencil and watching the clock through each of them, her thoughts orbiting helplessly around her father. Contrary to what her mother had promised back in July, Dad hadn't relented where college was concerned. In fact, he'd only dug in his heels all the harder, growing terser and more immovable each time Betty had raised the subject. By the time her junior year had begun, she'd stopped bringing it up. There was no point in beating your head against a brick wall. And in the months following the crash, Roger Campbell had become an edifice, as if he thought he could ward away all the dangers of a disordered world with his stoic silence.

And now here Betty was, well into the fall, when she should have been sending out early applications to coed colleges. She'd never had any intent of waiting until her senior year; she would do summer classes to earn her diploma early, exchange Roswell for the freedom of college life as soon as she could manage. But her window of opportunity was rapidly closing—not only for junior-year applications, but for senior year, too. If she didn't find some way to budge her dad on the subject, she would miss her chance altogether.

She was still ruminating on the enigmatic problems of her father as she walked home from school, and later, as she tended to her daily chores. By the time Juanita phoned with the breathless news that everyone was meeting at Vic's, Betty was sunk so deeply in her own thoughts that she left home without glancing in the mirror. She was halfway to the restaurant—could smell its intoxicating aroma of grilled burgers and frying oil—when she realized she was still wearing the same faded shorts and peasant blouse she'd thrown on to help her mother with the baking. She wore her old, scuffed saddle shoes, too, and she'd neglected to tie a silk scarf around her head, so the wind had blown her curls into a positive rat's nest and had dulled the glossy black sheen of her hair with a steady barrage of dust.

There was nothing for it now. Gatherings at Vic's were liable to break off at a moment's notice into drag races at the pecan orchard or bonfires at the lake, and no girl who had any hope of social status would be caught dead anywhere else. If she returned home to change and tidy up her hair, she was guaranteed to be left behind. So she pressed on, determined to pull off her laundry-line chic as an intentional stab at a gamine style. She hoped the other kids would fall for it.

When she came within sight of Vic's parking lot, Betty combed her fingers through her hair, trying to put her curls back into place. Without a mirror, the operation was hopeless. At least there were more interesting sights to distract the gang from Betty's ragged appearance. The girls were turned out in their brightest skirts, with necklines or cropped tops as daring as their mothers would allow. The boys' hot rods gleamed in the last of the day's light. Now and then an engine revved with a basso growl that drowned out the sugary music spilling from the restaurant. Carhops glided by on roller skates, trays balanced on their shoulders, their faces pinched in frowns of concentration.

Juanita spotted Betty and waved, then came scrambling across the hot pavement, her mouth already working on the latest gossip though Betty couldn't yet hear.

"Am I a mess?" Betty demanded.

"Gosh, no." Juanita stroked the embroidered ruffle at Betty's collar. "You look just like an old-fashioned princess. But with shorts instead of a skirt."

Old-fashioned wasn't what Betty had been going for, but she threw her arms around Juanita's neck all the same. It was good to have a real friend in the crowd.

"Say, Betty!"

She glanced over her shoulder and there was Jimmy Lucero, leaning against the hood of his Plymouth. A few boys hung around him, sporting the same short haircut that Jimmy wore—academy cadets, all of them, and strangers to Betty. None of the boys wore their cadet uniforms now, however. Jimmy was dressed in corduroy trousers, baggy and worn thin at the knees, with the sleeves of his white T-shirt rolled up to expose his arms. Betty had never noticed how nice his arms were, the muscles lean and defined, his skin brown as honey. But then, she'd hardly seen Jimmy for years, except in glimpses across town. She certainly hadn't been in his company long enough to exchange a word—not since his father's funeral, and that was three years ago.

"You know Jim Lucero?" Juanita loaded his name with a weight of significance. "He's an absolute dream."

Betty cut her friend a swift, apologetic look.

"Oh, go and get him," Juanita said with a laugh. "Would I hold you back from a prize like that?"

Betty approached Jimmy and his friends, adrift in a strange detachment. Part of her mind screamed that she ought to run home while she still could, or crawl under a rock and die, because surely death was better than walking right up to a gang of boys from the military academy when she looked like she'd crawled out of the laundry basket. The rest of her—a larger and deeper part—was stilled to a kind of meditative acceptance. Maybe it was only the hopelessness of her situation, the sheer ridiculousness of her circumstances, but some quiet force pulled her back from herself, and everything slowed around her—the boys roughhousing beside their cars, the flash of the waitresses' bare legs as they skated past. Even the music melted into a lazy lag, the notes disconnecting from one another and stumbling somewhere behind the singer's words. This wasn't a distance of space, but of time. She was struck by a sudden piercing clarity of the moment's frail transience. Someday, all of this would change. The girls' smart clothes would be thought as unfashionable as Betty's peasant blouse. Newer and sleeker cars would replace the hot rods. All those kids, so hip and vivacious now, would age into the same quiet despair that had swallowed their parents whole. Their own children would fill this parking lot, listening to music as different from this croony pop as modern music was from the crackling, muffled, Victrola sentimentality that their parents and grandparents favored. The carhops would be replaced by . . . someone else. Something else. Robots, maybe, like in the stories Betty used to read, servile and efficient, gliding on metal wheels. And one day the drive-in would shut down. The building would languish in its emptiness. It would degrade, as the whole town would, back into eternal desert. And all of this would blow away, dust on a future wind.

The premonition frightened her. It comforted her, too, because it meant that none of this mattered—her ratty blouse, her scuffed shoes, her wild hair. If nothing would last, then nothing was real. All the moments and the years yet to come were real, because there would always be more of them, always a new world constructing itself and expanding from any given point. What did the here and now matter, compared to everything that lay ahead?

As Betty strolled up, Jim gave a little jerk of his head, said to the other boys, "Scram for a minute, will you?"

They hooted about Jim Lucero getting a handful. That snapped Betty back to herself. Suddenly the present mattered far more than any unformed future. Her face burned, and for the sake of her dignity, she had to restrain herself from fussing with her hair again.

Jim was too cool to rise to his friends' bait. Mildly, he said, "She's an all right girl. Now beat it, before I beat you."

The academy boys retreated across the parking lot, gathered again at some other hot-rodder's car. Betty stood gazing at her childhood friend in bewilderment. The boy she had played with for a single winter was scarcely recognizable now. His features had grown strong and defined. He was taller, carried himself with a man's confidence that made her starkly aware of the year he had over her. One clear thought paddled its slow way through her mind: she ought to be the first to speak. The more popular girls at her school always had some gracious and charming comment ready, whenever any boy complimented them in the halls.

"Hi, Jimmy" was the best she could manage.

"It's just Jim now."

"Oh—I knew that." She hadn't known, in fact. "I don't usually see you at Vic's when the gang comes down."

"I'm usually too busy studying."

He propped his hip against the Plymouth. Casually, Betty did the same. She was pretty sure she looked like a scarecrow half–blown over by a stiff breeze.

"But tonight," Jim went on, "the Hawks are getting up a race out at the orchard. They've been running their mouths too much around town. All the A-Bombs are coming out tonight to put them back in their places."

The Hawks were the high school's racing club. Betty could only assume that the A-Bombs were a rival club from the academy. Not for all the money in the world would she have admitted to her ignorance.

"Say," Jim said, "can I get you a burger?"

"How about a shake? Chocolate."

He waved down a passing carhop to give the order. Betty willed herself to remain upright and poised, though everything inside her wanted to crumple. She knew nothing about cars or racing. A pang of sadness struck her. Where was the boy who'd built the model plane, who'd chattered about rockets and flights to the moon? She wanted to see that boy again, run with him under the stars while the Guff they'd made together ascended into the great black arch of the heavens.

One way or another, she floundered through the conversation. She made all the appropriate noises as Jim discoursed on the power of the Plymouth's engine, the slick builds his friends had made under the hoods of their own cars, how trounced and sorry the Hawks would be once the A-Bombs were through with them. When the hop came skating up with two shakes on a tray, Betty was grateful for the excuse to say nothing. She sucked on her straw, peeking up through her lashes now and then to watch Jim drink his own shake. His was butterscotch. She liked the way his Adam's apple moved when he swallowed.

After a minute, he said, "I guess I'll be showing up more often on weekends. I don't have to study so hard, now that I've been accepted into a university."

"Gosh, you have? Already?"

"Pasadena," he said. "The California Technical Institute. I applied last year, actually, as a junior."

She almost admitted that she was doing the same . . . trying to do the same. But what good would it do to talk about it if she couldn't make her dad relent?

"I'll be starting my studies at the Jet Propulsion Laboratory next fall," Jim said.

He felt a little shy at the admission. It was no minor accomplishment, for a small-town Mexican kid to land a spot in such a prestigious college. He'd studied and worked hard for it, had kept himself on the good side of the academy's dean so his transcripts and letters of recommendation would be flawless. He'd known for years that he would have to be perfect in his studies and his reputation to compete with the white applicants. And even though he had cleared his own high bar of perfection, still he hadn't quite believed that his efforts would be enough. Not until he'd received the acceptance letter from Caltech.

Betty seized his hand before she knew what she was doing. "Oh, Jimmy, you did it! Just like you always dreamed."

Then she realized how impulsive she'd been, how forward, and tried to let go. But Jim held on. She'd always been a pretty girl, and good company, too, back when they'd both been frightened, grieving children. She had grown up to be a real beauty, with the same intelligent light in her eyes, the same daring curiosity. That was what he liked best about Betty Campbell—the way her mind worked. It had always been what he'd liked about the girl.

Blushing, Betty said, "You've got a real chance to get out of this poky town—and stay out for good. Boy, I envy you. My folks used to be on board with sending me to college, but Dad won't hear of it anymore. He thinks he's got to keep me within arm's reach. As if I can't take care of myself. It isn't fair; all these years I've been working so hard to keep my grades up so I could get accepted to a good school. And then Dad goes and pulls the rug out from under me. How do you like that?"

"I guess your old man can't boss you anymore," Jim said. "Not when you turn eighteen."

"But how would I pay for school? I couldn't afford it without Dad's blessing."

"There are lots of scholarships now."

"For girls?"

Jim laughed. His thumb moved over her knuckles in a way that sent a wild, crinkly thrill up her spine.

"Of course, for girls," he said, "and in science, too. It was science that won the war, so everyone's gung ho to fill every program at every university right up to the brim. And women are welcome, from what I've heard. You ladies played a big part in the victory when you went to work in the factories. We aren't living in the Stone Age; no one thinks girls should be stuck at home, ironing and sweeping. Not anyone who's got his head screwed on straight."

"I wouldn't know how to get a scholarship."

"I can help with that—the applications, anyway. With my old man gone, I have to rely on scholarships, too. It's not as hard as you might think. Just keep your grades up—"

A shout: "Heads up!"

A heartbeat later, something silvery flashed between Jim and Betty. They leaped apart, barely holding on to their shake cups. A metallic clatter resounded from the hood of Jim's car.

"Flying saucer!" one of the military boys yelled. "Look out, Lucero, it's coming for you!"

Jim ran a hand over his hood, but the paint wasn't scuffed, nor was the body damaged. "Dang it," he bellowed, "you could have done some real damage, Marley! You're lucky if I don't turn you inside out!"

The projectile was still shivering on the ground—a tin pie plate, oscillating on its rim as it settled. Betty trapped it under her foot, and the thing went silent.

"What a bunch of drips," she muttered.

"You said it." Jim picked up the plate and flung it back at his friends, then gave them the bird, which made them hoot all the more. "Let's get out of here. Soon all the kids are going to be throwing that thing around, and I don't want this baby to get scratched. I've put too much time and money into her."

He opened the passenger door. Betty hesitated, heart pounding. She looked around for her friends and saw the girls watching her—Juanita and Christine, the rest of the usual gang. Even Millie and Theresa were staring in amazement. Betty slipped into the Plymouth. She had time to suck in one giddy breath before Jim got in behind the wheel and fired up the engine. The car's awakening raced all through her, shivering the particles of her physical substance until she felt as if there was no difference between herself and the thunderous sound. She had to bite back a squeak of surprise when Jim hit the gas and peeled out of the parking lot in a screech of rubber on pavement.

Once Vic's was out of sight, however, he slowed the Plymouth to a more reasonable pace. There was no point in getting traffic citations. Who could say whether something like that might endanger his future at Caltech? A guy like him couldn't be too careful about such things.

"What a bunch of goons," he said. "Everyone's still so damn hung up on that saucer story. Can you believe it? It's been months since it came down. And anyway, it was just a weather balloon. I don't see what the big deal is."

Betty clenched her fists to hide her palms, though there was no sign remaining of the old wounds.

"I wonder if we'll ever know what happened out there," she said. "I mean, was it a balloon, or was it something else? My dad said it might have been something the Soviets made. A spy plane sent to take pictures of our test ranges. And some kids think . . ."

Betty trailed off. Rumors about the saucer hadn't abated with summer's end. Plenty of kids in school thought the saucer had come from Mars or some other planet. Some said it was a time machine, and whoever had flown the craft now walked among them, a visitor from a distant future mingling unnoticed with the ordinary citizens of Roswell. She thought of the wild-eyed stranger who'd come to her house late at night, mere days after the crash. If Betty hadn't overheard his conversation with her dad—if she didn't know the man was a private, and friends with her father—she might suspect him of being the stranded time traveler. Why else would her hands have burned in his presence?

"Whatever it was," Jim said, "if anything crashed at all, and it isn't just some fake story, you can bet there's a scientific explanation."

She glanced at him. The sun had set, and only a lingering flush of gold remained low in the sky. The great, enfolding purple of a desert twilight had swallowed the town. Jim was barely visible in the dimness of his car.

"Do you really think so?" Betty said. "You think science has the answer?"

She wanted it to be true. She needed to believe that all of this could be explained through ordinary means—the crash, the wild rumors, the way her father, already altered by the war, had withdrawn even more into a private realm of persistent fear. Most of all, Betty wanted to believe that *she* was ordinary, that there was some plain and simple reason for . . . whatever had happened to her that night in early July, when she'd touched the scrap of metal.

"Of course," Jim said. "Science always has the answers. The trouble is that people misunderstand what they've seen, or don't know enough about the way the world works to get what's really going on—physics and chemistry and all that. So they fall back on superstition and religion and crazy, out-there stories."

He reached through the darkness, took her hand again. Betty laced her fingers with his, allowed herself to be carried off on a sweet, fast current of excitement. Jim liked the way their hands fit together, easy and natural. They'd always been a match.

"Say," he said, "why don't we go out to the Brazel ranch?"

"Where the saucer went down?"

She recalled the scrap she'd found that summer night, when she'd ridden in Dwight Carey's convertible to the ranch—remembered the prickling sensation that had afflicted her barely healed palms, merely from looking at the debris. She didn't want to go to the Brazel ranch. And somehow, she wanted nothing more in all the world.

"Whatever crashed," Betty said, "the Army took it away months ago. Kids have been going out to Brazel's place since the summer, looking for pieces of the saucer. No one has found anything, from what I've heard."

"I guess they would have been pretty thorough in cleaning it up. The Army doesn't go halfway on anything."

"Well, what's the point of going all the way out to Brazel's if we won't find anything?"

Jim chuckled. "Not finding anything *is* the point. Anything bigger and heavier than a weather balloon would have left some evidence. Scarring in the ground, burned sagebrush—that kind of thing. If we don't find any evidence, then you can bet there was never any flying saucer to begin with. Consider it a science experiment."

"What about the race?"

Jim had forgotten all about the Hawks and the A-Bombs. None of that seemed to matter, now that he and Betty were talking again, alone and honest, the way they'd done as kids.

He shrugged. "There'll be more races."

"I don't know, Jim. The ranch is private property."

Caltech passed through his mind again, but the possibility of being alone with Betty below the stars was more than he could resist. "There aren't any cops out there, and anyway, we won't disturb Mac Brazel. Or his sheep."

"But what if he sees us? Couldn't we get in trouble?"

His thumb moved again, back and forth across her knuckles. "I promise I won't get you into any trouble. Not unless you really want me to."

After that, she was ready to go anywhere with him.

Once they'd passed through the heart of town, Roswell vanished quickly. Betty's insides buzzed with anticipation, her stomach and her veins and her bones. She tuned and retuned the radio to keep the music playing as they sped through the hour that separated Brazel's ranch from the city limits.

Jim left the highway at a milepost that looked no different from any others. The turnout led to the sheep range on a rutted dirt road. The Plymouth slowed to a crawl, its tires chattering on loose stone. Headlights cut into the night, met one another in a far-off point. Animals skittered across the road—a family of ringtails, a slinking coyote with shining green eyes. Mac Brazel's house had no light on, a dark rectangle against the stars. It looked like the hole left over by a knocked-out tooth.

Jim drove for a while, then pulled over, cut the engine. The headlights blinked out.

"Is this the place?" Betty asked. She couldn't remember if this was where Dwight and the rest of the kids had stopped. One patch of desert looked very like another, especially at night.

Jim got out of the car, and Betty had no choice but to do the same. Clusters of sagebrush crackled against the door, giving up their sharp, dusty scent. The gray twigs scratched at her bare legs. Jim had already crossed the road to scramble up a low hill. His white T-shirt was vibrant under the starlight, making him stand out against the anonymous black land with a dreamlike emphasis. Betty felt as if she could reach out and touch him—wrap her arms around his waist, or his neck—though he was far away from her now.

She crossed the road, too, picking her way among stands of brush. The ground sloped ever so slightly, and she followed the upward pull of the subtle earth, followed the draw of that young man ahead of her—the bright, self-assured man who had once been her playmate.

They reached a summit of sorts, the highest point anyone could get to out there, and stood panting side by side. Betty turned in a slow circle. The earth revealed itself, a shallow, black curve. She'd heard the kids at school say that you could see the evidence of the saucer's crash, the track of its drag through desert varnish, broken shale, the sage burned where hot metal had barreled through. She had seen no such thing on her previous visit to the ranch, but the idea had stayed with her, growing more vivid in imagination the more she heard the rumor repeated. She had pictured a scar in the earth a mile long, wide as a school bus. Now she could see nothing but the unvaried, blue dimness of the land. There was no moon that night, only a white curtain of stars split by the lightless gulf of the galactic center.

They didn't do anything—nothing but watch the constellations move above the earth. After a while, Jim drove her home and promised to return the next evening to show her how to hunt for scholarships. He didn't even kiss her that night, though he wanted to, and Betty wanted him to do it. But it seemed to Jim as if things ought to progress more slowly between them. What they'd shared together in the past had been important, even sacred. And the oaths of honor Jim had taken at the military academy meant something to him. For all the world, he wouldn't bring dishonor on this girl. Not Betty Campbell, whose companionship had once been the tether that had anchored him to the world.

September spun itself out. Jim and Betty went out so often that she expected him to ask her to go steady, any day now. She already knew what her answer would be, and tried not to think of the next fall, when

Jim would be off to California and she would be left behind in Roswell. He helped her sort through brochures and pamphlets, showed her how to analyze a school's track record by the published material at the library. Together, they drafted letters of application for scholarships. At night, before she climbed into bed, Betty rewrote every letter at least a dozen times, choosing her words with meticulous care, determined to make the applications irresistible before she mailed them out to her chosen universities.

It all would have gone apple-pie perfect, if one of those requests for a catalog hadn't been delivered with the newspaper. The girl never had a chance to scoop it from the mailbox and hide it away in her bedroom. When she came home from a Saturday-night date with Jim, her dad was waiting up for her in his easy chair with a scowl on his face and the catalog resting on his knee.

For her rebellious attitude, she was grounded until Christmas break. No parties, no dances, and definitely no more dates with Jim Lucero.

It was the worst thing Betty could imagine. She cried for hours in her room, until Sunday came. She was so wracked by sorrow and exhaustion that her mother had no heart to force her out of bed, not even for Mass.

She spent the morning leaning against her windowsill, staring across the rooftops and the trees to the place where Jim's house was, three blocks away. She wondered if he ever looked across the neighborhood toward Twelfth Street, thinking of her.

Even after he left the Army, the memory remained. And it sent its roots through his soul—whatever a soul might be—and it grew until it was something more than memory, something more than experience. The sight and the feeling, the white light, the folding of all that had once been real into a greater, stranger awareness of what real *could be. He became more and less than what he was. He became—had always been—the moment itself, that glimpse through the mundane into a richer depth of understanding. Going through the motions of an ordinary life, working with his hands, his back, his humble and impermanent body, and paying the rent on his hole of an apartment, and eating and sleeping and waking every morning to the same, expected sun, he was transformed, though no one would have known it to look at him. Where there had once been order—a comforting chain of cause and effect, the familiar if-then of a linear life—he found a sacred unmaking, the detachment of all sense, and a rapid decay of the assumption that everything happened for a reason, that there* was *reason, that God—whatever God might be—had a plan.*

You might think such a revelation would fill him with despair. But now his every breath was a miracle. With all sense unmade, something new was created in its place—a deep well of holy awe for the senseless and the unexplained, for only that which can never be known can truly be called divine.

TRANSCRIPT page 7

BISHOP COTE: And what is it you're doing when you receive these wounds?

BETTY: Just things. Normal, everyday things.

FATHER KERRY: Can you elaborate on that?

BETTY: No. I mean, I don't know what you want me to say about it.

SISTER MARY AGNES: Betty is a perfectly ordinary girl, Your Excellency.

BISHOP COTE: That seems to be exactly our trouble, Sister. Stigmata are not known to occur unless the recipient demonstrates extraordinary faith. Praying all the time, for example, or having visions.

BETTY: It has nothing to do with praying. Not for me, anyway. It has everything to do with the saucer.

BISHOP COTE: How do you know that?

BETTY: *(no answer)*

FATHER KERRY: Can you tell us how, exactly, the flying saucer triggers the response, Betty?

BETTY: I have to be near a piece of it—the little pieces of metal some of the kids have picked up in the desert.

Or sometimes, I think talking about it is enough.

FATHER KERRY: Can you tell us more about that?

BETTY: Once, my dad's friend from the Army came to the house. He wanted to talk to my dad about the saucer. I . . . I hid at the top of the stairs to eavesdrop.

BISHOP COTE: Why did you do that?

BETTY: Because when I answered the door, just looking at the guy made my hands itch in the same places where they'd bled.

BISHOP COTE: And who was this man?

BETTY: I don't know his name.

BISHOP COTE: And when your hands haven't just itched, but have actually bled, how was the saucer involved?

CHAPTER SIXTEEN

October 11, 1947

Word at school was that all the boys from the military academy planned to attend Saturday night's sock hop, so Betty had spent the whole week thinking up and discarding one clever scheme after another that would get her to the dance in defiance of her dad's new rules. Most of the plans she concocted were too elaborate to succeed. Dad might buy a line about all the kids from church meeting for Bible study, but he would never believe that Betty would attend such an event of her own free will. Nor would he fall for a late-night study session with the girls from school. Not on a Saturday. Asking him to lift the restriction for a single night was out of the question. Roger never acted out of mercy where grounding was concerned; he was too much of a military man for that. He expected his children to see their duties through, just as he did, without shirking or complaint. There was a certain consistency to his morals that Betty had to admire, even when it annoyed her. But the issue of the course catalog had become a silent battle of principles between them, and Betty felt it was time she defended her own moral sense as rigorously as her father did his. She was his daughter, after all. If she didn't do what she knew in her heart was right, no matter the cost, she wouldn't be doing justice to the Campbell name.

Her opportunity came the evening of the dance. They had supper early, long before sunset. "Because your father is going fishing," Betty's mother explained as she stirred the pot of pozole. "I figured it was better to feed him ahead of time. You know how he gets when he's out on the lake. Sometimes he doesn't come home until late."

The pork stew was rich with spices, and Betty was hungry enough to eat the whole pot by herself. But she made herself pick half-heartedly at the dish, hoping she gave a convincing impression of infirmity.

"Are you all right?" her mother asked.

"I'm okay." Betty kept her eyes on her plate to hide her triumph.

"She gets this way once a month," her brother Billy said.

"What do you know about it, you little rat?"

Roger let his hand fall heavily on the tabletop. "Enough of that talk. At the dinner table, for goodness' sake! Bill, you'll be washing the dishes tonight, since you can't keep your language or your manners clean."

Betty stifled a smile and went on picking at her stew.

After supper was finished, before her father had a chance to leave for the lake, Betty filled the hot water bottle, allowed her mother to fuss with offers of raspberry leaf tea—the old-time remedy for cramps and other symptoms of the monthly malaise.

"I'll just go up to bed," Betty said weakly. "Try to sleep it off."

She hid in her room for a long time after her dad left with his fishing pole. Finally, her mother and brothers settled in for the night. She lingered near her window, watching the tail end of the sunset fade to an inky dusk. When nothing remained of the day but a slow swath of orange at the western horizon, she heard her mother run the taps in the upstairs bath. Betty's chance had come—and not a moment too soon. Her father might return from the lake at any second. She would have to make her escape fast.

Carrying her good saddle shoes in one hand, she slipped from her bedroom and down the stairs. Her brothers were in the sitting room, absorbed by a rerun of *Buck Rogers*, with the radio turned up loudly enough that she had no trouble sneaking past. In the kitchen, she paused to filch a chunk of corn bread the size of her fist, then let herself out silently onto the back porch. In moments, she had her shoes on her feet, and she was off, flitting like a ghost through the darkness.

The autumn night was cold, and Betty had brought no coat. Once her corn bread was gone, she hugged herself against the chill and moved as quickly as she could without breaking into a run. The gymnasium of the school would be plenty warm, once she got there, for the sock hop had been on for at least an hour. She didn't like the idea of arriving so late, but not attending at all was worse. And this might be her only chance to see Jim. She had told him over the phone, of course, that she'd been grounded for the crime of trying to get into college. But it was such a ridiculous reason, she felt as if Jim deserved a real explanation, face-to-face, of just how unbearable her father had become in the months since the crash.

The cold drew in more tightly as her thoughts turned to her father. Poor Dad—the war had already left him with a persistent fear, and that raw, vulnerable core seemed always to be exposed. Whatever he'd seen during his time in the Pacific, the experience hadn't left him any peace, not even years later. And then that *thing* had happened out on Brazel's ranch. Whatever her father had seen on the retrieval mission, the fear had settled deep, become as much a part of the man as his love and his honor and his strength were.

She could see the high school now, one more block down Main Street, light and music spilling from the open gym doors into the velvet darkness. A wave of guilt swept behind her, from the direction of home. Despite her dad's accusations of disobedience, this was the only time she'd actually rebelled against him in all her seventeen years. It didn't exactly feel good, but it didn't feel exactly bad, either. Like the rest of the adults in this one-horse town—like most of Betty's friends, if she were honest with herself—her father didn't seem to realize that there could be no going back. The world that had existed before the war, with its neat hierarchies and comforting order, might as well lie as far in the past as horse-drawn carriages and telegraph wires. The only place left to go was forward, into a remade world, into this bright, unfolding future—a future where women took their rightful places, shoulder to shoulder with the men, and didn't need to rely on their fathers or husbands for protection.

When she stepped inside the gymnasium, the heat of so many vigorous young bodies struck her, a lively burn against chilled skin. The boys from the audio club had rigged up a couple of turntables and lined the edge of a plywood platform with an impressive array of speakers. Benny Goodman filled the gym with the liquid wail of his clarinet. Vibrant skirts flared like monsoon flowers as girls spun in the arms of their partners, and everywhere the dancers' socks flashed as white as desert glare. Betty's previous attack of remorse was quickly forgotten. There wasn't anything better than a dance—not in a town like Roswell.

She scanned the crowd, searching for Jim's tall frame and his cadet's haircut. There were plenty of kids from the military academy escorting girls around the floor, but Jim was nowhere to be seen.

"Hi there, beautiful."

She turned, beaming. There he was, right by her side, sipping from a paper cup.

"I was hoping I'd find you tonight," Betty said.

"I was hoping I'd see you, too."

"You're the only reason why I came."

He laughed. "Come on. You'd be dancing whether I was here or not."

"I'd be grounded in my room," Betty said. "That's where I'm supposed to be now, but I gave my folks the slip so I could see you. Oh, Jim, my dad isn't ever going to give this up. He thinks he can keep me in some glass tower forever so nothing bad ever happens to me. He's losing his mind from worry. I don't know what to do."

"I guess you're not supposed to do anything tonight but dance."

She giggled and took his arm.

"Can I get you some punch?" he asked.

"I haven't worked up a thirst yet."

"We could do something about that," he said, "but you've still got your shoes on."

The other kids had left their shoes in neat rows along one wall of the gymnasium. She kicked off her oxfords and pitched them across the room. They landed close enough to the others.

Jim pulled her onto the dance floor as "Snafu Jump" began to play. The pounding toms and the high, bright squeal of the trumpet beat through their veins in perfect synchronicity. They'd never danced together before. Even so, they didn't miss a step, anticipating one another's moves with a smooth understanding that needed no words—only the meeting of their bright, hungry eyes and the grazing of a hand against back or shoulder or neck. This was what it all could be, Betty told herself—the new life, the new world that was coming, where male and female moved in sympathetic harmony. Why was her dad so afraid of this? Why did anybody fear it, and cling to the stuffy, old-fashioned ways of generations past?

Jim felt so drunk on the music, on the warm proximity of the beautiful girl in his arms, that for a moment he feared someone had spiked the punch. There wasn't another girl like her in all the world. Every time he lifted her for a dramatic twirl, he felt as if he were soaring up alongside her, with the gym and the music and the mundane world falling away below.

As the song reached its brass crescendo, Jim ducked his shoulders. Betty needed no other signal. She rolled across his sweat-dampened back and landed, breathless, on her feet. Only very gradually did she and Jim realize that all the surrounding couples had stopped their own dancing to watch the two of them. Betty blushed and hid behind her hands as the crowd whooped, applauding their unexpected performance.

One of the girls threw an arm around Betty's shoulders. "Say, you can really move!"

"Thanks. I guess I'm not so bad."

Tommy Wicklowe from chemistry class sidled up to her. "Can a guy get a spot on your dance card, Betty?"

She gave Tommy her most gracious smile. "In a few more songs. First I owe Jim another dance or two."

Tommy thumped Jim on his back. "Lucky so-and-so. The rest of us will have to try to keep up with you!"

The slow, chiming guitar of "Again" drifted from the speakers. Doris Day began to sing in her silky alto, and the crowd separated once more into couples.

Jim offered his arms. Betty slid into his embrace, and they swayed together, close enough that they could feel the pounding of one another's hearts.

"I don't care what my dad says," she told him. "He can't stop me from seeing you."

"Gee, Betty, you know I'm crazy about you, but I don't want to cross your old man."

"He can't control me. For heaven's sake, this isn't the Dark Ages. Oh, don't get me wrong, Jim—Dad's an all right guy. He means well, but he's living in the past. I've got my own life to live, and haven't I got as much a right as anybody else to say how my life ought to go?"

He pulled back a little so he could meet her dark eyes again.

"Of course you've got the right. But listen—I had to take an oath at the academy."

"An oath?"

"An honor code. We all had to swear that we wouldn't cause any sort of trouble or associate with people of questionable morals—that kind of thing. You might think it's silly, and maybe it is, but it means something to me. I mean to finish out my year at the academy in good standing so I won't have any trouble with Caltech next fall. That's what my dad would have wanted, and I intend to do his memory proud."

"I'm sure you do." Jim Lucero was the smartest, most honorable, most fascinating guy who'd ever lived; Betty was dead sure of that. How could any father help but be proud of him, in this world or beyond?

"That's why I can't take the risk of upsetting your dad," Jim said. "He could report me to the academy if I broke any of the rules where his daughter's concerned. And then it might be all over for me."

Betty sighed. She could see his point, even if she didn't want to.

"Why not let me talk to him?" Jim suggested. "Maybe I can convince him, man to man, that he ought to see things from our point of view. Maybe I can explain to him what my intentions are—that I'm not going to get you in any trouble. If I can get him to trust me, he'll ease up on you. He's got to."

"You always seem to be able to think your way through things," Betty said. "Wish I could do that. It'd save me loads of trouble if I could. All right—it might not help our situation if you talk to my dad, but I guess it couldn't hurt, either. As long as you don't tell him I came to the dance tonight. He'll skin me if he finds out I snuck out of the house."

When the slow song ended, one of the boys from the audio club announced a refreshment break, and the dancers drifted in the direction of the tables spread with punch and crackers. A bubbling energy filled the gymnasium, a buoyancy that surged on the chatter of so many voices. Betty accepted a cup from Jim. The icy sweetness cooled her and, like some magic elixir, seemed to drive back weeks of unanswered questions, all the bleak and pressing unknowns that had haunted her since the summer. Everything was going to be all right. She felt sure of that now. Whatever had happened to her that night, with her dad and his scrap of metal, it hardly seemed to matter anymore. The incident had been a passing mystery, a fantasy, a dream. This was real: her friends surrounding her with youthful cheer, the bold new world of opportunity that was throwing wide its arms in welcome. And Jim—him, most of all—with his good, sensible thoughts and his sturdy common sense, ready to shed a calm, rational light on everything, even on the problem of her father.

She fell into easy conversation with Jim, then with Juanita, who came squealing through the crowd to congratulate her on her dancing.

After a few minutes, all three of them noticed the knot of boys and girls that had gathered across the gym, near the speakers and record players. The group had drawn into a tight circle. There was something conspiratorial in their hunched shoulders, the cautious glances those kids threw, as if they feared one of the teacher chaperones might intervene.

"What do you suppose they're up to?" Juanita asked.

Betty shrugged. "Someone probably brought dope."

"They wouldn't be dumb enough to smoke it inside," Jim said. "And we'd smell it, besides. Let's go see what's up."

He led the way across the gym. As he approached the circle, some of his fellow students from the academy made way for him and the girls.

His buddy Frank Beam looked up eagerly, proffering a scrap of something paper-thin and silver-white. "Say, Lucero, get a load of this. Williams brought it from his house. Said his old man picked it up on the Brazel ranch where the flying saucer crashed. What do you think?"

The kids in the circle passed the scrap around, examining it, whispering over it, eyeing their friends to gauge their reactions.

"My pops was part of the recovery crew," Jeff Williams said proudly. "He said it was a whole ship, thirty feet across."

"A ship?" Juanita said.

"Not like a sailing ship—like the spaceships you see in movies."

"Oh, come on, Jeff," Juanita said. "That's silly. No one believes it."

Offended, Jeff drew himself up. "Anyone with half a brain believes it! My dad said there were dozens of men, all from the Army, except a few guys who were from the Pentagon—"

"The Pentagon!" Jim shook his head, chuckling.

Somebody called, "Quit pulling our legs, Jeff."

"I'm not pulling any legs!" Jeff's voice had risen a full octave. He was almost squeaking with indignation. "I tell you, some guys from the Pentagon showed up and made everyone at the base swear themselves to secrecy. On pain of *death*. My dad wouldn't have said it if it wasn't true—"

The boy went on defending his story, and Betty eyed the scrap of unassuming trash as it moved surreptitiously from hand to hand. It was smaller than the piece her father had shown her, but it seemed to be made of the same stuff—featherlight, paper-thin, and of a curious, silvery color that both reflected the light and seemed to pull all light into itself, blending its edges into the frank, solid reality around it. Her palms began to itch and tingle, just the way they'd done that night at Brazel's ranch, when she'd found her own scrap caught in the roots of the pinyon—the way they'd done when she'd opened the door and met that strange man's eye.

That's all in your head, she told herself. *It never happened.*

She wished the music would start again. That was all she wanted—to dance, to be the same kid she'd been before the crash had changed her and changed her father. She wished Jim would come away, leave the useless metal alone. She held tightly to his arm, pressing close beside him, her hands and even her feet prickling now with an electric energy.

When the scrap reached Jim, he took it gingerly between thumb and forefinger, held it up to inspect its properties by the sharp glare of the gym's fluorescent lights. The debris was about two inches wide and five long, ragged at one edge as if it had been torn away from something else. It had the smoothness and shine of aluminum, but even the lightest-weight metal would have had some detectable heft at this size. Whatever this was made of, it weighed almost nothing. Jim had the idea that if he dropped it, the scrap would drift airily to the ground like a feather. Betty was holding his arm, so he couldn't do much with one hand, but he managed to squeeze the object, curving it over his thumb. It bent readily, and when he released the pressure, it sprang back to its original shape without a crease or a dent.

"Now what in the heck could this stuff be?" he wondered aloud.

Suddenly, Betty gave a mewl of pain. She clenched her fists, hid them against Jim's body—hid her face, too, pressing herself against his shoulder.

Juanita turned to her friend, but before she could ask whether Betty was okay, she saw the girl's feet. Two spots of red were expanding through the crisp white cotton of Betty's bobby socks.

"My gosh, Betty," Juanita cried, "you're bleeding!"

Betty broke from the circle, ran for the bathroom. The gym and the dance and all her friends were lost in a blur of tears. She could hear Juanita shouting to wait, but she couldn't slow and wouldn't stop, wouldn't allow anyone to see. Blood pooled hot and insistent inside her clenched fists, and every step across the gym floor was slicker than the last.

When she reached the bathroom, she turned on the taps at the sink, held her hands under the cold water. The blood that had gathered in her palms ran down the drain, but there was more welling from the small, round wounds, and she shifted from one foot to the other, feeling a nauseating warmth congeal between her toes.

Juanita barreled into the bathroom. "Betty, what's happened to you?"

"Go away," Betty sobbed.

Juanita wasn't about to be deflected so easily. She crept closer, brushed Betty's hair back from her forehead, put an arm around her waist. Together, they stood and watched the water gushing over Betty's palms, circling in a pink vortex around the drain.

"I want it to stop." Betty's words came out strangled and small.

"We'll get you to the hospital," Juanita said. "The doctor."

"No! No one can know about this. No one!"

"But you're bleeding."

The girl shut her eyes, shook her head miserably. Her mouth was distorted with grief and fear, her breath harsh, her nose running.

"Did you cut yourself?" Juanita asked. "Maybe you need stitches."

"I didn't do this!" Betty almost screamed the answer. "It wasn't me!"

Juanita gathered paper towels from the bathroom's dispenser, began cleaning Betty's red footprints from the floor. "I know it isn't you. It's okay, Betty; it's okay. Just put pressure on your hands. That'll make the bleeding stop."

She folded more clean paper towels, tried to get Betty to lift a foot so she could remove one of the saturated socks, but Betty was frozen, shuddering as she leaned over the sink, and Juanita didn't think her friend could hear her anymore.

She crept to the bathroom door, put her head cautiously out. Jim Lucero was right outside, barring the way so no one else could get in.

"We've got to get her home," Juanita said.

"Is she okay?"

The poor girl didn't know how to answer. "I'll go and find her shoes. You go in with her, Jim. She's beside herself. I don't want to leave her alone."

Betty was only marginally aware of Jim's cautious, gentle voice, and she heard none of his words. Her eyes were fixed on her own reflection in the cracked, grimy mirror. She was staring into herself, into the inverted hollow of a place where the self she knew had been. She allowed Jim to remove her socks, one at a time. He pressed paper towels against the wound in one foot, bound them in place with his handkerchief. Then, with an apology, he reached into the pocket of Betty's skirt for her own hanky and treated the other foot in the same way.

By that time, the water in the sink was running mostly clear. The bleeding in her hands had slowed.

Juanita came back with Betty's saddle shoes and a pale, shaken look.

"Everyone's going to talk," Betty said weakly.

"Who cares what they say?" Juanita flared. "What do any of them know?"

"My dad's going to kill me when he finds out I snuck out of the house." Some distant part of Betty wanted to laugh—that of all things, getting into worse trouble with her father was her biggest worry now. Except, none of this was funny.

Jim said, "You only cut yourself. It happens all the time." *This* didn't happen, though—not to anyone, not ever. "Does it hurt? Can you walk, or do you want me to carry you out of here?"

"I'll walk," Betty said, more calmly than she felt. "It'll only make a bigger scene if you carry me."

Jim and Juanita helped her fit her bandaged feet back into her shoes. Betty pressed new pads of paper towel into each hand and took Jim's arm again, hiding her fists where no one could see. The three of them left the bathroom together, cleaving through a crowd of stares and questions and astonished laughter.

Once they were safely in Jim's car, Betty cried all the way to Twelfth Street. She pulled herself together just enough that she could beg Jim to stop at the corner.

"Are you sure?" he asked. "I can go inside with you, if you like—talk to your old man now, instead of later."

"No," Betty insisted. "I'm going to sneak back in the same way I got out. There's no point in making Dad sore on top of everything else."

"There's no chance your folks won't hear about this," Juanita said. "The story will be all over town by tomorrow afternoon."

"Maybe I can convince Dad it's a rumor." Even as she said it, Betty knew it was a futile hope.

Jim and Juanita watched her hobble up the block and cut through a neighbor's backyard. After a few minutes of agonizing stillness, a light flicked on in the upper story of the Campbell house.

"That's Betty's room," Juanita said. "She made it."

Jim put his Plymouth in reverse. "I'll take you home."

For most of the drive across town, the car was filled by a silence heavy with meaning. Neither knew what questions to ask, what answers would suffice.

Finally, Juanita could bear the pressure no longer. This wasn't the kind of thing anyone should speak of lightly, yet what else could she do but speak? "You know what that was, don't you?"

"It was nothing," Jim said. "No big deal. Betty cut herself somehow—that's all."

"Jim, come on. In both her hands and both her feet at once?"

He rolled to a stop outside the girl's house, turned to meet her eye. "That stuff isn't real. Stigmata? It's nothing but hysteria—or hoaxes."

"How do you know?"

"Because things like that don't just *happen*. The world doesn't work that way."

"It happened tonight," Juanita said.

"Whatever that was—whatever happened to Betty—it was real. Real things have rational explanations."

Juanita raised her dark brows, fixed him with a look that almost withered him. "Thanks for the ride," she said.

When he returned to his own home, Jim sat for a while in the driveway with his forehead leaned against the steering wheel, trying to make sense of the night. Everything had a down-to-earth, scientific cause. Even this. He couldn't see the answer yet. All he could see were the two dark spots on the sleeve of his shirt where the blood from Betty's palms had soaked in.

The memory remained, even after he left the Army, and filled him with reverent awe at the simplicity of the mirage that everyone called reality. But now and again, that ecstatic wonder gave way to a quiet suspicion that maybe he had lost his mind.

He had seen what he'd seen—of that, he felt certain, for why would the Army have made him swear those oaths and why had they threatened Mac Brazel if this had been a dream or a fantasy?

He'd seen it. He had obeyed the Voice and opened his eyes. He couldn't pretend his eyes were still closed.

But sometimes he wanted it to stop—the memory, the knowing.

It had set him permanently on the outside. In Roswell, yes, but everywhere else, too. He knew what he knew, that reality wasn't what it seemed to be, and around the sacred peace of that certainty, he felt the rest of the world—all the joy and connection and sweet, simple meaning he might have found in a life of contented ignorance—rushing in a vortex around him and spinning, bloodred, down a drain.

TRANSCRIPT pages 12–13

BISHOP COTE: Sister, you haven't wavered in your support of the girl's story.

SISTER MARY AGNES: No, Your Excellency. I'm quite convinced by my own observations that this is no hoax. Nor has Betty misunderstood what is happening to her.

BISHOP COTE: How long have you been in Roswell now?

SISTER MARY AGNES: Barely a month. My sisters and I arrived in mid-September.

BISHOP COTE: And can you explain, for the sake of our records, what an extern sister's duties consist of?

SISTER MARY AGNES: Certainly. Extern sisters aren't under the same vow of enclosure as the rest of our order. In addition to keeping the Hours each day and my duties in prayer, I do the necessary work of interacting with the world on behalf of my cloistered sisters— picking up necessities from the shops, for example. I also call on members of the parish as our priest requires. Since we arrived, however, most of my work has involved helping our handyman fix up the old farmhouse we've moved in to. The house and the grounds still need plenty of work; it keeps us both busy.

BISHOP COTE: This handyman—what's his name?

SISTER MARY AGNES: *(pause)* Does it matter, Your Excellency?

BISHOP COTE: Someone mentioned earlier that he's a friend of the Campbell family. I thought perhaps he might have also witnessed Betty's condition.

FATHER KERRY: The man's name is Harvey Day, Your Excellency. I hired him to work on the farmhouse. Actually, it was Roger Campbell who recommended Harvey to me as a hard worker who could get the place fixed up in accordance with the sisters' needs, and Harvey has proven to be a good worker, indeed. I understand he was discharged from the Army this past summer, but I must say, I find him to be an exemplary fellow. Sister Mary Agnes, are you well?

SISTER MARY AGNES: Yes, of course, Father.

FATHER KERRY: You've suddenly grown quite flushed.

SISTER MARY AGNES: I'm only warm. I'm still not used to the climate here. Roswell is a change from Chicago.

BISHOP COTE: Let us return, Sister, to your duties as extern. I'm interested in hearing how your work first brought you in contact with young Miss Campbell.

CHAPTER SEVENTEEN

September 11, 1947

On her first morning at the new monastery, Mary Agnes stepped out onto the porch of the old, white farmhouse and surveyed the grounds with a brisk, ready energy. The grounds were more beautiful than she'd thought the previous night, when she and her sisters had arrived.

Full night had already come when their train pulled into Roswell, pausing at the tiny depot just long enough for the nuns to disembark. The train had departed again in a great rush of noise and steam, and the sisters had huddled in silence, taking in what little they could see by night of their new surroundings. In Chicago, there had always been the soft, ambient glow of streetlights, of lamplight spilling from countless homes. Here, the world itself was swallowed by a huge, stifling darkness. A sickle moon had provided just enough feeble light to make out the humble, small homes of the town. The land beyond stretched away into a vast, flat emptiness. The air was so dry that it burned, and it left a mineral taste in Mary Agnes's mouth. Late as it had been, an insistent warmth had risen from dust and stone, a memory of the day's brutal heat.

A cadre of cheerful volunteers soon arrived to escort the nuns to the church, where the local priest offered a Mass to comfort and welcome them. Then they were driven to the site of their new monastery, situated on a large parcel of land just beyond the northern end of Roswell.

As the car had turned up a long, unpaved lane, Mary Agnes had peered through the windshield, into the consuming dark. There'd been precious little to see at that time of night. The lane vanished into a grove of stately trees, which grew so near one another that their trunks almost formed a natural wall. She'd been rather surprised to find such large trees in the desert, and had asked herself, amused, if she'd expected cactuses instead.

A simple sign made from a whitewashed plank had stood among the dim shadows of the lane. Its hand-painted black letters read *Monastery of the Poor Clares*.

Beyond the ring of trees, the grounds opened out onto several acres of empty field. At the heart of the acreage stood a great white farmhouse with a large porch and a Victorian turret that spoke of a time long past. Even by night, the house still possessed a certain elegance, though gaps showed in its siding and a loose gutter sagged from one eave.

"It used to be a sanitarium," the driver had said. "Tuberculosis patients, mostly. Don't worry, Sisters—the place hasn't been used for years. No disease hanging around now."

Sister Catherine of the Perpetual Sorrows—*Mother* Catherine now—had led the way up the porch steps, into their new accommodations. Mary Agnes had been too exhausted from two days of travel to take in much of the house's interior. She'd been left with only a fleeting impression of old-fashioned fireplaces and dark, polished wainscoting, with threadbare rugs covering the plank floors. The rugs were hand-me-downs, of course, from some generous soul in town. True to their name, the Poor Clares observed a strict vow of poverty, and used only what others gave them from the generosity of their own hearts. But despite a faint smell of mildew and age, the farmhouse had a homey appeal that came as a relief after days on a cramped, rocking train.

Now, in the benediction of morning light, Mary Agnes surveyed her new life with fresh, hopeful eyes.

The tight ring of trees—elms, she thought—enclosed some thirteen acres. The grounds were parched by the summer that had just passed, but the leaves were radiant with autumn color, shimmering in bowers of gold. A wind stirred, smelling of some exotic, woody spice, and the trees whispered in reply. Sunlight broke through the branches in mobile arcs, sending patterns of blue shadow and pearlescent light dancing along the earth. She hadn't expected to find such beauty in the desert. Only now, as her heart lifted at the sight, did she understand how anxious and unmoored she had felt since leaving Chicago.

The farmhouse door squealed open on its stiff hinges. Mother Catherine stepped out. The abbess closed her eyes, savoring the smell of the free, warm wind. "Isn't it delicious? Someone told me that smell is creosote bush. It's almost like the incense at Mass, I think. They say you can smell it before a rain."

"Rain in a desert?"

"Oh, yes—quite a lot of it, during monsoon season, or so I've been told. The rains come every summer and last into early fall. If we can expect to smell that heavenly scent for a whole season, then I believe we've found our own little Eden here in New Mexico."

"I hope this place comes to feel like home," Mary Agnes said. "It's been harder than I'd thought, to leave what's familiar."

"And difficult to adjust to our new roles." Mother Catherine laid a comforting hand on her shoulder. "You as an extern, after so many years in enclosure, and me—imagine it!—an abbess. Well, we must all do the work God gives us."

"I don't know how I'll manage. Goodness, Mother, I haven't spoken to hardly anyone but our sisters for twelve years."

"I remember that feeling. I was so frightened when I began externing. But have a little more faith, Sister—in yourself and in God. You'll manage just fine."

Mary Agnes hid her ironic smile behind the edge of her veil. That was the trouble; she'd never had enough faith. And now, with everything that had once been stable and familiar stripped away, she understood how badly she needed it. Despite twelve years of effort, faith had never taken root inside her. She wasn't even certain she could define the word—not with any real meaning.

Catherine shaded her eyes, gazed down the long lane that ran from the privacy of the monastery to the world beyond. "Here comes your first chance to prove how capable you are."

A cloud of dust billowed at the far end of the drive. A pickup truck came crawling up the lane, once a dark green but now so corroded by rust and a patchwork of paint that it was almost no color at all.

"That must be Mr. Day," the abbess said. "He's the handyman our priest has hired to do the manual labor around this place. And there is plenty of work to be done! You and he will stay busy, no doubt."

"I don't know what to do," Mary Agnes said. "I can't build, can't repair anything but holes in my habit. What good will I be to a handyman?"

Mother Catherine chuckled. "I'm sure Mr. Day will have plenty of work for you. He'll need you to run to the hardware store to fetch nails and things, or hold the end of his tape measure. For goodness' sake, Sister, don't look so pale! This won't be as much of a trial as you're fearing. Well, I must go back inside while Mr. Day is about. That's one thing *I'll* have to get used to again—remaining in enclosure. But we all know the rules. An abbess is not an extern."

Catherine slipped back into the house as the truck rumbled to a stop near the porch steps. Mr. Day climbed out, raising a hand in greeting. He wore a Stetson hat and a long-sleeved shirt, its tails untucked. His worn blue jeans were spattered with paint. Mary Agnes hadn't laid eyes on a man in the dozen years of her enclosure—maybe customs had changed. Yet she felt certain that Mr. Day was notably casual about his appearance, to say the least. Still, under the shadow of his hat brim, his expression was mild, even kind. He couldn't have been much older than Mary Agnes herself.

"Morning," he said.

Mary Agnes was filled by a giddy sensation close to dread. For a moment she could only stare at the man in bewildered silence. Then some small, distant voice spoke from a corner of her mind.

You know who you used to be. Before all of this, before you were a sister of the order.

Yes, she had once been a vivacious young woman, at ease among others—too much at ease. She recoiled from the idea of reaching into her own past. She had gained so much from her life as a nun—security, the peace of an uncomplicated life. And protection from the sinful nature that corrupted the spirit of every mortal man and woman. It felt almost like a sacrilege, to put Mary Agnes aside and become Patricia again, even in the smallest way, even for the good of her sisters.

Yet what else could she do? The nuns were counting on her to work effectively with Mr. Day—and after him, with any number of other people, in Roswell and beyond. Her duties as extern must begin. Allowing her old personality to rise to the surface seemed like the only sensible way forward.

Mary Agnes forced herself to descend the porch steps with a smile that felt like a lie. She wished there were someone else to introduce her; this was entirely too forward, to offer her own hand. But Mr. Day shook it without hesitation, nodding as she gave her name. Then he turned at once to his work.

From the bed of his truck, he retrieved a large toolbox and passed an empty tin bucket to Mary Agnes. "For holding nails," he said. "I mean to get the floor of that porch pried up today—as much of it as I can manage—and there'll be lots of nails to pick. Say, you'd better put some shoes on. You don't want to step on a nail."

"Sisters of our order never wear shoes, Mr. Day—not at the monastery, anyhow, and I'm the only one who will ever leave these grounds."

He met her eye with a startled look.

"It's part of the vow of poverty. It keeps us humble, like our founder Saint Francis—and Jesus before him, of course."

"Well, if you step on a nail, you're likely to get a case of lockjaw. You'd better stay away till I can be sure the place is cleaned up."

She wasn't upset by the suggestion. The prospect of remaining in close quarters with a man had left her heart pounding with anxiety. She retreated across the bare, dry acreage and busied herself with clearing away the branches that had fallen from the trees, piling them some distance from the lane. They would make a lovely bonfire, one of these nights. Her sisters would enjoy it.

As she worked, Mary Agnes kept one eye on the handyman—not out of any suspicion, but with a fixed fascination. He worked with an astonishing efficiency. In less than an hour, he had removed every rotted board from the porch floor and was already setting up a pair of sawhorses to cut the new wood.

By that time, Mary Agnes was thirstier than she'd ever been. Even in autumn, this place was hot—though it lacked the oppressive humidity of a Chicago summer. When Mr. Day waved to her with the all clear, she returned to the grounds and picked her way carefully up the steps and across the patchwork floor of salvaged boards and open gaps. She returned a few minutes later with a clay pitcher full of clean, cold well water and a cup for each of them.

"I think we've both earned a break," she said.

She sat on the upper step. Mr. Day joined her, removing his Stetson to wipe away his sweat. The pitcher stood between them, condensation gathering in diamond beads on its chipped surface.

She filled his cup and passed it to him. "We arrived so late last night, I barely had time to appreciate all the work you've done to the inside of the house. But it's really lovely; I know we'll be happy here."

"I had my work cut out for me," he said. "There were all kinds of problems with this place when I first took the job. And that Father Kerry fellow only gave me a couple weeks to get it whipped into shape before you ladies arrived."

"You've done a beautiful job. Of course, it isn't much like the monastery we came from, back in Chicago. That building was . . . oh, grand. A stately work of art, with a feel of history, inside and out."

He looked away, almost shy. "After living in such a fine place, this old farmhouse can't seem like much."

"It feels like a home," Mary Agnes said. "A real home. And I'm grateful to you for all the work you've done, Mr. Day. All of us are so very grateful."

He chuckled. "Don't go calling me Mr. Day, Sister. It's Harvey to you." He settled more easily on the step, poured himself another cup of water. "I'm glad to hear you're satisfied. I did some construction work when I was a kid, but it isn't my usual profession. And I've been wondering if I was worth anything at all, since I left the Army."

"So you were a soldier before you were a handyman?"

"I was a radar operator during the war. After, I was assigned to the airfield here at Roswell, but I didn't have any roots here, didn't know anyone except my buddy Roger. So when I left the service, I found myself a bit of an outsider in town. Working on this house has kept me busy, kept my mind on what's important. Kept me from going a little crazy, I guess."

The forgotten habits of the woman she'd been before were coming more easily now. It was no trouble to talk with this man. In fact, she felt so much at ease in his presence that she nearly forgot her name was Mary Agnes.

"Why did you leave the Army?"

On the instant, Harvey's easygoing attitude evaporated. His shoulders tensed, and he cast a long, silent look at her from the corner of his eye. "Call it a . . . a difference of opinion," he finally said. "Anyway, I intend to move on soon. I'll see this job through, of course, but I don't plan to stick around Roswell once the farmhouse is finished and I've got enough money to start my life over someplace else. By winter, I mean to be on the road."

"I'm sorry." Her face was burning, and not from the heat. "I didn't mean to pry."

"That's all right; I didn't take any offense. You know, you're an outsider in this place, too. We've probably got more in common than you'd think, to look at us."

He got up from the step and approached his truck again. He'd left the windows rolled down to keep the interior cool, and he reached inside without opening the door, withdrew a small, yellow box. When he returned to the porch, he passed the box to Mary Agnes.

It was a package of gumdrops. She gave a startled laugh and shook the box lightly. The candies rattled inside, and for a moment the memories of her childhood came crowding around. She no longer felt so far from home.

Mary Agnes returned the box to Harvey unopened. "We have rules about what and when we may eat."

"Can't wear shoes and can't have a gumdrop now and then?"

"It isn't exactly that. Strictly, I ought to share with my sisters."

Harvey shook a few gumdrops onto his palm. The candies caught the late-morning light with a nostalgic gleam. He popped one into his mouth. "Mmm. You're missing out, Sister."

Mary Agnes gave in with a playful laugh. "I think God will forgive me, this one time."

When she bit into a gumdrop, the burst of sweetness almost made her weep with its extravagance. But she didn't want to cry—not any longer. She and Harvey laughed instead, and she thought, *Maybe it won't be as hard as I'd thought, to serve in this new role. Maybe I really am where God wants me to be.*

CHAPTER EIGHTEEN

September 13, 1947

When Roger stepped inside with the newly delivered paper in his hand, the house was full of the smell of Rosa's baking. He paused, breathing it in, holding the comfort in his heart. For a moment, the richness of cinnamon and caramel and the warm, sharp tang of risen bread drove back the persistent fears that shadowed him. He could hear Rosa and Betty in the kitchen, their voices mingling as sweetly as the odors did, and though the empty hallway between himself and the ones he loved seemed too long and lightless a passage for him to cross, this evidence they were safe and content stilled the ghosts that haunted him.

When he entered the kitchen, Rosa looked up with her shy, girlish smile. She was packing a large basket with cookies and buns. "We're taking some things to the nuns at the new monastery," she said. "You could come along, if you like."

It wasn't the first time Roger had considered visiting the monastery. Hadn't he a right, after he'd helped Father Kerry find his handyman? And hadn't he a need? God knew he had that. Perhaps the sisters of Poor Clare could tell him what had happened to Betty that night in July, when Roger had come home with his proof of the unreal.

He watched his girl as she pulled a loaf of bread from the oven. Betty set the loaf on a rack to cool and slid her hands from the oven mitts. Roger could see no sign of her strange affliction; after two months, the wounds had healed without a trace. Yet he hadn't forgotten the sight of his child's blood, nor her stricken face, in all the time since he'd witnessed the terrible mystery.

There was too much in this world he couldn't explain, too much he didn't know. His homecoming from the war was supposed to be the end of the darkest chapter of his life. But the pages kept turning, and day by day, his fears closed tighter around him. Everything he couldn't explain, everything he didn't know, and all of it hanging over himself and his family, as near and bleak as the threat of Soviet incursion.

Maybe the nuns would know what to do about these endless fears, too. Maybe the sisters had some hidden magic, a direct line to God. They could call down a blessing that would finally free him of everything he'd seen and everything he knew, allow his mind to rest, allow him to believe once more in the sweet delusion of safety and control.

"No," he said to Rosa. "I'll leave you to it. I'm going to get caught up on the news, maybe listen to a radio program. But I hope you've saved one of those *conchas* for me."

He kissed her cheek and his daughter's forehead, then took the still-hot bun to the sitting room, where he turned on the radio and settled in his chair.

The nuns would have no better answers than anyone else had. Roger still accompanied his wife to church every Sunday, but he'd lost touch with the spiritual side of things years ago, long before the war, and now, the very idea of nuns and priests and Popes and saints left him with a faintly amused tolerance. God was a pleasant story people told themselves to make the wide, unraveling truth seem a little smaller and more tightly knit, a little easier to bear. Like the weather balloon. It was nothing more than a story, but one that must be told, if the world was to go on the way it had always done.

Roger had his own stories, pet narratives that kept things together despite the fraying edges of what was and what might be. Like the story that the Army knew best and had a damn good reason for swearing him to silence. Like the story that the war was over because it had been declared finished, and a victory, and the nations of a civilized and united West could prosper now without fear. And the dearest story of all, that if he kept his daughter close, he could save her from the ordinary dangers of the world, from the pain and the blood and the anguish, from fires that rained from the sky.

He didn't go with them to the monastery. But as Rosa and Betty began to depart, Roger got up from his chair and took a dollar from his wallet, tucked it into the basket among the cookies and fresh loaves of bread.

"For the sisters," he said.

Their God might be nothing more than a comforting fiction. But some stories were worth telling, even when you knew they weren't true.

~

While her sisters remained inside to work at the daily labors of an enclosed nun—cleaning, mending, answering letters—Mary Agnes once again joined Harvey outdoors. He had finished repairing the porch, and now they turned their attentions to the most pressing task: establishing a garden. The Poor Clares relied on charity even for their daily bread. Whatever food wasn't donated by kindly benefactors must be grown by the nuns themselves.

Mary Agnes followed Harvey around the grounds, holding wooden stakes in place while he drove them into the dry soil with a few blows of a rubber mallet. They strung twine between the stakes, marking out the rows where season after season the gifts of nature would flourish. When he pulled a pair of spades from the back of his truck and handed one to Mary Agnes, she braced herself for a difficult hour. Using only her bare feet for leverage, she would have to force the blade of her shovel down into the unyielding earth.

Naturally, Harvey, with his sturdy work boots, was much faster at the work than Mary Agnes was. By the time she had spaded up three or four feet of ground, Harvey had turned over nearly an entire row.

She was beginning to feel rather discouraged, and more than a little bruised along the sole of one foot, when she looked up to find two figures approaching down the long, dusty lane.

Gratefully, Mary Agnes laid her shovel aside and hurried across the dry grass to greet the visitors. She hoped they didn't notice her limping.

The newcomers were a mother with her teenage daughter. The woman held out a large basket, the contents of which were covered by a kitchen towel. As Mary Agnes accepted the gift with an exclamation of gratitude, she could smell cinnamon and a buttery richness wafting from beneath the towel. Fresh-baked pastries. She and her sisters would savor every bite. How long had it been since any of them had enjoyed a sweet?

Then she recalled the clandestine gumdrops she had shared with Harvey two days before, and she blushed. Perhaps she would allow her sisters a greater share of these treats than whatever portion she would take. That would be a fitting atonement for her unseemly greed.

"We wanted to welcome you to town," the woman said. "It will be such a blessing to have you sisters among us. I'm Rosa Morales Campbell," she added, laying one hand gently against her small, golden crucifix. "This is my girl, Betty."

"It's we who are blessed to live among such kind souls," Mary Agnes said. "I know I speak for all my sisters when I say I hope we'll be able to do much good for the people of Roswell."

Rosa lowered her eyes, and for a moment her warmth slid into something sad and remote. "Yes. We do need your prayers, Sister."

"We look forward to welcoming you into our chapel," Mary Agnes said, "to worship with us. Though the chapel isn't quite ready yet. We've all been hard at work, as you can imagine, turning this dusty old place into a proper monastery. Would you like to see the garden, though? We've just begun digging it today."

Betty glanced beyond Mary Agnes to where Harvey was still hacking away at the compacted soil. The girl's eyes widened, and she backed away, slipping behind her mother.

"Betty," Rosa said, "what's gotten into you?"

Mary Agnes offered the girl a sympathetic smile. "I was shy, too, at your age." Difficult to believe now, given how friendly she became with men only a few years later. "I had better get these wonderful things you've brought us inside, Mrs. Campbell. You can be sure my sisters and I will think of you when we enjoy them this evening, during our recreation hour."

As the mother began shepherding her daughter back down the lane, Mary Agnes called after them, "You're welcome here any time. If there's ever anything we may do for you, you need only ask."

By the time Mary Agnes deposited the basket inside the kitchen, where its contents were ogled and cooed over by her sisters, her foot had begun to feel better—which meant it was time for her to take up the shovel again and send it right back to its former agonies. Reluctantly, she returned to the afternoon's hot glare.

As she picked up the shovel, Harvey paused in his own digging to wipe the sweat from his brow. He gazed at the lane as if he could still see the visitors, though by that time, they had vanished beyond the elms.

"Wasn't that Rosa Campbell?" he said.

"Yes. Do you know her? A lovely woman."

"She's the wife of a friend—my old XO from the war."

It was on the tip of Mary Agnes's tongue, to ask him again about his time with the Army, and why he'd left. But she recalled the way he'd gone so tense and evasive the day before. She drove her spade into the soil and kept her peace.

Evidently, the Army was a sore spot with Harvey. She didn't want to endanger the man's friendly mood now that she'd begun to find some confidence in her role. Better to go on working peacefully at his side. She would honor his silence and allow Harvey to keep whatever secrets he held.

～

The skies in New Mexico were unlike anything Mary Agnes had seen, ever-shifting canvases of color and form, painted by the Creator's brush to express His every mood. That evening, after the sisters had observed Compline, the nightly hour of prayer, Mary Agnes spent her free hour walking the acres of the monastery, looking up now and then to watch the evening light progress through shades of saffron and flame, to rose, to the deep, settled purple of twilight.

"Hello!"

Mary Agnes turned. Sister Ann had just emerged from the farmhouse, and now she stood waving on the porch, a plate balanced on one hand. When Mary Agnes returned to greet her, she found that Ann's plate was heaped with things from Rosa Campbell's basket.

"These are the last of the cinnamon cookies," Ann said. "I thought I'd be good and see that everyone gets their share, rather than gobbling them all up myself."

Mary Agnes took one of the cookies and bit into it. The rich flavor was as vibrant as the evening sky. "Anyone would be tempted to eat the whole plate. What a talented baker Mrs. Campbell is!"

"We've received so many lovely things already from the women of Roswell," Ann said, "but I might like these cookies the best. This is already beginning to feel like home to me. I was so worried about pulling up my roots and moving away from Chicago, it's almost funny to think of it now. I'm glad to be here—really glad. Especially when I look up at that sky. Have you ever seen a sight so lovely?"

Mary Agnes cast her eyes up again. Above the golden sentinels of the elms, the violet dusk was giving way to a soft gray-blue, and the first stars gleamed like pearls against velvet. Bats crossed the sky in rapid flight, darting and turning on the wing in pursuit of insects. Crickets sang a joyful chorus from the tall grass, which had sprouted with the last rain.

"It certainly is a beautiful place," Mary Agnes said. "I hadn't thought to find so many pretty things in a desert. And the people I've met have been so friendly and helpful, too. I'll admit that I had my own fears on that count. Externing isn't easy after so long in enclosure."

In fact, her worries hadn't abated. She could only handle her new duties by allowing the long-buried Patricia to come to the surface, and that was a larger, darker fear of its own. But she didn't want to spoil Sister Ann's mood, so she kept her concerns to herself.

"This is all so new," Ann said, "for you and for the rest of us. But I came to the order in faith, knowing that God would use me for good."

"Knowing?"

On the instant, Mary Agnes wished she'd held her tongue. The question had asked itself before she'd found the will to silence it—torn itself free from the place of anguished self-doubt that seemed, sometimes, to make up the whole of her spirit.

But Ann was unfazed. She smiled and chose a cookie of her own from the plate, nibbled it thoughtfully as she spoke. "I've always had a sense that the Lord meant to use me for some greater purpose, ever since I was a girl. When I realized that His purpose was a humble one—I mean, when I felt the call to join the order—everything made sense to me. I knew then that if I only trusted in Him and went faithfully wherever He sent me, I couldn't help but do good. And I knew then, too, that even the small, quiet acts of a nun are not so small or quiet in God's estimation. There is so much good for us to do here, Sister. I can feel it, can't you? We've come to make the desert rejoice, and blossom as the rose, like Isaiah said. Well, I'm off to find more homes for these cookies. Blessings to you, Sister Mary Agnes."

After Ann had gone, Mary Agnes leaned against a pillar of the porch. She watched the bats in their haphazard flight with a good deal less happiness than she'd done mere moments before. Ann's rhapsodic experience of her own faith was a far cry from the silent battle Mary Agnes had waged these past twelve years—a war of the heart and spirit, a desperate fight to win a faith she had never really possessed. After so long a battle without any victory, she was starting to wonder whether it was still worth fighting for.

And then came the guilt, right on cue. She was always overwhelmed by remorse, whenever she allowed herself to dwell too much on this dilemma. Despite the peace and perspective she had gained from her time in the order, her reasons for entering enclosure had still been selfish ones. Certainly, Mary Agnes had never felt a conviction like Ann's, that God meant to use her for some greater purpose. Her sisters had placed a good deal of trust in Mary Agnes, as their sole contact with the outside world. Yet that trust was undeserved. Every one of the others had come to this order from a genuine desire to serve the Lord and His people. Mary Agnes had joined out of cowardly self-preservation, nothing more.

Her restless self-accusations drove her from the porch, back to the dim grounds. She walked among the bats and the shadows, past the newly dug garden and to the edge of the acreage, where the elms towered above her like the vaults of a cathedral, their tops whispering but lost to sight among the night's gentle fall.

"Sister Mary Agnes, hello."

Mary Agnes spun on her heel, biting back a shriek. Mother Catherine was seated among the roots of an elm, her back against the trunk, still and content as Buddha beneath his fig tree. Mary Agnes hadn't noticed her, despite the way her broad white collar stood out against the night. But then, Mary Agnes had been rather lost in her own dire thoughts.

"All right," the abbess said stoutly, "something is eating at you. It's plain to see. Help me up."

Mother Catherine reached up a hand, and Mary Agnes pulled her to her feet.

The abbess dusted the back of her habit with a due display of dignity. "I'm getting too old for this sort of thing. But I can't help it, on a night like this. I long to be out among nature. Now, tell me what's on your mind."

"Nothing of any real importance," Mary Agnes said.

The abbess eyed her through the darkness. "I've known you since you were an aspirant. You might fool some of the other sisters with a put-on like that. Never me."

She gave in with a sigh that was almost a sob. "Oh, Mother, why is my faith so small and weak after all these years?"

"Is it?"

Catherine looked so startled that Mary Agnes's guilt redoubled itself, just when she thought it couldn't possibly grow any heavier to bear.

"I don't know," Mary Agnes floundered. "I . . . I still have my doubts about my fitness as an extern." That wasn't untrue, and it was the only flaw she felt strong enough to confess to in the presence of her abbess. "Mother Superior—back in Chicago, I mean—told me once that God places us on the paths He means for us to walk, and all we need do to end up at the right destination is to keep moving forward in faith. But if I have my doubts about moving forward at all, doesn't that mean my faith is too small to guide me?"

"My dear, you aren't the first sister to feel this way."

Mary Agnes laughed bitterly. "Our old abbess said that, too—more or less."

"Good old Mother Superior. She is a wise woman, and I've wished for her guidance more times than I can count since we came to Roswell. Oh, yes, Sister, I also have my moments of doubt. But faith and trust are the same—or at least, they are two sides of the same coin. You may not think your faith strong enough to be your guide, but if you *trust* in the path God has given you to walk, the result will be the same."

That made sense. And it did nothing to ease the burden of Mary Agnes's guilt. "What if I'm not reading God correctly?"

"Reading Him, dear?"

"I mean to say, what if I'm misinterpreting His messages? What if I've wandered off my path and found myself on a path I was never meant to walk?"

Mary Agnes remembered the gumdrops and her face burned with shame. How easily she had broken the rules, how quickly she had given in to temptation—and for something as silly as candy! She had no more self-control than a child. She felt entirely too easy in Harvey's company, that was a fact. And after all that had happened with John, she ought to be more reserved in a man's presence, more mindful of her vows.

She said, "I can't shake this fear that I'm not cut out for an extern's life. That an extern's life is too much for me to handle. I . . . I find it so difficult to know what I ought to say and do around Mr. Day, for example."

"The handyman?" Mother Catherine shrugged. "My dear, the extern's life takes some getting used to after years of enclosure. But dealing with the people of the world is your duty now. This is the path God has chosen for you. It's new, but you'll soon get used to it. As for the question of what to say and do around men like Mr. Day . . . well, your vows will protect you from temptation."

They wouldn't. They hadn't. Mary Agnes already knew that much, to the pit of her miserable soul.

"As for reading God correctly," the abbess went on, "that's easy. Simply do whatever the church requires, and you'll never put a foot wrong. You can't; God's hand is on our church, dear. Honoring the guidance of our bishops and priests has been a tried-and-true method for countless nuns— and laypeople. And the saints, for Heaven's sake, for nearly two thousand years! Do you really think it won't work as well for you? Sometimes the best way to find your faith is to listen to what wiser voices are telling you. God is stronger than any sin, my dear. If you go where your faith leads, you'll always end up where He intended you to be."

The night's final bell sounded, soft and hollow across the monastery grounds.

"To bed," Mother Catherine said with a small, contented sigh. "Until we rise again in prayer. Farewell to this beautiful night—and farewell to your fears, Sister."

The abbess offered her arm. Mary Agnes took it, drawing comfort from the warmth and nearness of a nun whose experience and wisdom were so much greater than her own. Whose faith was so much greater than her own. Perhaps, she prayed, she would draw a little of that faith into herself, until she felt strong enough to walk this road without a sturdier soul to guide her.

CHAPTER NINETEEN

October 13, 1947

There weren't many men who looked forward to Mondays, but Harvey had come to anticipate them with the eagerness of a child awaiting Christmas morning. Sundays, you see, were reserved for worship alone, which meant Harvey had no business on the grounds of the monastery, and so he was obliged to spend the day in his apartment or fishing the Pecos River with only his thoughts for company. But Monday was the start of something good—the only good thing that remained in his life—six days of honest work, with each afternoon graced and brightened for two precious hours by the company of Sister Mary Agnes.

By now, a little more than a month after their first meeting, Harvey had come to feel their routine as an instinct. Whatever he might be doing—repairing the gutters on the farmhouse, or cutting the last frantic spate of autumn grass—he would look up just before the afternoon bell rang to dismiss the sisters to their individual labors, and he would catch sight of Mary Agnes emerging from the old white house. After so long in her company, he could recognize her at a distance despite the brown habit and black veil, which to a less discerning eye would make her anonymous among her sisters. But even from far across the grounds, Harvey could recognize her slight frame, her distinctive habits, the natural grace of her movements.

He watched her now, as she crossed the quiet acres with the spent leaves of the elms whirling golden around her. This was the only time in all his life when he felt like smiling, for only in Mary Agnes's company did he ever find any peace. Surely these sequestered nuns knew nothing of the saucer—nor did they know about the blue-ticket discharge that made him a pariah in the town. Here alone, he could be himself. Mary Agnes was the only soul in all the world who never judged him, and who posed no danger of talk about the saucer.

When she reached the shabby outbuilding where Harvey had worked all morning, Mary Agnes held up her usual offering—a large clay cup full of cool water. She had brought him the same gift every day. True to the name of their order, the Poor Clare nuns had little, but whatever they did have, they shared with an eagerness that always touched Harvey.

He drank the water gratefully and set the cup near his toolbox.

"And what are we working on today?" Mary Agnes asked.

"I hope to get this shed fixed up before winter," Harvey answered. "That way, you sisters can keep all your gardening tools out of the weather. They'll last much longer that way. But the walls are almost more holes than solid wood. I've got to pry all these rotted planks off the studs and get tar paper tacked up underneath. That'll keep the inside nice and dry."

"I can really be of some help this time." She lifted the hem of her habit to show her leather sandals. "Mother Catherine gave me a dispensation to wear them for any work that might involve rusty nails or other hazards. It feels strange, to wear something on my feet after so many years going barefoot. I think this is how horses and cows must feel, clomping around on their hooves."

They set to work on the inside of the shed, using pry bars to detach the soft planks from the walls. The space inside was close and dim, and each time Harvey brushed near Mary Agnes, a queasy thrill ran up her stomach, into her chest. She ignored the sensation, as she always did.

The abbess had said that Mary Agnes's vows would protect her from temptation, and she was determined to prove to herself that it was true.

Harvey wedged his bar behind a board and pried it away from the wall; the wood squealed against rusted iron, but the plank wouldn't fall.

"Dang it," he muttered, "there's got to be another nail somewhere on this piece, but I can't figure out where it is. It's too dark in here."

Mary Agnes gave a wry little laugh. "Would you like me to pray to Saint Clare? She's the patroness of clear sight, you know. Maybe she'll produce a miracle and fill this shed with light."

"The saint of clear sight," Harvey said. "I'll be. You Catholics really do have a saint for everything. How does one become the saint of clear sight, anyway?"

Mary Agnes related the story as they searched for the rogue nail—how Clare, bedridden and weak, had found herself unable to attend the Mass. Instead, the Mass had come to her, playing out in a miraculous vision on the wall of her cell.

"Long before movies had even been dreamed of," Mary Agnes said. "You might say that Saint Clare watched the first movie in all of history."

She located the nail by feel, set her bar under the board's edge, and pulled back with all her strength. The board fell away, and Mary Agnes turned to Harvey with an expression of considerable triumph.

"Maybe I ought to pray to that saint of yours, after all," he said.

She sobered then. "Are there things you need to see more clearly?"

For a moment he didn't answer, but turned away, mopping his brow with a handkerchief. Mary Agnes could sense a certain tension about him, though she couldn't decide whether it was reluctance or eagerness.

"Sis," he finally said, "my trouble is seeing things too clearly. More clearly than other people want to see them."

"What do you mean by that?"

Harvey didn't answer. He fetched the broom and began sweeping the loose nails into a neat pile. The burden of silence—the weight of his oath to the Army—had grown heavier than he'd thought it might. Every day he was possessed by an urge to talk about what he'd seen, desperate to find one soul in this lonesome world who might believe him, who might reassure him that he hadn't lost his mind. But he'd never forgotten the fear in Mac Brazel's eyes that day outside Ella's Bar. Nor had he forgotten Roger's warning. *Take it to your grave, and you might be able to keep yourself out of danger.*

"Do you really believe in miracles?" he asked. "Impossible things?"

"Of course," she answered, a little too insistent. "That's what God is all about, isn't He? Making the impossible manifest. That's the work of the Creator."

She still didn't feel any more convinced of God's capacity for the miraculous than she'd felt after taking her novice vows. But she had given a dozen years to this religious life. Surely Mother Catherine was right: if she trusted in the guidance of the church, she would find its truth eventually. What were her twelve years against the church's two thousand?

Harvey paused, considered her familiar shape and gestures through the umber shadows of the shed. No, he wouldn't tell her yet. But he might someday. He trusted her enough, to keep such an important secret. And why shouldn't he trust her? She was the only real friend he'd had since Roger. The only friend he'd found since his world had come apart at the seams.

That afternoon, Harvey wasn't the only soul in Roswell who was contemplating the torn fabric of reality. Jim had hidden himself deep in the stacks of the public library, a wall of books between himself and the rest of the world.

Since the sock hop . . . since Betty . . . since he'd tried to wash those spots of blood from the sleeve of his shirt, he had searched his own mind for answers but had found nothing but an endless corridor of ever more questions, reaching back into a primal blackness beyond his comprehension.

He had even gone to church that Sunday, taking the Host and kneeling with the rest of the congregation in prayer, but he'd found no understanding there, either—only a trembling awareness of how little he knew, how little anyone knew of this world and what lay beyond it—the priest included.

The library was his last hope for holding the old world together. For hours, he'd searched indices and pored over pages, desperate to find any explanation of the phenomenon he had witnessed, the mystery called stigmata. But there was little in any of the books he'd found, and nothing that could explain what had happened to Betty.

He turned from religious studies to medical texts, where he felt himself to be on more respectable ground. Surely the truth would be found here, in the fortress of science, protected by its solid walls.

But the science yielded no more answers than theology had done, and as the early October night drew in, Jim began to wonder if he'd found no explanation because there was no explanation.

Were there—*could* there be—some questions that had no answers?

The moment he allowed himself to entertain the thought, he reeled back as if from the edge of a cliff, for his mind had gone at once to the great mystery of the summer. The crash. The thing in the desert, the shadow that still cast itself aslant every hidden corner of Roswell. From the moment the Army had released its official statement, Jim had been happy to believe that nothing more unusual than a weather balloon had landed on Brazel's ranch. But what if . . . what if it really had been something different?

What if the Army had been hiding the truth, all this time?

The mere possibility made him sick. A cold sweat broke out along his back, and he wiped his brow on his sleeve.

The Army would never deceive. His father had been a good man, the very best of men, and his father had served with pride. The Army was worthy of the late Salvador Lucero's trust. And Jim, too, would serve someday with his father's same honor and pride.

It had only been a weather balloon. Nothing more than that.

He opened another medical book and went on scouring its pages for the truth.

CHAPTER TWENTY

October 15, 1947

The autumn radishes were growing well, and the carrots had finally begun to sprout. When Mary Agnes arrived at the edge of the garden with a tin pail full of water, the sight of the seedlings raising their frail, green arms to the sun sent a thrill of accomplishment through her. She and Harvey had nearly broken their backs digging that garden—and her sisters had helped, too, after Harvey had left the grounds each evening and the nuns could safely emerge from the farmhouse to labor out of doors. Combined with the new flush of green that had come over the acreage—the gift of one last rainstorm—those first sprouting plants seemed a sign from God Himself that despite the hardship of leaving their old lives behind, this new monastery would put down roots and thrive, even in the desert soil.

She watered the seedlings with the greatest care. The earth drank her offering with its usual thirst, and droplets beaded on the fine jade leaves. The sisters must plant cabbages next, and onions, too, for winter was around the corner.

A car horn gave a sudden squawk from somewhere close by. Startled from her thoughts, Mary Agnes nearly dropped the bucket. She found Harvey trundling up the unpaved drive—not in his usual rusty pickup, but in a long-nosed car, dull olive in color. The white star emblem of the

Army had once been painted on its side, but the star had been covered by a shade of green that didn't quite match the rest of the paint.

Harvey cut the engine and emerged with a grin. "Look what I scared up for you sisters. Well—really, my buddy Roger found it. I told him you've been needing a car up here at the monastery, and he got his hands on this decommissioned beauty. It took some work to get the engine back in shape, but it runs pretty good now."

"For us?" Mary Agnes circled the vehicle. "Harvey, you shouldn't have. I mean that, too. I'm not sure extern sisters are allowed to drive."

He chuckled. "You won't have much choice, once winter hits. There's never any telling what the snow will be like. If it's bad, you won't be able to walk the short distance to town to get the things you ladies need." He gave the hood a solid thump with his fist. "The Pope will never know, Sis—and if he finds out, you drive it anyway. Sometimes practicalities outweigh the rules."

"You're braver than I am," she said.

The boyish smile vanished. "I'm not brave, exactly. I'm just not ashamed of following my gut, even when I'm told to do otherwise."

Mary Agnes didn't press him, and his easy manner returned.

"Did you learn to drive before they made you a nun?"

She couldn't help smiling when he looked at her that way, so warm with friendship. She could almost laugh now, looking back on her foolish anxieties. It had been so much easier to step into an extern's role than she had feared. Now, she could scarcely remember why she had dreaded the change. The Father truly did place each woman and man on their rightful paths. That was a mark in favor of faith. Maybe here in Roswell, she would find a deeper trust in God, too.

"I never did learn to drive," she admitted. "I don't think any of our other sisters drive, either. Anyway, they're under vows of enclosure, so even if they'd been crack drivers in a previous life, it won't do them any good now."

"That settles it, then. I'll have to teach you."

He moved swiftly. There was a metallic jingle, a flash of sunlight on silver as the object he'd thrown arced through the air. Instinctively, she put up her hands and caught it. A key on a leather-tabbed ring.

"Get in." He opened the driver's-side door. "I'll have you driving like you were born to it, in no time flat."

Mary Agnes hesitated, one eye on the farmhouse. This time of the afternoon, her sisters would be engaged in work of their own—cleaning, preparing the next meal, opening the letters in which the faithful sent their petitions for prayer. Mother Catherine would be in her office, making up schedules for the next week's labor and corresponding with her fellow abbesses. She ought to consult with Catherine before she undertook something so audacious. But Harvey had made a fair point. The same storm that had brought its blessing of rain had stripped most of the leaves from the elms. Autumn had certainly arrived. If Mary Agnes hoped to secure the supplies her sisters would need for the long, harsh winter, the monastery must have a vehicle—and a sister who could drive it.

She slid behind the wheel. Her habit clung to the old, cracked leather of the seat and tightened around her. The car's interior was thick with heat and the sharp odor of diesel, and Harvey in the passenger seat felt entirely too close.

"Key in the ignition," he said.

She fumbled with the key ring, made several fruitless stabs at the slot near the steering wheel. Why wasn't the darned ignition bigger, or positioned in a more sensible place?

"Right foot on the brake pedal, left foot on the clutch."

Mary Agnes peered into the shadow of the footwell. There were three pedals, not two. "Which is which?"

"Oh, boy, Sister. We've got our work cut out for us."

Step by step, he walked her through the ignition process, which was more complicated than it had any right to be. Her bare feet trembled as she held down the leftmost and middle pedals. She couldn't make sense of the choke lever, no matter how he tried to explain its purpose.

Finally, when he was satisfied that her feet were in the right position and every switch and knob had been flipped or pulled or pushed as required, he told Mary Agnes to turn the key. The engine roared to life. The steering wheel shuddered in her hands.

"Now keep the clutch down," Harvey said. "Left foot. All the way down. Take your right foot off the brake. Now ease down on the gas pedal—the one way over on the right—while you ease up on the clutch."

She did exactly as he said. The car lurched and died.

They both fell to laughing.

"I'll never do it," she declared, breathless.

"Of course you will. You just need practice."

Practice was what she got that afternoon. After a dreadfully long and embarrassing half hour, she managed to move the car forward a few feet without killing the engine. Soon after, Harvey had her creeping around the monastery grounds in first gear.

When she was comfortable with steering and had learned how to brake without jolting the engine to an ignominious death, he directed her to the long dirt lane.

"Drive on the streets?"

"You'll have to get the hang of it sooner or later, if you want this car to be of any use."

Mary Agnes chugged the vehicle slowly down the lane. Dust lifted and swirled in front of the hood, forcing her to squint through a dazzle of reflected light. Beyond the wall of trees, the lane met the road. There she paused with the clutch depressed, the engine idling smoothly. The street was empty, but she couldn't seem to make herself pull onto it. Her extern duties had sometimes required her to leave the monastery grounds. Then, she had walked into the outside world. Driving felt different—more dangerous, and much too daring for a sister of Poor Clare.

Harvey urged her on. She fixed her mind on the winter to come, the needs of her sisters. Then she sent up a silent prayer and pulled onto the empty street.

As she crawled up the road, a wild sense of freedom began to eclipse all her previous hesitations. This car would allow her to range much farther afield in her duties. She could bring comfort and aid not only to the people of Roswell, but beyond—those who lived among the ranches and rangeland miles outside town.

"I think you're ready to learn how to shift gears," Harvey said.

"No, I'm not."

"Sure, you are! It's as easy as everything else you've learned today."

Mary Agnes huffed bitterly. None of this had been easy.

"Give it a little more gas," Harvey said.

She pressed her lips together in fear or frustration, but she did as he instructed. The Army car picked up speed. The engine's rumble rose in pitch until it whined with a frantic tension.

"What do I do now?" she cried in a panic.

"Press the clutch and take your foot off the gas, both at the same time."

She followed his instructions, though she couldn't suppress a shriek of fear. The engine ceased its high-pitched squeal. The car coasted along the street.

"Pull the gear lever toward you," Harvey said, "and push it up at the same time."

"What? That makes no sense!"

She reached for the lever above the ignition as Harvey did the same. His hand landed on her own.

A flare of fire burst in her chest. Desire ran like melted wax into her stomach, into her limbs. She lost all sense of clutch and brake and gas. The car shuddered and died.

Harvey's hand still lay on hers. She looked at him, though she didn't want to. No, she wanted to look at him, was compelled by that fiery longing in her flesh. But she didn't want to want this.

They were so near, so secluded in the warm interior of the car. And the lines around his eyes, the lines of his smile, were like the tracks cut by cool springs through desert stone. If she thought of John in that moment, or any of her old mistakes from the life she once had lived, they were distant thoughts, and fleeting. Harvey was a different man from John. And she was a different woman.

He pulled his hand away, retreated on the bench seat until he was pressed against the passenger door. "I'm sorry. I didn't mean to—"

Mary Agnes groped for the handle, let herself out of the car. She scrambled back toward the lane and the safety of the farmhouse. The pavement was hot against the soles of her feet as she ran, hot as the tears that blurred out the town. The wall of elms flashed past, and cement gave way to dust. The welcome cage of the monastery closed around her with its unchanging rules, its small but predictable comforts.

She fled past the farmhouse, to the far end of the acreage. There, below the bare autumn elms, she fell on her knees and covered her face with her hands. She could still smell the diesel on her skin. She would have done it—would have kissed Harvey, if he hadn't pulled away. Had her vows meant nothing, all these years? Was she so weak within her spirit, even after committing herself to the religious life, that one man could tear her away from God—even a practical stranger, whom she'd scarcely known for a handful of weeks?

All through that day, and across the bleak hours of the night, when she lay awake on her mattress of straw, the feel of Harvey's touch remained with Mary Agnes. In the middle of the night, when all the sisters rose from their beds to pray through the hour of Matins, she begged God for relief. She pleaded with all the angels to free her from the prison that she could feel, even now, assembling itself around her. Its iron bars were Lust and Longing and Desire, Self-Deceit and Independence. If she didn't find the strength to resist this temptation, the door would slam shut forever. Her soul would never be free.

As her sisters prayed for the sick, the lost, and the weary, Mary Agnes prayed for herself. These feelings for Harvey had stolen up on her so quietly that she hadn't even recognized them for what they were— not until that moment in the car, when he'd touched her.

And now, she couldn't help but see her situation in the plain, cruel light of truth. She hadn't left her old self behind, all those years ago when she'd taken her vows. These were the same feelings that had overtaken her good sense and led her down a road of trouble with John. The same feelings that had very nearly ruined her life for good. Was she truly so weak of spirit and will that she couldn't learn a lesson, couldn't keep herself out of the Devil's grip?

As her sisters murmured their prayers into the soft, dark ear of night, Mary Agnes cried within her heart: *Is this why you brought me here, O God? Did you tear me from the safety of enclosure only to confront me with the same lust that nearly destroyed me once before?*

Whatever the definition of faith may be, her heart was surely devoid of it, as barren of that essential virtue as the land beyond Roswell was barren of life. Faith was not for her; it wasn't *in* her, wasn't *of* her. And now she felt certain that she would never find it—not in Roswell, not back in Chicago, not anywhere in this stricken life.

The hour of Matins closed. The sisters returned to their beds in silent procession, but Mary Agnes didn't sleep. She curled into a ball on her hard straw mat, choking back her sobs but allowing her tears to flow as they would.

She must ask Mother Catherine, the very next day, to take this burden from her shoulders. Surely the abbess would appoint some other sister as extern, and Mary Agnes could retreat once more to the safety of the sequestered life. Restless, she rose from her bed. Her cell was in the upper story of the farmhouse, and from its small window she could see the dark rows of the garden carved into the midnight blue of the earth, the patient grounds waiting for the care and attention of the sisters, the great stoic wall of the elms with slices of night sky gleaming in lines of starlight between their ancient trunks. The long lane stretched from below out to the world beyond, and its flatness and paleness had picked up the shine of the stars, so it seemed a brightly illuminated road, running straight and true from the churn of sin outside to the place where Mary Agnes now stood.

With an effort, she calmed herself, stilled the wild flight of her fears.

Her old Mother Superior had told her that she must walk the path God had given her, if she was to find her purpose and her truth. If she had any small hope of understanding faith, she must place her trust in God, even when she felt the gesture was futile.

Surely, she prayed, *if You have brought me here, if You have made me to face again what I've run from all these years, then it's because I'm strong enough to overcome temptation. Because You wish me to know that I can't be destroyed again.*

Mary Agnes breathed in the quiet peace of the night. No, after all, she wouldn't ask Mother Catherine to take the burden away. In fact, she would bear it with a greater patience, with the suffering of the Bridegroom Himself. She would conquer her desires through prayer and dedication, as fitted a sister of the order. The wise voice of the church said it could be done. After two thousand years, surely they knew the way.

This time, she would overcome sin; she would be a woman in control of her own desires. This time, she would prove to herself that the deep, true faith of an avowed sister had been in her heart all along. She would feel its fire. She would heed its voice. When she found it, she would give herself over to the power of faith, and she would follow wherever it may lead.

The feel of a fire burning within you. The sound of a voice you can't help but heed. That was what it was like, to remember—and all he ever did was remember the light, the confusion of images that had sped past him, the moment when he'd found the words to make it all real, to understand what was there before him.

The experience stayed with him, as vivid as the first time, even months after the crash, even with the summer far gone and faded, with winter on its way. And he didn't know whether he would rather have forgotten, for the memory was somehow comforting in its terror and its bliss. It never changed, you see. He remembered it always in exacting detail, so it became the most solid and dependable part of his reality, this new reality that was his alone, a world in which he was isolated by all that he had seen.

Because the memories never changed and never abated, he could be sure that they were real. As real as the breath he drew, as ever-present as the remembered touch of Mary Agnes's hand, which burned like a fire inside him and commanded like a voice he couldn't help but obey.

TRANSCRIPT page 6

BISHOP COTE: And that was the first time you met Betty—the day when she came with her mother to the monastery?

SISTER MARY AGNES: Yes, that's correct.

FATHER KERRY: When did you first speak with Betty alone?

SISTER MARY AGNES: That was only a couple of weeks ago, Father. When you asked me to look into the rumors that a girl had experienced the stigmata.

CHAPTER
TWENTY-ONE

October 16, 1947

Father Kerry's office was hidden at the back of the church, in the cool, quiet shadows behind the sacristy. The room's close quarters and simple wood paneling reminded Mary Agnes of her old Mother Superior's office, back in Chicago, and as she settled into the chair opposite Father Kerry's desk, she was struck by a pang of nostalgia. Everything had been simpler then, before she'd come to Roswell and ventured beyond the safety of enclosure. Since she'd been forced to confront her feelings for Harvey, she had dedicated herself to prayer even more devoutly than she'd done before, but she found the man entirely too fascinating, his company far more pleasant than any working relationship ought to be.

Still, she reminded herself as the priest sorted through his papers, she hadn't suffered a lapse in morals. Despite that startling moment in the car—which really had been an accident—her relations with the handyman had always been cordial and appropriate. She may feel herself drawn to Harvey like water flowing down a hill, but nevertheless, she had held herself in firm obedience to her vows. That was something. For now, she would take it as a victory over sin.

Father Kerry seemed to have located the notes he needed. He looked up with a benign smile. "Thank you for coming, Sister. I hope you may be able to help me get to the bottom of a . . . well, I suppose we may call it a mystery, at this point."

All thoughts of Harvey stilled. "Certainly, Father. What can I do for you?"

His expression became thoughtful, even troubled. "Several members of this parish have told me that a . . . a rather unusual event occurred at a high school dance this Saturday past. Or, perhaps more accurately, there are rumors. Whether there's any truth behind the story remains to be seen. It seems a certain girl of this town may have experienced the stigmata."

Something bright and shocking crashed inside Mary Agnes. She sat forward on her chair.

"Now," the priest went on, "there may be nothing to it. You know how stories can run out of control, especially in a small town. Or it may be a simple case of young people fooling around, and other children misunderstanding what they've seen. But the fact is, I've received so many reports from the parents of Roswell, insisting that their boys and girls saw *something* happen at this dance . . . well, I feel I would be remiss in my duties to the community if I didn't look into the matter."

"And you need me to do the looking," Mary Agnes guessed.

"Can you spare the time? I don't wish to impose. I've been quite buried under correspondence with the bishop—keeping him updated on how our new monastery is coming along—among my other duties. Otherwise, I would see to it myself."

"Of course, Father. I'll be glad to help."

In truth, Mary Agnes was so eager for this work that her heart was already pounding in her throat. Father Kerry was right; the story was more likely to be rumor than not. But there was always the chance, however small, that a genuine miracle had occurred. Perhaps God hadn't torn her from safety merely to make her confront her own sinful nature. Perhaps He'd planned a greater purpose for Mary Agnes, all along.

Guided by the notes Father Kerry provided, she found the address that same afternoon. She paused on the sidewalk to consider the home of the alleged stigmatic. It was a two-story affair, with a classic pitched roof and covered front porch, the very symbol of an ordinary, ideal American life. If not for the adobe siding that was so typical of this desert town, it might have been any home in any place, anywhere in the country.

She started for the house but paused to look down in some confusion at a cluster of votive candles. The candles stood at the edge of the sidewalk, just where the dry lawn ended and the sidewalk began. A front yard was an unusual place to pray to the saints. But perhaps this was the custom in Roswell.

A footpath ran from the makeshift shrine to the front door. Mary Agnes took it, but the path seemed to stretch longer as she walked, the house receding from her as if God were dangling desire or salvation beyond her reach. When she arrived at the porch, she nearly gasped with relief. Someone had decorated the door with a wreath of dried grapevine, bright autumn leaves and the papery globes of strawflowers woven among its twigs.

Her hesitant knock was answered quickly. To her surprise, she found herself face-to-face with the same girl who'd visited the monastery with her mother in September. *Of course,* Mary Agnes scolded herself. *I should have recognized the name Father Kerry gave me.*

"Hello, Betty," Mary Agnes said warmly. "Do you remember me? We met last month at the monastery."

The girl eyed her soberly, taking in the brown habit, the wide white collar, the black veil. "I guess I remember you, Sister. Though . . ."

"We nuns do tend to look alike, don't we?"

The girl gave a timid smile.

"My name is Sister Mary Agnes. Betty, is your mother at home? I thought I might have a talk with her."

When she'd peeked out the window to find a nun coming up the walkway, Betty's stomach had lurched. Now an inexplicable panic set in. "Am I in trouble?"

"Goodness, no. Of course not. But I . . ." Mary Agnes chose her way carefully through this minefield. "I've heard certain stories about something that might have happened to you, Betty. Something important— something very difficult to explain. I thought perhaps your mother might know what's going on, and could shed some light on these rumors."

"But why do you want to talk to *her*?" the girl said. "Why not me?"

Mary Agnes looked at the girl more closely, noticing for the first time her expression of bewildered fear. "Do you want to talk? Do you need someone to talk to, Betty?"

The girl wanted to say no. She wanted to insist that everything was fine, that she didn't need a meddling nun sticking her nose into her business, making everything worse. Though Betty had been raised in the church, she didn't have much use for religion—had found the Mass and the traditions of Catholicism tedious and antiquated, nothing but laughable old superstitions with no use in a modern age.

But she did want her life to return to the way it had been before. People *looked* at her now, if she bothered to leave the house at all. And they'd begun leaving things outside, candles and framed pictures of saints, and bundles of herbs and other things that gave Betty a creepy-crawly sensation up her back, a feeling that she was being pulled into a realm in which she couldn't navigate, couldn't even find the horizon.

More than anything else, Betty wanted to return to the simple, predictable life she'd known before her hands had bled, before the crash in the desert had turned her dad into a different man. Even before the war, which had remade everything, the whole world, into something it wasn't supposed to be.

She had found no way back to normal on her own. Maybe this nun would have some answers.

She nodded.

"Where would you like to talk?" Mary Agnes asked gently.

Betty stepped back, pulling the door with her. "I guess you can come in."

It was then that Mary Agnes saw the gloves on Betty's hands—olive-brown with the fingers cut away. The girl noticed the direction of her gaze, said casually, "My dad's old shooting gloves from the war."

She led Mary Agnes to a comfortable parlor room, spotlessly clean. A few bright *nichos* adorned the walls, each housing the tiny statue of a saint. The home was pervaded by a rich smell of simmering stew, onions and beef and spicy peppers.

"You can sit anywhere," Betty said. "I guess I'm supposed to offer you something. Water?"

"No, thank you, dear. I'm fine."

The girl settled in an easy chair beside a large mahogany radio. She chewed her lip, waiting for Mary Agnes to speak.

"The house is so quiet. Your parents aren't at home?"

Betty shook her head, then added, "My folks had to go over to Lubbock to help my grandpa with something. They took my little brothers with them. They won't be back till late tonight."

"I see. Those gloves you're wearing. Are they to hide the . . . ?"

Mary Agnes trailed off into awkward silence. She didn't know what, exactly, she ought to call the holy wounds of Christ if their holiness hadn't yet been confirmed.

The girl slid the gloves from her hands, tilted them to reveal her palms. A chill or a fire ran through Mary Agnes. In the center of each of Betty's hands was a small, circular wound, red and frank against pale flesh.

Nothing has been proven, the nun reminded herself. *This might yet be a hoax.*

She cleared her throat. "I've heard that this happened to you at a dance on Saturday."

"That's right," the girl said. "But it wasn't the first time."

"It wasn't?"

"It happened this past summer. The night my dad came home from Brazel's ranch. He brought something with him, something he found in the desert, and when I touched it . . ." Betty lifted her hands again.

"I wore these gloves until my sores healed. I had my mother convinced that fingerless gloves are all the rage—can you imagine?"

Mary Agnes smiled. She couldn't help liking the girl. There was no hint of grandstanding or self-importance in Betty's personality. She seemed honest and thoughtful. Most of all, she seemed genuinely shaken by her experience.

"And then at the dance," Betty went on, "that was the second time. So I think whatever's happening to me has something to do with the saucer. Because, you know, that's what the kids were all doing at the dance. Playing with some little piece of metal, and they said it came from the saucer."

"A saucer?" Mary Agnes said. "I don't understand."

Betty stared in disbelief. The nuns were new to town, of course, but they'd been in Roswell long enough to know about the saucer. Nobody ever seemed to talk about anything else. "The *flying* saucer," she said, as if that explained everything.

Mary Agnes colored. "I'm afraid I still don't follow you."

"Gosh," Betty said with growing amazement, "do you really not know? Back in July, something crashed out in the desert, out near Corona. Nobody knows for sure what it was. The Army said it was a weather balloon, but I don't buy the story. Some of the kids say it came from outer space."

"Do you mean a meteorite?"

"No, like a space*ship*. Like invaders from Mars or some other planet. You know, a flying saucer."

Comprehension dawned at last in Mary Agnes, along with a healthy dose of skepticism. Maybe, after all, this mystery could be traced to the fertile imaginations of children.

"I see," she said. "I didn't realize they were called 'flying saucers,' these days. You must remember, I've spent the past twelve years living in a monastery. I haven't seen any of the movies or read the science-fiction stories."

Something fierce and wounded rose up in Betty, something rebellious. "This isn't science fiction, and I wish it was a movie. This is real. If you don't believe me, that's *your* problem, not mine."

A heartbeat later, Betty realized that she could exonerate herself. If she had the will to do it. If she could face the awful blood again, the throbbing pain. And all the answerless questions.

"I can prove it," she said.

Mary Agnes had gone quite still, watching the girl through a swimming sense of unreality. Betty gripped the arms of the easy chair, staring at Mary Agnes with a determined glower that sent a chill into the latter's heart.

Carefully, Mary Agnes said, "If you do have some evidence, I would be interested to see it."

Betty rose from the chair and left the parlor. She didn't tell Mary Agnes to come, yet the sister followed, compelled as if the girl were leading her by an invisible leash. Together, they walked through the house—past the framed portraits hanging in the hall of the Campbell family smiling together and into the kitchen, where Rosa's stew simmered on the range.

Betty stopped and opened a door—to a closet, Mary Agnes could see, set below the slope of the stairs. The gray tank of a water heater waited in the shadows.

"There's a loose floorboard back there," Betty said, "right in front of the heater."

The girl seemed to expect Mary Agnes to pry up the board herself. She entered the closet without a word and bent to probe at the floor. One of the boards gave, tipping under her fingers. She levered it up and set it aside.

"Now what?"

"There's a box down there," Betty said. She had looked at the container once—another occasion when her parents hadn't been at home—but courage had failed her before she could open its lid.

Mary Agnes emerged from the closet with a small box in her hands. "It's heavier than it looks."

"That's because it's a lead box."

"What's inside?"

For answer, Betty only shrugged.

Mary Agnes set the box on the kitchen table with ginger care. She opened the latch, eased the lid up on its hinges. Inside, there was nothing but a scrap of paper, blank and white, a little larger than her hand.

Betty watched from across the kitchen as the nun stared down into the box, her face a mask of perplexity. The girl's heart was thundering, her insides going weak and wobbly. The tingling had begun in her palms as soon as the lead-lined box was opened.

"My dad is in the Army," she said. "When the flying saucer crashed, he had to go out into the desert and help clean it up, take all the wreckage back to . . . wherever it is now. He hasn't been the same since. He was already bad, after the war, but now . . . I don't know if he'll ever be the dad I used to know."

Mary Agnes dipped into the box, withdrew the scrap of paper. No, it wasn't paper at all, though it was certainly light and thin enough. But the substance was much more rigid, and held a faint luminosity, reflecting the light from the kitchen windows with a curious, dreamlike vibrancy.

"What is this?" Her voice was scarcely louder than a whisper.

"A piece of the saucer," Betty said. "My dad kept it, though he wasn't supposed to. I've heard him and my mother arguing about it. She wants it out of the house. He refuses to let it go. I don't think he *can* get rid of it. It means something to him."

Betty drew in a long, deep breath. It did nothing to calm her stomach or steady her nerves. She raised her hands again so the nun could see her palms.

"Now," the girl said, "bring it here. Closer to me."

Betty kept her eyes fixed on the sister's face as she moved closer, one slow step at a time. The nearer that scrap of metal came, the more her hands tingled. Then they burned. She bit her lip but refused to look away from the nun, and though she wanted to clench her fists to hide the truth, she willed her hands to remain open, willed the sister to see.

When Mary Agnes was close enough that she could have laid the metal against Betty's skin, the burning intensified to a single, sharp stab.

Betty gasped. She felt the heat and thickness of blood in her hands. And in the nun's pale face, she found her vindication.

"Hail, Mary, full of grace," Mary Agnes whispered, "the Lord is with thee . . ."

Her eyes flashed up from the girl's bleeding hands, but Betty had dropped all her brave composure. The girl's face had crumpled into a mask of hopeless suffering.

"What's happening to me?" Betty sobbed. "I just want to know. What's happening, and why is it happening to *me*, Sister, please?"

~

She staggered and nearly fell, caught herself against a fireplace mantel— the hearth of polished wood. Staring, shuddering, she groped her way along the wainscoted wall, and her feet tangled in the fringe of an old hand-me-down rug because she was still wearing her sandals.

That was the first Mary Agnes knew that she had returned to the monastery.

Her sisters flocked behind her, alarmed and calling to her: *What's the matter? Are you well? Mary Agnes, you look like you've seen a ghost.*

She had no memory of leaving the Campbell home. No memory of walking—or running—back across the town. Time and life and mind, all a blank, wiped clean between now and the moment when she'd witnessed a miracle.

Her blind hands found the door to the parlor-turned-chapel. The hem of her habit conspired with her sandals to trip her, and she waded as if in a rising sea, through substance and space, through the months and the years and the long, long centuries of litany and prayer, past the benches where she and her sisters gathered each day, through Mary Agnes and Patricia Walton and all that she had been before, all that she would someday be. She fell to her knees at the foot of the cross.

A fire ran through her.

A fire so white and sharp it came from everywhere, it was *everywhere, and everything, pervading her heart and burning from within, from the place where the physical stuff of self once had existed.*

She was insubstantial now, translated in a flash of agonizing bliss to a soul without a body—not these hands that clutched one another in prayer, not this heart that beat, not these ears that heard the voice that sang from deep inside, from the place where the fire burned:

"What you saw, you did not see, and all that you witnessed, you saw as truly as God sees your heart. For the truth is all, and all is within you, and the All and the Within are the very heart of God, to those whose eyes are opened."

Through her tears, she looked up at the face of the Savior where He suffered on the cross. And the world she had known—a well-ordered world of Hours kept and prayers counted like beads on a string, a world made from the dictates of an ancient mother church and the authority of man—all of it broke into words without meaning. The shattered pieces went spinning, silver-white, past her awareness. The edges of every shard cut her as they passed, and what bled from her burning spirit was self and desert, and all that had gone before and all that was yet to come, and a red light of unmaking that plunged in fearful power from the endless black of a night sky.

She saw the faces of her sisters.

And Harvey with the sea behind him, the restless and eternal sea.

She saw blood falling on snow.

And her own face reflected in the mirror of eternity, like Christ's countenance, stricken by something too vast and sacred to be called merely rapture.

TRANSCRIPT pages 18–19

BISHOP COTE: Mrs. Campbell, would you say Betty is a good girl?

ROSA: Yes, of course. She has always been a good girl.

BISHOP COTE: And at church?

ROSA: Betty goes to church. *(pause)* Most Sundays.

BISHOP COTE: But she isn't especially enthusiastic about the Mass or the Holy Eucharist, is she?

ROSA: Most girls her age would rather spend time with their friends or daydream than go to church, wouldn't they? It doesn't mean she's a bad girl.

FATHER KERRY: Of course not, Mrs. Campbell. What His Excellency means is this. The church neither verifies nor disproves stigmata itself. Instead, it looks into the lives of those who have experienced the phenomenon to verify whether they have engaged in especially holy acts.

BISHOP COTE: Stigmata come to those who are unusually dedicated to prayer. Or those who have experienced some other divine mystery, such as holy visions.

ROSA: You're saying this can't be the stigmata because my Betty doesn't love going to church?

FATHER KERRY: Not necessarily—

ROSA: But she's been bleeding from her hands and feet, Father! What else would you call it, if not the wounds of Christ?

FATHER KERRY: Now, Mrs. Campbell, please don't get upset. We're all trying to understand what has been going on here, what has been happening to Betty.

ROSA: *Dios mío*, I don't know this world anymore.

SISTER MARY AGNES: Mrs. Campbell, I know this is upsetting, but—

ROSA: What I wouldn't give. What I wouldn't give, Holy Mother, if everything could go back to the way it was before. Everything is so mixed up now. I don't recognize my own life. That's the truth. I don't recognize anything.

CHAPTER
TWENTY-TWO

October 12, 1947

Betty had flatly refused to go to church that day, and now Rosa understood why.

She said nothing to Roger as they shepherded their two small boys across the parking lot to the family car. She said nothing as Roger drove them home, across the town so vivid in its brief flush of October green, the vermilions and golds of the changing season.

She said nothing until they arrived at the house, and then Rosa stormed up the stairs to her daughter's bedroom. She threw open the door, already ranting.

"Isabel Campbell, do you know what stories I heard about you at church today?"

"Mother, please!" Betty lay on her bed, curled into a tight ball with her back to Rosa.

"Mrs. Chavez told me after Mass that both her daughters came home from the dance spouting rumors about *you*, young lady." On the drive home, she had counseled herself not to go off like a barrel of dynamite, not to behave the way her own mother had done when Rosa had been a reckless, headstrong girl. But in the face of her mortification and fear, all the patience and good sense she'd talked into herself went flying out the window. "They said your hands and feet were bleeding. Like the wounds of Christ, Isabel. What have you done? What blasphemy is this? Sit up this minute and look at me."

Betty moaned, unfolded herself enough that she could hunch upright on the bed.

"It's bad enough, that you snuck out of the house against your father's wishes. But to make a scene in front of your whole school with some sacrilegious stunt!"

That was when Rosa noticed the gloves Betty wore—Roger's old shooting gloves, fingerless, large enough that the girl's hands were swimming in them. Then she saw the bandannas tied around Betty's feet.

A chill moved through Rosa, insidious and slow.

"Take off those gloves," she said, more gently than the storm that had led her into the room.

Betty's hands were shaking so badly that she could barely do as her mother commanded. When she pulled the gloves away, she revealed the strips of cloth that still bandaged the wounds on her hands. Spots of blood showed through, one at each palm.

Shuddering, Rosa sank onto the bed beside her daughter. Betty allowed her mother to unpick the knot of a bandage, and gently, Rosa exposed her daughter's hand.

The girl sniffed. She choked back a sob. "I don't know what's happening, Mama. I can't explain it. But you know I don't lie."

With a wordless cry of contrition, Rosa took the girl in her arms. "I know, my baby. I know, my girl."

She rocked her daughter until both their tears had dried.

"I believe you," Rosa said. "We should pray about this."

Betty pulled back with a toss of her head. "I don't want to pray. If God did this to me, then I don't like Him much."

That sent another kind of chill through Rosa. She could feel a dark hand clutching at her heart, and closing around her daughter, trying to pull the innocent girl off the path of light. But she didn't rage again, nor did she scold. She only kissed Betty lightly on her forehead and said, "I'll leave you alone for a while. I'm downstairs if you need me."

The boys were outside playing, and Rosa could hear her husband in the sitting room, tuning the radio. She paused at the head of the stairs. The silence between herself and Roger was like the long, black gulf of space, airless and uncrossable, colder than winter. She would cross it anyway, if she knew how—traverse this abyss of pain and fear and the ruthless memories of war. She would hold on to Roger, bring him back, pull her entire family back together. But she didn't know how to do it. She never quite knew what to say.

Rather than going down to the kitchen, or to the sitting room where Roger was, she slipped into the bedroom they shared. Pieces of her husband lay everywhere, his shirt and necktie arranged neatly on a hanger, his silver bill clip gleaming on the dresser, his good Sunday shoes peeking out from below the bed. And yet Roger had been nowhere since he'd returned from the front. There were women in town—Rosa's friends, some of them—who'd lost their husbands in the war. Her husband had come back in one piece, but sometimes she wondered if it wouldn't have been better. Better to have been made a widow rather than lose the man she loved a fragment at a time, over these cruel years that should have been the happiest of her life.

She fell on her knees before her little bedside shrine. Our Lady of Guadalupe gazed down at her, the gentle hands folded, the patient, forgiving eyes so soft with understanding, with a mother's love.

First the war, and then the thing that had happened in the desert, and now these marks on Betty's hands. Betty, of all the good but ordinary girls in Roswell, in all the world—Rosa's daughter, afflicted as the saints were afflicted. This would shatter the family all over again. Since Roger had come home, Rosa had felt one small thread of her life snapping after another. The life she'd always prayed for, the life she had known, had been unraveling in her hands for years now. She saw no way to mend the fabric of what once had been.

Why must it happen like this? she asked the Virgin in her heart.

Why a slow dissolution, when pain was so much easier to bear if it happened all at once? Because even in the most shocking catastrophe, the worst was over and done with right away. There was nothing left to fall apart just when you'd finally found some hope that you might put your old life together again.

She found little comfort at the feet of Our Lady of Guadalupe. All the same, when her prayers were finished, she took the small statue from its shrine and carried it to her daughter's room.

"Come in," Betty muttered when Rosa tapped at the door.

"I've brought a little someone to look after you," Rosa said.

Betty sat up on the bed, curious, but when she saw that it was only a statue of a saint, she wilted back onto her pillow.

"Come on," Rosa said, cajoling. "Look at her. She's pretty."

Betty made a muffled noise of protest, but she allowed her mother to place the statue on her nightstand.

"The Virgin of Guadalupe," Rosa said. "The special protector of all those who are holy—who have holiness in their hearts."

Betty looked up at her mother, though she couldn't see Rosa's face through her tears. "You do believe me."

Rosa smoothed the dark curls from her daughter's forehead. "I can't understand it, *mija*, any more than you can. But I know my baby doesn't lie."

It was the first time Betty had felt like smiling since the sock hop. She rolled onto her side, caught her mother's hand in her own. Despite the pain of the wound, Betty held on tightly.

Saints and angels—they were useless, as far as Betty could see, relics of a time when even less was known than now. God Himself was an outdated idea in this modern age, when science had an answer for everything, when science held the demonstrable power to unmake everything in a flash of atomic fire. But the little saint on her nightstand was proof that her mother, at least, believed.

Betty picked up the statue of Our Lady of Guadalupe, examined the small figure as she sniffed away her tears. The saint *was* pretty, framed by a radiant sunburst, with a patient brown face, a robe of rosy pink, with the great, dark curve of the moon below her feet. Betty ran her finger along the Virgin's mantle. It was bluer than an evening sky and teeming with stars.

~

The Hawks and the A-Bombs gathered that afternoon at the pecan orchard outside town, but sunset was well on its way, and no one had even suggested a race. Jim leaned against the hood of his Plymouth, watching the evening shadows run like ink across the orchard and the open range beyond, all the way to the Sacramento Mountains on the western horizon. He tried not to hear what the other kids were saying. But it was impossible to listen to anything else.

"That girl at the sock hop—"

"Betty Campbell. She's in my English class."

"She started bleeding."

"Bleeding?"

Betty was all anyone would talk about, all anyone could think about now.

"From her hands."

"And her feet. My girl was there; she saw the whole thing."

"Ask Jim about it—he was there."

"It's because of the saucer. Somebody brought a piece to the dance, and she touched it and suddenly—"

"Do you think the Army will take Betty away, too? Like they took the flying saucer?"

The kids all laughed at the thought. It made Jim want to spit. On them. It made him want to fight with somebody, which was stupid, he knew, but still he wanted to.

"It wasn't a flying saucer," Jim said, loud, so everybody else would shut up and listen. "It was a weather balloon. Jesus, you're a bunch of goons, you know that? Carrying on about a flying saucer when the Army already said—"

"Aw, who believes what the Army says?" That was Mitch Kromski, a Hawk. "You think they wouldn't string any old story along just to keep people in line?"

Jim narrowed his eyes at Mitch.

"They'll say whatever they have to say," Mitch went on, "to keep everybody from flipping their wigs."

"The Army wouldn't lie to the public," Jim said.

Mitch laughed at that. Everybody laughed.

"Whatever it takes to keep the sheep in their pen," Mitch said. "Keep 'em from thinking too hard about whatever's being cooked up right now in Soviet labs."

He made a noise like an explosion, mimed the low spread of a mushroom cloud. Everyone was still laughing, but the humor had evaporated.

"Are we going to race, or not?" Jim said.

He didn't wait for an answer. He got into his car and fired up its engine, turned right there without backing up first, so Mitch Kromski had to jump out of his way.

He didn't head back into town. Spurred by a restless energy, he drove the long, empty highways that crisscrossed the desert, racing the shadows and his own thoughts as the sun sank lower in the sky.

Whatever Mitch and the rest thought, Jim trusted the Army. His dad had believed in the virtue of service, the importance of defending home and principles alike. No way would his father have committed himself so completely to an institution that lied to the people it protected. Salvador Lucero hadn't died in service to a lie.

But the kids at the orchard hadn't been wrong. Whatever had happened to Betty at yesterday's dance, that funny piece of metal had caused it. Or the metal *seemed* to have caused it.

A weather balloon couldn't make a person bleed.

By that time, he'd driven far from Roswell. He was somewhere northwest of the town, closer to Corona than to home. He couldn't shake the thought of blood soaking through Betty's white socks, blood running pink down the drain in a spiral that kept going. There was no one on the highway behind him, so he slowed his car, took it out of gear, let it coast along the pavement till it lost its momentum and rolled to a stop near a certain milepost and a turnout onto a long dirt road.

Jim put the Plymouth back into gear. He left the highway, found the loose gravel and the ruts, crept through the dry rangeland into the heart of Mac Brazel's ranch.

By the time he reached the low rise, some two miles from the highway, the sun had disappeared behind the distant Sacramentos, but enough light remained that he could see clearly. He got out of his car and stood for a while at the top of the rise, arms folded against an encroaching autumn chill. Below him, the ground sloped away into a rocky bowl, its far side defined by a half circle of sandstone. There, at the curve of the bluff . . . that was where it came down. So all the kids said, the ones who refused to believe it was only a balloon. Jim didn't see anything unusual, no abrasion in the varnish of the stone, no char along the earth. But he couldn't take his eyes off the depression. A curious, deep quiet had come over him—had filled him from the place itself, which was stiller than stillness, suspended in a sacred amber that not even sound could stir, not even thought.

Somehow, he broke himself away. He left the dirt road and moved up to the crest, where he'd stood once with Betty to watch the stars, but he didn't look up at the sky now. He hunted among the sagebrush and the cholla, kicked at the roots of pinyons and scuffed his soles in the dust, searching, searching for something he knew he would never find.

Except, he did find it. In the very moment that light gave way to dusk, just when he'd convinced himself that he was a fool and he ought to leave, he uncovered something in the sandy earth. It was slick and flat and even though there was no light to speak of left in the sky, it sparked with a sly and revelatory glimmer.

Jim hesitated. He spent a good deal of time standing over the thing he'd uncovered, fixated and afraid to touch it. And then, all at once, he picked it up as if it were any piece of trash blown down Main Street.

Dust ran like water from its surface. It was clean and clear, a strip of material some seven or eight inches long, no more than two inches wide, thinner than paper and weighing almost nothing. He could see marks engraved in the metal, the strange spidery glyphs of a language he didn't know, purple, like the dusk.

All the long drive back to Roswell, Jim could feel that piece of metal like a slap across his face, though it only lay on the bench seat beside him. When he reached his home, he didn't go inside. He stood for a while in the driveway, trying to catch his breath amid a low, routine trill of crickets and the distant barking of a neighbor's dog. And then he took what he'd found into the garage. He turned on his work lamp, sat at the bench, bent over the scrap of metal as if he were in prayer.

The markings. They were writing of some kind; they had to be. Soviet, he told himself, though God knew he'd seen Cyrillic often enough, and the language bore no resemblance to these pictographs. The markings were impressed somehow into the surface, their edges faintly detectable with his fingers. He tried to make sense of them— turned the scrap this way and that, but no meaning emerged except the one meaning: that here was a thing he could not understand, and yet, at the same time, he understood perfectly.

Jim took his wire cutters and tried to snip off a piece of the metal. No matter how he held it, the substance wouldn't be cut, but only turned and slid itself between the blades and emerged again unharmed.

He plugged in his soldering iron, tried to burn it. The metal glowed a little, but it never melted or curled, didn't even release a thread of smoke.

Finally, Jim sat back and did the only thing he could do. He stared at the strange artifact where it lay on his workbench, and he let go of all his foolish certainties about the saucer and the Army, about the world and what lay beyond and around, about science and God and prayer and the ability to know. And outside, the crickets sang, and the dog barked, and the night was like any other night, like every night Jim had known.

CHAPTER
TWENTY-THREE

October 17, 1947

The day after she witnessed the miracle, Mary Agnes called again at the Campbell home, as soon as her duties at the monastery were finished and the bell tolled for all the sisters to disperse to their hour of personal time. She would have spent that hour walking, or reading in her cell, or writing a letter to her family back home. That was before she had witnessed the impossible, a genuine miracle, proof of the power and presence of God. Now there was nothing more pressing than the unassuming girl whose hands had welled with blood, nothing more worthy of her focused passion than the God who had caused such a sign to be given. Even while she'd prayed through the Hours, Mary Agnes had wrestled a fierce impatience, an eagerness to return to town and learn whatever she could about the miraculous child.

The afternoon was much cooler than any Mary Agnes had experienced since she'd arrived in Roswell. Winter was surely on its way. Or perhaps, she reflected as she made her way up the Campbell walk for the second time, a chill was only the body's natural reaction to the presence of something holy. She wasn't the only one who considered the two-story house with reverence. More candles had appeared at the edge of the lawn, bouquets of purple asters, handwritten prayers on scraps of paper held in place with small stones. Mary Agnes was almost tempted to leave an offering of her own, though she had nothing in her pockets, nothing to give but a sincere and trembling awe.

This time, Mrs. Campbell answered the door, wearing an apron and a half-startled, half-relieved expression.

"I've caught you at a bad time," Mary Agnes said.

"You've come to talk about Betty, I suppose."

Mary Agnes nodded.

"Give me a moment," Rosa said. "I'll take off this apron. We can talk out here on the porch if you like. My husband is inside, and I . . . I don't want to disturb him."

Mary Agnes settled onto one of the porch's wicker chairs. Aside from the growing shrine at the end of the walkway, the neighborhood was ordinary, lively with the sound of children at play. A damp, lazy smell of river earth drifted from the willow-lined ditch at the end of the street. Rosa emerged from the house carrying two tall glasses of ice water. Mary Agnes accepted hers with thanks. It would be good to wet her throat. She wasn't sure how to say what she needed to say to Mrs. Campbell.

Rosa sighed when she noticed the candles and flowers at the edge of her dry lawn. She didn't sit but went brusquely down the porch steps and out into the yard, where she gathered up all the offerings in her arms. She returned to the porch, kicked open an old, wooden tinder box with one scuffed house shoe, and dumped everything inside. Only then did she sink onto the other wicker chair with a long-suffering expression.

"Did Betty tell you that I called yesterday, while you and your husband were in Lubbock?"

"No, Sister." Rosa cast her eyes down. "She keeps to herself these days. We hardly hear a word from her."

"That isn't like her, is it, Mrs. Campbell? She seems like such a bright, confident girl."

"She has changed," Rosa said. "Since . . ."

Mary Agnes reached across the space that separated them, laid a gentle hand on the woman's wrist. "I know about Betty's affliction."

Rosa looked up, almost wild with hope. "You believe her?"

Believe—yes, Mary Agnes believed. She had never truly believed in anything until she'd seen the blood rise from the wounds in Betty's hands. She had only thought she'd understood, before, what the word meant. Believe.

"I witnessed it myself. Yesterday I called intending to speak with you, but Betty was here alone. She confided in me. And then she . . . showed me, Mrs. Campbell. She showed me what has been happening to her."

Rosa set her drink on the small table that stood between herself and the nun. She pressed her hands to her face, allowing the cool echo of the ice to push back the fever of her worries. "You don't know how hard it's been, Sister. Since Roger came home from the war. And everything has gotten worse since the summer. Since . . . whatever happened out there in the desert."

"The saucer," Mary Agnes said quietly. "I've heard."

"Now this. My poor girl."

Rosa hid behind her hands, but she couldn't protect herself from the terrible disorientation that was spinning around her, taking her world apart, one moment and breath and heartbeat at a time. The dark fears that had haunted her since the start of the war hadn't abated. America's victory over Germany and Japan hadn't been the end. For the Campbells, it had only been the start. No one talked about the war anymore, but Rosa could feel it, the specter of a hungry conflict that wanted to live on, wanted to go on consuming everything, money and spirit and lives and hope, for no better reason than its own perpetuation. That cloven-footed beast called War already held Rosa's life in its hands. It was only a matter of time before it ripped her apart for good, before it took Roger away into the blackness—and her children, too, her home, the safe little life she had once lived here, the life of quiet happiness, the only blessing she had ever asked of God.

"Does your husband know about all this?" Mary Agnes said.

Rosa looked up with a bitter laugh. "About Betty? No. I can't imagine that he knows. He never will if I can help it. In some ways, Sister, Roger was his old self when he came home from the Pacific. In others, he's a broken man. But since the summer . . ." She sighed, heavy with despair. "I know these changes in him have something to do with that . . . weather balloon the Army found in the desert. But Roger won't talk about it. I tried to get him to talk about it, once. He wouldn't. I can't press him, you see. If he's pressed on anything, it makes him feel . . . as if he's back in the Pacific, I suppose. I don't want to do that to him. I don't want to make him relive what he'd rather forget."

She was weeping openly now. Mary Agnes could do nothing but hold the woman's hand—small comfort, yet she hoped it made this poor, grieving soul feel less alone.

"I was so relieved," Rosa said, "when he came home in one piece. I thought: How lucky we are, when so many other families have lost their men. I told myself that all the things that were wrong with him . . . his temper, and his fears . . . they would heal, with time. And he might have gotten better, if not for this summer. The crash did something to this whole town. Turned us upside down, and Roger, especially. Now I don't think my husband is ever coming back again."

When her weeping had calmed a little, Mary Agnes released her hand. "What do you think happened, Mrs. Campbell? This past summer, I mean—the thing the Army found in the desert."

Rosa lifted her face, gazed into the distance. She seemed to look beyond the small, quiet homes with their evidence of small, quiet lives—the laundry lines hung with washing, the children's toys in the yards, the newspapers lying on porches waiting to be taken in. She saw past what was, into a wider what-is, and a wondering, bewildered expression crossed her face, fearful and shining with reverence.

"I don't know, Sister. I've asked myself a hundred times, a thousand times. Was it something from the war, a Soviet plane, maybe? Because it had to be something for Roger to feel the way he does about it, for him to fear it like he does. Was it something stranger? The kids, you know, they say it's a ship from outer space. And some of the ladies from church, they say it was an angel. Maybe it wasn't any of those things. Maybe it was nothing that could ever make sense to any of us. Do you see what I mean? Maybe God doesn't want us to know. Sometimes I think, when that thing crashed—whatever it was—that was God's way of . . ."

Rosa didn't know how to say what she meant. This was all too complicated for words—the feeling, the knowing, the not knowing, which seemed somehow more real and important than anything Rosa had known in her life. She stuck her finger into her water, stirred vigorously until the ice cubes spun in a tight spiral, around and around inside the glass.

Mary Agnes watched the ice cubes until they slowed. Rosa sighed again, and the children at the end of the street went on playing, the birds sang in the willow trees, as if this were still the same old world.

"I'd like to ask Father Kerry to open an official investigation," Mary Agnes said, "into Betty's affliction. If it's all right with you and your husband. I hope we might find some answers that way. I hope we might be able to put your mind, and Betty's mind, at ease."

"Yes," Rosa said quietly. "I suppose that's for the best."

"Would you like me to speak to Roger about it first?"

"No, Sister, no. It would be too much for him. I'll do it, when the time is right. I'll tell him the way it must be."

TRANSCRIPT pages 22–25

BISHOP COTE: I want to thank you all for coming here today, for being so generous with your time. I believe we've recorded everything we need to make our determination.

ROSA: Come, Betty. Let's go home.

BETTY: That's it?

ROSA: Betty. Get your coat.

BETTY: Aren't they going to say what happened to me? Don't I get any answers?

ROGER: Honey, I told you from the start that this was going to be a waste of time. Now let's get back to our lives and carry on.

(inaudible as Campbell family leaves room)

FATHER KERRY: Shall I shut off the recorder?

BISHOP COTE: Not just yet. We need a few more facts from Sister Mary Agnes first. But we are agreed, I think, that nothing has occurred here that might be of interest to the church.

FATHER KERRY: Yes, Your Excellency. That seems to be the case.

SISTER MARY AGNES: Wait. Forgive me, Father, Your Excellency—am I understanding correctly? After all this testimony, you believe that Betty Campbell has perpetrated some sort of hoax?

FATHER KERRY: It may not be a hoax. The girl might have tried to play a harmless prank, and then rumor ran out of control.

SISTER MARY AGNES: You think she's lying?

BISHOP COTE: Betty isn't an especially devout girl, to say the least. That's by her own admission, and by the testimony of her mother.

SISTER MARY AGNES: I suppose I don't understand, Your Excellency. What do Betty's personal religious feelings or habits have to do with this?

FATHER KERRY: The stigmata aren't known to occur in any person who's not of . . . shall we say, exceptional faith.

SISTER MARY AGNES: But I saw it with my own eyes, Father. I witnessed Betty's hands begin to bleed. I know she did nothing to cause it.

BISHOP COTE: The fact remains, Sister. The girl doesn't fit the profile of a stigmatic. She isn't devout enough to make the case compelling.

SISTER MARY AGNES: And what about me? I've taken religious vows; I've devoted my entire life to prayer. My

sisters and I rise in the middle of the night, for goodness' sake, each and every night, to pray. Am I not devout enough to witness a miracle?

FATHER KERRY: Your passion is understandable, Sister.
But the stigmata don't occur in girls like Betty, and
certainly not from science-fiction nonsense like flying
saucers. Somehow, the girl is perpetrating a hoax. It's a
sad thing to confront—lying and sacrilege in our own
community—but we must face the facts. No more
credit should be given to the story.

SISTER MARY AGNES: No more credit! The people of
this town have been leaving prayer candles and other
offerings at the Campbell home.

FATHER KERRY: A misdirection of faith. It will all blow
over, soon enough. False tales like this always do.

SISTER MARY AGNES: False tales! My sisters and I were
summoned to Roswell to bring the people of this town
back to God after something shook their faith. Now,
through Betty, the faith of many good people has been
restored—

FATHER KERRY: Through Betty, many good people have
been led astray.

SISTER MARY AGNES: I don't believe what I'm hearing.
I'm actually astounded, Father. Forgive me, but I am.
Something beyond our ability to explain has happened
here—possibly, a legitimate miracle—and you're ready
to turn your back on it, to write it off as a lie?

FATHER KERRY: Make-believe hokum like flying saucers are not sources of miracles, Sister. Please try to keep perspective.

SISTER MARY AGNES: I am keeping perspective. At Fátima, seventy thousand people or more witnessed a spinning disc in the sky, and saw it dance. That event was declared a miracle by the church. The first stigmatic in history—Saint Francis himself, who founded my order and yours—received his holy wounds as a beam of light from a luminous apparition in the sky.

BISHOP COTE: An angel, Sister. Not a ship from outer space.

SISTER MARY AGNES: How do you know what it was? How can any of us know? Maybe whatever crashed out there, outside this town, was something more than what the Army claimed it to be. Maybe it was something more than anyone can comprehend. Maybe in the time of Saint Francis, that thing would have been called an angel—

BISHOP COTE: Sister, not only are you speaking out of turn, but you're treading close to blasphemy.

SISTER MARY AGNES: I'm sorry, Your Excellency. Forgive me. It has been a long day. I've allowed my feelings to get somewhat out of control. Forgive me.

CHAPTER
TWENTY-FOUR

October 31, 1947

It was almost Day of the Dead.

Betty sat alone, in the lightless parlor room, with only a framed portrait of her late grandmother for company. The *ofrenda*, the little shrine where the departed were honored this time of year, seemed to stand out from the surrounding darkness with an eerie luminosity. Swags of flowers and the sugar skulls her brothers had clumsily iced floated on a raft of shadow. There among the decorations was Abuelita as a young woman, much younger than Betty had ever known her to be, sober in her portrait but beautiful, with the sharp brows and high cheekbones of a movie star, her old-fashioned hairstyle laced through with a silver chain and glittering *conchos*.

Betty could almost wish—she *did* wish—that she were with her grandmother now, out there somewhere in a misty other-land of ancestors and angels. With the dead. So far removed from this present world of humiliation that she could forget she had ever been Isabel Campbell, the stigmatic of Roswell. The stigmatic, or whatever she was. Whatever might explain the blood.

The house was empty. Her father was on duty at the base, and her mother was helping decorate the church for Sunday's observance of All

Souls' Day. Her little brothers had gone out trick-or-treating, so eager they'd left before the sun had even set. There had been no phone calls inviting Betty to Halloween parties—not this year, not after what everyone had seen at the sock hop. It was fine. Betty didn't have the stomach for a party, anyway. Not after yesterday's farce with Father Kerry and the bishop. Whenever she thought about the investigation—and she thought about nothing else—everything inside her crumpled in on itself, and she felt smaller than an ant, smaller than a louse, so small she was nothing, and deserved to be nothing.

They hadn't believed her. The priest, the bishop. They hadn't said so right out—not to Betty, anyway—but after she and her parents had returned home from the interview, no one spoke a word for the rest of the evening. They were all wrung out, disoriented, and Betty knew she couldn't be the only one who felt betrayed by the church. It was a wonder to her, that her mother had gone to help with the preparations for Sunday's service—and surely, Rosa had only done it out of stubbornness, to show Father Kerry that the Campbells couldn't be brushed off so easily. Betty didn't have the heart for such displays of spirit. She felt like a fool for thinking she might find her answers in the priest's hands. When had the church gotten anything right? Never, as far as she could see.

The sitting room smelled of the *ofrenda*'s marigold garland. Betty breathed the scent in deeply, held the sharp bitterness in her throat.

Day of the Dead. Land of the Dead. A better place, surely, than here.

Someone knocked at the door. Betty groaned and dragged herself out of her dad's easy chair. She had deliberately left the porch light off to deter trick-or-treaters. She'd even blown out the candles in her little brothers' jack-o'-lanterns. But the neighborhood children would try their luck anyway.

When she answered the door, however, she found Juanita on the porch, holding up a pair of rubber masks—a witch and a bright-red devil.

Betty sighed.

"Come on," Juanita said. "You aren't going to sit around in the dark like some kind of creep."

"Am too."

"I won't let you do it."

She tossed the devil mask at Betty, who caught it in self-defense.

"I can't go to any parties," Betty said. "First of all, I haven't been invited. And second, I'd rather die after . . . oh, Nita, yesterday was the worst. The priest thinks I'm lying! He didn't say so, but I know he does. I could tell by the way he treated me. How am I ever going to live it down?"

"We aren't going to a party," Juanita said. "We're going trick-or-treating."

"Aren't we too old for that?"

Juanita shrugged. "Yes, but who cares? No one will know who we are with our masks on."

That was what decided it for Betty. Since the sock hop, she had felt eyes on her everywhere she went—stares that followed her down the aisles of the grocery store when she helped her mother with the shopping, stares boring into the back of her head as she sat in her classes. Even Dwight Carey was acting strange around her. He wouldn't say hello in the halls of the school, but he sure stared enough for three boys. Betty had forgotten what it was like to move through the world unnoticed.

She stepped out onto the porch, pulled the devil mask over her face. "Perfect. Everyone's going to think I'm evil, anyway, once they hear that Father Kerry didn't believe me."

"He didn't believe you? Are you sure you didn't get him wrong?"

Betty the Devil shook her head.

"Well, I believe you." Juanita donned her own mask. "I guess that makes me a witch."

They roamed the neighborhood together, watching the children in bright costumes race from house to house. The small eye holes in

Betty's mask reduced the world to a narrow window, through which she saw only the innocent play of the town's youngest residents—not the suspicious glances of the men and women who'd heard the rumors, who wondered now whether that Campbell girl was a liar, or another unexplained wonder fallen from the sky.

The girls walked to Main Street and turned south. Among the packs of costumed children, no one looked twice at them. The Plains Theater was lit bright as Christmas, strings of golden lights chasing one another along its marquee sign. Betty and Juanita leaned against the wall of a service station, closed for the night, and watched the kids their own age file past the box office and into the Plains, where the latest Wolfman flick was playing.

"I don't know what I was thinking," Betty said, "going to the priest over . . . this."

"Who else should you have gone to?"

"Anyone else."

"But it makes perfect sense, Betty. Priests are supposed to know about these things. I know—why don't you go and see the nuns at that new convent?"

Betty scoffed behind her mask. It was that nun who'd come to her door, Sister Mary Agnes, who'd got the bright idea of having a formal interview with the bishop. Betty couldn't find any anger for the nun. Mary Agnes had obviously believed that Betty was sincere. Throughout the interview, the sister had tried several times to make Father Kerry and that arrogant, stick-in-the-mud bishop listen. But the men hadn't believed the nun's testimony any more than they'd believed Betty's.

"What would a bunch of nuns do for me," Betty said, "pray?"

Juanita just looked at her. Looked at her through the silly witch mask, with nothing to hint at her thoughts.

"Praying doesn't get you anywhere," Betty said.

"It does when nuns do the praying. That's what they're for, to get your prayers to God better."

"Oh, come on."

"Like the radio towers," Juanita said.

Betty laughed. It filled her mask with condensation, so she pulled it off, not caring now who saw her. "Shouldn't we be able to pray just fine on our own? Why does God get more complicated the more rules you put around Him? Nuns to make your prayers go farther, and priests and bishops to tell you that you can't really experience a miracle because you weren't holy enough to begin with, and Popes to say what God really meant and what He didn't. It's like the Army, isn't it?"

Juanita removed her mask, too, looked at Betty in confusion.

"I mean," Betty said, "it's like the saucer. Like what the Army *did* about the saucer. Took my dad out there to see what it was, and then, when they didn't like what they saw, they made up a different story. So everyone would believe they were still in control, they were still the same Army that won the war and knew what to do in every situation, even when something happens that no one knows anything about, like when a spaceship falls from the sky."

"Do you think it was really a spaceship?"

"I don't know," Betty wailed. "I just know it was *something*. It was something, damn it, because if it was only some ordinary thing, if it was just a balloon like they said, it wouldn't have done this to me."

Betty began to cry then—the great, wracking, hopeless sobs she only ever let out in the privacy of her bedroom.

Juanita pulled her into a hug, held on to her till the worst of it was over.

"I know it was something," Juanita said. "I believe you, Betty. I know."

Knowing. That was the problem, that was what Betty didn't have. There were no answers from priests or nuns, no clarity to be found in prayer. Her only hope for real knowledge lay at university—at any school that would take her. But her dad had set himself against the idea, and after yesterday's fiasco with the bishop, he was even less likely to give any ground.

One way or another, Betty had to get away from Roswell—away from the people who would only ever see her now as a saint or a liar, away from the crash itself, from the mystery that had come to dwell, somehow, in her blood.

CHAPTER
TWENTY-FIVE

November 1, 1947

For two days after she returned to the monastery, Mary Agnes accepted the decision her priest and her bishop had made. Or she told herself that she accepted the outcome of the investigation. Through her observation of the Hours, side by side with her sisters in prayer, she insisted within her own mind that she recognized the authority of these men of God; she lectured herself silently on their superior knowledge, their special fitness to discern the truth and to guide her through confusion and deception to a greater light. For two days, she reminded herself that she had stepped out of line—behaved shamefully at the close of the interview. It was a wonder Father Kerry and the bishop had forgiven her at all, and a testament to the worthy nature of their souls that they'd been willing to overlook her outburst with patience and grace. For two days, as she worked at her physical labors, as she held herself at a meticulous distance from Harvey—physically, emotionally—she scolded herself that she was only one woman. She lacked the broad experience the father and the bishop possessed—their education, their ordination, the superior discernment granted to those chosen by God and graced with His authority.

Now and then, she managed to convince herself. She managed to believe, for a few minutes at a stretch, that she agreed with their determination, that there was nothing remarkable about the girl Betty Campbell, that all of this was an unfounded rumor. Her own eyes had deceived her. Her lack of a higher understanding had left her vulnerable to being misled—by children engaging in routine mischief, or by the Devil himself.

These moments of acquiescence never lasted long. Mary Agnes couldn't seem to make her own obedience stick. And on the afternoon of All Saints Day, as she piled up refuse from the elms and the garden to be burned, the rebellious pull deep inside her built to a constant discomfort that she could no longer ignore. To accept the decision of the bishop and the priest would be to turn her back on a miracle—a sign she had been blessed to witness. And it *had* been a miracle, whatever Father Kerry and Bishop Cote believed. The fire burned now in Mary Agnes too hotly to be ignored. Faith had found her at last, a pure conviction of belief, thanks to the blessed hands of an unassuming teenage girl.

Mary Agnes knew what she had seen. She wouldn't blind herself now to the brilliant light of truth revealed—she couldn't, not even if she'd wanted to, not even at the command of a bishop ordained by God.

She stood back from the heap of tangled branches, watched Harvey scatter kerosene from a can. When he tossed a match onto the pile and the flames leaped up to devour, her eyes traveled up from the flame, found Harvey through the ripple of heat and veils of acrid smoke. She was struck by his presence, as if noticing him for the first time, and, in the same moment, as if seeing him through the long lens of a lifetime, through the ever-presence of eternity: his familiar gestures, his thoughtful demeanor, his capable body, so strong and appealing, and so near her own. The fire and the heat, and her offense at the bishop's denial, and the deep, clear pool of faith that filled her now, told her she knew what she had seen, and that she had seen truly—all of it combined with Harvey's presence to chafe her soul raw. She felt her vows as a stricture.

She felt the monastery, this life to which she had fled, as a cage for the first time in her life. And she knew, as the sparks leaped upward and the flames consumed, that not even her most diligent prayers would soothe her back to complacency.

Late that night, after her sisters had settled in their cells and the farmhouse descended into silence, Mary Agnes remained awake at her window. The chill of the coming winter pressed through the glass and left its touch lightly on her forehead, her cheek. She watched the tops of the bare trees move subtly against the dark sky. In the simple peace of the moment, in the seclusion of her heart, she allowed herself to look, for the first time, at that poisonous thing that had grown so large inside her, where her sisters couldn't see, where even she could scarcely discern it.

It was anger.

She was angry, so fiercely and bitterly angry, at the men of power who'd told her she didn't know what she had seen with her own eyes. Angry on Betty's behalf, too, that no one believed the poor child, who had displayed nothing but honesty and had spoken from her heart. Most of all, she was angry with herself. For listening to the priest and the bishop. For submitting to their will, for trying to bury the truth she knew because they had told her to do it.

She had betrayed herself. Perhaps, she had betrayed God, if God was still a thing she could believe in. If He existed, then wasn't this why He had brought Mary Agnes to Roswell—to witness a miracle and honor it, to know the great, impossible power of the Divine?

She pushed the first inkling of her doubt away. Yes, God was real, and He had chosen Mary Agnes to stand as advocate and defender of a girl whom no one else would believe. It must have been God's doing. What else could explain her life, her sacrifices, this strange path through enclosure and out again into the world? It was an immodest thought, but nevertheless, she couldn't deny its truth. Betty wasn't the kind of girl to whom these things happened, and yet the miracle had occurred.

When the bishop and the priest had denied Betty's story, both the girl and Mary Agnes had been wronged.

Such a simple act. Allowing herself to admit her anger, allowing herself to feel it. The smallest matter of internal friction, a giving inside that should have shaken the very earth, but moved nothing, not even Mary Agnes from the window. Yet a crack widened within her, a breach so small and insignificant she'd never noticed it before. Now she could feel it pulling apart, distorting the surface of her very identity like a flaw in a mirror. She saw twelve years of sacrifices she'd made for the church, and the lifetime of belief she'd given before she had taken her vows. Everything was bubbling and folding, the once-clear image of self, running like melted wax, losing sense and context. It frightened her, because she didn't know what she might find on the other side of that mirror-wall once its surface had been shattered.

There was no time to dwell on the question, however, for in that moment she looked down at the darkened grounds and saw a figure lying still in the grass—white blouse, bare legs below the skirt's hem. A bolt of shock ran through her, hard enough to make her gasp. She fled from her cell without thinking to shout for her sisters. Her only thought was to reach the fallen person as quickly as possible and give them aid if she could.

She pelted down the stairs in the dark, clinging desperately to the handrail. She was across the lightless farmhouse in a flash, but as she threw open the front door and her bare feet thudded on the porch, the figure in the grass sat up and cast a look over its shoulder, back at Mary Agnes.

Her first thought was: *Thank God that person isn't dead.*

Half a heartbeat later, she recognized the round, young face, the sober expression of inward searching.

Mary Agnes slowed to a walk, tried to catch her breath. "Betty," she said when she stood over the girl.

"Hello, Sister."

Betty lay back in the grass again. She didn't look at Mary Agnes. "What are you doing out here, and so late?"

"You told me I could come back anytime."

Mary Agnes thought back to their first meeting. The basket on Rosa's arm, the smell of cinnamon, Betty hiding shyly behind her mother. "Yes, I suppose I did."

"Anyway," Betty said, "I'm only looking at the stars. This is a good place to do it. I used to come here sometimes, before you nuns were here, when it was just the old, abandoned sanatorium. The trees block out most of the light from town and from the airfield—though they do it better in the summer, when they have their leaves."

"Do you mind if I join you?" Mary Agnes asked. "If you don't want me here, I'll understand."

"I don't mind."

She lowered herself to the cool earth, sat beside the girl with her knees drawn up under her sleeping habit. The grass was dry and crackling, and the grounds still pervaded by the smoky smell of the day's fire. She tipped back her head to take in the vast, encompassing arch of the Heavens. She had never been so aware of the stars—their number and extravagance. Once, they had seemed to her symbols of God's grandeur, His renewing power of creation. Now they looked cold, and far away, unfathomably distant, and she could feel the long, black gaps between each light pulling her into a labyrinth of questions. Never had she felt so small and alone.

"I know they don't believe me," Betty said.

There was no need to ask whom the girl meant.

"I'm sorry," Mary Agnes said. "It's my fault; I thought the whole thing would turn out differently. I shouldn't have put you through it."

"You were only trying to help."

"But I didn't help." Mary Agnes was quiet for a moment, searching for something more to say. All her words were useless. "I still want to understand it. I want to know what has happened to you, what causes it and why."

The girl gave a small, ironic laugh. "So do I."

"The stigmata is a gift from God," Mary Agnes began.

She was relieved when Betty cut her off with a cold, dry bark of laughter, for she wouldn't have known what to say, beyond that.

"A gift," Betty scoffed. "What kind of gift is this? Pain and suffering and fear, and everyone staring at me, wondering if I'm a freak or a liar."

Mary Agnes could think of no response. She lay back, too, in the grass. There was nothing to see now but the ring of elms and the dome of Heaven they contained. Nothing to see but her own frail inadequacy before the greatness of the mysteries.

"I don't believe in God anymore," Betty said.

"I can understand why." She had almost answered, *I don't believe in Him, either. Not anymore.* But she wasn't yet sure that was true.

"Nothing makes sense," Betty said. "I feel like I wrote down everything I know and think and believe, wrote it all out like a paper for school, and then someone took the pages right out of my hands and threw them up in the air. And now I'm picking them up and trying to put them back in order, but there *is* no order."

"I know exactly what you mean. I feel that way, too." Everything out of joint, out of context.

"If I could just find some path to follow. You know?"

Betty pointed up at the sky, and her hand moved subtly. It took Mary Agnes some time to realize the girl was tracing constellations, marking a path for herself among the faraway lights.

"Signs to point the way," Betty said. "A road with clear edges and a real destination."

Mary Agnes smiled, but it was neither warm nor happy. She blinked her tears away. "When I was back in Chicago, before I came here, my old Mother Superior said that if you only keep moving forward—if you follow the path God gives you, even if it doesn't seem like a path to you—it will lead you to the truth."

"Do you believe that?" Betty asked.

Mary Agnes didn't answer for a moment. She had never said the words aloud before, yet they were the truth. The path had led her to this. "I don't know what I believe now."

"I'm beginning to think that's the point," Betty said. "To put everything out of order, so nothing makes sense. That's why this happened to me. That's why it happened to all of us—the saucer, and the Army saying what they said. And nobody believing me, even when I had you to speak for me. I think maybe that *is* the point. If God had any hand in this—if God exists at all—He doesn't want us to know. He doesn't want us to know anything." She laughed again, a small, lonely sound. "I'm not making any sense, am I?"

Why did Mary Agnes recall, in that moment, Rosa on her front porch, stirring her glass with a finger? The ice cubes spinning in a tight whirl. "You make more sense to me than you might believe," she said.

"You aren't like other nuns."

Now it was her turn to laugh. Quietly, with more bitter in it than sweet. "I know."

"Sometimes I wish I could be out there," Betty said. "With the stars. They're so far away from here—did you know that? Some are so far off, it takes hundreds of years for their light to reach us. Or thousands of years. I'd like to be that far away."

"It makes me feel dizzy," Mary Agnes said, "to think about it. If they're so far away, but we can see them, then they must be—"

"Huge," Betty said. "Bigger than God. That's why I like to look at them. It's proof, isn't it, that some things really are too big for any of us to understand."

Mary Agnes didn't exactly feel comforted by that thought. She didn't quite feel unsettled, either. It was simply a fact—her smallness, the insignificance of one life in the greater array of Creation.

She turned her head on the grass to look at Betty. The girl continued to gaze at the stars, and her face, in profile, was picked out by starlight, sharp and illumined as if by a halo of consecrated fire. Betty was braver than she realized, braver than Mary Agnes could ever be. For she looked full into the face of mystery and found the cold clarity of truth. It, too, was a mirror's surface. Mary Agnes prayed that Betty's looking glass would never break.

CHAPTER
TWENTY-SIX

November 3, 1947

It didn't take long for word to get out that Betty Campbell was a faker and a blasphemer.

It started in the halls of Roswell High School, when Juanita Lopez entered the girls' bathroom to find Millie and Theresa sniggering at the sinks.

"Well, you know," Millie was saying, "she's been going around with Jim Lucero, so she thinks she's a real big shot."

"Everyone can see now that she's nothing but a liar," Theresa said.

Juanita walked right up to them. "Who are you talking about? Go on, spit it out."

The girls only looked at one another, then left the bathroom without a word to Juanita. Their nasty laughter echoed in the cold space behind them.

Mary Carper, whose husband ran the hardware store, heard all about the bishop's investigation and shook her head sadly at the November meeting of the Ladies' Rotary Club. "Something big will come of it, mark my words. Children these days think they can laugh in God's face, but He will not be mocked. I pray this girl sees the error of her ways and makes a good atonement for her sins." But that night, while she fixed supper, Mrs. Carper thought it was too bad that it had all come down to irreverence and sin. It might have been nice, to think of Roswell as a blessed place, a place where something miraculous could happen. A great, wide sadness opened inside her, and reached far back from her heart into all the years that had come before, to the place where she was still a girl of Betty Campbell's age. And that sadness stayed on her for days, and dragged everywhere behind her, no matter where she went, no matter how brightly and righteously she spoke. The sorrow never relented, and she didn't know why.

Cece Alvarado walked her three little dogs down Twelfth Street to the place where the road ended at the rectory and the Spring River in its willow-lined ditch. She walked the dogs up the other side of the street, and when she passed the Campbell home, she slipped the faded asters from her pocket and allowed them to fall at the edge of the yard, near the walkway, where the candles and the statues of saints once had been. Everyone in town was saying, now, that the story had been make-believe, or a trick played by kids. Cece thought it might still be true anyway. You couldn't believe everything you heard. And there was mercy in her heart for the humble child who'd been caught in a web of rumor. She talked to her dogs, but inside her mind, she was praying—for Betty Campbell, for her family, for everyone in Roswell who needed a miracle to be true.

Pilar Lopez stood in the yard, wrapped in her winter coat, smoking and looking up at the sky. She ought to make her daughter, Juanita, stop hanging around with that Campbell girl, now that the whole town was talking about Betty. But she remembered what it was like to be that age. You wouldn't know it to look at her, but it hadn't been so long ago. And she couldn't tell Juanita to stay away. Because what if it was true, after all? Bishops didn't know everything there was to know. Sometimes girls knew better than anyone else. Only nobody ever listened to what they had to say.

At the New Mexico Military Institute, Jim Lucero almost clocked another boy after he'd said something sneering and rude about that townie girl who was faking the wounds of Christ. Jim's buddy had to hold him back, one hand on his chest. "Remember the honor code, Jim. They could kick you out of Caltech before you even get there, if you're thrown out of school."

Something heavy and cold, a shadow of doubt, moved through the rectory. It made Father Kerry look up from his reading with a sudden clutch of fear. His heart was beating at a frantic pace, his forehead beaded with sweat, though he couldn't say why. The flash of a bright awareness illuminated, for one moment, his certainty that a true miracle wasn't subject to rules and hierarchies, didn't obey the whims of any church.

Then a loud, terse knock sounded at the rectory's door, and he pushed the thought away, set his book aside, drew his dignity and authority around him again. He wiped the sweat from his forehead.

"Sister Mary Agnes." He was surprised to find the nun on his doorstep, and more startled at the anger simmering just below her stoic expression.

"Father Kerry. May I come in?"

He stepped back, admitted the sister into the rectory.

As soon as he'd closed the door, Mary Agnes rounded on him. "You were wrong. You and Bishop Cote, both wrong about that girl."

"Sister, please. The investigation has concluded. Betty Campbell is not a stigmatic."

"She isn't a liar, either."

"The bishop and I have allowed that this might be rumor. Betty might have deluded herself into believing that her hands bled—"

"Nor is she suffering from any delusion. Why, Father, is it so hard for you to believe that a miracle might have occurred here?"

"Sister—"

She cut him off again. She wouldn't be deterred, wouldn't be silenced any longer. "How has attendance been at the church these past few weeks?"

Since the middle of October. Father Kerry understood what she was asking: since the initial rumors of a stigmatic in Roswell. He was forced to admit the truth. "More people have attended Mass than usual."

"Isn't that what the archbishop wanted? For attendance to rise, for more souls to return to the church after the disruption of this summer past? Wasn't that why my sisters and I were brought here to Roswell—"

"Sister, anyone might engineer a clever hoax. False stories may spur interest in the church for a while, but deceit is deceit, and no foundation for faith."

She looked thoughtful then, her anger falling away, her eyes seeming to gaze inward at some deeper, more personal quandary. "Then what is the foundation of faith? What, if not the things we've seen, the things we know to be true?"

"All the good things of God are contained within our church, Sister. You know this. Flying saucers aren't mentioned in the Gospel. How can such a thing give rise to a miracle? How can it be the foundation for anything, let alone faith?"

Her anger returned, a bright flash as she looked up and held his gaze, held it with a firmness of conviction that shook him more than he would dare to admit.

"You would deny a miracle because it doesn't look the way you expect it to look."

"If it doesn't look like the miracles our mother church describes," he said, "then it isn't a miracle at all."

Mary Agnes held him locked in her unyielding stare for one more heartbeat, then another. She turned from him abruptly, a dismissal, and the dark veil swung to hide her face. "I'll see myself out, Father. Good day."

CHAPTER
TWENTY-SEVEN

November 4–5, 1947

During the hour of recreation, after the last small meal of the day, the sisters gathered in the kitchen of the old farmhouse, mending their habits and winter stockings, or playing dominoes at the table while the whole group chatted and laughed. This was the lone hour of the day when the nuns did not observe a meditative and modest attitude. Now the nuns talked freely, discussing the prayer requests they'd received, sharing stories from their lives before they'd entered the order . . . and after.

This recreation hour was particularly jolly. All Souls' Day had just passed, the feast in honor of those who had departed in the faith, and stories flew around the old table of nuns who'd gone to meet the Bridegroom years ago, but whose quick wit and amusing antics were still fondly remembered. A fire blazed in the brick hearth, filling the room with its warmth and the nostalgic smell of woodsmoke. In anticipation of the Christmas season to come, Sister Ann had already decorated the mantel with cypress boughs and clove-studded oranges. White spangles of the year's first snowfall gusted past the window. Harvey had told Mary Agnes that this snow wouldn't last long. Most likely, it would be gone by morning. But on that night, the weather underscored the cozy contentment of the order.

Some of the mothers of the parish had brought offerings to the monastery—fresh-baked tortillas and cookies, and the beautiful, glistening rolls of deeply scored sweet bread known as *conchas*. The *conchas* were a specialty of the local women—and a novel delight to the newcomers from Chicago. Because the spirit of All Souls' Day still hung over the monastery, Mother Catherine of the Perpetual Sorrows had granted her indulgence, and the nuns nibbled freely on the abundance of sweets in defiance of their usual mandate to eat sparingly.

Sister Amata closed her eyes as she bit into a piece of chocolate-dipped shortbread, savoring the rich flavors. "There certainly are fine bakers here in Roswell."

"Pass me another of those buns, please," Sister Paula said. "I don't know when I've tasted anything so delicious."

Sister Margaret slid the basket of *conchas* down the table. "The wonders here never cease, it seems. We might even have a genuine miracle in Roswell."

Margaret turned to gaze at Mary Agnes, expectant. In fact, the entire order looked at her with raised brows, eager for some news of the bishop's investigation.

"Oh," Mary Agnes faltered, "I don't believe the bishop and Father Kerry found quite the answers they were looking for." She added hastily, "But I believe there's still more to be discovered."

Mother Catherine sniffed. "Surely, Sister, you aren't implying that the bishop conducted a faulty investigation."

"No, of course not." In point of fact, that was exactly what Mary Agnes was implying. "I only mean there's more to be understood before one can consider the case closed."

Paula and Margaret looked at one another in obvious bewilderment. Amata paused with her shortbread halfway to her lips.

"You remember," Mary Agnes said carefully, "that the archbishop wrote to our Mother in Chicago about Roswell. He said the town had gone through some . . . difficulties. Well, in my work as extern, I've learned a little more about those difficulties. It's all tied up with the case our bishop investigated—with this girl, Betty Campbell, and her affliction."

She did her best to explain what she could about the summer's crash and the rumors that still cast shadows over the town. The more she spoke of it, the more ridiculous it sounded, even to herself. And yet it was a fact that the story persisted. It was a fact that the tale was still exerting an influence over the people of Roswell. And it was undeniably true that fragments of whatever had crashed in the desert had caused Betty Campbell to bleed with the holy wounds of Christ. Mary Agnes would insist on that until her dying day. She had seen the miracle with her own eyes, whatever Bishop Cote and Father Kerry believed.

"Ships from outer space?" Sister Eugenia said. "That sounds rather far-fetched, Mary Agnes."

"I know it does, and I'm not saying the story is true. But it is . . . a mystery. We don't *know* yet what crashed in the desert, or why it affects this girl as it does. But something greater than all of us is at work here. Father Kerry told me that more people than ever have been attending Mass."

"We've had many visitors to the monastery, too," Amata said. "I hope by spring we'll have our chapel in sound-enough shape that we may welcome these good people in to pray with us."

Sister Ann rested her chin in her hands. "It's wonderful, to think that we've met the archbishop's goal already, bringing more souls back to the church. And we've only been in Roswell a couple of months!"

"But are more people returning to God because of us," Sister Paula asked, "or because of this girl's stigmata?"

"It doesn't matter which," Mary Agnes said, "as long as it serves God's purpose."

Mother Catherine arched her brows. "It certainly does matter, my dear. The one derives from God. The other derives from deceit."

"I truly don't believe that Betty Campbell has been deceiving anyone," Mary Agnes said. "I know her as no one else in this order does. She's humble and good-hearted, and hasn't gained anything positive by her affliction. She bears it with the suffering one would expect from a genuine stigmatic. Besides, I witnessed it myself, and I saw no evidence of a trick. Betty's wounds are genuine, Mother; they have to be."

"Our priest and bishop concluded otherwise," Catherine said.

"They might have been mistaken. Anyone may be mistaken, after all. Even priests and bishops are only human, and God works in mysterious ways."

"Not through flying saucers, He doesn't," Sister Paula said.

Mary Agnes tried to smile. "I know the saucer sounds like a silly story, but there's something to it. *Something.* I don't know what; that's the trouble."

"Best to let it go," the abbess said. "Now that the bishop has made his decision, there's nothing to be gained by continuing to chase after the story."

Mary Agnes ought to have lowered her face demurely in acceptance of Catherine's command. She couldn't seem to make herself give the proper display of obedience. The anger was still too loud inside her, tearing at her from the inside with spiked and frantic hands.

"There is something real happening here," she insisted. "Something no one can yet explain. Wouldn't it be a disservice to God, to turn our backs on His mysteries when He has sent such an obvious sign? For goodness' sake, a girl has received the stigmata. How can anyone ignore something like that?"

Mother Catherine gave a dry little grunt, which made the bitter thing inside Mary Agnes roar like a flame in the wind.

"Is this girl the praying type?" the abbess said.

Mary Agnes was forced to admit the truth. "Not more than most."

"Well, there you have it. Persons who aren't unusually devout in their faith aren't visited by the stigmata. It simply doesn't occur."

"But it *did* occur. Mother, I saw it myself!"

"What you saw was a clever trick."

The abbess spoke with such forgiveness and sympathy that Mary Agnes wanted to bite through her own tongue. She might as well be an especially gullible child, the way Mother Catherine was treating her now.

"It's not unheard of," Catherine went on, "for troubled souls to fake the stigmata. There's no shame in it, Sister. As you said yourself: we are all human, and fallible. Any of us may be led astray by those who seek to deceive."

Mary Agnes turned to Sister Ann, desperate for someone to stand beside her. "Don't you want to know? Don't you think it's a fascinating puzzle—that something crashed out in the desert, and now this girl—"

"Mary Agnes," the abbess said sharply. "Let's hear no more of this. The bishop himself has made his decision. It's not our place to question a man of such discernment."

"But I—"

"I fear for you, Sister, if you continue to moon over this story. It isn't fitting, for a woman of our order; you should be focused on holier things. This nonsense about flying saucers can only lead you away from what's truly important in this life: service to our Lord."

The clock in the parlor tolled out the time. The hour of Compline had come. Mary Agnes was grateful for the excuse to say nothing more, for she didn't believe she could have maintained a civil tone—not even to her abbess.

The sisters put their mending away and rose from the kitchen table, falling automatically into an orderly file. Together they progressed to their choir room, where they joined in nightly prayer and listened to the abbess recite the evening's Examen.

But all the while, Mary Agnes thought of metal in the desert, and blood rising fresh from a wound. She thought of the bright power of truth, how it burns in the atmosphere and lights the world, so nothing may hide in shadow.

~

That night, she dreamed.

She was walking through the desert. Skeletal plants snagged at her habit, and the parched earth under her bare feet was pale as the moon overhead. Far across the dusty expanse, she could see a massive, black shape hunched against the sky, a denser blackness than the night itself. She couldn't guess what that thing was—a stone formation or some bizarre construction of man, or the body of a slumbering giant. Perhaps it was God Himself, for the dark monolith pulled at her with a gravitational power, impossible to resist.

Mary Agnes stumbled closer. The land, the night, the very air was hostile to her presence, and yet she couldn't turn away. The dark shape against the sky called to her with an imperative no human heart could ignore. The nearer she came to the beacon, the greater grew her fear, until she was shuddering and weeping, but her feet refused to stop. In the lightless void of the unknown, something waited with outstretched hands. Something wanted to catch her and hold her fast, trap her in a snare of destiny.

She could smell an acrid, burnt odor among the desert sage, and she knew it was from the saucer. Uneven ground made her stumble, through ruts and over scar-like ripples of earth, as if some monstrous plow had been dragged across the land. She could see, now, that the dark monolith before her was a huge body of stone, curved like half of a bowl, and above its rim Mary Agnes could see all the stars of Creation.

Harvey was there somewhere, among the boulders and broken shale scattered at the foot of the bow-shaped cliff. She couldn't see him, in the dream. But she sensed him, a forceful attractor, lure and destination in one. Harvey and the great arch of stone were pulling her toward a splendid and hideous unmaking.

She was almost near enough now to touch the face of the cliff. Near enough to be swallowed by the force of all that was. But a sound came from the sky, from everywhere at once—a trumpet's blast, a bending and warping of the world, like the bones of the earth grinding and cracking under the constant weight of God.

When she turned back to look, a hot light blinded her, and she tried to cover her eyes. But she couldn't, couldn't stop herself from seeing the great circular *thing* that came hurtling from the sky, like the doom that fell on Sodom and Gomorrah, like the eyed wheels of divine messengers crying *Fear not* from the pages of her Bible. Glowing, shining with the light of the moon on its metallic skin, the object hurtled so close above her head that she could feel its terrible heat, could smell the ends of her hair burning. She could only watch as the silver wheel came down on a distant farmhouse . . . on the monastery where her sisters huddled in helpless enclosure.

The night burst with fire.

Mary Agnes sat up on her mattress, heart pounding in her throat. Sweat had soaked through her sleeping habit. The winter's chill bit through the damp cloth, into her skin. She lifted a hand to her face and found it wet with tears.

Something rattled and banged behind the wall to her left. Trouble in the bathroom. She wiped her eyes hastily on the sleeve of her sleeping habit, then hurried from her cell to help.

Sister Ann was wrestling with a toilet plunger. "Oh, Mary Agnes, thank goodness you've come. These old pipes—they're such a nuisance."

"The plumbing again?"

"It's almost enough to make me believe the pipes are cursed."

"I'll speak with Mr. Day about it when I see him at the next work hour," Mary Agnes said. "Until then, we'll all have to use the downstairs washroom and hope for the best."

She and Sister Ann both returned to their beds, but sleep didn't return to Mary Agnes. The moment she was alone again, the nightmare came back to mind. This was the same nightmare that had plagued her in Chicago, the same dark vision that had interrupted her waking prayers. The details had changed, of course. Now, the burning disc fell from the sky onto the bleak, pale desert of New Mexico rather than the high-rise spires of the city. But despite the setting, the dream was unchanged. Every haunting moment replayed itself in her mind, like a record whose needle has stuck in the wax—the terrible, compelling force drawing her through the night, the stone monolith with the stars watching slyly from above. And that monstrous, fiery *thing* that had come crashing down from the sky, eliminating the monastery, destroying all she knew in one sinister blow.

She was tired the next day during her hour of labor, and next to useless. Struggling for the words to explain the trouble with the upstairs bathroom, she stopped herself and pinched the bridge of her nose.

"I'm sorry, Harvey. I'm no good today. I didn't sleep well at all."

"That's all right, Sister." He leaned against the rusted wheel well of his truck. "I don't think I've had a good night's sleep since the summer."

"It's not just last night," she confessed. "I've been . . . distracted lately. You might have noticed."

Cautiously, he said, "I thought you might have been a bit tied up in your own thoughts, here and there."

Thoughts about him, Harvey assumed, with the usual pang of guilt that accompanied such musings. Ever since their first driving lesson, when she'd fled from the touch of his hand, Harvey had felt like a heel. He'd meant nothing salacious by the touch—hadn't meant to touch her at all, in fact; he'd only intended to help her shift the old car's gears. But it had been obvious from her reaction that he'd crossed a line. All these weeks, he had wanted to apologize—say or do something to make it right. Even bringing it up again seemed dangerous, the potential violation of another obscure religious vow. She was the best company he had, these days. Just about the only company that would tolerate him, with that blue slip pinned to his name. He would rather kiss a rattlesnake than push Mary Agnes farther away.

"I've been thinking so much about the saucer." She made the admission quietly, with a glance over her shoulder as if she feared another nun might hear.

Harvey perked up at that. "The saucer. You've heard about it?"

"Oh, yes. I've heard, all right."

Affecting a casualness he didn't feel, he probed at the conversation. "You don't think the whole idea of a flying saucer is bunk?"

Mary Agnes tossed her head. The black veil swung around her shoulders. "It's nothing I'm familiar with. But that doesn't mean it's bunk. The way *I* see it"—Harvey didn't understand the emphasis she put on that one little word—"there are plenty of things in this world I don't understand. Plenty of things that *no one* understands. And anyone who's not willing to call a mystery a mystery is foolish and arrogant and too puffed up on his own importance to . . ."

She pressed her lips together, reining in her mounting temper with evident will.

Harvey grinned in appreciation.

"Strange things in the sky are mentioned in the Bible," Mary Agnes said. "Did you know that?"

"I hope you won't think too poorly of me if I confess that I've never been much of a Bible reader."

"Ezekiel—a wheel inside a wheel that came from the north and hovered over the land. And in Exodus, the pillars of fire and smoke that led the children of Israel through the desert. Who's to say that God isn't mandating these same miracles even today? We think of them differently, that's all. Once, our forefathers called them angels or wheels in the sky. Today, we call them—"

"Weather balloons," Harvey said, chuckling.

She smiled at him.

He liked her smile. It made him think maybe the world wasn't such a desolate wilderness, after all.

He said, "I guess you get used to the unanswerable questions when you've taken up the religious life."

Her smile turned a little sad, at that.

Mary Agnes folded her arms, chilled despite the November sun, and looked away. "Not as used to it as you might think."

But the saucer wasn't bunk to her. And maybe she hadn't been as upset as Harvey had thought, that day in the car when he'd brushed her hand.

She might not think he was crazy, if—*if*—he told her what he'd seen that day in July. His eyes lingered a little longer on her face than he typically allowed. And when she met his eye once more and her smile returned, Harvey let himself feel it, right in the center of his heart.

CHAPTER
TWENTY-EIGHT

November 6, 1947

The fish didn't bite so late in the year, and anyway, by the time November came around, Roger could seldom get out to the lake at the magic hour, the low, lazy gold and quiet just before sunset and just after. It all happened too fast now—night coming down like a weight dropped, falling with a finality that took him by surprise, every time, and left him with too much darkness. There wasn't much he could do in the dark, besides walk the endless circles of his own thoughts, and he never liked the places that path led him to.

On that night, there would be no fishing, but he managed to reach the shore of Mirror Lake while there was still a little light left in the sky. The sunset huddled on the horizon, conspiring with the mountains, its tense back turned to the east, but night's advance was just slow enough that Roger could still see the land—the open ranges where the sheep ran, the eroded undulations of ancient hills, hardly bigger now than the ripples left in sand after the tides have washed over them, which he'd seen many times in the Pacific. He sat on the hood of his car, like he used to do as a kid. His dad would let him borrow the old Studebaker sometimes, and then he'd come out here to the lake and climb onto the nose of the car, where he could still feel the heat of its engine. He would listen to the crickets and the night birds and the wind moving like a tide moves across the desert. Like tonight. On nights like this one, he could almost believe that all the years of his life and the years of the war had never happened.

He hadn't been out there long when he heard the vibration of an approaching engine. Roger looked around. The car's headlights made him squint, but when the engine and the lights cut off, he blinked and saw that it was a cream-colored Plymouth, shiny and well-loved. A man got out of the car, tall and animated by that enviable vivacity of youth, a quick fluidity of movement. The kid had a regulation haircut. Someone from the base, Roger thought.

He considered sliding off the hood of his car and gathering some of his dignity, but then the kid said, "Mr. Campbell," and Roger realized it wasn't anyone from the base. They would have called him Colonel, for sure. He understood, then, who it must be—who would seek him out here, in the place where he came to be with his thoughts, or without his thoughts, as the mood suited him.

Roger allowed him to approach. He tried to remember his name, this boy whom Roger had forbidden his daughter to see. Johnny? No, Jim; that was it. And then he remembered that it was Jim Lucero, that he was Salvador Lucero's boy—a young man made fatherless by that greedy, still-living war.

"Evening, son," Roger said.

"Evening, Mr. Campbell."

Jim had his hands in his pockets. He shuffled his feet in the dust, looked anywhere but at Roger.

"How did you find me?" Roger said.

"Juanita Lopez—you know her? She's Betty's friend. She told me that Betty told her that you come out here to the lake sometimes."

More shuffling. The kid was searching for words, trying to choose them with care, and Roger admired that, the careful thought, because he knew, these days, how hard it was to think carefully.

"Look, Mr. Campbell, I know you don't like me much—"

That wasn't true. Roger didn't even know Jim. It was what he represented that Roger didn't like: Betty growing up, Betty removing herself beyond a father's reach. That wasn't this boy's fault. And yet Roger couldn't bring himself to say so.

"—but I hoped we might talk anyway," Jim said, "man to man."

It was a reasonable request. Roger granted it with a silent motion, an invitation to join him. After a moment of perplexity, Jim boosted himself up onto the hood of Roger's car and sat there beside him with his long legs stretched along the metal, watching the lake go blue-black in the cold twilight.

"Betty hasn't been herself lately," Jim said. "I mean, I don't know firsthand. I know you told Betty she couldn't see me anymore, and I've respected that, Mr. Campbell; I've kept away, though it's killed me to do it."

Except that night at the dance. Jim never found out whether Betty had told her dad about the sock hop. He didn't know whether Roger knew about Betty's troubles at all, though it seemed impossible that her own father could be that ignorant. It seemed as if the whole town knew.

"Some of Betty's friends have told me," Jim said. "They're worried about her. We're all worried about her. Isn't there something you can do—something we can all do—to help Betty be like her old self again?"

Roger considered the boy's words in cautious silence. How much did this Jim fellow know? About Betty, about what had happened to her—and what had caused it?

"You know I only want to keep my girl safe," he said.

"Yes, sir, I know. I understand that. I'm no danger to Betty, I swear—"

"There are bigger things out there than boys—men. More dangerous things. I could beat the hell out of you, son, and I wouldn't hesitate to do it."

Jim offered a half-frightened smile. He couldn't tell whether Roger was joking or not. Neither could Roger.

"But you're the least of my worries," he went on. "Bigger things. More dangerous things. Things a father can't do anything about." *Things a father can't begin to understand.*

"If you could just see your way to letting her apply to those colleges," Jim said. "I think it would do wonders for her—"

"No. No, you don't see what I see. You don't understand." But how to explain it without sounding like a fool, without sounding like he was as weak and helpless as he knew himself to be? "I can't protect her if she's out there, in some other place far away. I'd never get to her fast enough, if . . ."

If what? Jim wanted to ask. But he looked at the man through the dim remains of daylight, and he thought he saw the answer. Roger's stare was distant and too full of knowing. Jim thought his own dad might have come home looking the same way, if his dad had come home.

"If something bad comes out of the sky," Jim said quietly.

Roger met his eye and held it. "It was only a balloon."

"Then why . . . ," Jim began.

He didn't finish the question. *Why did it make Betty bleed?* Because he didn't know whether Roger knew, and he wouldn't betray his girl's trust, not for anything in the world.

Jim cleared his throat, tried a different tack. "Respectfully, sir, I would have thought the same thing, once—that it was a weather balloon. I would have said as much to anyone. I *have* said it."

"But not anymore."

"No, sir, not now."

Roger allowed the moment to hang, the pause to grow heavy with meaning.

Jim proceeded with all the care he could muster, working his way around the brittle edges of the man who sat beside him.

"I guess there are bigger things out there," the boy said, "things maybe none of us can do much about. I believe that now. There was a time when I thought there was nothing we couldn't know, nothing we couldn't explain and, well, *control*, I guess. I mean the Army, they were in control—or that's what I thought. And scientists. Engineers like my dad was. I don't think so anymore."

"Why not?" Roger asked. "What changed?"

Jim waited, working through his head, trying to find the best way to explain. Finally, he decided that seeing was best. Your eyes were easier to believe than any doctrine or command. "Hang on," he said, and slid from the hood of Roger's car.

Roger heard the door of the Plymouth open again, and soon the boy was back, standing at his side. Jim held something up for Roger to take, something long and thin, faintly luminous, even in the newborn night. Roger didn't want to touch it. And wanted nothing more; the object called to him in the loud, commanding voice of mystery. When he took it, he knew at once where it had come from. It had the same feel as the artifact that was still hidden, even now, in a lead box under the floor of his closet—weightless, thin as paper, with a curious tension and substance that resisted all force, even as it was, broken apart and fragmented.

"Where did you get this?" There was no need to ask. Nevertheless, Roger had to know, needed the confirmation like water.

"Brazel's ranch."

Roger nodded. He didn't take his eyes off the metal. And now he could see, asserting itself through the gloom, the faint tracery of purple along its surface. He tipped the piece this way and that, trying to make out the markings, but they were written in no language Roger had seen, not even during his time in the Pacific. A chill ran through him. A chill subsumed every part of him and replaced all that he'd known and all that he'd feared, blanked everything inside him until nothing was left but this cold acceptance of the inevitable.

"They're keeping something from us, aren't they?" Jim said quietly. "Something important. Something that . . ." Again, he stopped himself. He'd nearly said, *Something that can hurt Betty.*

"They have our best interests at heart," Roger said. "National security. That's the most important thing—this nation, this life, holding together. The world as we know it holding together. You've read about the bombs, or heard about them on the radio, but you don't know—you don't know what I know, what I learned during the war. Those damn bombs are more powerful than anything you can imagine, son, more dangerous than any monster you could dream up in a thousand years of dreaming. We can't risk it."

"Can't risk what?"

"Our enemies—the Soviets, and anyone else who might like to come up against us—our enemies getting the jump. Outclassing us with what they can make, what they can do."

Yet even as he spoke, Roger could feel the rapid rhythm of the chain, the dominoes falling faster. Every night the vast, empty desert was shaken by thunder from the sky—the fighter planes of the war replaced by jet engines, barriers of speed and velocity broken like a hammer to glass, and the tests out at White Sands and Trinity that kept going, more tests all the time, greater bursts of destruction, whiter heat, weapons that could eradicate life in radiuses wider than a city, in rings of fire that only ever grew. Mushroom clouds rising into the atmosphere. The war hadn't ended in '45, and he knew now that it would never end. It was a beast made of riveted metal, of engine and fire and speed, and it would go on eating the world as long as there were men left alive to feed it.

Whatever had crashed in the desert that summer, it was part of the war. It had come from the war. Everything was part of the war now, and came from it, and would live forever inside the hot sphere of its consequence and its endless rebirth. The military with its relentless invention; the wealth of this victorious nation; this small, unassuming town; the God its people worshiped; and Roger himself, and his family, his children, whom he was powerless to protect because they were already in the beast's belly, already swallowed and consumed.

"Mr. Campbell," the boy said. "Are you okay?"

Roger shook off his black thoughts. That was a thing he'd learned how to do—shake them off for a while, until they came again.

He handed the metal back to Jim. "Don't let anyone see that. You understand?"

"No, sir, I won't."

"I respect you, son. It takes some guts, to talk to a girl's father like this, man to man."

Jim didn't know what to say about that. He closed his fist around the strip of metal, and it bent in his grip, sprang back to its usual shape when he released it again.

"It'll be all right with me," Roger said, "if you come by to take Betty out sometime. Maybe tomorrow night. Maybe you can make her happy again. What do you say?"

Jim smiled. "I'd like that, sir. Thank you."

They went their separate ways, each returning to the town through a close, heavy darkness with only their headlights to guide them. Supper was ready by the time Roger got home, and he kissed his wife and ruffled the dark heads of his little boys with a lighter heart than he'd had for months or maybe years.

But as he ate, the black thoughts returned, faster than they usually did. He kept thinking about the metal that Lucero kid had shown him, the strange purple scrawl along its surface. It was a thing no one should possess—no one but the Army, who after all had everyone's best interests at heart. Who had a better shot than anyone at keeping such a dangerous secret and holding this fragile world together.

The next day, when he arrived at the base, Roger filed a report. That was what he was supposed to do, what he was expected to do as a loyal member of this military, a loyal citizen of the victorious United States. Young Jim Lucero would get in trouble for harboring a piece of the wreckage, but not too much trouble, nothing serious. And the secret would remain a secret, this quiet existence would sail on, carried by its easy current, unthreatened, unaware.

By the time Jim came to fetch Betty for their date, Roger was feeling rotten, even though he knew he'd done the right thing, the thing his superiors had told him to do. Because he hadn't said a word about what was hidden in the lead box under the floor of the closet. He couldn't give it up, that fragment of a nightmare, that proof of a greater power than all the powers he chose to believe in.

CHAPTER TWENTY-NINE

November 7, 1947

As Juanita was walking home from school that Friday, she spotted Betty coming out of the soda fountain, hustling up the sidewalk in her felt coat, shoulders hunched and collar turned up as if she could hide from the world.

"Betty!"

At Juanita's shout, Betty only walked faster. Juanita ran to catch up with her friend. She wasn't above running, not where Betty was concerned.

"I haven't seen you for three days," Juanita said. "Where have you been?"

Betty shrugged. "Not in school."

"Gee, Betty, your grades are going to slip. You can't let yourself go now, in junior year! What about college?"

"Oh, forget it! My dad's never going to let me go to college, and now I'm grounded, so I can't even see Jim, and he was the only one who was helping me write my letters, he's the only one who understands—"

When she saw Juanita's hurt expression, Betty reined in her temper.

"I'm sorry. It's not that you *don't* understand, Nita. It's just that . . . well . . . you believe, don't you?"

"Believe?"

Betty didn't know how to say it, didn't want to give words to the terrible truth, which would only make it stick fast, with no hope of fading into dream or rumor or misunderstanding. She held up a hand, palm raised to show the faint pink scar at its center.

"What, you don't believe?" Juanita said. "An honest-to-goodness miracle happened to you, and you think it was hokey?"

"I don't know," Betty muttered, hunching again inside her coat. "I don't know what it is. Nobody does; that's my point."

"You should go see those nuns."

"Nuns," Betty scoffed.

"Ask them for help."

"A fat bunch of help they already gave me. What could they do for me now?"

"Pray for you," Juanita said.

"Pray! What good does that do? Praying and saints and all that—it's corny, Juanita, it's nothing but superstition from the olden days, before people had any sense. Before we knew what the world was really like."

Juanita turned a startled look on Betty. "You think we know what the world is like now?"

That cut so close to the raw, tender truth that Betty went lofty and cold. "This is a modern age. We get our answers from science, not from religion. Jim said there's got to be a scientific explanation for all of this—for the saucer and . . . what happened to me. And he's right, I know he is. Answers don't come from nuns and saints. They come from modern thought, real thought—don't be such a square."

"Just think about it, will you? Maybe you won't get anywhere, but it doesn't hurt to try."

By that time, they'd reached the corner where they usually parted. Some kids had gathered on the far side of the street, boys and girls clustered together, passing a cigarette back and forth and coughing now and then. They all paused when they noticed Betty, stared at her in open curiosity or contempt.

"I hate them," Betty said. "I hate this, all of it, the staring and the whispers and people thinking I'm a miracle when I'm not."

Juanita hugged her, before Betty could flinch away. "You're still my best friend, no matter what. Even if you are a miracle."

They went their separate ways, but Betty could still feel the eyes of the other kids on her—the eyes of all of Roswell, from Main Street clear to her own neighborhood, sticking like a dagger in her back. When she reached home, there were more flowers and candles and things in the yard, and a fury hotter and wilder than any she'd ever felt came crashing up from inside. Before she could think better, she rampaged among the shrine, right out in the open where all the neighbors could see, kicking the candles into the street, stomping on the flowers, yelling with a wordless rage that didn't make her feel one bit better.

When her better sense caught up with her anger, she stilled herself and saw that one item remained in the yard, untrampled—a figure of Our Lady of Guadalupe, smaller than the one her mother had given her. A wave of guilt swept in to smother her rage. She snatched the little statue up and hurried to the end of the street, to the place where the dry ground dropped into a steep ditch. The Spring River had almost dried for the winter, lying along the bottom of the ditch in mirror stretches of still water, and all the willows had shed their leaves. Betty huddled among the roots of the biggest tree, gripping the tiny saint in both her fists.

She thought: *I might as well try it. Nothing else has worked.*

She forced her furious hands to soften and open, turned the statue over, considering it from every angle. How funny, that she'd been raised a Catholic, but had no idea how to pray. Prayer seemed like the kind of thing that ought to come naturally to a girl who'd taken her first Communion so long ago she could barely remember it now. But really, she'd spent more of her time in church thinking about her school assignments, or boys, or what had happened the day before when the gang had gathered at Vic's Drive-In, and if she ever heard a word Father

263

Kerry said to the congregation, that was enough right there to count as a miracle.

Besides, it didn't seem likely that prayer would do her much good now. Not after the way things had gone with Father Kerry and the bishop. She felt like a perfect dope—she should have seen this outcome long before it arrived, should have seen it when that nun Mary Agnes had suggested an investigation. When had any priest—any adult, for that matter—believed what a girl had to say?

Hey you, Betty said silently to the statue. *Is anybody in there? Do you care at all? Isn't anyone going to tell me what's happening to me, and why?*

The Virgin of Guadalupe gazed placidly back, her hands clasped around a secret she would never reveal.

Betty released a disgusted sigh. She dropped the statue among the willow roots and climbed slowly up the side of the ditch. All the gravity of the world pulled at her, and she would have let it take her, would have fallen into the riverbed if the mud hadn't looked so damn cold.

When she emerged from the ditch, she could only stare. Jim's cream Plymouth was parked at the curb, right outside her house. And there he was, stepping out of the car, already smiling at her in that way that made her feel like all her insides were melting.

"Hey, stranger," Jim called. "Long time no see."

Betty scrambled back to the street. She tried to put herself in order, brushing dirt and dead leaves from her coat and jeans, patting frantically at her hair. She realized she hadn't showered for days—why bother, when she hadn't been going to school?—and she wondered with a mortified flush whether she smelled like a wet dog, or worse. Maybe it wasn't too late to crawl back into the ditch and hide there until the end of time.

"What are you doing here?" she blurted.

"I came to see you, of course."

"But my folks—"

"I had that talk with your dad," Jim said. "You know, he's an all right guy."

She crossed the road, ignoring the candles and flowers she had kicked there, and stood beside him, silent and embarrassed and hopelessly, desperately thrilled.

"Your old man understands you better than you think he does," Jim said. "Anyway, he sure seems worried about you. He's pretty eager to see you get back to your old self again."

"Fat chance of that."

"He's willing to lift your restriction," Jim said. "In fact, he said he'd like it if I took you out tonight."

Betty withered. "I can't go out to Vic's or anyplace like that. You don't know what it's been like, Jim. I guess some of the other kids heard about that joke of an interview I had with the bishop. They've been awful to me ever since, watching me all the time and whispering about me behind my back, as if I can't see them doing it. Nobody believes me, Jim. I can't face them. I . . . I haven't been in school since Tuesday. My folks don't know I've been truant."

"I know you haven't been in school. Juanita called me yesterday afternoon. She told me all about it. That's how I got the idea to have that talk with your dad, see if I couldn't convince him that you need your pals now more than ever."

Betty wiped a tear on her sleeve. "Juanita's a good friend."

"She's been awfully worried about you. We all are—everyone who cares about you."

His words struck Betty with a fresh wave of pain. It seemed like the biggest lie she'd ever heard, that anyone cared about her now. Father Kerry didn't. And that stodgy old bishop who'd led the investigation— he'd barely even looked at Betty, hadn't seemed to believe that *she* was real, let alone her story.

And yet here was the evidence that she was loved. Jim had come to dig her out of her hole. And Juanita had called to make him do it. And her dad . . .

"What do you say?" Jim said. "Let's go for a drive in the old hot rod."

"I don't know, Jim."

"We won't go anywhere near Vic's. We won't go anyplace where you might run into other kids—not till you're ready. Deal?"

"Okay. But give me a minute to make myself look decent. I'm a real fright."

Jim waited in his car while Betty showered. When she returned to the yard, she'd freshened herself up in a clean pair of blue jeans, the cuffs rolled to her knees, and a smart fair isle sweater. Her dark hair had been tamed by a crimson ribbon. To Jim, she didn't look one bit prettier than she had when she'd come creeping out of that ditch, disheveled and red around the eyes. She was, would always be, the most beautiful thing he laid eyes on. He realized now that he'd thought so on that winter night, in what felt like another lifetime, when he'd heard her crying and had looked up to find a little, black-haired girl in a red pixie cap, vivid and isolated among the white blur of falling snow.

Jim opened the passenger door for her, which made Betty feel like a movie star, even in her blue jeans. She guessed not everything was quite as bad as it seemed.

They cruised well beyond the town, following the sun as it vanished in the western sky. The dusk of early winter usually came on quickly, but that evening, an echo of the sunset lingered warm and low along the gentle roll of the horizon. Doris Day came crackling over Jim's radio. Betty dared to scoot a little closer to him on the bench seat, and when he put his arm around her shoulders, she ducked her head and smiled.

"I hope you'll get back into school," he said. "It would be a real shame for your grades to slip before you apply to those colleges."

"Oh, Jim, you know I want to go, but my dad won't allow it." It was all she could do to fight back her tears. "It isn't fair. If I can learn enough about the world, I might learn what's the matter with me. But I won't learn anything new here in Roswell, and I won't be able to go anywhere else unless you can talk my dad into that, too."

"There isn't a thing the matter with you."

She pulled back a little, so she could look up into his face. "How can you say that? You saw what happened at the dance."

"You're still the same person."

Betty slumped against him. "I'm not so sure about that. I don't know what to make of this—everything that's happened to me. You said once that there's a scientific explanation for everything. There isn't for this."

"Maybe not yet." Jim gave a fond laugh. "Maybe you'll discover it at university. The scientific breakthrough of the century! Just think of that."

"If there's an explanation, then there's got to be some meaning. A reason I can understand. That's the trouble. I can't figure out what this *means*, what purpose there is to . . ."

She didn't know what to call it, how to discuss the thing that had happened to her. She didn't even think she wanted to discuss it—not after the way the investigation had gone.

"Nothing seems to mean anything now," she said. "Not anymore. Once, I thought there was some sense to life. I thought everything fit together like a story, everything happened for a reason, even if I couldn't see it. But I can't make any sense of this, Jim. If the bishop and Father Kerry believed me, that would have been one thing. If they had some answers, even really out-there answers, I wouldn't feel bad about it now. But they threw up their hands and walked away. Where does that leave me?"

Jim pulled her closer. She rested her head against his shoulder, which made his heart pound, and every nerve and cell of him was aware of her presence, the rightness of her presence, how easy it was to be with her.

He said, "I felt that way, after my dad died. Like there wasn't any sense left, like it wasn't the same world, and I didn't know how to get the old one back again."

They drove on through the lingering twilight, the lonesome rose-colored peace of the evening. The road lifted smoothly and dropped again, following the long, shallow curves of the ancient earth, like a sound wave fading into silence.

After a while, Betty said, "Did you ever? Did you get the old world back?"

He thought about it. A stretch of flat pasture opened along the crest of a rise, and he slowed his car, pulled onto the gravel at the side of the road.

"I guess no world ever comes back again, once it's gone," he finally said. "But I found a new one, so it doesn't bother me anymore. Not as much as it used to."

"I'd give anything to find some sense in all this mess."

"That's the trick. You *find* meaning by making it. That's what I learned, after Dad died. I decided I was going to carry on with his work, do all the things he can't do now. See, there might have been no good reason for him to die, but there's meaning to it now. Because I decided what to make of the loss. I decided I could do something about it."

He cut the engine. Betty looked out the window at the open pasture, flat and high above the subtle desert. "What are we doing here?" It wasn't the kind of place where anyone would go to park.

Jim opened his door. "Come on. I've got a surprise for you."

She scooted across the bench seat and followed him out into the cold bite of the wind. Night was closing rapidly, but the sky still held enough of a delicate light that every line and angle of the pasture stood out with a kind of lucid and insistent detail, the twisted, bare clumps of sage and the wire fence that ran for miles along the road.

Betty hugged herself against the chill, watched with growing curiosity as Jim opened the trunk of his car. When she looked down into the hollow of the trunk, she gave a cry of disbelief. There was the old Good Brothers' Guff, the model airplane they'd made ages ago.

"I can't believe you still have it," Betty said.

Jim smiled. He wouldn't have gotten rid of the plane for anything, not for all the money in the world. "You think it still works?"

He helped Betty scramble between the lines of barbed wire, then he passed the Guff across the fence to her. She paraded it into the sage, holding it high so the cold wind tugged at its wings.

Together, they found a bare patch of ground long enough to act as a runway. Betty set the Guff on its wheels while Jim banged the radio controller against his palm, trying to jar its old wiring back into place. When he nodded, Betty stepped back. He threw the switch. The propeller sputtered to life, and the plane began to crawl over the dim ground.

Faster and faster the Guff moved, and Jim and Betty ran together in its wake. When the plane lifted into the air, they howled, and the Guff skimmed beyond the ragged reach of sagebrush and creosote bush, up into the fading purple sky.

They watched the plane rise. The raspy whine of its engine dwindled to an insect's buzz. Betty held on to Jim's arm as the Guff arced and rolled through the air. She kept her eyes on its flight until she became aware of a new and significant stillness that said Jim was no longer watching the plane.

When she looked at him, he bent and kissed her. The feel of it ran through her like the burn of a religious ecstasy, a slow flame that spread from the inside out. She thought if she opened her eyes, she would see them both surrounded by a halo of fire. She understood, then, what it meant to pray. If she ever wanted to do it.

CHAPTER THIRTY

November 11, 1947

The hour of None, the midday prayer, dragged as slow as eternity. In the choir room, Mary Agnes sang with her sisters, and knelt before the altar to pray, but as the beads of her rosary passed between her fingers, she asked herself why. Why, these years of seclusion, these rituals, this God?

The question came not in a clap of thunder or a wave of grief, the way she had sometimes imagined a disastrous unmaking would come, but with the feel of a friend sitting close beside her, laying a patient hand on her shoulder, settling into a content and receptive silence.

Why?

In the middle of the abbess's prayer, Mary Agnes looked up. A slow, deep-rooted horror had beset her, strong enough that she might have gasped if it had taken her unawares. But she had seen this coming. For the past week and more, since the day she had marched to Father Kerry's rectory and challenged him, face-to-face, some part of her had known that the question would come, the doubt would come. The separation would come.

She looked past the bowed heads of her sisters, beyond the gilded cross and the painted images of saints, through the window to the world beyond. The elm trees stood bare in the clear, blue light of late autumn. Between the lines of their trunks, the sky was deep and cloudless, and she knew she would see, any moment, a giant of metal and flame—a great, burning, mechanical thing cutting through the peace in a red slash, trailing an apocalyptic light. But the wind only stirred the tops of the elms. And Mother Catherine's prayer went on, and Mary Agnes allowed the beads to slip through her fingers, as they always had before.

With her sisters, she lifted her voice in song. The words and the melody came to her without effort or thought, but spurred by that question, that single word, her mind delved deep into her past. Had there ever been a time when she'd found fulfillment in this religious life, in this church—or had she done, all along, what she'd been expected to do? As the song of praise rose around her, she examined her twelve years of service, and the years before that, when she'd been Patricia, the woman and the girl and the child. And she didn't know. She couldn't tell whether this life that had enfolded her was real and her own, or whether it belonged to someone else, whether it was any more substantial than a dream.

Yet now, at last, her faith was unshakable. She had found within herself a belief so vast and burning that she simply couldn't convince herself that there'd been a time when it had been otherwise. Logically, rationally, she knew—she remembered—that once she had lacked this very fire, that once faith had been a thing ill-defined and only halfway glimpsed from the corner of her eye. A true, earnest belief in the power of God hadn't come to Mary Agnes until she'd seen the holy sign for herself—until Betty Campbell had raised her red palms. If indeed God was the power behind such a display. If God was the right name for what she *knew*, now, existed—this sublime force that ran in an endless current from one heart to another, among all things, erasing the borders between people and the things they witnessed, between institutions and hierarchies and earth and sky, and real and unreal, so that everything reflected the All, and where she'd thought an edge might be found, she found instead only light. Like the metal she'd held in her hand. The boundaries of itself blurring into the background, its face shining back all the faces. Every explanation she'd heard from her church, from the cradle until now, seemed inadequate to describe or explain the greatness she knew and felt—an all-encompassing divinity too large and primal to be contained by ritual or rule. Too holy to care about the orders and hierarchies of men. That was the God she worshipped. That was the sacred light that had come, at last, to fill her heart.

The light had filled her enough that she had stormed into Father Kerry's rectory. Nothing had checked her that day; to throw her defiance in the priest's face had seemed as natural as drawing breath. She could scarcely believe now that she'd done it. And somehow, it seemed inevitable to her that she would. She *must* do it, for how else could any soul respond when the truth one knows is discarded before one's eyes? Mary Agnes knew what she saw that day in the Campbell home. She knew what it meant. That personal revelation of the divine force was holier to her now than any ancient rite of the church. Betty's affliction was a demonstration of the grand mystery that moved through all things. Father Kerry and Bishop Cote were mere men. What could men ever know of God?

The moment these dangerous thoughts found a shape in her mind—the moment they came to her as more than feelings, as *words*—a barrage of guilt nearly suffocated her. What if she was wrong—about Betty, about everything? After all, Mary Agnes was merely a woman. She was no better at discerning the truth than the priest and the bishop were. Surely Mother Catherine had been right when she'd said that these men, ordained by God to lead with wisdom and discernment, wouldn't steer this church into falsehood. The church itself couldn't have endured all these long ages if it was simply wrong. No establishment could have survived the flood of history with its traditions intact.

Guilt quickly gave way to anxiety, then to full-blown fear. Before the hymn of praise was half over, Mary Agnes had fallen silent, stricken by her own cold certainty that she would pay a price for her outburst at Father Kerry. The priest hadn't mentioned her impropriety in the days since the incident. He had performed the Mass for the sisters with his usual air of patient service. All the same, Mary Agnes felt like a fool and a sinner now—for behaving with such defiance, and for doubting

God's true and enduring church. How easily the Adversary worked his mischief, how gentle was the touch of his deceiving hand.

Mary Agnes ought to make a confession, ease her soul of this burden. But that would require confessing to Father Kerry himself. The very thought mortified her.

A thought that belonged to Patricia rose to the surface of her mind: Why should she admit that she had behaved inappropriately to the priest? He knew; he was there.

Then a thought that was hers, the nun's: confession would relieve the pain of sin, of doubt, of this sharp conflict that pulled her in every direction at once. Only through the methods of the church, tried and perfected through the centuries, could she draw closer to God.

She didn't know which voice to heed—that of the obedient sister, or the voice of this too-free, self-determining woman, Patricia, whom she'd thought long abandoned and forgotten.

She was trapped now in her dream—the nightmare of the burning disc that had plunged down from the Heavens. She must be, now, inside that dream. Nothing else made sense, nothing else could feel this way, and she expected at any moment to smell the stench of a chemical fire, to feel the heat of an imminent destruction. The monastery would be crushed under the weight of a fallen angel, with Mary Agnes inside. And she would be glad for an end to this suffering.

At the close of None, the sisters returned their prayer stoles to the closet and filed silently from the choir. The time of daily labor had come. Usually, afternoons lifted Mary Agnes in her spirit, for these were the two and a half hours she would spend in Harvey's company. Today, she was so distracted by her own dark thoughts that she scarcely managed to greet him when he arrived in his rusted pickup truck.

"I thought we'd tackle that upstairs bathroom for good," he said. "Get the pressure in that supply line fixed once and for all, so you sisters have no more trouble with it through the winter."

She gave a vague answer, and Harvey handed her the tool chest to carry. He noticed that Mary Agnes was distant, nearly distraught—of course he noticed, for her every word and gesture leaped in his aware-ness and his memory as if she were the only other person on God's earth, an untouchable Eve in a walled garden paradise. But there was no use in upsetting her further by asking what was wrong. When Mary Agnes wanted to talk about whatever was eating her, she would talk. That was her way, and Harvey knew her ways.

The bathroom wasn't large. Like all bathrooms in old houses, it was mostly an afterthought, a cramped cave of old, white tiles and jutting fixtures. Harvey had installed the shower himself, and it took up nearly half the space, so that he and Mary Agnes had to move carefully around one another, pressing and sliding and brushing sleeve of habit against back or thigh or the exposed skin of Harvey's arm. They did their best to work as quietly as the task would allow, for many of the other sisters were nearby, answering letters in the cells just down the hall or adjacent to the bathroom's walls.

Mary Agnes watched Harvey while they worked that day. Watched him openly, in a way she had never allowed herself to do, taking in his physical form, its striking capability and power, the compelling rug-gedness of his face, the dusting of stubble along his jaw. As he reached behind the toilet, frowning in concentration, she allowed her eyes to linger on the golden color of his arm—his skin, bared to her hungry attention—and when the sleeve of his T-shirt rose a little higher, the line that marked the boundary between his tanned skin and his pale, private, unmarked shoulder sent a rush of dizziness through her.

She was drawn to him. *Wanted* him with a longing she hadn't allowed herself to feel since she had been Patricia, who had loved John. On this day of catastrophic clarity, she saw this more starkly than she'd seen everything else. And why shouldn't she desire him? She had found more connection with this man than she'd found with any sister of her order.

"Hand me the crescent wrench," Harvey said.

Mary Agnes blinked herself out of her thoughts. She bent over the toolbox. "Which one?"

"Crescent."

She grabbed the first wrench she saw, held it out, but Harvey gave a little laugh and said, "That's a channel lock."

"I don't know—"

"It's all right," he said, rising from the tiles, "I'll show you."

And then he was brushing by. She leaned back, against the sink, but he was so close, so close as he passed her that they were practically in one another's arms. She could feel the warmth of his chest through her habit, and the warmth of his eyes as he looked down at her, and paused, the two of them face-to-face, mere inches apart.

Mary Agnes raised her eyes. Harvey was watching her with a half-startled expression. He could feel it, too—the fire of need and belonging that pulled them together, even when they were apart.

She tipped her head back, desperate for the kiss that would fall upon her vows and leave them a smoking ruin, the kiss that would set her free. Ever so slightly, Harvey bent to her—and hesitated. She could feel the presence of her sisters, their patient and obedient rhythms behind these very walls.

The bell tolled for Vespers, the evening prayer. The sound of it came shivering between them, and Harvey straightened a little, caught his breath.

Mary Agnes slid away from him, slowly, deliberately, holding his gaze.

"I must go," she said, "and pray." Though she didn't know what good prayer might do her now.

Harvey watched her disappear down the upstairs hall. She didn't look back at him, not once, but he could still feel that fire between them, a line of invisible light, tying him to a reality he hadn't known since the summer, since the saucer, since everything had come crashing down.

CHAPTER
THIRTY-ONE

November 14, 1947

When Jim asked Betty to a drive-in movie for a Friday-night date, she hesitated. He had convinced her to attend school again—for the sake of her college applications only. The other kids still whispered about Betty behind her back, and she could feel their stares, but at least no one had made any snide or insulting comments to her face. And Juanita had been a dear, fending off the cattier girls with her skewering looks so Betty never had to speak to them at all.

Still, venturing back into the town's social scene was a different prospect. At the soda fountain, at the roller-skating rink, at the drive-in theater, there were no teachers or principal to keep the teenagers of Roswell in line. Betty couldn't help but feel that Jim was asking her to accompany him into a jungle, its unseen shadows populated by fierce-eyed, predatory creatures. And she was their helpless prey.

But she couldn't expect to live the rest of her life shuttling between her bedroom and her classrooms. Even if she swayed her dad to the cause and got herself accepted into a university, there was more than a year and a half to go before her high school graduation. And she hadn't even sent off her applications yet; the hope that college life would spirit her out of Roswell for good was nothing more than a dream.

She would have to be seen in public again, one way or another. And doing so on Jim Lucero's arm—or in his slick, enviable hot rod—was better than a girl in her situation could hope for.

She regretted her decision from the moment Jim pulled into a space at the drive-in theater. She felt like a goldfish in a bowl, trapped where everyone could stare. The eyes of her peers cut into her, an invasion whether it was malicious or mild.

But once the film began and the kids settled into their cars to watch, her sense of unease ebbed. She even found herself enjoying the movie.

The story was about an astronomer who thought he was tracking a meteorite as it fell through the planet's atmosphere. But when he visited the crash site, he found a spaceship instead.

"No wonder they picked this film to show in Roswell," Jim said wryly.

As the astronomer crept closer to the smashed rocket, someone hooted from among the parked cars, "They filmed this flick out at Brazel's ranch!"

Laughter erupted among the audience. More jeers and smart-aleck comments flew around the lot.

"Come on," Jim muttered. "We can't even hear our own speaker."

"They'll quiet down in a minute," Betty said.

But the crowd didn't quiet. As the story played out across the flickering screen—the astronomer leaping back in surprise as a survivor of the crash emerged from the wreckage, sporting a bizarre Martian costume—the kids at the drive-in only seemed to grow more fervent with a wild, mischievous energy.

One boy even climbed onto the roof of his car, raising his fists as he shouted advice to the astronomer on the screen. "Call up the Army, buddy! Tell 'em you found a weather balloon!"

Jim leaned head and shoulders out his window, nearly knocking the portable speaker from his door. "Give it a rest, Johnson! Some of us are trying to watch the movie, here."

Betty clutched at his arm. "Don't draw their attention, Jim. I don't want to—"

There was no time to say more. A fist thudded into Jim's door. He turned from Betty in alarm, looked up to find Mitch Kromski leering down at him. Mitch had on his leather jacket, the Hawks patch displayed over his heart.

"You got a problem, Lucero?"

"Not with you, Mitch. Take a hike."

"'Take a hike,' says the guy who was too chicken to show up for the last drag race."

"I was busy," Jim said. "Mind your own business."

"Too busy to race for his friends. Well, the Hawks mopped the floor with the A-Bombs. Probably better you didn't see it. You would have cried more than you did when your old man died."

Betty gasped at the boy's cruel words, and Mitch ducked a little lower, peering into the Plymouth's shadows.

"Well, well, well," he said, "what do we have here? It's Roswell's own little miracle."

Jim's fist tightened on the handle of his door. "You'd better turn around and walk away right this minute, Kromski."

Mitch ignored him. "Look, everybody, the holy virgin of Chaves County has finally decided to grace us with her presence." His leering grin was all teeth, pointed like an animal's. "Or is she a virgin, these days? Guess we know what's been keeping Lucero too busy to face the Hawks like a real man."

Jim bulled his door open, knocking Mitch into the side of the next parked car. Betty gave a yell of dismay, tried to catch Jim's arm, but he was too fast. In an instant, he was outside, pulling Mitch up by the lapels.

Betty scrambled out of the car, too late to hold Jim back. A single blow sent Mitch sprawling on the ground, holding his jaw with a glassy, dazed expression.

Jim's knuckles hurt like hell, but there was a whirlwind inside him, roaring to drown out the pain. He advanced on Mitch, ready to kick him hard in the ribs. Betty's arms locked around his waist.

"Cut it out, Jim! He's not worth it!"

There was such fear in her voice that his rage deflated in an instant. Betty hadn't wanted to make a scene. She had wanted a quiet, normal night out, and what had Jim gone and done?

His body slackened. Betty dared to loosen her grip. If she'd felt the eyes of the town on her before, the sensation was a hundred times worse now. The whole parking lot was holding its breath, waiting to see what she and Jim would do next.

He put his arm around her shoulders, turned away from the writhing, half-stunned Mitch. "Let's get out of here, Betty. You're right—he's not worth it."

Mockery followed Jim as he pulled out of the lot.

"I'm sorry, Betty. I shouldn't have lost my cool. Mitch is such an ass; he always steams me. And when he said all that about you—"

Betty took his hand. "It was nice of you, to stand up for me that way. I don't think many guys would have done it. Not with the way all the kids are treating me at school."

"Are they still on your case?"

Betty nodded. "I can get through it, though. Once I've been accepted at one college or another, it won't matter anymore. Then it'll only be a matter of time before I can forget every jerk in Roswell. Never see any of them again."

The drive-in theater was a mile or two outside town. Jim's headlights cut through the darkness, illuminating some large object at the side of the road, far ahead.

"What's that?" Betty asked.

"Looks like someone's truck broke down."

Jim slowed the Plymouth as they approached. Sure enough, an old model pickup—once green, now more rust than any real color—was stalled at the shoulder. The hood was raised, and Jim could see a man working on the engine.

"I'll see if I can give him a hand," he said.

He pulled over. The old truck was idling, but not smoothly. Its exhaust pipe sputtered clouds of smoke.

The man with the pickup leaned around his vehicle to see who had come. In a flash of fear, Betty recognized him—the same man who'd come to the door that night in July. Her father's friend from the Army. The one who'd made her hands itch and burn with his mere presence.

She grabbed Jim's wrist. "Please, no!"

"Betty, what the heck's the matter with you?"

"Don't stop, Jim, please."

At that moment, the truck gave a renewed rumble, and its driver closed the hood. He offered Jim a friendly wave—one that said no help was needed.

"We're in luck," Jim said, mystified. "Guess he's all right, after all."

He pulled back onto the road. The Plymouth continued its smooth sweep into the town. Betty sagged against the back of the seat, watching through the side mirror as the truck and its unsettling driver vanished quickly in the darkness.

"I *would* have stopped," Jim said, "if he hadn't fixed it on his own. I can't just leave a guy stranded."

Betty knew it was an invitation for her to explain her reaction—even a demand. But this hadn't been a thing she could explain, not from the start.

"You believe me, don't you?" she asked. "About what's happening to me, and about the flying saucer."

"Of course I do, Betty."

The truth was, Jim might not have believed her once. He would have clung to his old insistence that everything had a rational explanation, even this. Not for all the money in the world would he have said so. He couldn't bear the thought of hurting her—and anyway, the past didn't matter when he believed so wholly now. That scrap of metal he'd found at the ranch, with its odd purple writing . . . it had changed everything.

The one thing he still knew, without a speck of doubt, was that Betty was telling the truth. He'd seen the reaction in her hands and feet with his own eyes. He'd be a fool not to believe, after that.

"What do you suppose it was, really? The saucer. Where do you think it came from?"

Her voice was plaintive and small, and huddled as she was against the back of the seat, Jim felt that she was very far away from him.

For a while, he couldn't even think up the words to answer. He'd heard every rumor the town could offer about the unknown object that had fallen from the sky. Those stories, too, had inverted everything Jim had thought he'd known about what was possible and what was not.

"I've heard a few things," he finally admitted, vague and hesitant. "Kids' dads in the Army who talked more than they should have."

"Tell me," she said.

"I don't know if any of it's true. And there are honor codes at my school, you know. We aren't supposed to do things like gossip. They can kick me out for it, and that would put me in real danger of losing my scholarship—"

"I won't tell anyone," Betty said. "But I've got to know what that thing was, Jim. There's got to be an answer somewhere."

Because the pain in her voice cut him to his heart, he relented. "Whatever the Army took off those ranches, it wasn't a weather balloon. Those photos in the newspaper, with the foil and the little sticks and Major Marcel—that was all planted. A setup."

"How do you know?"

"Some of my buddies from school—their dads were involved. Helped lay the whole thing out and brought in reporters from the papers so they could see what the Army wanted them to see."

Something small and cold moved inside Betty, the quiet acceptance of a truth she already knew.

"What do you think it was?" she asked.

"Heck, I don't know. I wasn't there. Who knows which of the stories is true and which is crazy rumor? Or outright lies."

"But if you had to guess. What was it, Jim?"

Helpless, he shook his head. "It's got to be something the Soviets made. Doesn't it? Now the race is on to see who can get a rocket into space first, and the Soviets have something to prove, since the war ended so badly for them. We were allies then, but they don't exactly love us now—and that's an understatement. So it's got to be . . . I don't know, a spy plane? A rocket that couldn't get out of the atmosphere?"

But that writing on his scrap of metal. The strange hieroglyphics were burned into his memory. The saucer wasn't Soviet. He couldn't bring himself to speak the truth aloud.

Betty hesitated. She had asked herself a thousand times if the wreckage might be stranger still, but she had never dared to give voice to the question where anyone else could hear. Jim wouldn't laugh at her or brush away her fears. She could trust him, of all the people in the world, of everyone in Roswell.

"What if it came from somewhere else?" she said.

"Japan? China?"

"No, I mean . . . somewhere else. Outer space, like in the movie. I've heard some people say it might have come from another planet. Do you think it could be true?"

The suggestion seemed to pull the very air from inside the car. For a moment, Jim found it absurd, that he was doing anything as ordinary as driving along the highway, that he was doing anything as ordinary as existing. Outer space. *Of course not,* he told himself. *That stuff's for the movies, for magazines and radio shows. It isn't real. It couldn't happen. Not in a place like this.*

"I only wonder," Betty said, "because why else would I . . . why would this happen, with my hands and my feet, if it was only some rocket from the Soviet Union?"

Jim shrugged, giving every appearance of a lightheartedness he didn't feel. "Why would anything from outer space make you react the way you do, any more than a rocket would?"

Betty stared at him for a moment. Then she laughed. Roughly, unexpectedly, the amusement gushing up inside like the sweet salvation of a spring. "You're right. I never thought about it that way, but you're right. Oh, Jim, it's all so ridiculous. Nothing makes sense anymore."

By the time they reached the town limits, they were both laughing, and holding one another's hands.

He dropped her off outside her home. The kiss he gave her lingered, and she would have stayed longer in his car if she didn't feel her father's impatience, his endless anxiety straining at the edges of the night.

"How about a burger and a shake tomorrow?" Jim said.

"Maybe." She gave him one last kiss and slid from his car.

The night was cold but serene, full of the crisp smell of the Spring River among the willow roots. A perfect sickle moon hung bright and sharp in the sky.

The moon gave enough light that Betty could see the word painted on the first step of the porch: "LIAR." She stared at the step for a long time before she realized the message was meant for her.

CHAPTER
THIRTY-TWO

November 15–17, 1947

Harvey was shaking, his hands and his arms and even his legs jumping a little as he downshifted the old pickup and turned up the monastery's long, dusty drive. He guessed he was feeling more anxious than he'd realized. The scrapbook lay beside him on the bench seat, jittering as the truck rolled along the lane. Now he wondered why he'd brought the thing, and whether he was really going to go through with this crazy idea. But he'd already decided to do it. That day in the bathroom, when Mary Agnes had stilled herself so close to him that the warmth of her body had become his own, and he'd felt that if their lips had touched, everything he knew and everything he was would flow from him into her, and he would receive, too, all of her into him, whatever her vows would allow her to give—that day, that moment, he'd known he couldn't keep this from her. For better or worse, she would know. She must know, if she was to know Harvey. But not the whole story—not yet. Most days, he couldn't even admit the whole story to himself.

He cut the engine outside the farmhouse. Mary Agnes was already coming from the garden, waving, her bare feet whisking through dry grass, a basket hung over an arm. Her smile always did something to him, but there wasn't much point in thinking about it, or what had happened—what had almost happened—in the bathroom that day. No point in longing for what he couldn't have. Still, though he knew he could never be with Mary Agnes the way his heart demanded, he needed her to know who he was, what truths had come in to replace the old, conventional Harvey with someone new and wiser and remade.

She lifted the basket as he stepped out of the truck. "Look at all these radishes! Our second harvest, and this batch of radishes is better than the first. I've got a few carrots, too. I've been busy in the garden while you've been *late*, Mr. Day."

"Sorry about that," he said. "This old truck has been giving me trouble lately. I had to sweet-talk her into starting today, and it set me back awhile. I think the old girl might be on her last leg. Father Kerry might have to spring for a truck of his own, if he wants me to keep hauling lumber and nails for the monastery."

"I hope we won't need more lumber until after the new year," Mary Agnes said. "I've heard more snow is expected, and it's going to stick this time. With luck, all the repairs you've made so far will hold until drier weather comes our way."

"Speaking of my repairs, how is the upstairs bathroom holding up?"

Her eyes skated away from him, across the grounds, and she blushed, which was more noticeable than it might have been on other women, thanks to the sharp lines of black veil and white undercap that isolated her face. Neither of them had forgotten what had passed between them in the upstairs bathroom. Nothing—it had been nothing, no violation of her vows. And yet it had been everything, all the shock and fire of a revelation, all the longing of every soul.

"None of my sisters have reported any more trouble," Mary Agnes said. "I'll figure out which saint we ought to pray to, so we can keep our good fortune coming."

She left her basket on the porch step. They made their way around the perimeter of the farmhouse, inspecting gutters, prodding at suspicious patches in the siding, making a list of tasks that must be completed before the snow came. When they'd finished, they found themselves back at the truck, and Harvey began to shiver again. The time had come.

"Well," Mary Agnes said briskly, "where shall we start?"

"I hoped I might show you something," Harvey said, "before we work on anything else."

His change in demeanor—suddenly cautious, almost shy—wasn't lost on Mary Agnes. For a moment, she was ashamed, for she thought their encounter in the bathroom was to blame. It may have been chaste on the surface, but it hadn't been chaste in her heart. And now she wondered whether he might put up some wall between them. He could do it, no doubt, with the same speed and efficiency with which he built all things.

"All right," she said. "What do you want to show me?"

Harvey retrieved the scrapbook from his truck before he could talk himself out of it. He passed it to her without a word.

She held it for a moment, looking at its blank cover in some surprise. Maybe this had nothing to do with the bathroom, after all. She set the book on the pickup's hood and flipped quickly through the pages. Each contained an article clipped from a newspaper or magazine, and every headline blared about flying saucers.

"I've been keeping that book," Harvey said, "collecting all those articles, since the summer. I guess you could say I have a special interest in the subject."

"I suppose you do," she answered faintly.

Mary Agnes had no idea that there'd been sightings and even potential crashes of flying saucers far beyond Roswell. The scrapbook was fat in her hands, its paste-stiffened pages almost turning by themselves. And there were so many pages. Harvey must have gathered stories from every state.

Feigning a casual air, he said, "I thought you might like to see it, since you're so interested in the local saucer story. If you want to hang on to it for a while so you can read them all, you're welcome to."

That evening, when her sisters gathered in the kitchen for the recreation hour, Mary Agnes declined to join them. She slipped instead to the choir room, the enclave of worship where the nuns gathered several times each day for chanting and prayer. The choir had once been the parlor of the farmhouse. Now its only furnishings, besides the gilded cross, were the two rows of benches that faced one another down the length of the room and a donated organ that stood beside the fireplace.

Mary Agnes settled on one of the benches with Harvey's scrapbook in her lap. Slowly, she paged through the book again, reading every article, every word.

The first story was from Los Angeles, dated February of 1942—mere months after the Japanese raid on Pearl Harbor. The story described an apparition of lights above the city that had sent Los Angeles into a positive panic—an understandable fear, considering how quickly the war had boiled over. She read the article twice, and in her imagination, the air-raid sirens screamed and the rounds tracked into the sky like reverse comets, chased by tails of fire, but the menacing lights never fell, never moved, only went on watching the humans below with a cold, imperious stillness.

She read of pilots encountering things like white pie pans in the sky, flying twice as fast as any known aircraft could move. And housewives watching enormous, glowing balls drift slowly over their neighborhoods before zipping straight up into the atmosphere, gone in a blink. She read of flying propane tanks, chevrons of light, black cubes within glasslike spheres, all of them moving as nothing could move, all of them defying any explanation the Army or the government tried to give. Minnesota. Oregon. Arkansas. New York. Clippings from Canadian newspapers, clippings from Mexico. And yes, there was a story from her home state of Illinois. It seemed no place in North America had been untouched by the phenomenon in the summer of 1947. She wondered whether the same could be said of Europe, of Russia, of Japan.

But only Roswell boasted of having captured one of the objects. Harvey had documented the local story in the final pages of his book.

First the admission that the Army had come into possession of an unknown craft—a "flying saucer," according to the *Roswell Daily Record*—and then the correction in the *Morning Dispatch*, assuring the public it had been nothing more alarming than a weather balloon.

Mary Agnes studied the photograph that accompanied one of the Army's denials. A uniformed major squatted among a careful arrangement of debris, holding up one limp edge of some wrinkled substance that bore no resemblance to the white metal she had handled in the Campbell home.

The sound of a footstep on the choir threshold brought her from her daze; she looked up with a flash of guilt. Mother Catherine was watching from the doorway, an unreadable blankness on her face.

"Sister Mary Agnes, are you well?"

"Yes, of course, Mother."

"I thought perhaps you weren't feeling yourself, since you didn't join us for recreation."

"Oh—no, Mother. I only wanted to do some reading."

"The hour of personal reflection is the time for reading. It's important to be with your sisters during recreation."

"Yes, Mother, but—"

Catherine swept into the room. There was no time to close the scrapbook, and such a gesture would have only underscored Mary Agnes's guilt. She sat immobile, the articles about Roswell's flying saucer crash exposed on her lap, as the abbess loomed above.

"Sister, I've warned you already about focusing too much on this ridiculous story. It's a lot of salacious nonsense, undeserving of your attention."

"Mother, this isn't just a story. There's something real happening, something bigger than anyone suspects. These articles prove it."

"Then it's best left to newsmen. For goodness' sake, Mary Agnes, the bishop himself has already looked into this incident and has found nothing worthy of his time."

"That was the matter of Betty Campbell, not the saucer." Mary Agnes knew she sounded like a sulking child. She couldn't seem to help herself.

"Not so many days ago," the abbess said, "you were insisting there wasn't any difference between the two. I've been in the order longer than you have. I've seen sisters led into doubt, even into immorality when they've given too much credit to worldly things." She sat on the bench, too close for Mary Agnes's comfort. "Please heed me, Sister. I'm telling you this for your own good. You've pledged your time and your thoughts to God. Putting worldly matters before Him will only lead you from this path. Now will you promise me you'll devote yourself to your duties and your sisters—nothing more?"

Mary Agnes's cheeks burned, though whether from embarrassment or anger, she couldn't have said. "Yes, Mother. I promise."

~

On Monday afternoon, when Harvey arrived for his usual work session, Mary Agnes wasn't her usual self. The habitual cheer had been replaced by a heavy silence. She was pensive, her thoughts turned inward to a place Harvey knew too well.

She returned his scrapbook without a word.

"I guess you understand the trouble now," he said.

"'Trouble.' That word doesn't go far enough. Something big is happening, Harvey, something beyond anyone's ability to explain. And I can't help but feel it's tied up with the local girl."

"The local girl?"

She looked up at him with evident surprise. "You haven't heard the story?"

He gave a small, uncomfortable laugh. "I haven't exactly been popular in the gossip circles since I left the Army. If there's a story going around, you can be sure I *haven't* heard it, and you can be sure I'm the only one."

Mary Agnes did her best to explain Betty's strange case as she and Harvey crossed the grounds. She kept the girl's name out of it, however. Betty was still a child, after all, and it didn't seem right to talk about her private affairs behind her back—not even with a trusted friend.

By the time she'd recounted everything, she and Harvey had reached the small, shabby outbuilding that served now as a garden shed. Mary Agnes ducked behind it. There was no danger that she might be overheard, so far from the farmhouse—not by any of her sisters, nor by the abbess—but still she felt the compulsion to hide while she said the rest. She was disobeying her abbess's orders, after all.

"Now that I've read those articles, I'm more certain than ever that something real is going on with . . . that girl. The bishop and the priest dismissed it because it didn't fit with their neat ideas of what's possible and what isn't. I can't imagine what these things are—" She couldn't quite bring herself to say the words. "Flying saucers." There was still a part of her that knew it was too absurd to be true, and she couldn't believe—even after all she'd seen. "I don't know why they affect this girl the way they do. But something is happening, something real, and I can't understand why so many people are trying to pretend otherwise. The bishop—"

"And the Army," Harvey said, "with those tales about weather balloons."

"Yes!" She peeked around the corner of the shed again, just to be sure there was no one listening. "Do you know what I think? I think the bishop and Father Kerry are deliberately turning their backs on this mystery. Because it *is* a mystery. It challenges what they already believe to be true, and they're afraid. They're afraid of losing their faith over it. Or maybe they're afraid of losing their power."

Harvey's heart was racing now. He'd been right to trust her, right to let a little of his secret out. "That's what I think about the Army," he said. "Things being the way they are with the Soviets, the Pentagon can't let on that there's something better than our own planes in American airspace. They'd be risking too much—panic, riots—and worse, the Soviets would use any hint of weakness here in America to do God knows what. So they've decided it's best to pretend it never happened, despite all those news stories, despite saucers being seen in every state across the nation."

"I can't stand for it," she said bitterly. "Leaders of the church who fear to face the unknown? *My* faith is strong enough to look a mystery full in the face and still find God at its heart. I don't think it's unreasonable to expect that a priest and a bishop ought to do the same."

"You really do understand. You don't think I'm crazy."

He reached out, caught both of her hands before he could think better and restrain himself. He'd been carried off by the sheer, sweet relief of knowing that he'd found an ally in this hostile world—but the moment he touched her, he was jolted back to his better senses. Surely, Mary Agnes would withdraw from him, and he would be left knowing once again that he had pushed her too far beyond the boundary of her vows.

At once, he tried to pull away, but her small, work-hardened hands tightened and held him fast. She ought never to have touched him. But a touch no longer felt to her like sin.

For a moment, nothing existed for Mary Agnes but the bright pulse that beat like a heart between herself and Harvey, the rising of some great, tremulous chord of music that only she could hear. The monastery grounds and the farmhouse, the abbess's rules, even the great austere power of the church itself receded and vanished. They were nothing but themselves—a woman and a man, trusting and needing one another, finding their way to one another through the sacred mystery of life.

That night, when she stood at the window of her cell, watching moon shadows chase one another across the grass, she could still feel the warmth of Harvey's hands. She pressed her palms to her lips. The tears she shed were of gratitude, not shame.

CHAPTER
THIRTY-THREE

November 18, 1947

Betty wasn't watching where she was going; that was the trouble. And she was running late. The bell for her first class would ring in less than fifteen minutes, and she was still blocks away from Roswell High. She should have left the house half an hour ago, but she hadn't been able to tear herself away from all those letters she and Jim had written over the weekend, applications to every university they could find that accepted coeds into their science departments. None of the letters felt right to her. Every sentence had to be perfect; it was imperative that she should make the best possible impression on those colleges, especially since she was only a junior, and most of all, since she was requesting scholarships. Her future and her fate depended on each word, for nothing else would get her out of Roswell. Each sentence *must* be perfect.

Finally, with the clock ticking away the relentless minutes, she had scooped the whole stack of letters up with her books and headed out the door. She would perfect the applications during her classes, after her regular work was finished. But as she hurried toward the school, even class time felt too far off, and the task too urgent. She read the topmost letter as she walked, repeating her own words quietly to herself, and wondering with a terrible, sinking dread whether the letter's recipient would think her capable or foolish.

She never saw the collision coming until her papers exploded into the air and her strapped pile of books landed with a thud on her toes.

"Oh, I'm so sorry!"

The voice was familiar. Dazed and panicked, Betty blinked and found herself face-to-face with Sister Mary Agnes.

"Are you all right?" the nun said. "I was so distracted, looking through the monastery's mail. Oh, dear, your papers are everywhere. Let me help. It's the least I can do, after smashing into you like a battering ram."

Betty and Mary Agnes scrambled about, retrieving letters and pieces of mail from the sidewalk outside the post office. When they'd collected everything, Betty shuffled her papers back into some kind of order and hugged them tightly between her books and her chest.

"It was my fault," she said. "I wasn't watching where I was going."

"Neither was I," Mary Agnes admitted.

She considered Betty for a moment. The girl had always had a serious demeanor—at least, in Mary Agnes's acquaintance. But now a greater sobriety hung over Betty. Her face was pale, her eyes darkly ringed as if she hadn't been sleeping.

"How are you, Betty?" the nun asked, hesitant and cautious.

Betty shrugged. "Okay, I guess."

That was far from the truth. She had promised Jim she would return to school, but it hadn't been easy to keep that promise. The whispers and stares had only gotten worse. Her father had scrubbed the paint off the porch step, wouldn't allow Betty to help. She had watched him do it through a hot blur of tears. Every day she knew, she *knew* something worse was coming. Someone would say something cruel to her face, or her home would be defaced again. She was becoming a burden to her family, a source of relentless shame.

"Thanks for helping me pick these up," she said. "They're application letters to some colleges, and I've been awfully worried about getting them written out just right."

"You're going to college," Mary Agnes said. "How wonderful!"

"Well, I hope I'm going." *Please,* she prayed—though to what and to whom, she had no idea—*please get me out of this town.*

"I've been rather worried, myself," the nun confessed. "Harvey—that is, Mr. Day—has been teaching me to drive. This afternoon, he's making me get out on the highway. I'm all jitters over it. Driving in town is one thing, but out there, at high speed . . ."

"You'll do all right," Betty said. "I've got to get going, Sister. School will start soon."

"Yes, of course. I won't keep you longer. Good morning, Betty. I hope your day is a happy one."

Mary Agnes watched the girl rush down Main Street. The morning was bright and clear, and a crisp, blue light seemed to surround Betty like the protective wings of an angel. After all that girl had suffered, surely someone was looking out for her, or so Mary Agnes prayed.

As she turned toward the old Army car, something moved at the corner of her vision—a sheet of paper caught among the ornamental shrubs that lined the sidewalk. Mary Agnes retrieved it—one of Betty's letters, neatly addressed to the theological seminary at the University of Redlands in California.

"Betty!" she called, waving the paper above her head.

But if the girl heard, she gave no sign.

Mary Agnes folded the letter carefully and slipped it into the pocket of her habit. She would call on Betty that afternoon, when her driving lesson and the girl's school day were finished. Until then, she had worries of her own to occupy her. The challenge of the highway still lay ahead, and Mary Agnes had no idea how she would rise to the occasion.

Nor could she imagine what it might be like to spend an hour with Harvey alone, entirely private in the car, far from the watchful eyes of her sisters and the abbess.

When Harvey arrived at the monastery, Mary Agnes was so wracked by nerves that she could barely speak. He chuckled at the sight of her, pale and wide-eyed as if she were about to be sent off to war.

"There's nothing to be afraid of," he said. "It's easier to steer when you're going faster. You'll see."

From the monastery, they headed north into the desert, and all too soon, Roswell was dwindling to a speck in the side mirror. At first, Mary Agnes gripped the wheel tightly. Whenever she saw a vehicle approaching in the opposite lane—a shimmer in the distance, resolving slowly into solid form and definite speed—her heart would pound and her breath would come short until the other car had blown past in a rush of noise and metal.

But mile after mile, her fear began to abate. Harvey had been right. It was easier to drive at higher speeds. The car moved more smoothly, and less fussing was required with the gears. She even began to enjoy the smooth glide of the highway, the easy company of the man at her side.

"Where should I go?" she asked.

"Doesn't matter. Take any road that catches your eye. I know them all; I can get us back to town again, so you won't be late for your prayers."

Every road was much like the others. Mary Agnes turned now and then, and soon she was quite lost, with nothing but desert sweeping away to all sides, no hint of the town or the Army base on any horizon. The land astonished her with its pale beauty. Never had she imagined a desert could be so lovely, so serene. Here and there, patches of snow still clung in the shadowed depressions of long-eroded hills. Waves of buff grass rolled into the distant blue of far-off mountain ranges. The earth was as bright as the sky, everything saturated in an all-encompassing light. Flocks of sheep moved along the low crests of rangeland. The last flowers of autumn, called back to life by the melting snow, lay along the contours of the land in swaths of orange and intense reddish pink.

"You've been so quiet," Harvey said.

"Concentrating on the road."

He accepted that without comment, but it wasn't entirely truthful. Mary Agnes had been too evasive lately, dealing with the abbess and her sisters—even with herself—in a manner that wasn't entirely honest. She didn't like the feeling. Any woman who'd accepted the responsibility of religious vows ought to have no use for lies, even little white ones.

"I suppose I've been upset lately," she admitted. "Ever since I sat in on that investigation—the one I told you about."

A quick thrill of relief went through Harvey. Not upset at him—not for the incident in the bathroom, not for the scrapbook full of his strange obsession.

"You mean the girl from town," he said.

"That's right. Your book—all those newspaper clippings—made me see it so clearly. How willing everyone is, the Army and the church and the government, I suppose, to pretend that all of this is under their control, that they understand the world—oh, just perfectly, thank you very much. But no one understands what has happened here. Not with the saucer, and not with that girl I spoke of."

"No, Sister, I don't believe they do understand. Maybe the Army and the church don't understand the first thing about anything. Maybe no one really does."

"And yet they ignored me. The bishop and Father Kerry."

She could feel her anger rising again, cresting like an oily, black wave in her stomach. Her disappointment, her frustration—the sheer insult of her sincerest testimony disregarded—none of those feelings had gone anywhere. They'd been simmering darkly inside, all these weeks since the investigation. She had paid little mind to the feelings, but nevertheless they remained. And that, too, was a kind of lie—one she told herself—to disregard her own emotions, to accept the disrespect those men of the church had shown her.

The force of her feelings cracked her voice. "It's so upsetting, not to be believed. I know what I saw. And yet they told me I saw nothing."

Harvey watched her for a while in silence—her hands tight on the steering wheel, her fierce, determined face turned to the endless line of the road. He knew in that moment that if he told her everything, she might be frightened or horrified, might end up as lost and troubled as he was. But she would believe him.

"Take that turn up ahead," he said quietly.

"Where? I don't see a turn."

"At the milepost."

"That's a ranch road, Harvey. Who knows where it leads to?"

"I know what it leads to. Take it easy; bring the car down to first gear. You don't want to turn too fast onto gravel."

Somehow, Mary Agnes knew that if she left the paved highway with Harvey, she would steer herself deeper into sin. Without hesitation, she did as he instructed—a Patricia thing to do, running toward iniquity.

The pavement gave way to chips of loose stone.

"It's all right," Harvey said. "Driving on gravel is the same as pavement, really. You only need to slow down a little more."

The road ran on for a few miles—to nowhere, as far as Mary Agnes could see. The gravel rumbled under the tires, and a haze of white dust obscured her vision. She was beginning to think she ought to ask Harvey how to turn around on such a narrow track, so they could head back for Roswell. Then she realized that he hadn't said anything for several minutes. A stillness had come over him, a deep sobriety that filled Mary Agnes with a subtle, new fear.

The road climbed a gradual slope. When they reached its low summit, the land fell away again, into a shallow bowl of sagebrush and yellow stone. Mary Agnes stepped on the brake, seized by the sharp awareness that she had seen this place before. But that was impossible. She had never been here in her life—hadn't even ventured outside the town limits before that afternoon.

Then she looked more closely at the small valley below. Its far end was dominated by a sandstone bluff, curved like half of a bowl's rim.

Mary Agnes drew a quick breath. This was the place from her nightmare. She was certain of it, though in her dream, she hadn't seen the place by daylight. Still, there was no mistaking the hulking shape of that bluff, the distinctive curve of the stone. She stared, not daring to move. A hawk circled on a weak winter thermal, small and dark in the glaring sky. Neither she nor Harvey spoke.

After a long spate of silence, Mary Agnes fumbled with the gear shift and crept down the far side of the hill. The closer she came to the bluff and the circular depression at its foot, the more she could feel the weight of the place pulling her in. There was a hush to the land, a reverence like the silence of the monastery. And a thick compulsion in her throat, a need to get closer to that place, and closer still.

They reached the floor of the small valley. The bluff was just ahead now, so close that Mary Agnes had to lean forward over the steering wheel to see its top, pale and sharp against the sky.

"This is the place."

Harvey's voice was so hoarse and thick that Mary Agnes stopped the car again, fearing he might be in some distress. When she looked at him, he seemed undisturbed, despite the intensity of his stillness.

"Except for the snow," he said, "it's still the same as . . . on that day."

He opened the passenger door, got out, and started walking.

A rapid fear overtook Mary Agnes. The emptiness of the car, Harvey's absence, was a void great enough to swallow the world. She cut the engine and scrambled out, calling to him. But Harvey didn't slow down.

She pursued him, still clumsy in her unaccustomed sandals. The soles broke through crusts of snow and ragged ice tore at her feet. She waded through the sagebrush that clawed at her habit the way it had done in her dream, through exposed patches of damp, sandy soil that broke and slid underfoot. Harvey was upset—fearful, somehow. He needed her. She could help him, and wasn't that what she wanted? Wasn't that why she had come to Roswell—to do real good in this bare, stricken world?

Near the foot of the bluff, among a scatter of pale stones, he slowed enough that Mary Agnes could catch up to him. By that time, she was panting with the effort.

"Harvey, what's wrong? What is this place?"

It was the setting of her nightmare—she was sure of it—and yet it didn't feel menacing now. The coincidence was strange, no doubt, but there was no danger evident, no strangers hiding among the rocks, no wild beasts watching from the bluff with hungry eyes.

And yet, Harvey was shaken, his face white as ash, his eyes wide with a fervor Mary Agnes had seen sometimes in her sisters, when the fire of God ran through them, when the mysteries of the divine were laid bare in their hearts.

He turned abruptly from the bluff, looked at her so directly that she felt his attention, his very spirit, strike into her mortal flesh. Mary Agnes didn't break his gaze, though the force of that intimacy ran through her, the thunder of a monsoon storm.

When Harvey finally spoke, his voice was little more than a whisper. "I need to tell you something, Mary Agnes. I've got to tell someone. I can't keep it quiet anymore."

She nodded. Couldn't have spoken, then, to save her life.

He drew a ragged breath, squeezed his eyes shut. Over the shuddering of his own heartbeat, which was loud in his ears, he could hear Roger's warning. He hadn't stopped hearing it since that evening on Mirror Lake. *Keep your mouth shut. Not a word to anyone about what you saw. Take it to your grave, and you might be able to keep yourself out of danger.* Surely Mary Agnes was safe to tell. A nun who only interacted with anyone outside her sect when necessity demanded. A woman pledged to God, dedicated to a life of service, to doing no harm to anyone. If any soul in this world was safe—if he could lay this burden at anyone's feet—it was hers.

The hawk overhead gave a small, distant cry, and Harvey drew a breath.

"The night the saucer crashed," he said, "I was on duty, monitoring the radar. A big storm was moving through, and I picked up something strange on the radar. I don't know how to explain it."

He did his best to describe the impossible things he'd witnessed that night, how the craft on his oscilloscope had moved like no manmade thing could.

"Once we were sure the craft had gone down—hit by lightning, I guess—that was when all hell broke loose. Since I'd identified the location where the bogey crashed, they brought me along on the recovery crew."

"Recovery?"

She didn't like his grim nod, nor the way he pressed the heel of his free hand against one eye, as if he could drive back the memory by physical force.

"When we got out here," he said, "we found a thing I can't explain, even now. The more I've thought about it, all these months since it happened, the less sense I can make of it. We came down the hill back there, to this bluff. And right up there, where the cliff face meets the ground, was a . . . a vehicle of some kind. A craft."

"A plane?"

"If it was an airplane, it wasn't like any I've seen in my life—not even a Soviet plane, nor a rocket. It was silvery white, kind of round, kind of pointed at one end, though the point was all smashed into the rocks. Not like anything I've seen, and believe me, I've seen a few pictures of strange Soviet inventions. Our spies are pretty good, you know. They get a lot of interesting shots out of Russia."

He gazed up at the bluff, tracing his thoughts back into memory.

"I knew at first sight, no military or government on Earth had made that thing. It just couldn't *be*; it couldn't have come from our world, the way it looked, the way it moved on radar, and when you handled the pieces that had fallen off of it, the way the metal moved in your hand, sort of healing itself and turning out perfectly smooth."

Mary Agnes shuddered, wrapped her arms tightly around her body. She knew what he meant. She hadn't forgotten the unnatural lightness of the thing Betty had shown her, the silver-white scrap hidden beneath the floorboards of the Campbell home.

"And then," Harvey said, "the major told me to go up there to the bluff and take a closer look. Look for 'survivors,' he said—my God. I couldn't refuse, but you know, I've come to think I would have gone anyway—would have volunteered, if I hadn't been ordered. There was this curiosity inside me. No, 'curiosity' isn't the right word, it isn't strong enough. I *had* to know. Like I was being compelled, commanded. Like an instinct was inside me, controlling me, to know what that thing was, to *know*. So I crawled up this bluff, and the closer I got, the harder it was to turn back. The craft itself had me on a line. It was reeling me in. I had my Geiger counter out in front of me like a sidearm, like it could save me if . . . if something popped up out of the wreckage to attack. But I didn't see any survivors. Didn't see anything but the craft itself, maybe thirty feet wide in all, with a hole ripped in its side big enough for me to put my head and shoulders in."

He fell silent. He had longed for months to unburden himself of this catastrophic truth. Now that he was finally doing it, he almost felt as if he were committing some vast and unforgivable sacrilege.

"So that's what I did." His voice took on a high note, strained and vulnerable, like a young boy about to break into tears. "I don't know how to say this. I don't know how to make you believe what I saw. *I* can't even believe what I saw; it was flat-out impossible, but I saw it, all the same. The closest I can come to explaining is this: that craft was bigger on the inside than it was on the outside. I leaned into the gap in that thirty-foot-wide object, and inside, I found a . . . a room, a huge, white room, at least a hundred feet to any side, maybe bigger, with a ceiling maybe twenty feet high. I don't remember much about the room itself, other than its size. There were chairs, kind of, all made from a smooth material like crystal, but chairs for sure, the kind a pilot and crew might sit in. And flat surfaces like dark glass. Maybe they were radar screens, when the craft was functioning. But the *size* of it. It was enormous on the inside, as big as a movie theater—bigger—the biggest room I'd ever been in, so huge it should have gone straight back into that bluff, and far above where the roof of the craft was, and even far below, into the ground. But somehow, all that space was contained in one small, flattened aircraft. Not more than thirty feet long.

"I could only stand to look inside for a few seconds. The feel of it disoriented me so much that when I pulled myself back out, everything was spinning around me, and I could barely stand. I don't know how I got down the bluff without falling and breaking my neck. When I was sure I was in the real world again, where everything was its proper size and shape, I spewed up everything in my stomach. I was sick for days after, too."

In the silence that followed, Harvey felt wrung out, depleted. He had given her the facts, but they were inadequate to convey the greater truth—that putting his head into a gap and finding the very substance of reality inverted, perverted, decimated—it had changed him. Changed everything. Because if even space and substance could be proven false, then what was all the rest of it? Time and tradition, institutions and war, and nations and enemies and governments and gods—what did any of it matter? The great victorious power of the Allies was as much an illusion as outside and inside had been, as big and little and real and unreal; none of these words had meaning any longer. Nothing but the meaning Harvey might choose to give.

Mary Agnes tried several times to speak before she finally managed a few words. "What happened to it? The craft?"

"Army took it all away. Every scrap of metal they could find, too. Loaded it up on trucks and hauled it off to God knows where, to do God knows what with it. Roger said they took it to Ohio, to reverse engineer it. Maybe they only meant to hide it, so no one else will know. Can you imagine what it'd do to the world if ordinary folks knew about this? If ordinary folks even suspected that such a thing could exist, that such a thing is out there, in our skies, so much faster and more powerful than any human fleet could be? See, I understood, when the Army told the newspapers it was a weather balloon. It didn't sit well with me, to spin the truth that way, but I understood why they did it. Better to let folks think the Roswell saucer was a case of mistaken identity than visitors from another planet. Or time travelers from a thousand years in the future, or whatever might explain that damn craft. I don't know where it came from, or how far it flew to get here. But I know for sure that it was real."

"This is why you left the Army," she said.

He nodded. "I understood their reasons for telling folks it was a balloon, but I couldn't go on upholding that story, either. The guys who only saw the outside might be able to carry on with the lie—the guys who didn't see what I saw. They gave me a blue slip—not exactly a dishonorable discharge, but close enough that it doesn't make a difference. Nobody trusts me now—not in a place like Roswell, where everyone has ties to the Army. The only reason why I have my job at the monastery is because the church pays less attention to Army politics than the grocer or the postmaster do, or the guys down at the hardware store. Do you think I'm crazy, Sister?"

"No. Never."

"Don't tell anyone," he said. "Please. If word gets out—if the Army knows I've told anyone—it could be bad for me. Real bad. I don't want any trouble. All I want is to make enough money that I can get out of here, go off and start my life over somewhere else."

"I won't tell a soul," she said. "I promise."

"But you believe me, don't you?"

There was such desperation in his eyes that Mary Agnes took his hand. She shouldn't have done it, but his soul was crying out for comfort. And why had she come here, if not to ease what suffering she could?

CHAPTER
THIRTY-FOUR

November 19, 1947

After the midnight prayer of Matins was finished, the nuns returned to their cells. Mary Agnes remained awake, pressed against her door, listening as her sisters resumed their interrupted sleep. When the upper floor of the monastery was perfectly still, she crept from her room and crossed the old farmhouse, quiet as a breath.

In these earliest hours of morning, the world was still enfolded in the soft embrace of night. She made her way through the empty shadows of the monastery and down the stairs, groping along its walls, sliding her bare feet forward in mistrust. The straight, smooth path of the religious life had vanished beneath her. She was lost in a wilderness of perfect order.

She slipped back into the choir room. The smell of incense still hung thickly in the air. The old parlor windows admitted a wash of starlight, which reflected off the gilded cross hung upon the wall, so the limbs and sorrowing face of the Savior stood out from the darkness, sharp as a rebuke.

She fell to her knees before the cross, gazed up at the figure in a silent plea for His mercy. What Harvey had described to her the previous afternoon was so strange, so impossible that it simply couldn't exist—not in this ordinary, safe reality. She had always known a world that was carefully arranged in accordance with God's design, where humankind was the beloved pinnacle of Creation. No wonder the Army had sought to cover up the story. No wonder the bishop and Father Kerry had brushed off Mary Agnes's testimony. Truth held the terrifying power to rip the fabric of reality to pieces.

Mary Agnes already felt as if she had been torn apart. The substance of her life and self hung from her now in tatters. She had thought God had brought her to Roswell so she could find her path, yet she had been cruelly tested at every turn. First her attraction to Harvey, then her testimony before the bishop being dismissed out of hand. And now the mystery of the saucer. If Harvey's story was true, then the God Mary Agnes knew and served simply couldn't be—this God of laws and commandments and predictable order. There was nothing in the Bible that might explain the stark impossibility Harvey had witnessed. Nothing in all the long history of the church, in all its teachings or in any sermon delivered by Christ Himself. Harvey had described a thing beyond this God of order and physics, the author of a Creation that was easily measured and predicted. Perhaps what Harvey had seen was even beyond the power of God to create. They couldn't both exist in the same reality.

She clutched her rosary until the beads impressed themselves painfully into her palm. She pleaded with Mother Mary to intervene on her behalf, with Saint Clare to raise her blessed light and drive the shadow of doubt from her heart. But the darkness remained, and Mary Agnes couldn't help but ask herself what it would mean for her, if the saucer was truly beyond explanation. For if Harvey had told the truth—if he'd seen clearly that day, when he'd looked over the threshold of this reality, into another world—then Mary Agnes had sacrificed the best years of her life to a fallible institution that had no more claim on the truth than the Army had.

She couldn't accept that. Couldn't allow herself to believe that she'd given twelve years for nothing, had hidden herself away in enclosure for nothing, had preserved herself from the threat of sins that didn't even exist.

Yet Harvey was no liar. Mary Agnes was sure of that.

Then he had misunderstood what he'd seen. Eagerly, she grasped at that feeble straw. It was all that could save her now from plunging over the cliff. Harvey had spoken in earnest, but he'd been mistaken. His eyes had played tricks on him, that day in the desert. Or he had dreamed the whole thing—a nightmare so vivid it still seemed real to him. Perhaps he had temporarily lost his wits. One way or another, he had made a mistake. That was all this was, an innocent mistake.

It wasn't lost on her that the priest and bishop had said much the same thing about her own experience. But she had to believe that Harvey was mistaken. She needed the world to hold together—the order and the meaning of her vows, the clear delineation between this safe inner landscape of obedience and the treacherous realms of sin and damnation that waited beyond. Here, God's laws were cut-and-dried, and every woman knew where she stood and what she must do for the sake of salvation.

Let me see clearly again, Mary Agnes prayed, *if it be for the greater glory of God and for the good of my soul.*

But Saint Clare gave no answer. The hour slipped away in silence. The only sound Mary Agnes could hear was her own tears falling on the hard, bare floor.

CHAPTER
THIRTY-FIVE

November 20, 1947

"Cadet Jaime Lucero. Come in."

Jim stepped inside the office of Major General Waxman, superintendent of the New Mexico Military Institute. He stood at attention, facing the general's desk. His heart pounded so frantically, he felt sure the vibration of his pulse must be visible—his jugular vein twitching or the lapels of his uniform giving a subtle jump to betray his nerves. But he held himself still and alert, waiting for the major general to speak. The first deep snow of the year had fallen early that morning. A sharp glare bounced off the snow and through the office window. Jim had to squint against the brightness and the pain.

"I've received some concerning reports about your behavior," Waxman said. "It seems you were involved in a fight at the drive-in theater last week."

There was no evading the truth. "Yes, sir."

"I have to say, Lucero, I'm disappointed in you. You've managed to conduct yourself flawlessly through years of schooling here at the institute, and now, months before graduation, you're fighting with hoodlums like Mitchell Kromski? I don't have to tell you that this kind of behavior violates this academy's honor codes."

Olivia Hawker

"No, sir, you don't."

"Explain yourself, cadet."

Jim chose his words with care. "Sir, I only engaged with Mitchell Kromski in defense of a young lady. I thought it would have been a worse violation of the academy's honor code to allow him to slander and harass a girl."

"Yes." The superintendent glanced at one of the papers on his desk. "Betty Campbell is the young lady in question, correct?"

"Yes, sir." Jim could feel the color draining from his face. Each moment slowed to an agonizing crawl.

"Cadet, recite the code for me."

"Sir?"

"You heard me."

Jim swallowed hard. The fierce light of winter was lancing his brain. "A cadet will not lie, cheat, or steal, nor tolerate those who do."

"So what are you doing hanging around with a delinquent like Betty Campbell?"

He was so startled by the question that he forgot himself and met the major general's eye. He shifted his gaze again, holding the posture of a subservient cadet with a well-trained intensity of focus. "Sir, Betty Campbell is not a delinquent. She's a respectable girl."

Waxman sighed. "I've already spoken with the principal of Roswell High, and he has confirmed that this Campbell girl has been truant often throughout the fall. And her reputation for truthfulness is . . . not good, to say the least."

"Betty isn't a liar, sir. I've known her for years."

"It's a well-known fact that this girl has been making up stories to bolster her own importance."

Jim was shaking now. There was no chance that Waxman didn't see. "Sir, I know Betty hasn't made up any of those stories. I would swear to that. Whatever has been happening to her, it has something to do with the flying saucer—"

Waxman's hand slapped down hard onto his desk. The crack was loud as a rifle's report, and Jim snapped to a more fervent attention.

"Damn it, cadet, that was no flying saucer. We know the explanation; the Army confirmed that it was a balloon, and continuing to spread stories that contradict your leaders will certainly get you expelled. Do I make myself clear?"

"Yes, sir." Jim was amazed that he could speak at all.

"You need to think long and hard, son, about your future. If you fail to uphold this academy's honor code, you'll be suspended. And if you're suspended, you could very well lose your scholarship to Caltech. You won't get another warning, Lucero."

"Yes, sir. I understand."

That afternoon, Jim lingered in the front yard of his house. Hands deep in his pockets, he kicked uselessly at the snow. The cold bit into him and burned his lungs. None of it felt worse than the sinking, hollow sickness in his gut. The yard and the street and the whole quiet neighborhood looked exactly the way they'd looked on a long-ago December day, when he'd found a little, black-haired girl crying in the middle of the road.

What could he say to Betty? He cared for her, more than any girl he'd dated. But he had his future to think of, his father's memory to honor. There was too much on the line, too many complications.

Later, as the long, blue shadows of winter gave way to the coming evening, Betty knelt on the rug in her bedroom. She gazed up at the small statue of the Virgin of Guadalupe, which still stood on her nightstand, splendid in her bright, starry robes.

Betty had been attending church since she was an infant in her mother's arms, yet she had never prayed, not with any real intent, not because she meant it. The girl couldn't be certain that she meant it now—didn't know whether she really believed that any greater spirit was out there listening to the silent plea of her heart. But she had searched for answers in books and newspapers. She had, to her bitter regret, placed herself in the hands of the bishop and the priest. No authority or institution had managed to illuminate the unseen corners of the truth. Maybe, she thought now, the only way to see into the heart of the unknown was to walk the path of mystery.

She closed her eyes, concentrated on the image of the saint. At first, nothing was any different from the way it had been before, when her eyes were open. Little by little, she felt her inhibitions recede. Doubt drew back like a summer haze retreating before the sun. Her doubts didn't vanish completely; they only withdrew far enough that something else could come in, something warm and tremulous.

Won't you please guide me, Betty prayed. *I'm lost, and I don't know how to find my way to the truth again.*

The late afternoon was undisturbed by any miracle. No visitation from the saint, no angelic choir descending to beat back the darkness of confusion or shine a holy light of understanding. But the small, quiet warmth kindled a little, and she felt for the first time that there might be some reassurance, some reason out there in the wider world. She would find it someday.

There was a tap at her door.

"Just a minute!"

She scrambled to her feet, dizzy from rising so quickly. When she opened the door, her head was still swimming, so that when she saw Jim Lucero standing in the hall, at first she thought he wasn't really there.

"Betty," he said. "Is it all right if I come in? I've got to talk to you."

She sat on her bed, but Jim wouldn't join her. She could tell by the look on his face that something terrible had happened, but he couldn't seem to speak at all, and only paced the room.

"What *is* it, Jim?" she finally demanded. "You can't ask to talk to me and then say nothing. It isn't fair."

"You're right," he said hoarsely. "This isn't fair. But it's what I've got to do."

He took Betty's hand, held it in both of his own. From a numb, cold distance, she listened as he explained. About his school superintendent.

The honor code. He wasn't to see her anymore. He didn't want it to be this way, but—

She tore her hand from his grip. "So your principal thinks I'm a liar, too."

Jim could give no denial. He looked down at the braided rug below his feet, its bright colors a mockery. If this was the honorable thing to do, why did it make him feel so rotten?

"Everyone in this town thinks I'm lying." All the previous mercy of distance vanished, and Betty collided with her own emotions, hard enough to knock the wind from her lungs. She gasped for air between her sobs. "They all think I made it up. They think I'm doing it for attention. I thought *you* believed me, Jim. I thought—"

"I do believe you."

He tried to catch her hand again. She flinched away, and the mistrust in her eyes burned him.

"Go away," she said. "I don't want to see you anymore. You aren't the guy I thought you were, Jim."

What could he do, then, but leave?

As he descended the stairs, the front door opened. Roger Campbell stepped inside his home, dropped his keys in a dish on the bureau. Only then did he seem to notice Jim's presence. Roger looked up, startled, and when his eyes met Jim's, such a look of remorse and shame came over the man that he might as well have been a whipped dog.

Jim didn't know what to make of Roger's expression. He didn't think much about it till later that evening.

That afternoon, Harvey and Mary Agnes worked together to finish the siding on the garden shed. But she wasn't her usual cheerful self. Quiet and withdrawn, she assisted Harvey ably enough—holding the end of the tape measure, fetching his tools as he called for them—but her brow was furrowed, her eyes distant, and Harvey was plagued by a constant trepidation, an instinctive certainty that he had erred in confessing his story.

They passed nearly two full hours in that stiff, awkward state. The shortening day lost its brightness quickly, fading to a featureless gray that allowed them just enough light to see the final nails as Harvey pounded them into place.

"That's done," he said, when the last piece of siding had been hung. "This shed ought to hold up to a few more monsoons, at least."

"I'm sure we'll all be grateful to you in the years to come." Her voice was small and distant, distracted.

"Now come on," he said. "Don't be like this."

She looked up swiftly, eyes wide and startled. "Like what?"

"Mary Agnes, you've been . . . not like yourself. Today. And yesterday. Ever since . . ."

He didn't finish the sentence, didn't like to admit, even to himself, that he'd done the thing he'd promised Roger and himself he would never do. Told someone about the saucer. Opened his fool mouth. Damn it, he'd thought he could trust Mary Agnes.

"Of all the people in the world," he said, "I thought you would believe me. Or accept it, even if you couldn't understand."

Guilt rushed in like a flood. She took a few eager and desperate steps toward him, would have clung to his arm if she dared to touch him. "Oh, Harvey, you've got me wrong. I do believe you. That is, I believe you saw *something* unusual, even if you're mistaken about what you saw."

He watched her levelly for a moment, stern and silent in the fading light. "I'm not mistaken."

"But you have to be. What you described . . . a thing that's bigger on the inside than the outside, a space going back into that bluff and down into the ground and, oh, I don't know what else, a room the size of a football field! Contained inside a thirty-foot ship? It can't be real, Harvey; it just isn't possible."

"Every bit as impossible as the local girl," he said.

"Girl?"

"The one whose hands bleed. The miracle you witnessed yourself—you told me, remember? The priest and the bishop didn't believe you, any more than you believe me now."

She deserved that sting, and she knew it. Yet she couldn't yield to his argument. If she did, the tender core of her religion—of her very identity—would be exposed.

"What you spoke of," she said, "what you thought you saw—it couldn't happen in a world like ours. We have physics, for goodness' sake, Harvey. Reality works in a certain way."

"You, a woman who believes in an all-powerful God so much that she took vows to serve Him. You, of all people, can't allow that maybe what I saw was also a kind of miracle? The impossible happening even though everything we know about the world, about reality—"

"But that's just it, don't you see?" Her voice had risen, all of its own accord. She was close to shouting at him, but she couldn't seem to rein in her temper, nor the fear that had surged inside. "My vows. Don't you understand? What you saw—what you thought you saw—goes beyond even the miracles God has given us, beyond what's written in Holy Scripture, beyond what the church has documented."

"Documented by men like your priest and bishop, who wouldn't listen to you, Mary Agnes, who wouldn't believe, even though you *know*—"

"If it's real," she said, close to tears now, "then it contradicts too much of what I know of God. What the church knows. Too much of what I've spent the past twelve years of my life believing and serving. And I can't, Harvey—I can't turn my back on this." She gestured helplessly at her own self, her body robed in a homespun habit, the bare feet and black veil. "This is my security. It's what keeps me safe. Either you were mistaken, or what you saw was real. And if it's real, then twelve years of my life have been wasted. And worse, everything I know about God and the world, about order and sense and about myself—it all falls apart. I can't let it fall apart. I've given too much of myself to turn my back on this life now."

All the fire went out of Harvey then, all the anger. He felt nothing but pity for her, for she had built a cage around herself, around her mind. The bars of that cage were vows—only words—but Harvey knew how unbending those bars could be. He'd sworn his own share of oaths in the Army, and he didn't take them lightly, not even the one he'd broken.

He picked up his tool chest without another word, nodded with what he hoped was a sufficient display of acquiescence, or at least sympathy. She would rather think him crazy than accept a truth that broke her world into pieces. He couldn't blame her for that, but still it hurt. It hurt worse than leaving the Army had, worse than the blue slip that made him an outcast in this place. It hurt worse than his own shattering had agonized him, that day when he'd looked beyond the barrier of what is, when he'd seen into a catastrophic truth too great to be contained by the small.

～

Whenever Jim felt down, wrenching always picked up his mood, so the minute he got home from Betty's house, he changed into his old, grease-stained blue jeans and a T-shirt that was more holes than not. He turned on the work light and left the garage door open to let in what little remained of the day. He slid under his Plymouth on an old plywood creeper, but then he just laid there on his back, shivering with the cold, staring up into the guts of his engine and wondering dully what he ought to do—about his car, about Betty, about everything. He had a sense that he ought to fix something. And everything in his life needed fixing. He couldn't figure out where to start.

After a long while, fruitlessly holding his wrench against his chest and smelling the sharp, oily smell of the car's underside, he heard an engine cut outside the house, the hollow, metallic thump of car doors shutting—two, one after the other. Jim turned his head, squinted from the well-lit garage into the deep gray of evening. Two sets of feet were approaching up the driveway. Even lying on his back with his vision restricted by the car above, he recognized the fastidious shine on the men's shoes, the distinctive greenish brown of their trouser cuffs. These were Army men, and no mistake.

Jim slid out from under the Plymouth, scrambled to his feet.

The men were both big, imposing. One of them, with the triple mark of a sergeant on his sleeve, Jim recognized—for there weren't many Black men in Roswell. This sergeant had given a lecture at the academy only a few weeks before. Jim struggled to remember his name. The other, Jim had never seen before. He was even taller and broader than the sergeant, his complexion ruddy and flushed, with close-cropped, red bristles showing at the brim of his hat. The two silver bars of a captain flashed on his epaulets.

Three years collapsed; Jim was fifteen again, watching the Western Union messenger approach with that telegram in his hand. He forced the image away. This was a different time, and he was a different boy now. He was a man, with years of honorable, dedicated service as a cadet to his name. There was nothing to be afraid of.

Yet he was afraid.

"Jaime Lucero," the captain said.

"Yes, sir."

"I'm Captain Armstrong. This is Sergeant Roosevelt." He spoke brusquely, almost aggressively. It was clear that he would brook no nonsense—not that Jim had intended to give him any. "We've come to speak with you about a very serious matter."

The blood began to pound in Jim's face, then in his ears. He could barely hear his own thoughts over the thump of his heartbeat. Had word of his fight with Mitch Kromski made it all the way to the base? His kowtowing to Waxman should have been enough to set that right. And breaking up with Betty—that should have been enough, too, to satisfy their damned honor code, their precious oath.

"You've got something that belongs to the Army, son," Captain Armstrong said.

Jim blinked, shook his head in a daze. So this wasn't about Mitch. Or Betty. What in the hell were they talking about?

"I don't think so, sir." Jim tried to keep his voice light, his demeanor helpful. No point in landing himself in more trouble. "There must be some mistake."

Sergeant Roosevelt lifted an eyebrow. "Have you ever been out to Mac Brazel's ranch?"

The world went still around him. His thoughts, his breath, the day itself all vanished in a vast, white blankness of understanding.

The metal. The scrap of metal he'd taken from the crash site—that was what they were talking about. That was what they were after.

Slowly, through the thick shock of understanding, he saw the captain's mouth moving, heard his voice as if it came from underwater, or across a great distance.

"You're risking your future, son," Armstrong said. "At the Military Institute, and at your university."

They had taken his silence for denial.

"Hand over what you took now, and we'll call your record clean. If you cooperate, there'll be no reason to contact the dean of Caltech— you get me, son? A kid who messes around with the United States Army isn't going to hang on to any scholarship, I can tell you that."

They'd taken his silence as refusal, and now they were threatening him.

Fury leaped up in Jim—fury and a sick, cloying disgust. He wanted to deny their request—their command—tell them to get lost, that he wasn't afraid of them and there was nothing they could do to him. The strange piece of metal with its mysterious purple writing was too fascinating, too important to let go. It was proof that something big had happened there in Roswell, proof that a bigger reality might exist somewhere beyond the confines of what was already known. They wouldn't say a word to Caltech. It was all a bluff.

Jim opened his mouth to tell them so, but the sergeant spoke first.

"I don't think you understand how serious this matter is, young man. It's a matter of national security. Do you know what the Pentagon will do to protect the security of this nation?"

Jim swallowed hard. He shook his head.

"It's a big desert out there," Roosevelt said. "Wouldn't be hard for a kid like you to get lost and never find his way back home again."

Cold struck Jim full in the chest, fast and hard like the impact of a bullet. Kill him. They would kill him—have him killed. That was what Roosevelt had meant.

They wouldn't go that far, he told himself. *Not the Pentagon, not these goons.*

The Army was the good guys, the soldiers for a righteous cause. They didn't stoop to murdering civilians, not even over matters of national security.

Jim told himself all that as he glanced helplessly between Roosevelt and Armstrong. He could no longer believe it. After all, the Army had lied outright about the crash. His little scrap of debris, with its indecipherable writing, was proof of that. If they could lie to the public about something so important, they might be capable of anything.

When he managed to speak, his voice was hoarse. "Hang on. I'll get it for you."

It didn't take long to retrieve the scrap. He'd been keeping it in a shoebox under his bed. In the privacy of his room, he held the metal in his hands, tilted it in the glow of his desk lamp to puzzle one last time over the strange hieroglyphics, the bright purple symbols of no language he'd seen.

The saucer truly had been something inexplicable. Something whose mere existence had the power to unmake society, to bring the United States and its allies to their knees. Why else would the Pentagon cover it up? Why else would the Army lie?

Why else would they be willing to threaten witnesses with death? And if they were willing to make those threats, they were certainly prepared to see them through.

Anger and disgust made him clench his fists. The metal crumpled in his grip. All this time, all these years, he'd made the Army his idol, had shaped himself into the obedient cadet they wanted him to be. For what? The Institute made him swear that damn oath of honor, to tell no lies and to associate with no one who lied, and all this time, the captains and the sergeants and the majors and the generals and God knew how many more all had lied, to Jim, to the whole damn country, to everyone. Betty's father—he hadn't lied, exactly, but it could only have been Roger Campbell who'd ratted Jim out. Nobody else had known he'd kept this piece of wreckage.

And Waxman. The major general had forced him to break up with the girl he loved for honor's sake.

There was no honor left. Not in the Army.

Jim's grip relaxed. The miraculous metal sprang back to its former shape, unblemished, the purple markings sharp and clear in the lamplight.

He returned to the driveway, handed the scrap of debris to the captain without a word. There was a long silence as Armstrong and Roosevelt inspected it, took in the strange writing, allowed the shock to settle into them, too, the way it had long since done into Jim.

Finally, Roosevelt said, "Is this all?"

"All I had, sir."

The sergeant held his eye. Jim didn't blink.

"You sure about that, son?"

"Yes, sir, I'm sure of it. I took an oath to always speak the truth. I take my oaths seriously. I take honor seriously, even if some others don't."

Roosevelt nodded. "You've done the right thing, young man."

They left him then. Got back into their car and drove away, business concluded, nothing more to say. Jim stood in the driveway, his arms folded tightly across his chest, watching their car dwindle up the street. With a great effort, he held back the tears of helpless anger that wanted to gather and fall. All this time, ever since his father's death, all he'd wanted was to do the right thing. If he'd done the right thing now, in handing over his prize—in breaking Betty's heart—then why didn't it feel right to him?

CHAPTER
THIRTY-SIX

November 21, 1947

Betty's blue jeans were dirty. Her tennis shoes were soaked with melted snow, and her feet were so cold they hurt, but she didn't care. What was the point in caring? She leaned against the corner of the hardware store, watching the cars crawl up and down Main Street, their tires hissing in the gray slush. A wind gusted across the town, smelling of ice and the exhaust of traffic, tumbling a few stray pages of a newspaper down the wet sidewalk.

She watched the paper flap and roll past her like a wounded bird. A pang of recognition struck her. Every page of her life was out of order, and blowing away, beyond her reach, beyond her power to repair. There was no use now in trying to read her own story, no sense to be found in the past or the present. She didn't see much hope for the future, either. Not if she remained in Roswell.

A police car rolled past. Betty stood up straighter, locked eyes with the cop inside, daring him to pull over and confront her on her truancy. It was a Friday, and she ought to have been in school, but now that Jim had broken things off, she couldn't make herself face her fellow students again, nor the teachers who watched her with suspicion from across the classrooms. Jim's encouragement had kept her chin up through the hard times. Merely knowing he was on her side had stopped her ears to the whispers, blinded her to the sly, amused looks of her peers, and given her the fortitude to fix her attention on a future she could believe in. But now he thought Betty was a liar, just like the rest of them. Like everyone in that town. What was the point of going to school? Her grades would slip, and she would never get into any college, but that didn't matter now. If everyone in town thought she was a juvenile delinquent—Jim included—then she might as well be one.

The trouble with being a delinquent was that it was neither fun nor interesting. In movies, dangerous and exciting things happened to the kids who skipped school to commit petty crimes. They smashed windows and painted dirty words on brick walls with the wild glee of untamed animals. They smoked reefer and danced as if they were possessed by a liberating devil. Hardened criminals chased them through dark alleys, and they ran their mouths at the authorities with an adult impunity that always sent a thrill up Betty's spine. They engaged in breakneck drag races to the accompaniment of rowdy jazz soundtracks. All Betty was doing was holding up the wall of the hardware store and freezing half to death in the slush and the wind.

Without any company, she had no choice but to dwell in her thoughts. Those thoughts were a spiral corridor, leading endlessly back to the place where they'd begun. There was no path forward now. But there might be an *out*, if she could find the road.

As morning gave way to midday and the sharp winter sun glared off the whiteness of the town, she left the corner she'd been haunting and wandered through the streets. She was hungry, but she had no money in her pockets, and she couldn't go back home until the usual hour, or her mother would know she'd been skipping classes. Mom was the last person in all the world who still believed that something real had happened to Betty—Mom and Juanita. She couldn't disappoint her mother now; it would only break her heart. So she walked, restless, angry, without aim or destination. Hunger turned to a gnawing ache, and her thoughts gnawed on one another until everything inside her was eaten away, and all that was left was a deep, hollow pain. The only streets she avoided were her own and Jim's. One neighborhood looked exactly like any other, sleepy and small and frozen by the snow. Every house was the same, every street the same, and all the people inside those houses believed what their neighbors believed, what they'd been told to believe by the bishop or priest, by the Army, by the superintendent of the academy. Not one person looked up to see for themselves what was real.

She spent an hour or two in Cahoon Park, throwing snowballs at the old pioneer building, tossing rocks from the footbridge so they punched dark holes into the fragile, new ice on the Spring River. When she thought the school day might be nearing its end, Betty followed the river's course back through town, jumping ditches and crossing culverts until she reached Main Street again. She made her way slowly up the sidewalk, eyes down, her cold-chapped fists hidden in the pockets of her felt jacket. As she passed Eller's dress shop, the door swung open too fast for Betty to avoid it. She collided with the customer who'd been leaving the shop—an old woman with a package tucked under her arm. The package fell to the wet sidewalk.

"Sorry," Betty said, bending to pick it up.

When she straightened, the woman was looking at her with a scowl of offended disgust.

"You're that girl who's been mocking God, aren't you?"

Fear stole Betty's breath. She shook her head.

"Yes, you are," the old woman sneered. "Trying to put on airs. You're nothing but a blasphemer. You'd better repent of your sins, girl, before it's too late."

Betty shoved the package into the woman's arms, then turned and ran up Main Street toward home. She was out of breath and half blinded by tears by the time she reached Twelfth Street.

When she threw open the front door, her mother called from the kitchen, "Betty, is that you? Are you home already?"

Betty didn't answer, but ran up the stairs and shut herself in her room, shaking from the ordeal, weak and weary with a hopeless sorrow.

She scooped the stack of letters from her desk and collapsed on her bed. She looked through them, one by one—the addresses, so neatly written, of universities in Texas and New York, Iowa and California. The hopeful salutations, each sentence carefully composed, every word brimming with her dreams and ambitions.

Useless, those dreams. She knew now that she couldn't face anyone in this town. So she wouldn't be going back to school, not ever, which meant the stack of letters served no purpose. They'd all been a waste of time.

She slipped into the upstairs bathroom, found the little box of matches, and stole down the stairs again with the letters rolled in her fist. She carried them across the street, to the ditch where the river ran. She was surprised to find the small statue of Guadalupe lying where she'd left it, discarded among the roots of the willows.

For a while, Betty stood and stared at the saint, half expecting the little wooden Virgin to sit up and speak to her. *Some help you are,* she thought, and kicked Guadalupe into the river below. The statue skittered across a shelf of half-formed ice and disappeared into a patch of unfrozen water.

Betty crouched among the willows, hidden from sight of the house. She struck a match, touched it to the corner of a letter. The flames blossomed hungrily. In moments, the paper was consumed, curling to black ash. Only the corner Betty held between her fingers still burned. She let it go. The fire snuffed itself as the ruined scrap of paper floated down to the river. She didn't return to the house until every application was burned.

Her only hope now, her only chance for a life she could bear, was to get out of Roswell. Now. That very evening, if she could manage it. She would go to some other town—*where* hardly mattered—anyplace where no one knew her name, anyplace where no one had heard of a flying saucer. Maybe she would work in a diner to support herself. It wouldn't be the life she had dreamed of—learning the mysteries of flight, joining in the great human endeavor of leaping off this planet, into the black divinity of space—but it was better than remaining in a town where she would be afforded no dignity, where the truth would never be believed.

As she crossed the street again—calm now, settled into the inevitability of what she must do—she asked herself *how* she could leave Roswell. There was only one practical answer that Betty could see. She must take her father's car. When she thought of how angry he would be, how disappointed, she wanted to cry all over again. She fought back the tears, needed a level head now. Her future—what little remained of it—depended on staying cool and rational.

Dad will hate me for it, she told herself, *but everyone thinks I'm a delinquent now. So I might as well be what they want me to be.*

In her bedroom, she packed a few necessities into a travel bag. She scrawled a hasty note on a blank sheet of paper and left it on her pillow. Then she watched from her window until she saw her father's car turn down Twelfth Street, gray as a phantom in the gathering dusk.

Betty waited at the threshold, listening. The front door opened. Her father called out his usual greeting, and yes, there was the clink of his key ring as it landed in the catch-all dish beside the door. His voice traveled through the house, into the kitchen where he struck up a conversation with Betty's mother.

Now was her chance. She crept down the stairs, careful to prevent her bag from bumping into the wall and giving her away. At the front door, she closed her fist around the key ring so it would make no sound, eased it into the pocket of her coat. Betty paused with one hand on the doorknob. In the kitchen, her parents sounded so cheerful, like they hadn't since the summertime. Her brothers were clamoring for a story from Dad. Mom was laughing fondly at the boys' jokes. The house smelled of cinnamon from her mother's baking. They would all be better off without her. Their lives could go on with no more shame, once she'd gone for good.

Betty slipped out and shut the door as quietly as she could manage. She wouldn't have much time to get the car away. She'd never really driven—just twice, and even then, she had only driven up and down Twelfth Street with her father in the passenger seat to guide her. But the principles were simple enough, and how much different could it be to drive across town, or out on the open highway?

The engine was still warm from her dad's trip home from the base, so she managed to start the car quickly. As she rolled up Twelfth Street, a determined peace settled over her, and a confident ease took the place of her anger. She was really doing it—getting away. Leaving forever. Let everyone who'd doubted her, everyone who'd called her names or spread ugly stories, fade into the past, into what she left behind. Let all the people who'd put candles and flowers in the yard fall behind her, too. What did they know? Nothing. Nobody knew anything about this world or what lay beyond it. But Betty would sure as hell find out what lay beyond Roswell.

The town was gone soon enough, and she accelerated onto the open road. A blue twilight covered the land and drew her into an intoxicating distance, a promise of far horizons and the unknown things that waited beyond. It was the first time she felt really good, really hopeful, since all this trouble had started. Maybe all along, the answer to her troubles had been this. To go. To refuse to acknowledge what had happened to her, or what she once had been—to keep moving in the direction of a mystery.

She managed to travel a few miles beyond Roswell before she hit a patch of ice. The steering wheel jumped in her hands. The car fishtailed across the highway. The world lurched and spun in a confusion of snow and pavement and darkening sky. She didn't even have a chance to scream.

～

The hour of Vespers had come. The sisters had donned their choir stoles and had just begun chanting the evening prayer, their voices joining in a subtle harmony, when a frantic pounding cut through the liturgy. All the sisters fell silent, looking at one another in shock. No one had ever dared to interrupt the Vespers prayer—or any other Hour.

Mary Agnes rose from the bench. "I'll go and see who's at the door."

She crossed the old farmhouse alone. A vertiginous sense of danger seized her, as if she were walking along a tightrope strung between two skyscrapers. She was certain that if she looked down, she wouldn't see the threadbare rugs of the monastery but rather an endless plunge into disaster, a drop into a different world. Something was terribly wrong.

She opened the door to find Rosa Campbell, breathless and disheveled and red-eyed.

"Sister, help me, please. It's Betty."

She thrust a piece of paper into Mary Agnes's hands. Mary Agnes blinked at it for several long moments before the words resolved into a stark and horrible sense.

I'm sorry for what I did, but I know you'll all be better off without me. I love you forever.

Everything that was in Mary Agnes flashed to ice—her mind, her heart, her spirit.

"She took the car." Through the swim of Mary Agnes's thoughts, Rosa's voice came distant and small. "Roger phoned the police, but we don't know where she's gone, Sister. We don't know how to find her."

"She must have driven somewhere," Mary Agnes said. "We've got to find her before . . . before anything happens."

Rosa seized both of Mary Agnes's hands, shook her with a mother's purest desperation. "Pray for us, Sister, please. Pray for my baby."

Gently, Mary Agnes pulled away. She would do much more than pray for Betty.

She took the keys to the old Army car from their hook beside the door.

≈

Jim leaned back in the driver's seat, staring off into the typical commotion of rumor and horseplay that filled the parking lot at Vic's. He had placed an order for a burger and fries, even though he wasn't hungry. Since he'd broken things off with Betty—since he'd broken her heart—everything had tasted like dirt. Besides, he couldn't stop thinking about those two men, Armstrong and Roosevelt, their grim threats, the steady, cold promise in their eyes. The Army wasn't what he'd thought it to be. No, not by half. He'd hoped to find honor and purpose as a soldier, had planned to do his father's memory proud. How could he serve with honor when the whole outfit was built on deception, ran on deception the way an engine runs on gasoline? And they'd taken Betty from him. Waxman had taken Betty. Roger Campbell had taken his proof of the crash—for only Betty's dad could have ratted him out to Armstrong and Roosevelt.

A pack of Hawks strutted past, puffing out their chests to show off the club patches on their jackets.

"There's the slugger himself," one of them jeered.

"Get lost," Jim said, "unless you want a piece of what I gave Kromski."

"Say, where's your girlfriend, Jim?"

Another of the Hawks made a stupid whistling sound, wavering his hands through the air in mimicry of a Hollywood flying saucer.

"I said get lost."

Jim stepped out of his car. The Hawks scuttled back a few paces.

At once, Jim's friend Marty Silvers appeared at his side, laid a restraining hand on his shoulder. "Take it easy, Lucero. You know what Waxman said."

"Who cares about Waxman?"

"Come on, Jim. Don't let these clowns get the best of you. You're a cadet; you've got more honor than to fight with jerks like them."

Honor. What did honor matter, what did oaths of proper behavior matter when the guys at the top were all lying through their teeth? He could throw it all away without regrets—forget Caltech, forget university altogether. What did it matter now? He'd planned all along to smarten up in college, bring his engineering know-how back to the Army and take up where his dad had left off. But he'd be damned if he'd have anything to do with the Army now.

One of the Hawks spoke up. "Didn't you hear the news? That wacky Betty Campbell has run off. Stole her dad's car. She's no good, guys, I tell you."

"What are you talking about?" Jim said.

"My dad's a cop," the Hawk insisted. "They've got an APB to search for her old man's car. That cuckoo chick stole Daddy's car and drove off. Probably going out to look for more saucers."

Stricken, Jim stared at Marty. "She doesn't know how to drive."

"Easy, Jim. She'll be all right. The cops will find her—if the story is even true."

"With this snow on the roads, she could get hurt. Bad." Jim pulled his key ring from his pocket.

"Whoa," Marty said, "what do you think you're doing? Waxman said you've got to stay away from that girl."

"Betty could be in serious trouble. If Waxman has a problem with me maybe saving a girl's life, then too bad for him. I'd rather be insubordinate and right than follow his damn honor code and be wrong."

Marty hesitated only a moment longer. Then he stepped aside, clearing the way to Jim's car. "Be careful," he said. "And good luck, Lucero."

Jim didn't know where to begin searching. Betty might have gone in any direction. The desert outside Roswell was vast and lonesome, crossed by endless miles of highway. He tried to think his way through the problem, tried to use common sense and his rational mind, as he always did. If she'd taken her dad's car, she would probably have driven north. It was the fastest way out of town from her neighborhood.

That was as far as rationality carried him. His vision kept blurring from the tears he refused to shed, and as he navigated Main Street, driving as fast as he dared in the slick conditions, he found himself repeating the same thoughts over again, a prayer chanted to a remote and heartless God.

Please let her be okay. If she's okay, I'll take everything back. The academy doesn't matter. My scholarship doesn't matter. Just let her be all right.

∿

Harvey took it slow as he pulled onto the westbound highway. The snowfall had stuck this time, compacting onto the roads in slick patches and refreezing in the bitter chill of evening. He didn't quite trust the old truck's tires in such conditions, but Alamogordo was only a little more than a hundred miles away. If he drove carefully and took his time, he could make it there before midnight. And he couldn't stand the thought of remaining in Roswell for one second more. Not now that Mary Agnes had decided he was crazy.

He had packed everything he wanted to bring with him in his old Army rucksack—a few changes of clothes, some basic tools, and of course, the scrapbook that contained all the evidence for his own sanity. He would have liked to bring a piece of the saucer with him, but he'd never found a scrap of his own. That didn't matter, really. His memories of the event were vivid enough.

The highway cut through the high pastures and open plains, and Harvey gave the pickup as much juice as he dared, reveling in the freedom. The untouched snow of the rangeland lay silver and soft along the earth. The sky was as wide and high as his new possibilities. Somewhere beyond Alamogordo lay Arizona, and beyond that, California, where he would make his new home, start a new life. A blue slip counted for less out there. He cranked down his window, let the winter cold strike him full in the face. The highway may have been slick, but it was paved with promise that night. He drank it in with the frigid bite of the wind.

A car loomed out of the darkness ahead, pulled to the side of the road. Harvey slowed to a crawl. He could see a small figure darting around the vehicle, taking mincing steps in the snow and struggling to raise the hood. As he came closer, the figure's flowing, dark robe and white collar nearly stopped his heart. It was Mary Agnes, stranded on the shoulder.

Some luck. Just when he thought he was free.

He couldn't drive on by and leave her. He wouldn't have done it to any woman, but especially not to Mary Agnes.

When she looked up from her efforts with the car hood, Harvey could see the tracks of tears down her face. He cut his engine and slid out of the cab, hurried to her side.

"Harvey!" she cried. "Thank God it's you."

"What are you doing out here on the highway, at this time of night? And in the snow, to boot?" He looked down at her feet. The thin sandals she wore for driving gave her no real protection from the snow. "Good God, Mary Agnes, you'll cut yourself on this ice. Get back in the car."

"Something's wrong with it," she said. "I don't know what. I can't keep it running, and there's no time, no time!"

Gently, Harvey took her by the shoulders, steered her to the passenger side of the car. He made her sit on the seat, tucked her feet safely into the floor well.

"Tell me what's wrong," he said. "Take a deep breath and tell me."

She explained her trouble with the car. He could tell by her description of the rough idle and sporadic banging that it was only a clogged filter on the carburetor, a quick roadside fix. But she was still upset about something, talking with a rising panic that sped his heart.

"Betty Campbell is missing. The police are out looking for her, but—"

"Betty. Isn't she Roger's girl?"

"She may be in danger, Harvey. We've got to find her."

"Sit tight. I'll get this old thing running again, and then we'll find her. You'll see, Mary Agnes, we'll find her. It's going to be okay."

He retrieved a small flashlight from his truck and held it in his mouth. Then he dove into the carburetor, working as quickly as he could. He had no idea whether things would be okay. The fear and misery in Mary Agnes's eyes made him suspect a tragic outcome. There seemed to be deeper currents moving here, complexities he didn't understand. But he knew one thing for certain: if any member of Roger's family was in peril, he wouldn't rest until he'd done all a man could do to help.

When he had the filter cleared and back in its place, he told Mary Agnes to turn the engine over. She scooted across the seat and worked the ignition. The engine fired up readily, and Harvey slammed the hood shut.

"Move over," he said. "I'm better at driving in snow."

Mary Agnes retreated again across the bench seat. Harvey slid in behind the wheel, pulled the car back onto the road.

"I didn't know where to look," she said. "I only know the police were headed north and south. I picked a different direction."

"There are a lot of places a girl might get to out here in the desert."

She hesitated, eyeing his determined profile as he glowered at the snow. She was burning to ask the question, and afraid of learning the answer. "Where were you trying to get to," she finally said, "out here in the desert? You weren't out on a joy ride, Harvey. Not in this weather."

"I'm leaving Roswell. For good. I can't stay in a place where I tell the truth but no one believes me. It's more than any man can put up with."

He was referring to her. Mary Agnes knew it; she could feel it in the bluntness of his words, the accusatory heat of his sidelong glance.

They drove on in silence. Minutes dragged with the weight of hours. Explanations and excuses and compromises kept forming themselves in Mary Agnes's mind and fading again before she could find the courage to speak.

Harvey tensed at the wheel. "What's that?"

She leaned forward, bracing herself against the dash, squinting into the night. Far ahead on the highway, on the opposite side of the road, something round and white hung just above the earth. As they drew nearer and the headlights flooded the scene, she realized the pale, circular thing was a white-walled tire. A heartbeat later, the grim truth struck her full in the chest, knocking the breath from her body.

A car. Turned upside-down in a ditch across the road.

Harvey slowed the old Army car; it skidded a little across the pavement. Mary Agnes was out of the car before it came to a full stop. She scrambled across the road, heedless of the rough crenelations of ice that cut past the straps of her sandals.

"Betty!" She tripped over the hem of her habit, fell down the slope of the ditch. A frigid dampness soaked her habit, the cold biting into her chest and arms. She picked herself up quickly and pressed her hands against the driver's-side window, staring into the wrecked car.

Betty lay inside, motionless along the vehicle's roof. The girl didn't respond, no matter how loudly Mary Agnes called to her or pounded on the glass. Mary Agnes wrenched the door open, took Betty's hand, tried to pull her from the wreckage. She felt the girl's fingers twitch.

"She's alive, Harvey, but I can't get her out!"

It was all Mary Agnes could do to force herself away, making room for Harvey to do his work. Sobbing, she clawed her way up the icy ditch to the surface of the road and watched as Harvey sank to his knees, leaned his head and shoulders inside the car. A moment later, he backed out, slowly, carefully, cradling Betty in his arms.

As Harvey rose to his feet, the girl's head lolled. One of her arms fell limp at Harvey's side. He picked his way out of the ditch, placing each foot with care. As he gained the road, something dark and round blossomed on the ground below him—three perfect circles of red, vivid against the snow.

Mary Agnes looked up in shock—first at Betty's exposed palm, where the fresh blood welled, then at Harvey's face.

"Open the door," he said. "We've got to get her to the hospital, fast."

CHAPTER
THIRTY-SEVEN

November 22, 1947

"Your girl is very lucky, Mr. Campbell." The doctor smiled, his eyes warm with the unexpected pleasure of delivering good news. "We'll keep her here at the hospital for observation—one more day at least, maybe two. A concussion like hers needs to be followed closely. But I think we can expect her to make a full recovery."

Roger shook the man's hand, more vigorously than he should have done. "Thank you, Doctor. You don't know how glad I am to hear it."

When the doctor had departed the waiting room, Roger wrapped his arms tightly around his wife. He pulled Rosa close, burying his face in her hair with its sweet, familiar scent, savoring the fact of *her* in his arms—this half of his heart, this woman who was his world. This woman who had given him that precious girl in the hospital bed, the girl he'd come so close to losing.

The hour was half past midnight. Roger didn't know whether he was too tired to keep his eyes open, or whether he expected never to sleep again. Rosa loosened her grip on him, tried to pull away, but Roger held her more tightly still. He never wanted to let her go.

"I thought I could keep her safe," he said against his wife's cheek.

"Oh, Roger, dear."

"All I wanted was to keep her safe, but we almost lost her, Rosie. Like that. Almost lost her in a blink."

Gently, Rosa stepped back, held her husband by his broad shoulders. "There are things in this life we can't control. There are things we can't protect our children from, no matter how much we might want to."

"I know."

"It's not any reason to stop living. It's not any reason to stop our daughter from living her own life."

He sagged against Rosa again, hiding his tears on her shoulder. "What's a man for, if not to protect his family? But there's so much I can't do. So much I can't understand."

Her hand moved slowly on his back, small circles, quieting him and stilling his fears. "Maybe Betty will find a way to understand. Someday, Roger—if she gets out there and explores the world. If she follows her own path in her own direction."

He understood Rosa's meaning. He sniffed and gathered himself, took her small, warm hand. He wouldn't hold Betty back any longer. If college in some far-off city was what she really wanted, then she could go. He would let her go. The girl was bright, after all, and this world was a different place from what it had been years ago, before the war, before all sense and order had fallen from the sky. Betty was strong enough to command her own fate. And Roger would have to find the strength to stand back and let his girl fly free.

"Where is she? I've got to see her!"

Roger turned at the commotion. Jim Lucero had blown into the hospital like a storm. The boy was trying to shake off the two nurses who clung to his arms.

"Jim. Over here, son."

The nurses let him go, and Jim rushed across the waiting room, red-faced, his eyes filling with tears.

Roger tried to put a comforting hand on his shoulder, but Jim stepped back.

"Fat chance, Pops. You think I don't know it was you who sent those two Army creeps after me? Where's Betty? I want to see her."

"She's all right," Roger said. "Thank God, she's going to be okay."

The better part of Jim's fear and outrage left him in a great, shuddering sigh. He covered his face with his hands, and this time, when Roger put his arm around Jim's shoulders, the kid didn't pull away.

"You were out looking for her, too, weren't you?" Roger said.

Jim nodded, still hiding his face.

"Thank you, son, for looking out for her. Thank you for caring about my little girl. You won't get any more trouble from me. I can promise you that."

At last, the boy looked up. "Why did you do it? Why did you tell them? You don't know what it was like. They . . . they threatened me. My life. They might have killed me, for God's sake."

Roger shook his head. He couldn't meet the kid's eye. "I thought I could hold everything together if I followed all the rules, did everything the way they said to do it. But the cover-ups and threats haven't made the truth go away. It's still there, under everything. We can only pretend for so long. Sooner or later, the truth catches up with you—with everyone. Can you forgive me, son? I'll understand if you can't, but . . . but for whatever it's worth, I'm sorry for putting you through it."

"I don't know."

Jim stepped back to consider him. Roger looked older than when he'd seen him last—old and tired and possessed of a calm resignation that had a fair amount of dignity in it. He thought with time he might come to trust Betty's father, maybe even to like him. After all, both of them knew what was true and what wasn't. That was something they shared in common.

"Can I see her?" Jim said again.

"The doctor said she can have visitors tomorrow. He wants her to rest undisturbed until then. But I'd be very glad if you'd come back then. I think she wants to see you, too, Jim. I think there's nothing she'd like better."

Roger put out his hand, tentative and almost afraid. If the boy didn't want to shake, didn't want to forgive him, that was well enough, and understandable.

Jim hesitated only a moment, then took Roger's hand.

"You're a good man, Jim," Roger said. "Your father would be proud, if he could see you now."

~

Mary Agnes didn't return to the monastery that night. After they'd delivered Betty to the hospital—after a swarm of doctors and nurses had descended on the girl and taken her away for emergency treatment—she drove Harvey up Main Street and parked outside the hardware store. She'd watched as he'd let himself through the street-level door. A short while later, a light came on in one of the second-floor windows—Harvey's apartment. She kept the car idling at the curb until the light went out again, and even after, she remained. Now and then, a lone car passed on Main Street, but the town always descended again into a deep, self-contained stillness, an island of quiet, adrift in a larger, darker sea, the desert beyond dreaming of its well-kept secrets.

She slumped in the driver's seat and laid her forehead against the steering wheel, trying to think her way through the dissolution of her faith. No, not her faith—that was as strong as ever, as hot and bright as it had been on her first sight of the miracle, the blood rising from Betty's palms. It wasn't her faith that was fading, but her belief—in the order, in the church, maybe in the God they claimed to know and serve.

She had never stopped believing the witness of her own eyes. Betty's stigmata were no hoax, whether Bishop Cote could comprehend the miracle or not. And Harvey's touch had triggered the girl's bleeding. What did it mean? Somehow, Harvey himself must carry the essence of the saucer. Its mystery and power had transferred to him, sunk into him, and it reflected from him like the radiance of a saint. He hadn't lied—of course he hadn't—nor had he misunderstood what he'd seen.

His encounter with the saucer had been no dream. That unknown disruptor, that breaker of reality, had left its impression on Harvey for good. That was the truth. She could no longer deny it.

That word—"truth"—mocked her. For the unknown seemed franker and more factual now than the version of reality she had accepted without question all these years. Harvey had said the saucer was bigger on the inside than it was on the outside. Not even God could make such a perplexity—at least, not the God Mary Agnes had known. He was a deity of order and rules, of hierarchies and causation. What Harvey had seen—what Harvey had touched and experienced—turned reality on its head. It reduced the God Mary Agnes served to a small, powerless thing. Or it rewrote the rules of God, remade Him after a pattern the church refused to recognize.

This church, with its commandments and rituals, its rules of salvation and sin. What if it meant nothing? The very thought saddened her, terrified her—it was so opposed to everything she'd been taught and all she'd been raised to believe.

But what had God given her eyes for, if He hadn't meant for her to open them, and see?

Trembling, sick with fear, she forced herself to try on a dangerous, new idea, to feel its fit and texture. What if there was no sin? What if there had never been any sin, and sin was only a feeble invention of man, a tool used to prod and herd and control the frightened masses?

She wore that idea for as long as she could stand it. She felt its weight drag at her heart. If there was no sin—if she and John hadn't wronged the Lord but had merely done something innocent and human—she would have had a very different life. She might have married John, might have gone on loving him. She might have kept her career as a switchboard operator, made friends in the city, and lived a life full of joy and excitement, a life vibrant with discovery and adventure. She might have had a family. Not with the baby she'd lost, of course, but there might have been other children. Suddenly her heart was a great void of longing, pulling her down into an agonized awareness of all she wanted and all she lacked.

Mary Agnes gasped from the pain, and that deep breath stilled her thoughts.

It wasn't too late. She might find that life still. There was a chance, however small. Harvey hadn't left Roswell yet.

Mary Agnes shut off the engine. Her painful feet made her hobble as she crossed the road, but she found the side door unlocked, and she slipped inside, moved quietly up the stairs.

In an upper hall, she paused. She didn't know which of the several doors led to Harvey's apartment. She closed her eyes, trying to orient herself to the memory of his light in the window. It had to be the first door on the left. She tapped timidly. A momentary panic overwhelmed her—what if she'd chosen incorrectly? How would she explain herself to the person who answered—a ragged nun disrupting their sleep in the dead of night? But she heard a shuffling on the other side, and when the door opened, there he was, a slow, glad surprise spreading across his face.

"Can I come in?" Her voice was shaking. All of her was shaking.

He stood back, allowed her to enter. Then he closed the door behind her, and they were alone together.

"Is something wrong?" Harvey flicked on a light. "Is there news about Betty?"

She didn't know how to do this. The things that passed between women and men were no mystery to her—not after John—but still they were a great and sacred enigma.

"I don't want to stay away from you anymore." She moved toward him but didn't dare to touch. "I'm afraid. The order is all I've had. There's nothing for me out here in the world, nothing but you. I barely know you, Harvey. What if I can't count on you to stay?" The words were pouring from her now, desperate and hopeful, trying to make him understand. "But I'm more afraid of living a life without you. Without trying to make this work, together. You trusted me. With your story about . . . the thing you saw in the desert. You trusted me, and I must have faith. I believe you. I know you told the truth. I can't understand what you saw, but I know it was real."

Suddenly his arms were around her—she was in his arms, encircled by a sweet fire. His mouth met hers, and the kiss distilled and slowed every sense to a concentrated awareness of nothing but him.

She realized her hands were scrabbling at his back, and when she found the lower edge of his T-shirt, she understood that she wanted to touch him, his bare skin, warm and smooth beneath her hands. She lingered over the feel of his body. The shape and solidity of his muscles, the curve of his ribs. The bright, ecstatic reality of this moment. She hadn't imagined that mere carnality could feel so blessed, so divine. For all the great waves of fervor and awe that had run through her in the monastery, she had never known the greatest bliss might come from the union of man and woman, from a union of hearts, of minds.

He led her down the hall to his bedroom—stumbling and falling against the walls, for they never broke that hungry kiss, never disentangled their arms from one another until another door had closed and, in the pale starlight of the window, they had clawed away one another's clothing.

She found it wasn't so difficult to bare herself, after all. Not before the heat of this sacred fire.

CHAPTER THIRTY-EIGHT

November 23, 1947

Betty's head ached—every joint in her body, too. But she didn't hurt as badly today as she'd hurt on the first day, when she'd opened her eyes to find herself in the sterile, white stillness of a hospital room. She guessed it was an improvement. Small steps, the doctor had told her. One small step at a time would lead her to a complete recovery.

This was a new sensation, to simultaneously feel like the luckiest girl in the world and the biggest jerk who'd ever drawn a breath. She had put everyone she knew into a full-blown panic; she had acted like an absolute fool. And yet, after having rolled her father's car into an icy ditch, she knew her survival was nothing short of a miracle. She was grateful—no, "gratitude" wasn't a strong enough word for what she felt now. Betty was delirious with the thrill of being alive. And she wished there were a rock she could crawl under so she could disappear forever. How on earth was she going to live this down, on top of everything else? She glanced at her hands where they lay at her sides, exposed on the coverlet. Each was bound with a clean, white bandage. *Again.* The rumor mills of Roswell would churn over the name Betty Campbell until the next Ice Age came.

The door eased open slightly, and Betty's nurse peeked in. "You have a visitor, Miss Campbell."

Betty nodded. It hurt her head to do it.

She had expected her parents again, or maybe Juanita, who'd already dropped by three times with successively larger bouquets and get-well cards from the girls at school. Anyone would have been welcome, for most of the time Betty's only company was the little statue of Our Lady of Guadalupe, which her mother had placed on the rolling table beside the bed.

Sister Mary Agnes was the last person Betty had thought to see. The nun entered the room with a sad, solicitous smile.

Betty struggled to sit up.

"Please." Mary Agnes raised a hand to stall her. "You need your rest. I only wanted to stop by to see for myself that you're all right. When I heard the news that you were recovering, I couldn't quite believe it—though of course, I was praying for you."

"You found me. That's what my mother said."

"Mr. Day and I found you. It was he who pulled you out of the car; I wouldn't have been able to manage on my own."

"Thank you," Betty said. "I think you saved my life—you and Mr. Day." The girl's face fell. "Though I don't know what I'm going to do now. Stuck in Roswell for good, with this reputation."

"You aren't stuck, Betty. You've got college to look forward to. You must keep your focus on the future. What's done is done. All that matters now is what lies ahead."

Betty began to weep with a suddenness and force that appalled her. She hadn't cried one bit since she'd woken, groggy and sore, in the hospital bed. It seemed all the tears, all the terror and relief, were catching up with her now.

"I can't go to college," she said. "I burned all my application letters—every one. Oh, why was I so stupid? What did I do it for? I wish I could go back, Mary Agnes. I'd do everything differently if I could."

The nun smiled, a spark of amusement in her eyes. "You didn't burn all the letters."

Mary Agnes reached into the pocket of her habit, drew something out, and passed it to Betty.

The girl unfolded the paper carefully. She stared at it for a long time before she recognized her own handwriting, the neatly copied address at the top of the page. The University of Redlands—its divinity college, in California.

"Where did you get this?"

"You dropped it that day outside the post office. Remember?"

Betty laughed, which made her head pound, but despite the pain, she felt good, good enough that she wanted to keep laughing forever. "They don't even teach science," she said. "Not much, anyway—not in their school of theology. I only applied to this university because they accept girls, and because it's in California."

"Do you have a special interest in California?"

Betty didn't answer that question. The only interest she'd had in California was the fact that Jim would be there. What did that matter now? He'd broken things off; he thought she was a liar and a fake. At least Redlands was more than two hundred miles from Caltech. Assuming Betty could get into the school, there was little chance she would run into Jim by accident, which would make her life more unbearably mortifying than it already was.

"I suppose I'll send the letter," Betty finally said. "I don't have any interest in studying theology. It's kind of the opposite of science, isn't it? But if I can get in—if this school gets me out of Roswell—I might become a devout believer, after all."

"A school of theology might not have been your first choice," Mary Agnes said, "but it might be where you're meant to be. Back in Chicago, my old abbess told me once that if you follow whatever path God gives you, no matter how strange or hostile that road may seem, it will lead you to the place where you're meant to be. It will lead you to the truth."

"Do you really believe that?" Betty asked.

Mary Agnes gazed out the window to the white world beyond, to the far horizon that lost itself in a wash of brilliant light. "I didn't," she said. "For a long time, I didn't. But now I see that my old abbess was right. And I believe you'll find the same truth, Betty, if you have the courage to walk whatever path opens to you, and you see the journey through to its end."

Betty looked at the statue on the table beside her. The Virgin of Guadalupe watched her with patient eyes. The gilded stars that covered her mantle shone in the winter light, as numberless as Betty's questions and bright with the promise of truth.

The nurse tapped lightly at the door again. "Miss Campbell, you've another visitor. A Mr. Lucero. Shall I send him in?"

"Jim!"

Betty tried to sit up again. Mary Agnes pushed her gently back onto her pillows.

"What's he doing here?" Betty gasped.

Mary Agnes chuckled. "I guess he's come to see you."

"I'm a fright! If only I had a comb and some lipstick."

Mary Agnes took in the girl's bruises, her mussed hair, the blue-black circles around each eye—a consequence of the concussion. "You're beautiful," she said.

She slipped from Betty's hospital room as Jim entered, bearing a bouquet of pink roses. He held the door for Mary Agnes, gave the sister a respectful nod. When he and Betty were alone, he approached her bed with shamefaced hesitation.

"I'm awfully glad you're okay," he said.

Betty's smile was brittle. "So am I."

"I tried to see you yesterday, but you were asleep. And the day before that, but your dad said to come back later." He squeezed his eyes shut. "When I heard you were missing, I about went crazy. I searched for you, Betty. And when I couldn't find you, I—"

"You're not supposed to be seen with me, Jim. What about the academy, the honor code? What about your scholarship?"

He fell onto the chair at her bedside, clutched her hand with a fervency that made her eyes and throat burn.

"I don't care about any of that," he said. "Major General Waxman can go stuff it. I should have told him so in the first place. I know you're not a liar, Betty. It doesn't matter what other people think. I know you." Jim lifted her hand, turned it over. He pressed his lips against her bandaged palm. "And I know this is real."

$$\sim$$

It wasn't Sister Mary Agnes who left the hospital that day. As she drove the old Army car back to the monastery, she repeated the name in her mind dozens of times, hundreds of times, trying to learn the truth of it again. Patricia Walton. She was Patricia Walton now. A distant part of her had always been Patricia, watching the life of Sister Mary Agnes from some suspended place out of time, from the velvet darkness between the stars, with a mild curiosity and a great, eternal tenderness. Patricia Ann Walton. By the time she pulled up the long lane that led to the monastery, the name Mary Agnes no longer had anything to do with her. She was a bright, hungry hollow of eagerness and longing, ready to receive the new life that would soon pour itself in.

The wall of elms stood bare, their branches laced and fragile with ice. The winter light had taken on a thin, blue quality, a sense of a new year fast approaching. She parked the car outside the old, white farmhouse and paused for one last look around. Little more than ten weeks had passed since she and her sisters had arrived in Roswell, since the woman who had once been Mary Agnes had first laid eyes on this place. She'd expected then that this monastery would be her home until her dying day. How swiftly a life could change when confronted by the great mysteries.

The nuns would be in the choir room now, at the tail end of None, finishing the afternoon prayer. No doubt, the sisters had heard her pulling up the drive. She would wait outside until they let her in—if they let her in. She wasn't a part of their private world. Not any longer.

The women inside were singing one of their hymns. The music came to Patricia faintly through the walls, so soft and indistinct it might have been a dream or a far-off memory. She closed her eyes, allowed the song to find the deepest place of her heart. The wind moved easily, carrying the year's last incense of creosote. The monastery would forever be a place of unrivaled beauty, full of the most earnest and generous love, and rich with the gifts of these women's spirits. She felt a deep sadness at parting with this family of many years, but her sorrow was tempered by the joy of new discovery. What prospects waited beyond the walls? The thought had frightened her once. It still frightened her, a little. But she knew, now, how to find the sure path. And there were many more paths that would reveal themselves out there in the wide, unknowable world.

The farmhouse's front door opened almost as soon as the hymn was finished. Sister Ann came running down the porch steps, the white oval of her stricken face isolated by her veil.

"Mary Agnes!" Ann clung to her, trembling. "Oh, I've been so worried about you. We've all been terribly worried. When you didn't come home last night, Mother Catherine thought she might call the police. She thought you'd been abducted."

"I'm all right. No need for these tears."

When Ann released her, Patricia removed the rosary from her rope belt, then untied the belt, too. She passed these relics to her friend.

Ann looked down at the belt and rosary with a dawning awareness. When she met Patricia's eye again, there was such grief in her expression that Patricia had to laugh.

"It's all right, Ann. Each of us must take the road we're given."

All the sisters had gathered on the porch by then, watching with mingled concern and relief. The abbess made her way to the edge of the porch, implacable and silent.

"I suppose Mother Catherine wants to speak with me," Patricia said quietly. "I'd better get this over with."

The abbess's office was small and confining. Mother Catherine of the Perpetual Sorrows sat at her desk with her hands clasped and her all-seeing eye fixed sternly on Patricia.

"Suppose you tell us exactly what's been going on," Catherine said. "You didn't come home last night. You had us all worried sick."

Patricia wasn't about to give the abbess any details. The full story was between herself and God—the God she knew, which was not the God of this church.

But her sisters did deserve some explanation. "I'm sorry I've made you worry. Everything happened so quickly, there was no time to speak to anyone properly, or to send a message. But I suppose you were right, Mother. I've been led away from this life by other concerns. The mysteries of the church aren't for me to contemplate—not anymore. There are other mysteries I'm meant to pursue."

Catherine's face burned with some emotion Patricia couldn't read. Anger, probably. "You've removed your belt and rosary. Does this mean you've broken your vows?"

"Yes."

It amazed her, how easy it was to make that admission, how light her heart felt at the sound of one word. If she still thought the church had any real bead on the truth, that confession would have crippled her with as much guilt as the vow-breaking itself might have done. But there was no shame in her now. Inside, there was only a smooth, easy sense of forward motion, of moving on.

"I think it's best that you return to Chicago." Catherine took up her pen, began jotting a note on one of her papers. "Externing was obviously a mistake for you. Returning to enclosure is the wisest course for—"

"No, thank you. I've made up my mind to leave the order."

Mother Catherine recovered quickly from her surprise. "I'll need to write to the Vatican. Petition for your dispensation."

351

"Thank you, but that won't be necessary." Patricia rose from the bench. "I'm leaving the church, too." She wanted no bill of good standing with an institution that held no truth for her. Patricia's God—the God of love—needed neither petitions nor dispensations. He required only the sincerest effort of an honest heart.

She led the way out of Catherine's office and found the sisters gathered outside the choir room, whispering together, wide-eyed and anxious. She allowed them all to surround her, one last time, with their warmth and kindness.

"I love you all so much," she said to them—all of them, the abbess included.

Then she kissed Sister Ann on the cheek, a final farewell, and left the order forever.

She had nothing to her name, nothing but her habit, blowing loose around her body in the sharp autumn wind. She walked the long lane, and the cold, yellow earth of the desert worked its way past the straps of her sandals and between her toes. She only looked back once, when she reached the ring of elms. Her sisters were there on the porch, watching her go. She raised a hand in grateful parting.

In the world beyond the monastery wall, she pulled the black veil and white cotton cap from her head. Another gust of wind pushed at her, and she closed her eyes, reveling in the feel of God's fingers through her short hair, the hair that had hardly been uncovered for twelve long years. She held cap and veil aloft in one hand and let them go. The wind took them, tumbling their wings of black and white down the broad, empty street.

When she found her way back to Harvey's apartment, he opened the door as soon as she knocked, as if he'd been waiting all day for her return. She stepped into the warmth of his arms.

"My name is Patricia now," she said. "Which is funny. I barely remember how to be Patricia."

He smiled, holding her gently by the shoulders. His hands ran up and down her arms, driving away the last of the chill. "That means you get to figure it out all over again."

"Can I stay here for a while? I only need a place to live until I find some work. Maybe I can go back to the switchboards. Are there any switchboards in Roswell?"

"You can stay with me as long as you like," he said. "I hope you'll stay a good, long time. Forever, if you want to."

"I can't live with you as an unmarried woman. It would cause a scandal."

Harvey stepped closer. She could feel the heat of his body through the thin, homespun cloth of her habit. "Who cares what other people think?" he said. "None of them has a bead on the truth, anyway."

He bent, then, and kissed her. The kiss lasted a long time.

CHAPTER
THIRTY-NINE

January 8, 1948

After the new year turned, Betty haunted the mailbox every day until an envelope arrived from California. The neat, typewritten address read *Miss Isabel Campbell*. She let the rest of the mail fall to the ground, tore open the letter from Redlands, and scoured the page with a trembling energy, half-eager, half-terrified.

> *Dear Miss Campbell,*
>   *On behalf of the Dean of Students, I am pleased to accept your letter of application to the theological seminary at the University of Redlands, and to extend the offer of a scholarship for—*

Betty's howl of triumph and relief brought the neighbors to their windows and set Cece Alvarado's three little dogs to barking.

By the time her father arrived home from the airfield, Betty had reread the letter fifty times at least, and each time she still ended up shivering with excitement. When Dad's keys fell into the dish beside the door and he called out his usual hello, Betty drew a deep breath, but it wasn't enough to steel herself for the task that lay ahead. Only when she'd taken up her statue of the Virgin of Guadalupe and whispered a prayer into the Lady's ear did she feel steady enough to do what must be done.

She found her parents in the kitchen, kissing over a bubbling pot of Mom's pozole.

"Dad, can I talk to you?"

Roger broke away from Rosa, regarded his girl with the same tenderness he'd felt when he'd held Betty in his arms for the first time. She was no longer that small, helpless bundle. She was bright and determined and honest, and she'd come through enough suffering to do a grown man in. Betty was a young woman any father could be proud of. She was strong enough to look after herself, now.

He followed her into the sitting room, took his usual place in the easy chair beside the radio. Betty perched on the edge of the sofa, anxious and fidgeting.

"I've been accepted into a college, Dad. Even with the school I've missed, my grades are good enough that they're willing to take me this fall."

"Before high school is finished?"

"It is finished for me. I've got to get out of Roswell. Try to understand, Dad."

He didn't like the idea of Betty leaving the nest at such a young age. But on the other hand, he was damn proud of his girl. *Must have got her brains from her mother,* he thought.

"They're giving me a scholarship," Betty said. "It's enough money that I'll be able to do four years on my own." She swallowed. Next came the hardest part. "It's in California, near San Francisco. That's where I'm going in the fall."

Roger felt a severing inside, and a deep, visceral ache. Once he'd accepted that he couldn't keep Betty from her future, he'd hoped she might find a school in Santa Fe or Albuquerque. Maybe west Texas, at the worst extreme. San Francisco was so far off, it might as well have been on another planet. And it wasn't lost on him, what his daughter had said. She was going. She hadn't asked his permission.

When he was certain he had his feelings under control and there was no danger of unseemly tears, he nodded. "I'm proud of you, honey. Real proud. Your mother and I have set a little money aside. We'd meant to give it to you when you married someday—to help you and your husband buy a house of your own. I want you to have it now instead. Use it to take proper care of yourself while you're off at that university."

"Oh, Dad!"

She flew across the room, landed in his lap, and clung to his neck, exactly the way she used to do when she was a tiny thing.

There was no hope now that Roger would keep his tears at bay. "On one condition," he said, choking up. "I want you to write me regularly and let me know how you're doing. So I don't have to worry about you."

She kissed his cheek. "I'll call, too, at least once a week. And I'll come home to spend every holiday with you and Mom and the boys. I promise."

She didn't like the idea of returning to Roswell, not for any reason. But she would do it for her family. They were worth a little trouble, worth a little pain.

~

Neither Harvey nor Patricia owned much. They managed to pack everything they needed, everything they cared to bring out of Roswell, into the panniers on Harvey's motorbike. It wasn't much—a few changes of clothes, the tools Harvey could use to scratch out a meager living, the money he'd got from selling his old, rusted pickup truck. And the scrapbook that proved there was more to this life than most people dared to believe.

Harvey cinched the pannier closed. "Where are we headed, anyway?"

"California might be nice."

"It's a big state," he said, laughing. "Anyplace in particular?"

"No." She leaned across the bike to kiss him. "Let's go wherever the wind blows us, wherever the road wants to run."

"What if the wind blows us to Las Vegas? To one of those wedding chapels?"

It took a few startled beats of her heart before Patricia understood the suggestion. "Harvey!"

"Is that a yes?"

For an answer, she kissed him again.

"Mary Agnes!"

Patricia broke away from Harvey, blushing, and found Betty Campbell running down Main Street, waving a piece of paper above her head.

"There's someone I've got to say goodbye to," Patricia said. "Give me a minute, will you?"

She hurried up the street to meet Betty with a long embrace.

"Look at you," Betty said, pulling back to take in the sight. "Blue jeans and sneakers. You could fit right in at Vic's Drive-In, if your hair wasn't as short as a boy's."

Patricia ran a hand through her shingled hair, laughing. "It'll grow out—eventually."

"I never guessed you looked so hip underneath that habit and veil."

"Neither did I."

"I tried to find you at the monastery," Betty said, "but all they'd tell me was that you weren't there anymore, and you weren't coming back. No one in town knew where you'd got to, either."

Patricia explained as best she could—how she'd been lying low at Harvey's place until after the holidays, after the snow, when they could take to the road and find a new place to belong.

"I suppose it was hard to find me," she added, "because I've changed my name. That's to say I've gone back to who I was before. I think. My name is Patricia now. No more Sister Mary Agnes. She belongs to the past."

"I get it," Betty said. "Patricia is your future. And here's my future."

She handed over the letter, watched Patricia's face as she read the news. By the time she reached the end of the note, she was beaming.

"Betty, I'm so glad. It's almost exactly what you'd hoped for. I know theology wasn't your first choice—"

"But it's the right choice," Betty said. "I think I might find my answers there."

She lifted a hand, palm up. The trace of a scar showed, pink as a new sun rising.

Patricia took the girl's hand, closed her fingers to hide the scar. She was dreadfully certain that Betty would find the opposite in her study of theology—no answers, but questions that ran deeper the more thoroughly she pursued them. But there was beauty in the pursuit itself, and a certain satisfaction in the inscrutable nature of God.

"Say, where are you and Mr. Day going?" Betty asked.

"Wherever the road takes us."

"To California?"

Patricia smiled. "Maybe."

Betty fished a scrap of paper and the terminal stub of a pencil from her jeans. She pressed it to a shop window and copied out the address of her college.

"Here's where you'll find me, come the fall. If you're in California by then, come and see me. I'm sure we'll have loads to talk about."

There was no more reason to linger in town. Patricia returned to Harvey, climbed onto the bike behind him, and wrapped her arms around his waist. He fired up the newly restored engine. It roared like a rocket, and its heat was like the fire of the stars. They headed north out of town. The wind was sharp and free against their faces, and the blue winter sky burned along a beckoning horizon.

Patricia looked back only once. Roswell was dwindling behind her, Main Street stretching and vanishing, a long, straight line into the past. But she could still see the small figure of Betty Campbell waving, sharp and clear against the shadows of the town.

EPILOGUE

The years flew on, into an accelerating future. The nations of the world made their pacts, established their blockades. The atomic bomb proliferated, spread around the globe, and its fire became the phantom that haunted innocent sleep. Neighbors began to watch one another with suspicion. Joe McCarthy had his eyes on everyone. In Korea, the great powers of this new world found an excuse to make war again. Nothing ever really ends.

But though the shadow of the bomb darkened every thought and every day, there was still joy to be found. The future is forever unknown, which means all things are possible—even love, even hope, even that which seems inconceivable.

After a year or so of wandering, Mr. and Mrs. Day settled in the city of Berkeley, California. Their ideas about this world and what lay beyond it were far-out, by the standards of a polite society, but in Berkeley they found a community of radical thinkers, voyagers of the mind who listened with interest to Harvey's thoughts on time and space and what might traverse them—thinkers who contributed philosophies of their own. By the time their first baby was on its way, the Day home was known as a wellspring of free thought, giving rise to the kinds of ideas that could tear down blockades and bring citizens shouting to their feet. The kinds of ideas that would make McCarthy gnash his wolven teeth. Not a weekend went by that Patricia and Harvey didn't entertain the poets and protestors, the trippers, the subversive professors, all those who knew that reality was bigger on the inside than it seemed on the outside and the only way to discover the truth of this world was to get on your knees and put your head inside the wreckage.

Jim Lucero was the star student of his cohort at Caltech. By the time he graduated with honors, the Korean War was underway, and the Army was eager to put his sharp mind to use, burning a path to another lucrative victory for the United States. But Jim had found a better way to honor his father's memory. War planes no longer interested him. He had fixed his sight on broader horizons; he had turned his attention to the stars. When the Ames Research Center of San Francisco came courting, he accepted their offer without hesitation. At Ames, he would work on the problems of blunt-body reentry, the first and most critical step to bringing a manned spacecraft back into the planet's atmosphere. The question of whether humankind could leap from the face of the earth and venture into the stars was still unanswered. But Jim wanted to know. He was ready to dedicate his life to the sacred mystery.

The Ames laboratory wasn't the only thing that drew him to San Francisco. It wasn't even the most powerful lure. Betty had just begun her master's at Redlands. She had found a deep, quiet fulfillment in her studies, and reluctant to leave the resonant mysteries of theology behind, she was already eyeing a doctorate, maybe a career as a professor. She never did find an explanation for the affliction she had suffered as a girl in Roswell, that singular, strange year when a flying saucer had crashed to the earth. But by that time, stigmata were her least pressing question about the miraculous and the divine. She knew she would never find the answers, but that was no longer the point of her studies. She longed only to know how deep the well of mystery ran. She would spend her life immersed in those waters, swimming joyfully toward a bottom she would never reach.

The four of them—Betty, Jim, Patricia, and Harvey—spent evenings together, as often as their busy lives would allow. They would meet on the sandy stretches of the Bay shore, talking, laughing, remembering all that had passed. Betty, with her new diamond ring, would cradle Patricia's baby and kiss his soft cheeks, and Jim would toss the boy up to the sky, up to the atmosphere that would soon be no more a barrier to humankind than the veil between sleep and dreams.

Best of all were the nights when they drove out to Half Moon Bay, where the lights from the city dimmed to nothing. Sometimes they flew the old model plane high above the sand and the waves. Sometimes they only sat, side by side, where the ocean met the land, looking up into the endless heavens.

None of them saw anything in the sky that they couldn't readily explain. All the mysteries that had visited them in the summer of '47 seemed content to remain in the past. But they saw the light of the distant stars, and that was miracle enough.

AUTHOR'S NOTE

When I was twenty-one years old—which, as I sit writing this note, was more than half my lifetime ago—I saw something in the night sky I still can't explain.

I was sitting in a hot tub in a suburb north of Seattle with two friends. For no reason any of us could name (we all compared notes later, reassuring ourselves and each other that, yes, this really had happened; it was real), we all stopped talking at the same time and looked up. It was a clear summer night, and a V of five lights was moving steadily from east to west. Each light was about the same size and color as the stars, indicating a very high altitude. There are three major military bases in western Washington, all of which have active airfields. It wasn't unusual to see aircraft moving in formation at any time of the day or night.

What happened next *was* unusual.

The five lights scrambled suddenly, whipping around one another in an intricate motion, as if they were trying to braid themselves in midair. I can't accurately describe the *strangeness* of their motion. It wasn't only the speed at which they moved—which was far faster than I'd ever seen any aircraft maneuver—but the tightness and precision of their movements. All five of these lights darted at ninety degrees relative to one another and zipped back again, each pinging around the others so rapidly they seemed to jumble up the very concept of visual perception. Those of you who are old enough to remember cassette tapes, think back to the sound a tape would sometimes make if you pressed "play" and "fast forward" at the same time—a bubbling garble devoid of all sense. Now translate that sensation from sound to sight. That was the way the lights moved . . . until they didn't. In a blink, they snapped back into their tidy V, and the whole arrangement shot off to the south, with the point of the V still aimed to the west.

For a long time, my friends and I could only stare at the now-empty sky.

Finally, I said, "Did you guys see that?"

"Yep," Friend 1 said.

Friend 2 said, "Let's go inside. I don't want to be out here anymore."

It took me many years to realize it, but that night—that sighting—marked the beginning of all the biggest and most important changes in my life. None of these changes were immediate or came with any fanfare, but they did come—most notably, the dissolution of my very strong faith and my identity as a member of my church. Seeing something impossible with your own eyes changes the way you think about the "big questions": our purpose as humans and our relative power; the Powers That Be, whether they be God or government; the very nature and basis of reality. In the two years that followed my sighting, I would begin questioning the tenets of the faith I was raised in, the faith I'd only recently chosen to be baptized into and for which I still had, on that clear summer night, a newly confirmed member's sincere enthusiasm. When I officially left my faith at the age of twenty-three, the process was remarkably easy. I didn't suffer the protracted doubt or shame that so often impacts others who leave a high-control religion. I just left. And though many people in my religious community tried to convince me that I was choosing the wrong path, that my soul would come to grief unless I returned to the fold, their threats and warnings never had the least impact on me. I knew—I had seen for myself—that there was something bigger out there than any human conception of God. And I knew that nobody really understood what was possible and what wasn't.

I'll spare you the full discourse on my two subsequent decades of spiritual sojourning and will stick to what's relevant to this note: namely, that I have found a deep and sacred communion with the divine, one that grows more wonderfully perplexing and mysterious the more thoroughly I explore it, and which bears no resemblance to any organized religion. I will tell you, too, that I've remained fascinated by the phenomenon of the UFO ever since my sighting. This will probably surprise most of my readers. One would expect a dyed-in-the-wool UFO nut to gravitate toward sci-fi, not historical fiction. (Let me state, for the record, that I am almost as obsessed with history as I am with UFOs.)

Of all the old tales of unexplained objects in the sky, the Roswell Incident might be the best known. It is certainly the most enduring. All one has to do to conjure up images of flying saucers and little green men is say the name "Roswell." The story, on its surface, is a fairly simple one. Shortly after midnight on July 3, 1947, an anomalous object was detected on radar at the Roswell Army Air Field, home to what was, at the time, the only airborne atomic weapons in the United States' arsenal. A large thunderstorm was moving through the area, and the object disappeared from radar. A few days later, William "Mac" Brazel, a sheep rancher near Corona, reported that he'd found some sort of metallic wreckage on his land. He spoke first with a local journalist, John McBoyle, and then with the sheriff.

From there, the standard account of the Roswell Incident runs as follows: a few individuals, including Major Jesse Marcel, went out to Brazel's ranch and found some metallic and wooden debris. They collected this stuff and brought it back to the base, where they determined that it was the wreckage of a high-altitude weather balloon. In the meantime, McBoyle got ahead of himself and reported that the Army had captured a "flying saucer." The Army had to set the record straight, and the next day they released an official statement that the alleged saucer was nothing more than ordinary meteorological equipment—a case of mistaken identity.

That's the story most people know. But it isn't the whole story. I'll circle back to Roswell later.

What many people don't realize is that the crash on Mac Brazel's ranch was only one incident in a much larger chain of events. In the field of ufology (that's the study of anomalous aerial phenomena), a collection of concurrent sightings is known as a "flap." Late June through mid-July of 1947 saw one of the largest single flaps in world history. At least eight hundred—and possibly more than a thousand—sightings were reported, from civilian and military witnesses, from nearly every state in America and from many Canadian provinces, as well. The headlines I used in Harvey's scrapbook are real, taken from archived newspapers from the summer of '47.

The Cold War had just begun, and the Pentagon took these reports of incursions into US airspace very seriously. The initial assumption was that these objects were some sort of Soviet technology, created and deployed to spy on US military secrets, or to actually menace American civilians with the threat of nuclear bombardment. In response to the summertime flap, a top-secret operation was initiated and tasked with investigating the sightings. In early 1948, Project Sign began its work— but its members soon realized that although many sightings were easily proven to be cases of mistaken identity (ordinary or experimental domestic aircraft, windblown trash, flocks of birds), a significant and alarming number couldn't be explained so simply. In fact, some couldn't be explained at all.

Far too many reports, some corroborated by radar and other data, indicated that there were objects in United States airspace that not only outperformed the most cutting-edge technology America possessed but also seemed to defy physics altogether—indicating that Soviet innovation was unlikely to be behind these phenomena. Objects were recorded traveling up to eighteen hundred miles per hour, stopping abruptly in midair and reversing course in the blink of an eye, and maneuvering with incredible precision at speeds that were frankly impossible. More confounding still, many of these craft were described as having no wings, no propellers, and emitting no apparent exhaust, making their means of propulsion a complete mystery. Most perplexing of all was the fact that many of these unexplained sightings seemed to involve intelligent control. The "flying saucers" behaved in ways that one would not expect from windblown refuse or flocks of birds. The objects tailed or evaded military aircraft, sometimes appeared to respond to the thoughts of observers, and showed an unsettling interest in the bases where top-secret nuclear technology was being studied and refined.

Obviously, with the Cold War already well underway, the government couldn't admit that its best weapons and vehicles were hopelessly outmatched by far more sophisticated craft. Civic unrest might well ensue, and worse, the Soviets might learn of and exploit American weaknesses. So Project Sign was quickly replaced by Project Grudge, which was itself replaced in 1952 by Project Blue Book. The specific mandate of both Grudge and Blue Book was to find mundane explanations for sightings, no matter how implausible those explanations might be (swamp gas, pelicans, etc.). The goal was no longer to find out who was behind the anomalous objects but rather to keep the public from thinking about those objects, or talking about them, or even believing that they existed at all. Thus, faith would continue in the unconquerable might of the United States military. Grudge and Blue Book did their work so thoroughly that, for decades, if anyone admitted to seeing something strange in the sky, they were ridiculed, even made into a social outcast. People soon stopped reporting their sightings altogether, including military pilots, who nevertheless continued to encounter highly advanced and intelligently controlled aerial phenomena with astonishing regularity.

Okay, this sounds totally ridiculous. Top-secret military operations whose purpose was to come up with any old, mundane excuse for UFO sightings so that nobody would know how weak the US military was by comparison? That sounds like conspiracy-theory nonsense . . . but we now know that it's a historical fact.

In 2017, the *New York Times* published a groundbreaking article titled *Glowing Auras and "Black Money": The Pentagon's Mysterious U.F.O. Program*. The article admitted that the US government had, despite decades of denial, been running special programs to analyze reports of UFOs (and, some insiders claim, actual UFOs themselves) since at least 1947. That article initiated a cascade of more investigations, which culminated, in 2021, in the formation of a new Congressional committee to openly investigate the United States' history with unexplained objects in the sky, and to form and fund such task forces as would be deemed necessary to learn whatever could be learned about these incursions into national airspace. It was through these Congressional hearings that the world learned the truth about Grudge and Blue Book—that the mission of these operations was not to get to the bottom of the mystery but rather to hand-wave the mystery away, to protect America's reputation as an indominable military superpower, and to scare off future reports with the threat of public and professional ridicule.

Project Blue Book officially ended in 1969, but government efforts to deflect and discredit UFO sightings continued throughout the remainder of the twentieth and the beginning of the twenty-first centuries. However, the idea of otherworldly apparitions in the sky has always held sway over the human imagination. Despite the best efforts of the Army and the Pentagon, the Roswell Incident didn't fade away. As Blue Book came to a close, interest in the Roswell crash suddenly rekindled, and the "weather balloon" of New Mexico became the fervent focus of amateur ufologists across the country.

These citizen-journalists were both thorough and intrepid, seeking out and tracking down witnesses to the events of early July 1947. Between the late seventies and the mid-nineties, the accounts of dozens of firsthand witnesses were carefully assessed and assembled to present a compelling picture of what actually happened in the desert northwest of Roswell.

Compelling evidence exists to support the idea that either two craft crashed between July 2 and 3, or one craft went down—almost certainly struck by lightning—and scattered a large debris field between Mac Brazel's ranch at Corona and a second crash site near Socorro. Brazel noticed the storm, for it was of unusual size and strength. He watched the lightning striking repeatedly in a single place, as if drawn to something metallic. Stepping outside, he saw a large, metallic object, which he took to be an airplane, hurtling across the sky toward Socorro. The next morning, he found a large field of metallic debris scattered across his land that his animals refused to approach. But he didn't report the incident until July 7. By that time, he'd visited the town of Corona and had heard rumors of flying saucers that were sighted in recent days. Recalling the metallic object he'd seen during the storm, he wondered whether the debris littering his land might be more than ordinary trash. That was when he traveled to Roswell, to report what he'd found.

The Army quickly apprehended Mac Brazel. He was held in jail for a week and made to swear oaths of secrecy. His life and the safety of his wife and children were threatened if he should ever break his silence.

Meanwhile, the Army mobilized, for now they had not only the location of Brazel's debris field, but another location near Socorro, reported by archaeologists working for universities in Michigan and Pennsylvania who thought they'd witnessed the crash of a small airplane.

The Brazel ranch yielded a swath of metallic debris about three quarters of a mile long and several hundred feet wide. The second site, near Socorro on the Flats of Saint Augustine, featured an actual vehicle of some sort. It was disc-shaped, about thirty feet across and roughly twelve feet high at its thickest point. It's unclear whether the Roswell Incident involved a single craft that began disintegrating over Brazel's ranch, or two craft—one of which exploded over Brazel's ranch and the other of which fell to earth mostly intact, save for a split in its hull.

The most unsettling feature of this story might be the fact that many direct witnesses reported bodies being recovered at the Socorro crash site. Consistent reports from firsthand observers state that there were four inhabitants of the craft. Two were deceased when the Army arrived, one was in the process of dying, and one was still alive. They were described as being small, with large, hairless heads and large eyes. All four were taken away with the craft itself, which was flown on a B-29 from Roswell Army Air Field to Wright Field in Ohio (now Wright-Patterson Air Force Base), where experimental research and reverse engineering on captured enemy vehicles had been conducted since World War I.

Major Jesse Marcel was a real man, a highly respected and thoroughly experienced intelligence officer with a specialty in nuclear technology. He led the recovery efforts at Brazel's ranch. Although he went along with the Army's story that it was just a weather balloon, and even posed for pictures with some mylar-like substance to set the public's fears to rest, from 1978 on (once he no longer cared to uphold the oaths of secrecy he'd taken), Marcel insisted that something "extraterrestrial" was behind the Roswell Incident. He freely admitted that the photos he posed for were a setup and that the material he's handling in those photos was not the material he and his men gathered on the Brazel ranch.

The real debris, Marcel said, was "parchment-like" and silvery or white in color. Extremely lightweight and thin, it nevertheless could not be damaged. Creasing, wrinkling, or crushing it was pointless; it simply sprang back into its previous form, with no mark on its surface. Neither could it be cut or burned. And some of the pieces were marked with purple-pink writing that bore no resemblance to any language Marcel had ever seen. He compared the writing to ancient Egyptian hieroglyphics, though he said that this was not an exact match, either. The comparison simply conveyed the strangeness of the markings he observed.

Marcel wasn't the only witness to see purple-colored "hieroglyphic" markings on the recovered debris. Several others gave the same information in interviews, many of whom did not know Major Marcel personally and would have had no occasion to hear the story from him.

John McBoyle, a reporter with Roswell's local radio station, was indeed threatened by an Army officer with suspension of the station's broadcast license if he reported on the saucer (and he did see the Brazel debris field for himself). McBoyle made the report anyway, calling in the story to his colleague Lydia Sleppy in Albuquerque. Sleppy was indeed interrupted on her Teletype machine as she typed up the story for release. The FBI was clearly monitoring the wires for outgoing communication about the saucer that had been recovered in the desert.

Speaking of threats from government agencies, many of the witnesses, including Mac Brazel, were contacted by two personages from the Army, a red-haired Captain Armstrong and Sergeant Roosevelt, who threatened them with dire consequences, including death, if they ever spoke of what they'd seen. The threat seemed to stick for a couple of decades, but by the late 1960s, witnesses were talking, and the real story of the Roswell crash began to revive.

The Poor Clare monastery was founded at Roswell in 1948, not 1947, and the decision to locate a new monastery in that sleepy desert town likely had nothing to do with the flying saucer crash. But because I've always found the idea of the UFO to be tinged with a blush of the spiritual, I liked the idea of tying the two events together. I'm not the only one who has noticed a remarkable connection between UFO sightings and religious visions or apparitions, either. Such luminaries as Carl Jung, Jacques Vallée, and John Keel have noted the similarities between reports of religious visions and reports of UFOs. A modern researcher on the subject, Diana Walsh Pasulka, professor of religious studies at the University of North Carolina Wilmington, has even written two excellent books on the topic: *American Cosmic* and *Encounters*, both of which I consulted while working on this novel. If you are interested in exploring the remarkable parallels between religious experiences and UFO experiences, I especially recommend *American Cosmic*, an engaging and very readable deep dive into the subject. It's among my favorite nonfiction books on any subject.

While I'm speaking of authors, I must mention Vallée and Keel again. Both authors conducted extensive interviews with UFO experiencers from around the world. Each interviewed several people who claimed to have looked inside a "flying saucer," typically during military recovery missions like the one depicted in this novel. In every case, those who saw inside the craft reported a distinctive distortion of both space and time. Though the craft appeared to be little larger than an automobile from the outside, the inside revealed a space so huge as to be disorienting, variously described by witnesses as the size of a movie theater, a football stadium, or a cathedral. Although no such observation is recorded by any witnesses of the Roswell crash, I found it to be such a fascinating idea that I gave Harvey the same experience.

My other major deviation from the witness accounts of the Roswell Incident was to leave the bodies of the "pilots" out of the story. I did so for one simple reason: this isn't a story about alien visitors, or time travelers, or whatever strange intelligence might be behind the anomalies in our skies. It's not a story about solving the mystery behind the UFOs. It's a story about mystery itself—what effect the unexplained and the unexplainable has on our lives, how mystery can change the ways we see and interact with one another, with religion, and with reality itself.

In addition to the authors and books already mentioned, I must acknowledge *Witness to Roswell* by Donald R. Schmitt and Thomas J. Carey, and *A Right to Be Merry* by Mother Mary Francis, PCC, for details of the founding of the Poor Clare monastery at Roswell. I also relied on the documentary *UFOs: The Secret History* directed by David Cherniak, and most especially, a very thorough yet private archive maintained by a man whose identity I will keep private. I don't know whether this fellow wants the world to know that he's been documenting the Roswell Incident for decades. I confess that I found his stash of private documents through the kind of ancient Google-fu known only to those of us who are old enough to have been around the internet almost since its inception. Nothing about this man's public-facing website mentions UFOs (rather, his website is dedicated to a very respectable career as a field biologist), and I only gained access via some mild and good-natured hacking. Nevertheless, his incredibly well-cited, cross-referenced, and thoroughly documented trove of information on the Roswell Incident was very helpful in the writing of this novel. My fellow UFO nerd, I salute you.

I hope you, reader, have enjoyed this story. It's true that we never learn why the saucer caused Betty's stigmata. But the point isn't to know. The point is to *not* know, to accept the holiness of mystery and the ever-broadening horizons such a mystery provides.

My sincerest thanks to my editor and publisher, Danielle Marshall, for trusting me to write such an unusual work of historical fiction, and for the insightful comments that refined and deepened this story. Thanks also to my copyeditor, Jaye Whitney Debber, and my proofreader, Tiffany Taing.

Thanks also to the many fine people who are doing big work and small work in the realm of ufology—particularly my friend Shawn, whose personal videos of UFOs are something truly remarkable; Darren King of the *Point of Convergence* podcast; and Kelly Chase of *The UFO Rabbit Hole* podcast. If your curiosity about UFOs has been piqued by this story and you'd like to learn more but you need a sensible, rational entrée to the subject, I can't recommend Kelly's podcast highly enough. It is excellent, and it makes the very concept of UFOs approachable and accessible.

Most of all, thank you to my wonderful readers, who continue to support my books with so much enthusiasm—even the slightly weird books, like this one.

Olivia Hawker
May 2024
Victoria, BC

ABOUT THE AUTHOR

Photo © 2018 Paul Harnden

Olivia Hawker is the *Washington Post* bestselling author of *October in the Earth*; *The Fire and the Ore*; *The Rise of Light*; *The Ragged Edge of Night*; and *One for the Blackbird, One for the Crow*, a finalist for the Washington State Book Award and the WILLA Literary Award. Olivia resides in Victoria, British Columbia, with her husband and several naughty cats. For more information, visit www.hawkerbooks.com.